"Lucy thinks *you're* her father?"

"That's what I said," James agreed with fine irony. "Look, it's no business of mine but wouldn't it be better to tell her the truth?"

Jenna shook her head. "I can't...and I can't tell you either." To her horror she started to cry. She tried to stop and found she could not.

"Hush...it's all right," James murmured, enfolding her in his arms. It was wrong to let him take control like this, but it was heavenly to feel the burdens shifted off her shoulders, even if it was only momentarily.

"I have a proposition to put to you," James told her quietly. "Maybe now isn't the time—"

"If it's another offer to buy the Hall, then the answer is no," she told him tautly.

"Not exactly." His voice was carefully neutral. "What I actually had in mind was that you and I get married."

Books by Penny Jordan

HARLEQUIN SIGNATURE EDITION
LOVE'S CHOICES

HARLEQUIN PRESENTS

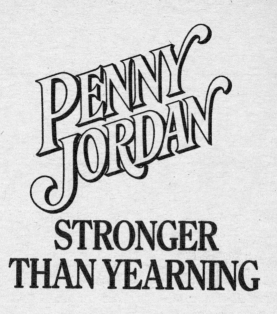

PENNY JORDAN

STRONGER THAN YEARNING

Harlequin Books

TORONTO • NEW YORK • LONDON
AMSTERDAM • PARIS • SYDNEY • HAMBURG
STOCKHOLM • ATHENS • TOKYO • MILAN

Harlequin Signature Edition published June 1988
Second printing November 1988

ISBN 0-373-83205-2

Originally published in Great Britain in 1986

CHAPTER ONE

Now that she was here, she had a curious feeling of anti-climax almost as though an inner voice was warning her not to go on but to bury the past and put it completely behind her. She silenced it using the strength of will she had honed to a fine keenness over the years. 'Cold' and 'hard' were how some people described her: business adversaries who had learned too late that her cloud of Titian hair and almost breathtakingly feminine features were not signs of weakness, ploys to soothe the male ego, but a banner of her determination to succeed as what she was and not because she was willing to use it.

She had lost count of the number of men who had invited her to their beds. She had left the majority of them with their egos bruised and their desire cooling to resentment. What did she care? Her rejection of them had given her some small measure of satisfaction, but that was not why she rejected them. She was a woman whose emotions ran deep and secret, some so secret that no one knew of them, and the strongest of all those emotions was the one which had brought her here to this remote Yorkshire village, to this house . . . on this particular day.

Harley, her closest business adviser, had expressed surprise when she told him what she intended to do. He had wondered verbally that she should even have heard of the auction of some remote manor house in Yorkshire, never mind want to attend it with the

5

purpose of buying it. When he had questioned her reasons she had simply shrugged, her cool remote air infuriating him, as it still did on occasions.

'It will make a good headquarters,' was all she would tell him, and she said it in a tone of voice that warned him against arguing with her.

A small frown touched Jenna's smooth forehead. It was annoying that she should feel that small sense of let-down. Today should be a milestone in her life. From the point of view of return on her capital alone she ought to be feeling elated. She shuddered to think what her accountants would say if they knew of the amount she had spent in secret on garnering every scrap of information there was to be garnered about the Deveril family. And at last it had paid off. A hundred yards in front of her stood the house.

The first Deveril to build on this spot had been one of William the Conqueror's knights. The family had gone from strength to strength until the death of Richard III. All four sons of the family had fallen at Bosworth but they had had wives, and one of those wives had produced a posthumous son whom Henry VII had pardoned and forgiven for his father's misdeeds. For a while the family had languished, keeping close to their Yorkshire estates, but then one of the daughters had caught the eye of Prince Hal, and whether it was because he retained a soft spot for her or not, the Deverils did extremely well out of the sack of the monasteries during the Reformation.

That was when the original property had been demolished; a fine new house, built with an eye to beauty rather than defence, sprang up on the site of the old.

It was more than fifteen years since she had last seen this house. Then, she had looked back on it as she left the village, swearing eternal hatred to those who lived in it. How very young she had been! Of course, her hatred had faded, and with it over the years the hotly burning need to wreak vengeance on those who had caused it. But Jenna's desire to exact atonement had never entirely faded. The news eighteen months ago that Alan Deveril and his son, Charles, had both died in a car accident had shocked her into realising the futility of wasting her life in impossibly unrealistic dreams of challenging fate. All she had been left with was a residue of bitterness, intensified by the news she had received later that as there was no direct heir, the house now stood empty.

Out of all the people she had once known in this area, she only kept in touch with one couple, her old headmaster and his wife, and it was they that she and Lucy were staying with now. Lucy! She sighed involuntarily as she thought about her rebellious fifteen-year-old daughter.

Lucy hadn't wanted to come with her to West Thorpe, but Jenna had insisted and for that insistence had had to endure sulks and silence during the long drive up from London. Lucy! The gulf that had recently sprung up between them pained her. Most parents encountered some problems with their teenage children she knew, but she was not most parents; she was a single parent, and Lucy had been increasingly demanding recently about her right to know the identity of her father. Jenna, of course, had refused to tell her. Her mouth compressed as she reflected wryly that although she might be able to control her own business and a staff of a dozen or so people, when it came to controlling her daughter . . .

She resumed her study of the house. The main Tudor building with its mullioned windows and fancy brickwork had been added to by a Georgian Deveril, whose rich bride's dowry had enabled him to employ Robert Adam to design a new wing. She had never been inside the house; the Deverils were not the sort of family to invite the village children into their elegant home. Alan Deveril had been a snob of the first water. It had always been his intention to arrange a marriage between Charles and a wealthy heiress — someone whose parents were eager to trade their money for the Deveril name and title. Her mouth compressed again, bitterness darkening her green eyes to stormy jade.

'Jenna, there you are.'

She turned at the sound of Harley's voice, frowning slightly. 'You must be mad to think of taking on this place,' he said frankly as he came up to her. 'It's riddled with damp . . . half the windows are rotten. It will cost an absolute fortune to put everything right, and to what purpose? You could get yourself a modern office block in London for a tenth of the cost and far less hassle.'

The petulance in his voice made her smile faintly. Plump and slightly balding, he nevertheless considered himself something of a ladies' man and dressed accordingly. His expensive pale grey suit and toning silk shirt looked very out of place in the tangled undergrowth of the house's gardens. He was perspiring slightly, Jenna noticed, something he always did when he was nervous. Poor Harley, he had a hard time sometimes keeping up with her, but he was an excellent administrator, fussy to the point of irritation at times, but fanatically methodical, unlike herself. It had taken a long time for her to build up her interior design business to the standard it had reached; now, although very few people might recognise her name, she could almost pick and choose her clients. It had become something of a cachet to claim that one's interiors had been designed by Jenna Stevens.

'It will make an excellent showcase for our craftsmen,' she said lightly, 'and besides I'm sick of London.'

Harley Thomas sighed, knowing he wasn't going to get any more information out of her than he already had. At times infuriating, always calmly controlled, there was still a vulnerability about her that made him anxious. He couldn't remember when he had seen a more beautiful woman. Her bone structure was delicately feminine, her eyes large and deeply green, her skin porcelain pale, her hair a thick mass of red-gold curls. At twenty-nine, she could easily have passed for twenty-three or -four if it hadn't been for her air of cool self-possession. Tall and slim, her curves were nevertheless femininely voluptuous, especially her breasts. Unlike him, her clothes did not betray her as a city person, her sleek tweeds fitting her as naturally as though she had worn them all her life.

'Where's Lucy?' she asked him, flicking open the pamphlet outlining the details of the house.

'Sulking in the car,' he told her wearily. 'God, Jenna, have you thought of the trouble she's going to give you if you do move up here? She's dead against it.'

'So she says, but she'll be at school most of the time.' School! That was another of Lucy's grievances and probably a justifiable one, but what alternative had she had? As a busy woman building up her career she had not had the time to devote to a growing child. At first she had managed with a housekeeper and Lucy had attended a local school in London, but then as Jenna's business had expanded, she was required to

be out more and more in the evenings and had been
worried about Lucy's isolation from other children her
age. In the end, the decision to send her to boarding
school had seemed the only answer, and until recently
she had thought Lucy enjoyed her school. It had been
carefully chosen, being neither too lax nor too strict,
and she was always meticulous about visiting her and
keeping time free during the school holidays to spend
with her. Only last summer, she and Lucy and two of
Lucy's friends had spent six weeks in the Aegean. It
was the old story . . . she needed to work to support
them both and yet by working she was forced to
abandon her traditional role as mother.

She made a pretence of studying the leaflet in front
of her, not wanting Harley to see her concern. Once
he suspected she had doubts, he would do everything
he could to dissuade her, Jenna knew that. But it was
only a pretence because she knew the facts about the
house off by heart. She had never been inside the
main part of the Hall, but already she could visualise
its rooms, feel its air of timelessness . . . sense the in-
bred belief of those who had lived there of their right
to be the privileged few. But now, they no longer had
that right. If she was successful at the auction the Hall
would be hers, and, ridiculous though it was, her need
to own it . . . to possess that which had once belonged
to the proud Deverils who had so disdained those
lower down the social ladder than themselves that
they were not permitted to put a foot inside the place,
was a strong motivating force in her life.

'Well, are you going to go inside?'

She was, but in her own good time and alone.
'Later,' she said non-committally, adding, 'look, why
don't you take Lucy back to West Thorpe, it's going
on for lunchtime. I'll join her there later.'

'Would you like me to stay overnight?'

When she had rung Bill Mather to tell him that she and Lucy were coming up to Yorkshire he had instantly insisted that they were to stay with him and his wife, Nancy, but there was no spare room for Harley and to be honest she didn't want him there, trying to pressurise her into changing her mind.

If she bought the Hall, even at the reserve price, it would take every spare bit of cash she had, and even then she would have to borrow heavily. But it would be worth it. It would be worth every single penny.

'You go back to London,' she told him. 'The Sedgerton contract should be in from the solicitors soon and I'd like you to go over it for me . . . I'm not sure I trust them completely . . . '

It wasn't unknown for some of her wealthy clients to try and wriggle out of paying for her work, and for that reason Jenna was insistent upon watertight contracts.

Harley leapt as eagerly at the bait as she had hoped. 'I'll get on to it the moment it arrives. How long do you think you'll stay up here for?'

'Just until after the auction.'

So she was still determined to go ahead. He sighed gustily. Privately, he thought she was mad even to contemplate buying such a vast, and undeniably crumbling pile. He shuddered to think what the bank would say, and of course, it would have to be bought in the company's name, especially if she intended to use it as a showcase for their work. Who on earth would come all the way from London up here, though?

Almost as though she had read his mind, Jenna drawled laconically, 'They aren't all devoid of money and taste north of Watford, you know, Harley. There's a vast untapped market up here and if we get in first, it could prove an extremely lucrative business.'

'But our contacts, our craftsmen, they're all in London.'

'So we'll pay them to travel — or find more.'

He knew her stubbornness of old, knew it and in many ways admired it. Not many women of her youth and with her commitments would have left a safe, well-paid position with an established firm to set up on her own, but she had. He had first heard of Jenna through a friend whose apartment she had decorated. He had gone to her initially to find out what she could do for a small Chelsea Mews flat he had bought and which he wanted modernising in order to sell at a profit. He had walked into her office to find it in chaos, paper everywhere, and her vivid, haunting beauty had almost robbed him of breath. He soon learned that under the chaos was a very keen business mind, but her untidiness had him itching to put things in order.

When she had let slip the fact that she was looking for a business administrator, he had leapt at the chance to join her, and even to this day wasn't sure if he had actually angled for the job or if she had simply let him think he had.

Their partnership worked well. She was a generous employer, content to leave the administrative side of the business completely to him, and he took a pride in the neat lists of schedules and work plans he kept locked away in his desk, carefully monitoring the progress of each contract, checking that all flowed smoothly.

Initially he had been almost desperately in love with her, but he soon learned that it was pointless. She was the only woman he knew who seemed to be

able to live her life without a man in it. In all the years
he had worked with her he had never known whether
she had a lover and, if so, who. On balance he rather
doubted it, which seemed incredible, given her start-
lingly good looks and the fact that she had a fifteen-
year-old daughter. Proof positive, surely, that once
there must have been a man. And that she must have
been extremely young . . .

He wasn't sure of her exact age, she looked younger
than she was. What had happened to Lucy's father?
Had he been married perhaps? Had they quarrelled?
Had he perhaps been a boy as young as she must
have been? Was it Lucy's conception and birth that
had soured her against men? None of them were
questions he would have dared to ask her, and over
the years his love had faded to admiration tinged
with a wistful yearning that things might have been
different.

Left by herself, Jenna walked towards the house.
Sharp knives of tension speared her stomach. Those
who knew her would have been stunned had they
known how she was feeling. Jenna never betrayed
any emotion, any weakness and yet here she was,
dreading setting one foot inside the house she had
come so far to see and yet knowing that she must.

The Hall was rectangular and dark. Someone had
painted over the elegant Georgian plasterwork in
a revolting shade of brown, so that even the light
pouring in through the high windows did nothing to
alleviate the gloom. Dust and the smell of damp per-
meated the air. A double staircase curved up to the
first floor, the stairs elegant and shallow. All Jenna's
inborn sense of colour and fitness rebelled at what
had been done to this once-gracious room.

Two sets of double doors led off the hall with

another two single doors further towards the back of it. This main entrance was in the new wing of the house and, as she knew from the sketch plan she had, contained a large drawing-room, the library, a dining-room, and another room which was described as a 'back parlour'.

Although badly scratched, the mahogany of the double doors into the drawing-room seemed firm and dry; the brass handles and locks decorating them were probably the originals, Jenna reflected, marvelling at the workmanship that meant they opened outwards easily despite their weight without so much as a squeak.

The drawing-room was at the far end of the new wing, and, from the smell of damp pervading it, had probably suffered the most neglect. A leaking downspout, or a hole in the roof, Jenna decided knowledgeably, studying the betraying mould-stains discolouring the faded silk wallpaper at the far end of the room.

Over the years, the original Adam design had been mutilated as only the Victorians and Edwardians had known how, but she could see how the room once must have looked and how it could look again. Against her will, Jenna found as she walked through the dusty neglected rooms that she was slowly falling in love with the house, the one thing she had made no calculation for at all. Against all reason, its neglect called out to her, making her ache to restore it to what it had once been. Moving from room to room she forgot why she had originally come here, and knew only a powerful feeling that the house had to be hers. It went against all logic and reason, but it was strong enough to blot out everything else, even Lucy, waiting for her at the Mathers', even the fact that originally she had wanted the house simply because it had once belonged to the Deverils, everything. She had heard of love at first sight, but had never envisaged herself falling so deeply in love with a house that the thought of not owning it caused actual physical pain.

Not even the open evidence of damp and the knowledge that it would need a fortune spending on it could put her off. Already she could imagine how it would look; how it would come to life under her expert care and love.

On the first floor, a galleried landing overlooked the main hall with four doors leading off it. Jenna had already noticed several paintings hanging on the walls — the house was being sold complete with contents — but this was the first one that had caused her to spare it more than a passing glance. The portrait was of a man, dressed in clothes of the late Georgian era. His dark hair was worn unpowdered, curling close to his skull, and the painter had somehow managed to capture on canvas the sitter's aura of intense masculinity. A cynical rakehell character, Jenna suspected moving closer to the portrait.

The words 'James Deveril, aged 32, 1817' were painted on the frame, and it seemed to Jenna as she studied him that the dark blue eyes watched her, coolly mocking her.

As far as she knew most of the Deverils had been fair-haired Saxon types whereas this man was dark, his hair as jet black as a gypsy's, his skin tanned as though he had spent some time in hotter climates than Yorkshire's.

Fascinated by him against her will, Jenna wondered who he was. It shouldn't be difficult to find out — the Deveril history was well documented in the local library as she already knew.

What on earth was wrong with her? she chided herself, moving away. The moment she entered this house she had been acting in a manner totally foreign to her normal behaviour.

She walked from the Georgian wing into the old, Tudor part of the Hall. Here the rooms were small, oddly shaped, the windows mullioned and the ceilings beamed. The Georgian wing fronted the house and the original Tudor building ran at right angles to it, a good-sized courtyard was at the back of the building enclosed on two sides by the house itself and on the other two by stables and outbuildings. Now neglected and weed-covered, Jenna could already see how attractive this area could eventually be.

Beyond the house lay the grounds, which included a small park planted with specimen trees, collected by an adventuring Deveril who had had business interests in the West Indies, but the rich farmland that lay beyond the house's immediate environs was being sold separately. Not that she would have wanted it, Jenna admitted, studying the plans at the back of her sale pamphlet, the land that went with the house afforded it plenty of privacy. She remembered as a child cycling past the lodge gates, intensely curious about what lay behind the protective ring of trees that hid the house from sight.

Today wasn't the first time she had visited the house, though; there had been one other occasion on which she had been here. As she stepped out through the back door into the derelict yard her mouth twisted bitterly. On that occasion she had made the mistake of ringing the front doorbell, and had been sent round to the servants' entrance for her pains. 'Servants' entrance', dear God, how antiquated it all seemed now, ridiculously so; the hallmark of a family desperate to preserve the old 'us' and 'them', 'master' and 'servant' image. Then she had been totally over-awed, embarrassed and humiliated. How naïve she had been! A true product of her remote village upbringing by a spinster great-aunt.

Having finished her inspection she walked back towards her car, lost in memories of the past.

'Nice car!' The unexpected intrusion of the deep male voice into her thoughts unbalanced her, and she swung round tensely, colour flushing up under her skin as she found herself being studied by a pair of openly appreciative male eyes. The visual impact of coming face to face with a man so similar to the portrait of James Deveril, which she had just been studying, made her usual cool poise desert her, and she could only glance from him to her scarlet Ferrari in disorientated bewilderment.

'Sorry if I startled you!' His eyes crinkled in warm amusement, laughter tingeing his voice as he added, 'You look as though you've seen a ghost! Have you? They do say that one of the wives of one of the Deverils walks sometimes at full moon . . . though no one's ever seen her during the day.'

He had a faint accent that she couldn't place, and angry at herself for her bemused reaction, Jenna threw him a cold look. The laughter died from his eyes immediately, and he sketched her a briefly mocking bow, drawling lightly, 'Sorry if I spoke out of place, ma'am . . .'

He was dressed in jeans and a checked cotton workshirt, his hair tousled, the open neck of his shirt revealing a deep vee of tanned flesh and the beginnings of a tangle of dark hair. Who was he? He was so like James Deveril that he must have some Deveril blood somewhere . . . but why not? There had been several

Deverils in the past who had taken what they considered their *droit de seigneur* over the village girls; this man could be the descendant of one of them. He couldn't be a legitimate member of the family; there weren't any alive.

'Thinking of buying it, are you?' He nodded towards the house as he spoke, his eyes lingering on the full thrust of her breasts as she turned to unlock her car.

Seething inwardly Jenna ignored him, hoping that he would take the hint and leave her alone, but when he kept on prowling appreciatively round her car, she began to suspect he was deliberately trying to infuriate her, and she snapped shortly, 'Look, I can see that you consider yourself something of a local Don Juan, but I'm really not interested. If I were you I'd get back to work before your employers discover that you're missing.'

She had expected him to be disconcerted by her put-down, but instead he merely laughed, stepping away from the car as she slid in to fire the engine. The car needed servicing and was being rather temperamental. It refused to start, despite several attempts to get it going, and all-too-conscious of his amused scrutiny, Jenna willed herself not to give way to temper.

'Here, let me.'

His arrogance left her breathless, stupefaction giving way to fury as he opened her door, turned the key in the ignition and the car fired right away.

Closing the door for her he gave her a wide, taunting smile, and said, 'Some cars are like women; they respond best to a man's touch.'

Chauvinist! Much as she longed to throw the insult at him, Jenna restrained herself. Why get so het up about the sexual insolence of some village lout who obviously thought of the female sex as no more than male chattels.

She was still fuming when she reached her destination. Although deference wasn't something she expected to receive from her peers — of either sex — there had been an air of insolent amusement about him, an easy, but none the less distinct, self-assurance that had jarred on her. Mere farm labourer he might be, but for all that he had made it plain that he considered himself superior to her simply by virtue of his sex, and that made her seethe. It had been a long time since she had come up against such blatantly arrogant maleness and it had unsettled her. Implicit in the look he had given her as she drove away had been the suggestion that had he so wished he could have mastered not only her car but her as well. No man could look at her like that and get away with it.

For goodness' sake, Jenna chided herself as she parked her car in the drive of the old school-house and climbed out, why was she getting in such a state over some country Lothario?

Since she had left the area her old school had been shut down but Bill Mather, the headmaster, had been allowed to purchase the school-house. Built in the Victorian era, it had an air of solid respectability and stability. This was the first house she had ever truly called home, she thought, as she ignored the front door in favour of walking round to the kitchen. She had come here as a frightened, ignorant girl of barely fifteen, having been virtually thrown out by her great-aunt, her clothes in a battered suitcase and a two-week-old baby in her arms. She sighed faintly, anticipating the conflict now to come with that same 'baby'. Lucy had objected strenuously to coming to Yorkshire, mainly because Jenna herself had been so eager to do so. What had happened to the easy friend-ship that had once existed between them? Sometimes these days she felt as though Lucy almost hated her. Was she being selfish in wanting to buy the house? Lucy still had several terms to do at school, even if she decided to leave after O levels; she had always com-plained about the smallness of their London flat. Here she could have as much space as she wanted. Perhaps even that horse she had nagged her mother for last year.

There was no sign of Lucy as Jenna walked into the Mathers' kitchen. No doubt she would be sulking in her room. Lucy had made her dislike of the Mathers more than plain, because, Jenna suspected, she be-lieved that like Jenna herself they knew the identity of her father and were conspiring with her mother to keep it from her.

Of course Jenna could understand why Lucy want-ed to know her father's identity, but it was something she just could not tell her ... She bit her lip won-dering how many people living in the village could remember that summer nearly sixteen years ago. She had changed of course. Then, she had been a pain-fully thin, milk-skinned child with red hair and enormous, frightened eyes. All that was still the same was the colour of her skin ... even her hair had turned from carrot to rich Titian. No, she doubted if anyone would recognise her. She hadn't had many friends. Her aunt had never really mingled with the other villagers, and besides, she had always been con-tent with Rachel's company.

Rachel ... pain pierced through her. Fifteen years her sister had been dead and even now Jenna's grief was as fresh and sharp as it had been then. Rachel had been everything Jenna had not: three years older, warm and extrovert, with a personality that drew people to her. There had not been an ounce of malice in her nature. Naturally warm-hearted she had naïvely believed that everyone else was the same; trusting and eager to please, she had paid a terrible price for her naïvety . . .

'Jenna!'

She tore her thoughts abruptly from the past as Bill Mather walked into the kitchen. 'I thought I heard your monster of a car arrive. How did it go?'

The grey eyes weren't quite as keen now as they had been fifteen years ago, but they were still kind and wise.

'I fell in love with the place, totally and for ever,' Jenna told him honestly.

He and his wife were her only bridge between the present and her past; she loved them with an intensity that went so deep that it was something she could never talk about. Without them . . .

The faded grey eyes showed concern. 'Jenna, my dear, are you sure you're doing the right thing?'

'If you're questioning my motives, I admit that initially it was a macabre need to gloat that brought me here. I wouldn't be human if I didn't harbour some resentment.'

Bill Mather smiled wryly. 'No, of course not, but you mustn't let your bitterness over the past mar the present, Jenna.'

'You mean I should forget what happened, forget how the Deverils killed my sister . . . how they . . . '

Emotion boiled up inside her, pain reflected in her eyes as they met his.

'Jenna . . . Jenna . . . of course not . . . but, my dear, Alan and Charles are gone . . . the family is gone . . . '

'Not quite.' She said it quietly, her face pale

and strained as she looked at him. 'There's still Lucy . . . '

'Yes. Jenna, do you think it's wise to conceal the truth from her? The child has a right to know that . . . '

'That what? That her mother was brutally raped by her father and left pregnant . . . abandoned and left to die giving birth to the child she should never have had? Is that what you want me to tell her?' She was shaking with emotion, sick with the force of it. Fifteen years had done nothing to lessen the sense of sick despair she always felt when she thought about her sister. Beautiful, lovable Rachel. 'I want to buy the house,' she said quietly. 'I want to buy it for Lucy, because it is hers by right.' She remembered with bitter clarity how she had visited the house with Rachel, just after Rachel had discovered her pregnancy. Her sister had been distraught with fear and shame, frightened into telling Jenna about the brutal attack she had endured.

She and Charles Deveril had met by accident. Rachel had been attending college in York and he had seen her waiting at the bus stop and recognised her as someone from the village. He had offered her a lift, and Rachel had naïvely accepted, but instead of driving her straight home, he had taken her down a deserted farm track. There had been tears in Rachel's eyes and voice as she described the way she had fought against him, only to be overpowered. Terrified by what had happened and too frightened to tell their aunt, Rachel had tried to put it from her mind. Their upbringing had been a strict one and neither girl was promiscuous: at eighteen, Rachel had still been a virgin.

It had been Jenna who had insisted that they must

go up to the house, naïvely sure that when he knew
what had happened Sir Alan would insist on Charles
marrying her sister. But after ringing the front doorbell they had been sent round to the back, and Sir
Alan had accused them of making the whole thing up
and had even threatened to call the police, claiming
that Rachel was trying to besmirch the Deveril name.

It was only later that Jenna discovered that Charles
had something of an unsavoury reputation with
women, and that he had been expelled from school
because of certain allegations made against him by the
parents of a girl in the village near to the school.

What had followed had been a nightmare of con-
spiracy and fear. Rachel had bound her to silence,
making her promise to say nothing to anyone. A tall,
slender girl, she had disguised her pregnancy with the
then fashionable loose clothes, refusing all Jenna's
entreaties to visit a doctor or tell their aunt.

She had started in labour one Saturday afternoon
when they were both in York; a passing policewoman
realising what was happening had taken them both to
hospital. What happened there had been a nightmare
to Jenna, bewildered and confused, alone in the wait-
ing-room until a doctor suddenly appeared, grave-
faced, questioning her gently, until she broke down
and told him the whole story. 'My sister . . . please let
me see her,' she had begged when she had told him,
and she had known instinctively by his silence and
tension that something was wrong.

'I'm sorry . . . '

'She's dead, isn't she . . ?' Jenna could remember
even now how those words had burst from her throat,
panic and pain clawing desperately at her stomach.
Rachel could not be dead. She was only eighteen —
people didn't die having babies these days.

But Rachel had. Rachel, whose narrow frame wasn't built for easy birth, whose life might have been saved had the doctors known what to expect. 'She should have had her baby by Caesarian section,' the doctor had explained quietly to Jenna, but because it had been too late, there had been complications.

Complications which had resulted in her sister's bleeding to death, her life flooding away on a dark red tide that the nursing staff had not been quite quick enough to conceal from Jenna as the doctor gave way to hysterical pleading and allowed her to see Rachel for one last time.

As she looked at her sister, she had heard a faint mewling cry, and had stared, totally stupefied at the tiny bundle held by one of the nurses. Until that moment she hadn't given a thought to Rachel's child.

'A little girl,' the nurse told her softly.

'Give her to me.' Jenna had been barely aware of making the demand, but as she looked upon the tiny screwed-up face of her niece she made a vow that somehow she would find a way to keep her sister's child, and that somehow the Deverils would be made to pay for Rachel's death.

It hadn't been easy — far from it . . . Painfully, Jenna dragged her thoughts away from the past.

'I'd better go up and see her,' she told Bill, referring to Lucy. 'Oh, by the way, the most curious thing . . . I saw a portrait in the house — of a James Deveril, quite unlike the rest of the family — very dark . . . and then just as I was leaving this man came up to the car. He was almost identical to him . . . the living image in fact.'

'A trick of heredity,' Bill told her. 'It must be. There are no Deverils left. The solicitors made an exhaustive search before putting the Hall up for sale. It happens occasionally.'

'Yes . . . After all, Lucy is far from being the only Deveril bastard to be born around here.'

Bill Mather heard the bitterness in her voice and sighed. The effect of her sister's death had left scars on Jenna that he doubted would ever heal. Fifteen was such a vulnerable age to be exposed to the agony of losing a deeply loved sister, and especially in such circumstances. He had never ceased to admire the way Jenna had shouldered the responsibility of her niece, the way she had forged a new life for herself — and a very successful one at that — but it grieved him that she was still alone, still so wary and sharp with men. They couldn't know, as he did, that it cloaked a very real fear, a dread of betrayal that had been burned into her soul with Lucy's birth and her sister's death.

It would take a very special sort of man to break down the barriers Jenna had built around herself: a man with the strength to appreciate her need to be self-sufficient, to have her career, her escape route from the pain of emotional commitment. He would need patience too . . . patience to undo the wrongs of the past, and the intelligence to see past the beautiful façade Jenna presented to the world, to the woman beneath.

The kitchen door opened and his wife walked in. They had been married for over forty years and were still as happy together as they had been on their wedding day. Their one regret was that they had no children.

'Have you spoken to Jenna?' Nancy asked him. He had met her, a brisk Yorkshirewoman, during his first teaching job near Thirsk. A farmer's daughter used to hard work and the uncertainties of life in the Dales, she had a down-to-earth common sense that was sometimes worth more than any educational degree.

'I tried to . . . but it's very difficult.'

'It's not difficult at all,' Nancy corrected him crisply. 'You simply have to point out to her that she must tell Lucy the truth. The child has a right to know. Jenna's always listened to you before.'

'She isn't sixteen any longer, Nancy,' he said gently. 'I can only advise her now, not command. She wants to protect Lucy. Think how you would feel learning that your mother had been the victim of a vicious attack by your father.'

'Jenna should have told her years ago. I mind I told her often enough. Has she made up her mind about the old Hall?'

'She says she's fallen in love with it.'

'Fallen in love with a pile of stones and mortar?' Nancy Mather snorted derisively. 'She wants to find herself a man to fall in love with. It's past time she did. Unplucked fruit only withers,' she added forthrightly. 'You only have to remember that great-aunt of hers to know that. Where is Jenna now?'

'Gone upstairs to see Lucy.' He sighed faintly. 'She's going to have problems there. Lucy's determined to oppose her for no better reason than setting her mind against everything Jenna is in favour of.'

'Well, that's teenagers for you. I don't agree with Jenna buying the Hall, though. She's not still doing it because it belonged to the Deverils, is she?' she asked sharply.

'I don't think so. Oh, I don't say that wasn't what originally motivated her, but her desire to buy it now is entirely because she loves it. I could see it in her eyes. By the way,' he added, 'do you know anyone hereabouts that looks like James Deveril? You remember, we saw the portrait of him the last time the hunt ball was held there.'

'Aye, I remember,' Nancy agreed with a smile. 'I doubt any woman looking on that face could forget. A right tearaway he looked. Dark as a gypsy with eyes as blue as cornflowers. No, there's no one hereabouts who looks like that. Plenty with the Saxon Deveril looks, but he was a one-off, as I recall it.'

'Yes, something of a black sheep of the family,' her husband agreed. Since his retirement he had amused himself by studying the Deveril family with a view to writing about them, and he remembered that when he had questioned Sir Alan about his mysterious ancestor, his host had responded with thin-lipped displeasure.

'Not a true Deveril at all. It was said at the time that his mother had been unfaithful to her husband, and he was the result. I have her diaries in the library. It seems she cared more for him than she did for her other children, although in the end she had to pay. He was caught poaching on a neighbour's estate and shipped off to the West Indies. Bad blood always tells,' he had added pompously.

Poor lady, Bill had reflected, listening to his host, if her husband had been anything like as dull as the present holder of the Deveril title, no wonder she had been unfaithful. Sir Alan took a pride in the Deveril name which far exceeded its actual importance — at least that was Bill's view. Personally, he found both Sir Alan and his son unpleasantly Victorian in their attitudes to life. Charles in particular had an arrogance that was intensely jarring. Bill had never liked him and had always considered there was something slightly shifty about Charles . . . something that aroused an atavistic dislike, and he could not deny that both the Deverils, father and son, had behaved extremely badly over Rachel. The poor girl had been too ignorant and young to realise that the law would have been on her side, and Sir Alan had managed to terrorise her into keeping her pregnancy a secret, claiming that no one would believe her story, and that *she* had been the one to entice Charles.

Had he ever suffered any guilt? Bill wondered. The girl's death had been a nine-day wonder in the village, especially when Jenna returned from York, with a baby she said was her dead sister's, refusing to name the father, but insisting stubbornly in the face of her great-aunt's outrage that the child was not going to be adopted. Both of them would have ended up in council care if he and Nancy had not stepped in. Jenna was like a daughter to them, Lucy a granddaughter, for all that they had not seen her since she was a child. He knew that Jenna was concealing Lucy's parentage from her with the best of motives, but it was still wrong. He would have to try to talk to her again . . . Nancy would let him have no peace until he did so.

CHAPTER TWO

OUTSIDE Lucy's room Jenna paused, gathering together all her self-control before she knocked and opened the door. Lucy was lying on the bed reading a comic. She turned her head sullenly in Jenna's direction, scowling fiercely as she looked at her.

'I don't care what you say,' Lucy burst out defiantly, 'I won't live here. I won't!'

Sighing, Jenna sat down on the bed and studied her niece's turbulent features. Lucy took after her mother in looks, her hair the same warm, dark brown that Rachel's had been. She also had Rachel's grey eyes, but whereas Jenna remembered her sister's expression as being a placid one, Lucy's was normally defiant. She looked towards the window, not seeing the view beyond it, wondering why it was that she and Lucy seemed to be so constantly at loggerheads. Of course, she could understand Lucy's desire to know more about her father, it was a quite natural one, but how could she tell her the truth?

Perhaps it would have been wiser to have made up a father for Lucy when she was too young to question what she was told too deeply, but now it was too late for that.

'Darling, you're forgetting, you'll be at school,' she said in a placatory voice. 'And you can always spend part of the holidays in London. I'll probably keep on a flat there.'

'School!' Lucy's voice was thick with loathing. 'I

29

hate that place, I hate everything about it. Why do I have to go there?' She turned to face Jenna, anger turning her eyes almost black. 'But, of course, we both know the answer to that, don't we? If I wasn't at boarding school you wouldn't have so much time to devote to your precious career, would you?'

It was an argument they had been through many times before and once again, patiently, Jenna explained to Lucy that she needed to earn a living for them both, that she needed to go out to work.

'Yes, but there was no need to send me away to school, was there?' Lucy challenged. 'You could have sent me to a day school. I don't suppose you ever really wanted me anyway, did you?' she threw out bitterly. 'If you'd been able to have an abortion in those days, I suppose that's what you'd have done, isn't it?'

Genuinely shocked by Lucy's outburst, Jenna could only stare at her. 'Well, isn't it?' Lucy challenged fiercely.

'Lucy, Jenna, lunch is ready,' the calm interruption of Nancy's voice cut through the tension in the small room.

'You're quite wrong, Lucy,' Jenna said, fighting to appear calm, and not to betray the dreadful shaking that was threatening to overcome her. 'But now isn't the time to discuss this. We'd better go down and have lunch, otherwise Nancy will wonder what's wrong.'

'You mean she hasn't already guessed?' Lucy laughed bitterly as she got up off the bed and sauntered towards the door. Before she pulled it open she turned and stared defiantly at Jenna. 'You needn't think I'm going to leave it like this because I'm not. Somewhere I have a father, and one day I'll find out who he is and nothing you can do will stop me!'

She had gone downstairs before Jenna could call her back, and although over lunch Jenna made an effort to respond to Bill's interested questions about the old Hall, her mind was not on them. There was, of course, no real way Lucy could find out about her parentage, but Jenna's heart ached for the pain of the younger girl wishing more than anything else that she could tell her the truth, but fearing that she had left it far too late. The relationship between herself and Lucy was so delicate now that she half feared that if she did tell her the truth, Lucy would not believe her.

And what good would it do, anyway? None that she could see.

'So, what do you think the old Hall will go for?' Bill asked when they were drinking their after-lunch coffee. 'The reserve price?'

Jenna grimaced, 'I'm hoping so. Even at that it would take more than my existing cash resources.'

Bill put down his cup and looked at her thoughtfully. 'Jenna, are you sure you're doing the right thing? I accept that you've fallen in love with the house, and I can quite see that it would make an excellent headquarters from which you could expand your business, but in view of the fact that Lucy doesn't want to move up here, and, well, the past . . . '

'I've made up my mind,' Jenna told him curtly. 'Don't ask me to explain why, Bill. I don't really know myself.' She made a tiny helpless gesture, oddly heart-tugging in a woman normally so invulnerable, and Bill could not help but be touched by it. 'All I do know is that I must own the old Hall. For it to be mine will satisfy some need in me. I can't explain it any better than that.'

'Mmm, well . . . You know best.'

'Dear Bill.' Jenna got up and ruffled his grey hair. 'What would I have done without you and Nancy to support me?' He was the only member of his sex with whom she allowed herself to be herself — the only man she did not either dislike or despise.

'We only did what any caring human beings would have done in the same circumstances, Jenna. It was your misfortune that in both your aunt and in Alan Deveril you came across two of the less attractive specimens of human kind.'

Jenna shrugged. 'I suppose I can't really blame my aunt. After all, she was very much a product of her time. She'd done her duty as she saw it, by taking in Rachel and myself in the first place.'

Bill watched her, noting the brief flash of pain that crossed her face. He had never been able to understand how Helen Marsden had been able to turn her fifteen-year-old great-niece from the door, especially when she had been carrying a two-week-old baby in her arms. Helen had known that the child hadn't been Jenna's, but that had made no difference. Thank God he had happened to be out walking the dog that night and had seen Jenna trudging down the lane, tears cascading down a small face that had been oddly fierce and determined despite her plight, even then. Lucy had been clutched in one arm, a battered suitcase in the other.

At first Jenna had refused to stop and talk to him, but he had managed to coax her into the house and once there, Nancy soon had the whole story from her. She hadn't wanted to stay, but Nancy had insisted. The next morning, while Jenna was still deep in an exhausted sleep, he and Nancy had sat down and talked about the situation. Jenna was flatly refusing to give up her sister's child, and there was no reason why she should, at least in Nancy's eyes.

When Jenna eventually woke, they had put it to her that she stay with them, at least for the time being. At first she had been reluctant to agree. She knew Bill only as the headmaster of the local school and Nancy not at all and she was patently truculent — reluctant to trust them — but gradually Nancy had persuaded her.

Still too young to leave school herself, Jenna had had to leave Lucy with Nancy during the day while she attended her classes. She had always been a hard-working girl, and intelligent, but then she worked like someone driven, Bill remembered. He had found her one night in the sitting-room poring over her books. When he had questioned her as to why she was still working at that time of night, she had told him fierce-ly that she needed to leave school as quickly as she could with as many qualifications as she could get, so that she could find a way of supporting herself and Lucy.

'And what will you do about Lucy, Jenna?' he asked her quietly now, coming back to the present. 'I'm afraid she isn't going to accept coming to live up here very easily.'

'No, I know, I'm hoping when she goes back to school she'll settle down a bit better.' Jenna bit her lip, an endearing childish gesture in so polished a woman, and frowned quickly. 'When I was upstairs with her just now, she said she hated school. She even accused me of sending her to boarding school because I want-ed to be rid of her. It wasn't like that at all, Bill.' She turned to him, her eyes appealing for understanding. 'I could have sent her to a day school, yes, but that would have meant her coming home sometimes to an empty flat, crossing London alone, I didn't want that for her. I thought at least at boarding school she would be safe and secure, with other girls of her own age.'

'Lucy's a teenager, Jenna,' Bill reminded her, 'and like all teenagers, she's going through a very painful growing period — something I know you missed out on.'

'I didn't have time for growing pains.' Jenna admitted wryly. 'I was too busy fighting to prove I was grown up enough to keep Lucy. I was terrified the authorities would take her away from me. And so they would have if it hadn't been for you and Nancy, agreeing to stand as our foster parents until I was old enough to adopt her legally.'

'Well . . . we wanted to do all we could to help you, Jenna, but as far as Lucy's concerned, now, today, I think the root cause of the problem is this conflict between you concerning her father.'

'Yes,' Jenna agreed quietly, 'but what can I do, Bill? I can't tell her the truth now. I just can't. Perhaps I should have made up a mythical father for her years ago, but somehow I never thought about it. I ask myself, what would Rachel want me to do, and I can't help feeling she would want me to protect her daughter.'

Bill sighed, knowing that Jenna's refusal to tell Lucy the truth sprang from a genuine desire to protect her but not sure that he agreed with her. If she wasn't told the truth, Lucy would go through life constantly wondering about her father. He accepted that to be told the facts now would cause her considerable distress, but Lucy had more of Jenna's strong nature than either of them realised — enough he was sure, when the initial shock had died down, to accept what she had been told. He felt that in the long run it was better for Lucy to have the anguish of knowing the truth now, rather than the unhealed wound of not knowing her true parentage.

'I hope there isn't going to be a lot of competition for the house,' Jenna commented, changing the conversation. 'When I originally found out it was going up for auction I wanted it because it had been their house, but now I've been round it, seen it . . . ' She shrugged and smiled wryly. 'Ridiculous, I know, but I want it so badly, Bill. Too badly, perhaps. When I went inside I . . . it was the strangest feeling, as though somehow I had come home.'

'I haven't heard that there's been much interest locally.' Bill was avoiding looking directly at her, and Jenna guessed that he was more affected than he wanted her to know by her brief revelation. She had never found it easy to talk about her feelings — Bill knew that. Jenna loved both Bill and Nancy with a love almost as strong as that she felt for Lucy, but she had never been able to put her emotion into words. She knew that people often found her cool and unapproachable and she preferred it that way. Not for the world would she have wanted to admit to anyone how frightened she was of emotional commitment, of laying herself open to pain and betrayal. Strange, she had not thought so deeply about her own innermost feelings for years, and now was hardly the time to become involved in the complexities of self-analysis, she reminded herself wryly.

'Of course,' Bill went on, 'one never knows about out-of-the-district buyers. But I shouldn't think you'll have anything to worry about. After all, the building is extremely run-down and in a rather remote part of the country. Large houses such as the Hall are notoriously expensive to run. What time is the auction?'

'Eleven o'clock tomorrow morning,' Jenna told him. 'I had intended to take Lucy with me, but in view of her present mood I was wondering if you and Nancy could keep an eye on her for me?'

'Don't worry about Lucy, she'll be fine with us.'

Jenna bit her lip. She hadn't missed the way Lucy had taken to watching Bill, and remembering her own early teenage years, she suspected that, like her, Lucy was suffering from the lack of a caring male presence in her life. Would Lucy also grow to womanhood seeing men as an alien and somehow threatening sex? That wasn't what she wanted for her. So what could she do about it? she derided herself mentally. Marry?

Who? Harley? She repressed a brief grin at the mental picture conjured up by her thoughts. Poor Harley. There had been a time when he had fancied himself in love with her, but she suspected that if she made any romantic overtures to him now he would run a mile. Marriage wasn't for her. She could never envisage herself giving up her freedom; her right to remain in control of her life and her career . . . and yet . . . seeing the looks Bill and Nancy sometimes exchanged, the depth of understanding and caring that existed between them, there had been instances when she had felt deeply envious.

Bill and Nancy were lucky, she told herself. She only had to think of half a dozen or more of her close acquaintances to remind herself of the disillusionment and pain that marriage could bring. She was right to remain contemptuous of the male sex. She would be far better employed worrying about what her accountants and the bank were going to say when she broke the news of her latest acquisition to them. She repressed another grin as she visualised herself telling them that she had bought the house because she had

fallen in love with it. Hardly good business practice.
No, somehow she would have to convince them that
with the acquisition of the Deveril house her business
would flourish, as indeed she believed it would.

It had been hard work to go from being a short-
hand-typist, working in a pool with other girls, to
owning her own business. It had been her good
fortune that she had soon grown bored with the hum-
drum routine of the typing-pool and had applied for
another job. That job had been the first stepping-stone
to her present career. She had been exultant when
John Howard took her on as his personal secretary,
and had made an excited telephone call to Bill and
Nancy to tell them all about it.

'An interior designer?' Nancy had been inclined to
be slightly disapproving, thinking that Jenna would
have been wiser to stay with the insurance company,
but Bill had supported her. Her plans for going to uni-
versity had been abandoned when Rachel died. Bill
had tried to argue her out of it, telling her that he and
Nancy would take care of Lucy for her, but she had
been adamant. Lucy was her responsibility, her only
link with her dead sister. If she went to univer-
sity Lucy would be five or six before Jenna was
qualified . . . . Lucy would not be Rachel's child but
Nancy's and Bill's, so instead Jenna had concentrated
on gaining some secretarial skills, determined to find a
job and a home for them both just as soon as she
possibly could.

Getting a job had been relatively easy. In those
days, secretarial jobs weren't that hard to come by,
and by studying the national papers she had managed
to secure an interview with a London-based insurance
company without too much trouble. Finding somewhere suitable for herself and Lucy to live in London

was a different matter. And who would look after
Lucy while Jenna was at work? Her salary was small
. . . not large enough to support both of them, but instinct told her that if she was going to succeed anywhere it would be in London, and not the quiet local
market town in Yorkshire. So she had been forced to
agree with Nancy's view that Lucy should stay with
them. It had been hard, those first six months in London, saving every penny she could from her salary,
living in a dismal but cheap women's hostel so that
she could travel back to Yorkshire every weekend to
see Lucy . . . And then had come the job with John
Howard. He had paid her well, delighted to discover
that she had an almost instinctive flair for colour and
design. It had been at his suggestion that she had attended night school, and she had learned a good deal
from him, sensing that he was not a man who represented any threat to her.

He had not, as many people had suspected, been
her lover, but his wife had been suspicious and jealous enough for him to tell Jenna after she had worked
for him for two years that he felt it best that she
looked for a job elsewhere. She had been stunned,
shocked, gripped with a furious sense of disbelief. She
had worked hard for him, and for herself, saving,
scrimping, putting as much money on one side as she
could so that she could move out of her hostel and
find a small flat for herself and Lucy. She had it all
planned out. Lucy could attend nursery school while
she worked. She would find herself a neighbour with
small children who would be glad to earn a few extra
pounds a week taking Lucy to and from school, and
now, all because of a spoilt woman's wholly irrational
jealousy, her plans would have to be changed.

Sensing how distraught she was, but not knowing

the reason why, it was then that John Howard had tentatively suggested that she go into business herself. He would help her financially in the early stages, he had offered awkwardly, and although pride had urged Jenna to refuse his guilt-induced offer — after all, she had done nothing to warrant being dismissed, nothing at all, no matter what his wife might think — caution had whispered to her to wait. How she had hated Marian Howard, she remembered grimly. Although they had never met, she had seen photographs of John's spoilt, beautiful wife. They had no children, and from what John said Marian seemed to spend her life in a ceaseless round of shopping and socialising. Now, because she was jealous of Jenna, Marian was forcing John to dismiss her . . . and because of his wife's insecurity she would lose her chance to have Lucy with her.

'I could put quite a lot of business your way, Jenna,' John had offered, warming to his idea, unaware of the battle going on inside her.

Jenna thought rapidly. She knew quite well what business John meant. As an established, socially prominent interior designer, he was often approached by women who wanted to boast that their living-room or bedroom had been designed by John Howard, and yet these same women, when told how much it would cost them to drop his prestigious name into the envious ears of their friends, often had a change of heart; when they did go ahead and commission him they were always difficult to please. Jenna had had the unrewarding task of soothing more than one of them. But it would be a start, a chance to prove just what she could do, an opportunity to establish herself financially, to have Lucy living with her, and although her pride was outraged and demanded that she refuse to be bought off, she heard herself saying coolly that it sounded a good idea.

Of course it had not been easy. There had been problems ... snide remarks ... whispered comments that John had backed her financially because she had been his mistress, but she had weathered it all and had long since paid back the small capital John had loaned her, with interest, and now ...

Now she was a successful, prominent interior designer herself, as courted and fêted as John had been. One of the reasons for her success had been her ability to keep ahead of the trends, and now she sensed a mood in people to return to the past — a desire for craftsmanship rather than gimmickry — so she had slowly set about building up a pool of craftsmen and women, each an expert in their own field.

If she moved to Yorkshire she would have to start again, she told herself later that evening as she prepared for bed. Of course, she could retain many of her contacts but others ... A tiny thrill of excitement curled upwards through her stomach. She wanted the challenge of a new venture, she admitted to herself, and more than that she ached to start work on the old Hall: to restore it, to cherish and love it. Half hysterically she reflected that while other women her age had love affairs with the opposite sex, she was embarking on a love affair with a house. But what about Lucy? Guilt and despair mingled inside her. Initially everything she had done had been for her sister's child, for Lucy, so that she wouldn't suffer as she and Rachel had done. She had wanted so much for her ... had wanted her to have the security of love and money as she and Rachel had not. She had never quite lost the conviction that had Rachel come from a more moneyed background, from a family where there was someone to stand up for her and support her, that Alan Deveril would not have been able to browbeat her as he had, that Charles would not have got away with what had been a violently brutal rape. But instead of protecting Lucy all she seemed to have done was alienate her. How could Jenna explain now to Lucy how she had been conceived . . . who and what her father had been?

Lucy was so achingly vulnerable, and although she tried to hide it from her, Jenna was acutely aware of her vulnerability. Sometimes she ached inside for her niece, but it seemed nothing she did could make Lucy happy. She could of course always agree to stay in London. Should she? But London was too full of pit-falls for a young and rebellious teenager. If she gave in to Lucy on this issue, all too soon there would be others. Staying in London was not really the crux of the problem between them: it was Jenna's refusal to discuss Lucy's father with her, and at the moment she could see no way of solving that problem without causing her niece pain and possible emotional damage. She drifted off to sleep with a frown on her forehead, still worrying about Lucy.

When Jenna first opened her eyes, it took her several seconds to remember where she was. She shook her head, wonderingly, a bright skein of hair clouding her vision until she pushed it away. It had been years since she had slept so heavily or so well. Must be something to do with the cool, crisp, Yorkshire upland air coming in through the open bedroom window, she thought wryly.

It had also been years since she had woken up in the morning possessed by the faintly breathless sense of excitement she was now experiencing. A sense of excitement she suspected most women would equate with the appearance in their lives of a new man. Her mouth curled derisively. Jenna was no fool. She knew that her attitude towards the male sex was an unusual one, just as she knew that in many ways it sprang from what had happened to her sister. She also knew that all members of the male sex were not like Alan or Charles Deveril, but knowing that had never stopped her from freezing off any attempts men made to make contact with her. It wasn't that she hated the male sex; it was more that she felt nothing for it in terms of sexual responsiveness. Or had trained herself to feel nothing for it, she thought rather wryly.

What had come over her? It wasn't like her to be so deeply self-analytical . . . and that she should be now was faintly disturbing. Unbidden, an image flashed across her mind: a man, tall, with a dark shock of hair and amused blue eyes. The man in the portrait at the old Hall. Quickly she dismissed the image and its disturbing nuances. What was the matter with her? She was as nervous and on edge as a teenager facing her first date. Excitement, that was all, she told herself as she slid out of bed.

A narrow beam of sunlight barred her body, penetrating the fine silk of her nightgown, making her glance briefly downwards to frown slightly over the slender gold of her body where it was revealed by her nightgown. Her own body was something she rarely gave much attention to. She was as slim and as supple as Lucy, and yet her body was quite unmistakably that of a woman and not a girl, her breasts full, her curves feminine. Another image slid into her mind and with a cold shock she realised she was visualising how yesterday's dark-haired stranger had looked at her.

Too intelligent to practise self-deception, Jenna acknowledged as she banished the image, she suspected that her contempt for the male sex sprang from a deep-seated need to protect herself from the same sort of agony her sister had known. Where sex itself was concerned, her feelings were even more confused. She had never met any man who aroused in her a sexual desire that was strong enough to overcome all her deeply buried fears. Perhaps because she equated sex with what had happened to Rachel. Whatever the case she had been scrupulous about not passing on her own feelings to Lucy. She desperately wanted Lucy to have everything she herself had never had. That was why it hurt so much when Lucy had flung her heedless adolescent accusations at her.

As she dressed, an unusual surge of optimism swept through her, banishing all her doubts. Who could tell? Perhaps once Lucy had accepted the fact that Jenna intended them to move to Yorkshire, she would grow to love the old Hall as much as Jenna herself did. Lucy was at a difficult age, Jenna reminded herself fairly, but in another few years she would be an adult. Perhaps then they would be able to talk about Rachel, Jenna thought contemplatively, acknowledging that she would like to talk about her sister with someone, to share her memories of her, and who better than Lucy? As it was, only Bill and Nancy had known Rachel, and could share her memories with her. Maybe that was why she was so afraid to let a man into her life, she reflected. Because if she did so, she would have to tell him about the past, about Rachel and Lucy . . .

What was she really afraid of? she asked herself, as she tugged a brush through her hair and studied her reflection pensively in the mirror. That a man might reject her because he thought she had had an illegitimate child? Or that if she cared deeply enough about someone to tell them the truth they might not share her view of the enormity of the crime against her sister. It had been a long time since she had examined her own deep feelings so intensely, perhaps too long.

In London, with a growing, demanding business to take up all her time and Lucy to worry about, there never seemed to be an opportunity to sit down and think about herself. Or was it that she didn't want to dwell too deeply on her own emotions or lack of them? Harley had accused her on more than one occasion of being a-human. Who knew? Perhaps he was right. A self-mocking smile curved her generous mouth. What would they say, all those men who had striven so hard to get her into their beds, if they knew the truth? That far from being a cool, composed, experienced woman, she was in reality no more than a frightened, inexperienced virgin. The thought was ludicrous enough to make her laugh. What did it matter? No one was ever likely to know the truth, apart from herself.

Once again, irritatingly, a mental image of the man who had admired her car with words and her body with his eyes flashed across her mind, the blue eyes taunting, the curl of his mouth suggesting with arrogant maleness that he knew everything there was to know about her sex. Why had she allowed him to antagonise her so intensely? The man was a stranger, someone she had never met before, nor was ever likely to meet again. Shrugging aside the memory of how he had looked at her, Jenna went downstairs.

'Sorry I'm so late,' she apologised to Nancy as

she walked into the kitchen. 'I can't think what happened.' She wrinkled her nose ruefully. 'I haven't slept so deeply for years. Where's Lucy?'

'Gone out,' Nancy informed her drily, adding bluntly, 'I know you won't like my saying this, Jenna, but it's high time you told her the truth. If you don't —— ' She broke off as they heard a car outside.

'Funny!' she exclaimed, her forehead puckering in a frown. 'I wasn't expecting Bill back so soon. He's driven down to the village to get some more bread. There's nothing wrong with young Lucy's appetite, whatever else might be ailing her.'

But it wasn't Bill who came to the kitchen door. It was Lucy, her eyes shining, her cheeks flushed, and with her, to Jenna's complete consternation and shock, was the man whose features had so annoyingly impressed themselves upon her mind, to the extent that twice during the last half an hour she had recalled them in vivid detail. As she looked at him, she realised that her memory had not played her false. His eyes were as intensely blue as she remembered, his skin as healthily tanned.

'Lucy, where on earth have you been?' she asked her niece frostily, dragging her attention away from the male figure lounging in the open doorway and forcing herself to concentrate instead on the teenager's flushed and rebellious features. What was Lucy doing with this stranger, a stranger whose overt sexuality made her mouth compress in bitter contempt? He flaunted his sexuality like a banner and it disgusted her, riveting her attention until Lucy spoke.

'Out!' The pert toss of the dark hair which accompanied the defiant challenge only increased Jenna's perturbation, but she managed to mask her fear with a coolness she was far from feeling.

How many times had she warned Lucy against the folly of talking to strangers; any strangers. It made no difference that every instinct she possessed told her that this man was definitely not the type who needed to waylay young girls in order to obtain sexual satisfaction.

'I'm afraid the fault lies with me.' His words fell into the thick pool of silence, stagnant with antagonism, that had fallen on the kitchen after Lucy's defiant remark, and it goaded Jenna unbearably to know that beneath the conventional apology he was probably laughing at her.

'I met your daughter down at the Hall and offered to give her a lift back here. It seems that you and I are going to be in competition at the auction this morning.'

Jenna's eyes left his face and darted to Lucy's. What had Lucy been doing down at the old Hall? For now her concentration on her niece was something she could use as a defence mechanism to block out the shock of what she had just been told. *He* wanted to buy the Hall. Her mouth curled unwittingly into a bitter smile. So much for her initial assumptions about him.

'And what exactly were you doing down there, Lucy?' she questioned curtly, trying to blank out the feeling of tension invading her veins. What had happened to the excited euphoria with which she had woken up? It was gone, banished by the presence of this dark, mocking man.

'I just wanted to see what it looked like.' Lucy's reply was sulky.

'Without telling anyone where you were going?' Jenna knew she was overdoing her chastisement, and that it would be wiser to keep her criticisms until they were alone, but something about the enigmatic scrutiny of the man watching them was driving her on. It was as though somehow they were locked in some sort of secret battle . . . If that was the case, establishing her parental authority over Lucy was hardly likely to win it, Jenna reflected, slightly ashamed of the way she had spoken so sharply to the younger girl. She wasn't so far removed from her teenage years herself that she could not remember how touchy and vulnerable a teenager's pride was. Her voice softened slightly. 'I'm sorry, Lucy,' she apologised, curling her fingers into her palms and refusing to look in the direction of the sardonic stranger. She didn't want to see him gloating over her apology. 'I shouldn't have snapped at you like that but . . . '

'She shouldn't have accepted a lift with me.'

Once again the cool drawl raised tiny goosebumps of prickly resentment on Jenna's sensitive skin. 'My fault again, I insisted. It seemed foolish to let her walk when I was coming this way . . . ' He shrugged powerfully broad shoulders, this morning encased in a thick navy jumper that added to his ruggedly masculine appearance.

'Really?'

The moment she spoke the coolly dismissive word, Jenna knew that she had fallen into a carefully baited trap.

'Yes.' He ignored her cool withdrawal and smiled instead at Nancy. 'If I might come in for a second?'

He was still standing just by the door, and Jenna watched with narrowed eyes and a prickling sense of foreboding as Nancy coloured slightly and said quickly, 'Oh, my goodness, of course! Please do.'

He was a charmer all right, Jenna thought critically, but even if Nancy was not immune she was. She was

looking at him, studying him as he walked into the
room, watching the lean, long-legged way he moved,
his movements as fluid as those of a great jungle cat —
and just as dangerous — when suddenly she was
conscious that she was staring and that, worse, he was
aware of it. The look he gave her as their eyes clashed
made her feel as though he could see right into her
mind and read every thought in it. He knew how antagonistic she was to him. A fine shudder of
apprehension rippled through her body. An outright
reaction to her antipathy she could deal with, but
somehow his deliberate refusal to show any response
at all was unnerving.

'Well, thank you for bringing Lucy back for us,
Mr . . ?' Jenna paused and he obligingly filled the space
for her. 'Allingham,' he told her laconically, 'James
Allingham.'

His name meant nothing to her, but the smile that
curled his mouth without reaching his eyes chilled
her.

'Lucy tells me you're hoping to buy the Hall and use
it as a headquarters for your business interests,' he
commented, observing her, Jenna noticed, with eyes
that were suddenly almost frighteningly watchful.

'Yes,' she agreed, not knowing what else to do.
Who was this man? Obviously not the farm labourer
she had originally supposed. He might be wearing casual clothes — a checked shirt, a thick sweater and a
pair of cords — but they were expensive casuals. It
irritated her now that she had allowed his blatant
sexuality to blind her to the fact that he was a
potential rival for possession of the Hall. 'And you,
Mr Allingham,' she challenged, lifting her head and
looking directly into his eyes, letting him know that
she wouldn't be easily intimidated, 'what is your

purpose in wishing to acquire the property?' It crossed her mind that he could quite possibly refuse to tell her, but he didn't.

His smile widened, but still did not reach his eyes. 'Well, as to that,' he drawled, making her remember that she had previously thought that his heritage wasn't entirely British, 'my ancestors originally came from here and I kinda thought it would be rather nice to keep the property in family hands.'

Jenna went white, a small gasp escaping her lips before she could stop herself from betraying her shock. James Allingham was a *Deveril*! No wonder she had felt so antagonistic towards him, she reflected bitterly. Her senses must have known what her mind had not. Don't be ridiculous, she chided herself mentally, her antagonism had initially sprung from the fact that he was so overpoweringly and blatantly male, and nothing else. Even so, it was a shock to discover that he was related to the Deverils.

Suddenly she remembered the portrait she had seen in the house and how stunned she had been on first seeing James Allingham's resemblance to it. Just for a moment all her old hatred of the Deverils surged up inside her, but she had herself under control almost immediately.

'Really,' she exclaimed in a marvelling voice. 'You do surprise me. I had heard that the solicitors made extensive enquiries and had decided that the Deveril family had completely died out.'

'So, I believe, it has,' James Allingham agreed, with mocking urbanity. 'But there is a connection none the less. One of my ancestors was born here in this village. His mother was the wife of the then Sir George Deveril.' His mouth twisted slightly as he added,

'Unfortunately, he fell into disgrace and was packed off to the Indies. Once there he married the daughter of a wealthy sugar planter.'

Jenna froze, and as though sensing her disbelief James Allingham said coolly, 'Oh, it's all quite true, I can assure you, but the father of the girl whom James Deveril married insisted as part of the marriage contract that James change his surname to Allingham.' He shrugged. 'The story goes in our family that James wasn't all that reluctant to part with a surname he despised.'

'A most romantic story, Mr Allingham,' Jenna said crisply, suddenly understanding why James Allingham would want to possess the house. No doubt like her he harboured a feeling of resentment against the Deveril family, but she must not start feeling sympathy for him, she told herself sharply. That was what he wanted . . . what he was angling for.

'Yes, isn't it?' he agreed, giving her a bland smile, the glint in his eyes telling her that he was amused rather than annoyed by the coldness in her voice.

Bright patches of colour stained her high cheek-bones as she happened to glance at Lucy and saw that the younger girl was enjoying seeing her bested by James Allingham. Hard on the heels of her initial anger came pain. What had happened to her and Lucy? They had once been so close. But she knew what had happened. Lucy resented her refusal to discuss her father with her.

It was infuriating that James Allingham should so easily have got the better of her and in front of Lucy too, but what was more infuriating was that he was making it clear to her that he felt he had a greater right to the Hall than she did. Her chin went up, her eyes unknowingly flashing warning signs at him.

'Well, it's a most interesting story, Mr Allingham,' she conceded graciously, 'and I can quite understand why you should want to buy the old Hall.'

'The auction is due to begin in half an hour,' he commented briefly, glancing at what Jenna could easily recognise as an extremely expensive gold watch. What she could see of his wrist beneath the cuff of his woollen shirt was well muscled, covered in fine dark hairs and extremely masculine. For some reason the sight of it disturbed her, setting off tiny flurries of sensation in her stomach.

'Why don't I give you a lift down there?'

His arrogant assumption that she would want to travel with him infuriated Jenna, her fury fuelled by the unfamiliar sensations she had just experienced. Part of her realised, or at least suspected that he was deliberately trying to get her off balance, and yet even knowing this, another part of her still reacted to what she suspected was a deliberate encouragement of her anger. No doubt her red hair had already betrayed to him her quick temper, and perhaps he hoped to push her into some sort of hasty hot-headed reaction which would unnerve her before the auction. She had come across this sort of tactical manoeuvre before and thoroughly despised it. Her upper lip curled slightly. He was everything she most detested in the male sex, she thought furiously. Arrogant, an overweening belief in himself, a masculine air of superiority that she longed to challenge, but most of all, an amused and slightly taunting manner towards herself, as though she, like Lucy, was little more than a child. He could not be more than thirty-six or so: the seven-year age-gap between them was scarcely large enough to warrant his almost paternal mockery of her. It was on the tip of her tongue to refuse him when Nancy suddenly interrupted, 'Oh, what an excellent idea. You know you said your car wasn't behaving very well,' she reminded Jenna.

'Then it's all settled.' The smile James Allingham gave Nancy was pure sexual coercion, Jenna told herself distastefully, refusing to admit to the strange feeling she experienced when she saw the warmth in his eyes as they rested mischievously on the older woman's plump face.

She had already noticed that Lucy seemed ready to hang on his every word and she was not very pleased when the girl burst out impulsively, 'Oh, Mother, surely you aren't going to go ahead and bid for the house now? Not when you can see how much James wants it. After all, it *did* once belong to his family.'

Jenna had to grit her teeth together to stop herself snapping at Lucy's mock-virtuous tone. No doubt it would suit Lucy very well indeed if she were to back out of the auction, but she had no intention of doing so. And as for the house once belonging to James's family . . . Anger and pain — both were there inside her. Oh, Lucy, if only you knew, she thought wryly. But Lucy did not and how could she tell her? Her smile for James Allingham was tight and slightly bitter. 'Yes, I can quite see that Mr Allingham has a valid claim to the house, Lucy,' she agreed, 'but as I'm sure he is aware one can't allow oneself to be clouded by emotion when it comes to business matters.'

As she swept towards the door, Jenna thought she heard Lucy mutter rebelliously, 'Or when it comes to any matters . . .' but even as she stiffened and was about to turn, she heard the inner door slam as Lucy walked into the hall.

'A very attractive young lady, your daughter,' James Allingham remarked a few seconds later as he settled

her into his car — a Mercedes saloon, she noticed
absently as she fastened her seat-belt.

'I think so.' Her cool voice was meant to warn
him not to trespass any further, but James Allingham
refused to take the hint.

'There's just the two of you, or so she tells me,' he
persisted. That he should ignore her warning and
continue with his line of questioning angered Jenna
even further.

'That's right,' she agreed, knowing as she did so that
her voice sounded brittle, defensive almost, and that
angered her even more.

'She also tells me that she doesn't want to come back
and live in Yorkshire.'

Impossible not to miss the amused, half-victorious
sidelong glance he gave her as he put the car in
motion.

'You and Lucy seemed to have had an extremely enlightening conversation,' Jenna said tartly. 'At least,
enlightening as far as you were concerned.'

He shrugged and met her cold glance with an easy
smile. 'I bumped into her as I came out of the Hall. We
got chatting.' He shrugged again. 'She seemed to be in
need of someone to confide in. Sometimes strangers
make the best listeners. I take it you do still intend to
bid?' Another sideways glance.

Jenna was infuriated. 'Why shouldn't I? Because of
that little sob-story you've just told us?' She managed
an arctic, derisive smile. 'Oh, come on, Mr Allingham, I
wasn't born yesterday, even if Lucy was.'

'Meaning?' His voice was as cold as her own now,
and somehow slightly intimidating, making Jenna
uncomfortably aware of the fact that she was alone
with him in his car. Wild thoughts of his kidnapping
her . . . holding her captive somewhere until the

auction was over, flooded into her mind, only to be dismissed as more rational reasoning took over.

It gave Jenna a brief sense of satisfaction to know that she had got under his skin and broken through that air of easy confidence at last.

'Oh, it's not that I don't believe you're telling the truth,' she told him, her own confidence restored.

'I'm relieved to hear it.'

The sardonic inflexion beneath the words momentarily rang warning bells but Jenna ignored them.

'Then why the antagonism?' he questioned, throwing her off balance by the unexpectedness of his question.

'Surely I don't need to spell out for you the fact that you used what you learned from my daughter in an effort to dissuade me from bidding for the house?' Jenna said by way of explanation, hoping that he would not probe any further.

'Meaning that you don't give a damn whether your daughter wants to move up here or not?'

The injustice of his calmly delivered comment stung. That wasn't what she had meant at all, but she was too honest to be able to refute completely what he had said. 'Of course I do,' she snapped, 'but I happen to believe that at fifteen Lucy is not old enough to know where she does or does not want to live. *I* don't consider that London is exactly an ideal environment for an impressionable teenager.'

'She tells me you sent her to boarding school,' he commented, changing tack.

Dark colour flamed in Jenna's cheeks.

What else had Lucy told this threatening stranger? And he *was* threatening . . . every instinct Jenna possessed told her so.

'That's right.' Her curt, clipped voice warned him

against any further intrusion, but, as before, he ignored it.

'Do you think that's wise, for a mother to completely abandon the upbringing of her child to others?'

For a moment Jenna was so angry that she had to clench her hands tightly against the leather of the seat to stop herself from coming out with the first biting retort that sprang to her lips.

'I *am* a single parent, Mr Allingham,' she said at last, 'and in common with other single parents I have to earn money to support myself and my daughter. Much as I would love to spend more time with Lucy it just hasn't been possible.' Inwardly she was shaking with temper. How dared he? How dared he criticise her like this?

'Oh, come on now, I don't believe that.'

Against her will Jenna felt her glance drawn to his. His eyes were cold and watchful where her own were hot with resentment. 'A woman with your . . . assets,' he said softly 'would never have any problem in finding a man to support her . . . and her child.'

His implication stunned her. There were a thousand things she could have said: that she loathed his sex and would never, ever allow herself to be dependent on a member of it, that she preferred to be independent, that —— Bottling up the violent emotion clamouring for release inside her, she gritted through her teeth, 'But I happen to prefer paying my own way through life.'

Now he smiled at her, but it wasn't a pleasant smile. 'A rather masculine way of looking at things, wouldn't you say? Most women prefer to have a husband to lean on for both emotional and financial support.'

'Yes, no doubt,' Jenna agreed crisply, 'and a good many of them discover later in life just how fragile that support is when their husbands leave them for someone else. Someone younger and fresher. I have no desire to marry, Mr Allingham,' she told him in brittle tones, too carried away by her feelings to watch what she was saying, 'even if that means that I don't have as much time to spend with Lucy as I would wish. She's a teenager and at the moment, as all teenagers are wont to do, she's apt to feel herself hard done by.'

'Umm. Lucy told me that she didn't have a father.'

A sensation of pain lanced through Jenna. She could feel him watching her. 'Are you widowed, divorced?'

She longed to refuse to answer his impertinent questions, but pride would not allow her to do so. 'Neither.'

'So . . .'

The way he murmured the word made Jenna suspect that he had already known what her answer would be. 'You must have been very young when Lucy was born.'

'Old enough.' She wasn't aware of how much bitterness there was in her voice, only a profound sense of relief as the Hall lodge gates came into sight.

'And that's why you hate my sex so much, is it?' he pressed. 'Because Lucy's father deserted you. Left you to bear the burden of parenthood alone?'

As they went up the drive, all Jenna wanted was to escape from his questions and his proximity. 'Is that what you think?' she snapped at him. 'It fits neatly into all the psychiatrists' theories, doesn't it?'

She was conscious of the glance he gave her, but

because of the other cars parked ahead of him, he had to stop, and the moment he did so, Jenna unfastened her seat-belt and got out of his car without waiting to see if he was following her.

The cool morning air soothed her flushed cheeks and her temper. It had been foolish to let him get to her so easily. She shrugged dismissively as she walked towards the house. After today, once the Hall was hers, she would never see him again. But would it be hers? The doubts she had refused to give weight to since he had first made her aware of his intentions now surfaced.

For all that it needed a good deal of money spending on it, the old Hall was not being auctioned cheaply. James Allingham would be as aware of the reserve price as she was herself. In order to buy it, he would need to be a reasonably wealthy man. Without false modesty Jenna knew that many people would consider her to be very comfortably off, but for her to buy the Hall and restore it she would need to employ her company's assets. Hence her decision to use it as the company headquarters.

What line of business was James Allingham in, she wondered. He had mentioned that his ancestors had included a sugar planter, but with the abolition of slavery the finances of these once-wealthy men had waned. His accent was American — but only faintly so. Shrugging impatiently she cautioned herself to put him out of her mind and to concentrate instead on the coming auction. But James Allingham and the house had become strangely intertwined, and it was becoming impossible to think of one without the other. Straightening her spine, Jenna vowed mentally that she was not going to let him best her.

There was a martial glint in her eyes that Harley

would have recognised — and deplored. Normally extremely cool and level-headed when it came to business matters, Jenna could occasionally be provoked into a certain rashness — the curse of her red hair and turbulent temperament, she acknowledged as she walked into the house.

CHAPTER THREE

THE auction was being held in the large Georgian drawing-room in the newer part of the house. When Jenna made her way there, she found the room less than half full, which was reassuring. The auctioneer was already in place, studying some papers in front of him, and Jenna suspected that the small group of by-standers gathered together to one side of him were probably more curious than actively interested in bidding.

Jenna had already been in contact with the firm of estate agents, who were acting as auctioneers, on several occasions in connection with the house and up until this morning she had felt that she stood every chance of securing the property at the reserve price. She saw James Allingham come into the room and saunter across it to stand almost opposite. There was no smile in his eyes now, and Jenna felt as though they were two opponents facing one another prior to joining battle. She wondered if anyone else in the room was as aware of the animosity between them as she was herself. She was in little doubt that James Allingham had sought her out so that he could gauge the competition he might have in the bidding, and she was aware of a tiny frisson of fear running over her skin as the bidding began.

Gradually as the minutes ticked by the more half-hearted bidders dropped out. Soon it was down to Jenna, James Allingham, and one other, a bluff beefy

Northerner, who, Jenna heard someone next to her whisper, was a builder.

When they reached the reserve price her stomach nerves knotted in tension. The builder dropped out, and Jenna felt herself tense as she saw James Allingham coolly raise his hand.

Dare she try to outbid him? She bit her lip worrying at it, knowing down to the last thousand pounds how high she could go, and then desire overrode caution and she raised her rolled pamphlet, forcing herself not to glance across the room at James Allingham as she did so.

She was conscious of a stir of interest around her as the bystanders began to realise they were witnessing a tense duel between the dark-haired man and the red-headed woman. Caution vanished as Jenna was urged on, both by her desire for the house and her desire to triumph over James Allingham.

The price crept inexorably upwards and Jenna's heart sank as she realised she could not continue bidding for much longer. Already she was way, way over her self-imposed limit and Harley would be having a fit if he was here with her.

She saw James Allingham's brief nod to the auctioneer after her own latest bid.

'Another thousand . . . am I bid another thousand?' The auctioneer looked encouragingly at her and Jenna knew she should bow out, but she couldn't do it . . . not with so many speculative pairs of eyes watching . . . not when she wanted the Hall so desperately that she was ready to mortgage her very soul for it . . . not when losing meant James Allingham winning. She raised her hand, curling her fingers into her palm to prevent them from trembling. Out of the corner of her eye she was aware of someone approaching James Allingham and touching him on his shoulder.

The auctioneer was declaring her bid. Unlike her he probably could not see the smaller man standing almost behind James Allingham and whispering urgently to him.

'For the last time . . . at one hundred and eighty-five thousand pounds . . . going . . . . '

Jenna saw James Allingham frown and turn towards the dais, but his companion was still talking to him. He frowned again, very deeply, his attention distracted from the auctioneer. Jenna held her breath, waiting to hear James Allingham interrupt the auctioneer with a raised bid, but suddenly for some reason all his attention was concentrated on his companion.

'Gone! At one hundred and eighty-five thousand pounds!'

Jenna was so engrossed in watching James Allingham that she was barely aware of what the auctioneer was saying. Across the width of the room he lifted his head and looked at her, but somehow his gaze was unfocused, as though he wasn't really seeing her . . . as though he wasn't even really aware of where he was. What on earth could his companion have said to him to take his attention so completely away from the auction? Jenna knew that whatever it was she ought to be grateful to the other man but, strangely, she felt cheated, as though somehow her victory was unfairly won — by default almost.

The auctioneer was heading towards her, claiming her attention, and when Jenna looked again James Allingham had disappeared.

The old Hall was hers! Even now Jenna could hardly believe it. She had spent the rest of the day sorting out all the formalities connected with the purchase. A telephone call to her bank had secured for her the increased mortgage facilities she would require and Jenna quailed a little as she contemplated the financial burden she had taken on. She was in no doubt about her ability to pay off the mortgage eventually, but initially it would be a struggle.

She gave a brief mental shrug. She would just have to hope for some good commissions locally in the early months.

A small voice inside her reminded her that fortune was seldom so kind. Harley would go mad, she acknowledged as she took a taxi from the estate agent's office back to Bill's and Nancy's.

Instead of feeling excited, enthusiastic, she was conscious of a flat, let-down feeling. Telling herself it was merely reaction she walked towards the front door.

Lucy was sitting sulkily in front of the television. She barely glanced up as Jenna walked in.

'Well, how did it go?'

Thank heavens for Bill, Jenna thought, sinking into the chair he indicated. 'I got it.'

'You don't sound too pleased about it.'

'I had to pay over the reserve price.' That was the excuse she was using to herself to cover her lack of enthusiasm and it certainly seemed to deceive Bill.

'I hope you haven't taken on more than you can handle,' he warned her worriedly. 'Old houses like the Hall gobble up money.'

'I know, but as I intend to use it as a showplace for the craftsmen I employ, I'm hoping to be able to set a certain amount of the cost off as a business expense.' Jenna hoped she sounded more confident than she felt. Her accountants had cautioned her against hoping for too much when it came to convincing the tax authorities of the authenticity of her claim.

'Even so . . . ' Bill was still frowning, but he smiled briefly as Nancy came into the room carrying a tea tray.

'I heard you come in,' Nancy told her. 'How did it go?'

'She got it,' Bill answered for her.

'Oh. What happened to James Allingham then? He didn't strike me as a man who would easily give up something he wanted.'

Jenna agreed with her, but she only shrugged. There had been something odd about the way James Allingham had suddenly lost interest in the bidding . . . no . . . not lost interest, she corrected herself . . . it had been as if something more important had demanded his attention. But what could have been more important than securing the house he had told her in no uncertain terms he intended to have?

'I wonder where he comes from,' Nancy mused. 'He had a faintly American accent.'

'I doubt that we'll see him again,' Jenna interrupted. Lucy had turned round to look at her and a spasm of alarm shivered down her spine as she saw the look of bitter disappointment cross the girl's face. Was Lucy in danger of forming a crush on James Allingham? The thought was distinctly disquieting even though Jenna knew that it was unlikely that they would see him again. However, she had enough problems with Lucy already without adding any more.

'So . . . what do you intend to do now?'

It was two days since the auction and Jenna was sitting in the kitchen with Bill, drinking coffee. She cupped her hands round her mug and stared thoughtfully at it.

'I'll have to go back to London — I intend to keep
an office going there. Richard Hollis, my assistant, will
run it. We've got several contracts on at the moment
but nothing that Richard can't handle.' As she talked,
she was mentally going over the work they had in
hand. None of it was threatening to prove difficult
and she felt that she could with perfect safety hand it
over to Richard.

'I can't move in to the Hall — not yet. Far too much
needs to be done, but on the other hand it's going to
be hard work supervising everything from London.'

'Why not stay with us?' Bill suggested.

Jenna shook her head. 'No. It wouldn't be fair on
you and Nancy,' she told him. 'I'll be coming and
going all the time, using the telephone. One of the
first things I'll have to do when I get back is to find
out if any of my craftsmen have contacts up here.' She
would also need a good architect, she reflected, and a
sympathetic builder. Until she knew the Hall was hers
she hadn't allowed herself to think too much beyond
the auction but now the auction was over and . . .

'And Lucy?' Bill questioned, watching her.

'I took her out of school to bring her up here with
me. She's due back next Monday.'

'She won't like it,' Bill warned her.

Jenna nibbled worriedly at her bottom lip. 'I know
she won't, Bill, but what else can I do? A London day
school is out. I've seen what those kids get up to, you
haven't. The way she's behaving at the moment I
couldn't trust Lucy not to get in with some wild
crowd.'

'Perhaps that's what's wrong,' Bill suggested
quietly. 'Perhaps you should trust her, Jenna.'

He watched her shrug and persisted. 'Yes, I know
you only want to protect her, but can't you see? In her

eyes, by refusing to talk to her about her father, by refusing to listen to her grievances, you're refusing to believe her worthy of trust, and her views worthy of being respected.'

Bill had taught teenagers for many years, Jenna recognised, and she could also see that what he was saying made sense.

'I don't know, Bill. Perhaps at the end of this term, in the summer . . . There's nothing I want more than to see her happy, but she says she hates Yorkshire. More to spite me than anything else, I suspect. At least at school she has her friends. I just don't know what to do.'

She was more worried about Lucy than she wanted to admit. The way her niece had sprung to champion James Allingham had reminded her that Lucy was balanced very precariously between childhood and womanhood. With the problems that existed between them at the moment it would be all too easy for Lucy to decide to throw off the yoke of childhood and seek solace for her grievances in open rebellion.

'She lacks a man's presence in her life. You both do, Jenna.' Bill's quiet criticism wounded her, and she put down her mug, getting up and pacing angrily up and down.

'Oh, for God's sake, Bill,' she exclaimed. 'Don't you start! What am I supposed to do? Go out on the streets and grab the first man who walks past?'

'Don't fly up at me,' Bill chided her. 'Sit down and we'll talk about this calmly.'

Unwillingly she did so.

'You know I've never interfered in your life, Jenna, but I hate to see what's happening to you. You should have a husband and children of your own. I . . . '

'Bill, the days are long gone when a woman wasn't complete without a man at her side. I don't want a husband, and as for children . . . I have Lucy. For heaven's sake, at Lucy's school more than half the girls are from single-parent families. It means nothing nowadays.'

'Does it?' She could feel Bill watching her.

'Perhaps to you, Jenna, but not to Lucy. If you're not careful she's going to start looking for a father substitute for herself and I hate to think where that could lead. Look, I'm not suggesting you marry the first man who comes along simply for Lucy's sake, I *am* telling you that she needs a male influence in her life that she can identify with, whether that man is her actual father or someone else, and the person best equipped to provide her with the right sort of male influence right now is you. I know that what happened to Rachel hurt you badly, Jenna, but all men aren't like that.'

'I know that.' She got up again, pacing tensely. 'I'm not a complete fool, Bill, it's just that . . . well, I've never met any man who I would want to give up my freedom for. Sometimes I wonder if I'm capable of sexual love,' she added bleakly.

She heard the scrape of Bill's chair as he got up, and then the weight of his arm round her shoulders. 'With that hair, and your temper . . !' His eyes were laughing at her. 'You're capable of it all right, but somehow you've managed to train your mind to tell you that you're not.'

Three days later, back in London, Jenna found that she couldn't get what Bill had said out of her mind. On Sunday she was taking Lucy back to school, and although Jenna had tried on several occasions to talk seriously to her niece, Lucy had proved extremely unco-operative. Every time Jenna asked her if she had a moment to spare, Lucy was either on the point of going out, or she had to speak urgently to a schoolfriend, or there was something else of equal importance she had to do. Jenna was no fool, she knew that Lucy was deliberately punishing her because of her refusal to discuss her father, but what could she do? As she waited for the coffee to perk, Jenna heard the newspaper plop through the apartment's outer door. It was Thursday and she had several appointments that morning, most of them connected with the Hall in one way or another. Richard had proved a marvellous help, taking all the work on hand off her shoulders so that Jenna could concentrate on organising the initial work on the Hall.

Harley had proved at first disbelieving and then disapproving when she told him how much she had paid. Like Lucy, he was sulking with her. Sighing faintly, Jenna opened the kitchen door and called out to Lucy. The younger girl was spending the day with a schoolfriend who, coincidentally, had also been off school, and they were going shopping together.

Jenna's first appointment of the morning was with the firm of architects she normally used for any major reconstruction work required by her clients; she was hoping they would be able to recommend a Yorshire-based firm of architects to her. She had already unearthed a professional guide that listed builders qualified to work on restoring period buildings, and she was slowly going through it, writing down the names of those within reasonable travelling distance of West Thorpe.

'Lucy, come on, you're going to be late!' she called again, pouring out a cup of coffee and walking into the small hallway to get the paper.

The front-page headlines were familiarly depressing and Jenna glanced at them briefly before turning to the gossip column. The previous evening she had attended a party thrown by one of her clients to show off her new décor, and her hostess had told Jenna that she had invited several society columnists. The moment she opened the paper on the society page a photograph caught Jenna's eye. She stared blankly at it for several seconds before reading the caption beneath it. 'Millionaire James Allingham returns to Britain following the deaths of his father and stepmother in car crash!'

There was no mistaking the dominatingly masculine features of the grim-faced man in the photograph, even with his expression stripped of all emotion save for a certain dark bleakness.

Several days ago James Allingham flew to New York, following the tragic news that a car driven by his step-mother, Lorraine, had been involved in a multiple pile-up on a New York freeway. Allingham, who was in Yorkshire at the time, arrived in New York just in time to see his father before he died. His step-mother, Lorraine, died later in hospital, his step-sister, Sarah, being the only survivor of the accident. A millionaire in his own right, James Allingham shares an inheritance from his father of the latter's large art collection and a chain of hotels throughout the Caribbean. Allingham's own fortune was founded on the holiday and marina complex he developed on the Caribbean island of St Justine which he inherited from his grandfather when he was twenty-one. Since

Allingham is not married, and has always led a somewhat peripatetic life, it will be interesting to see if he now succumbs to the blandishments of one of his many female 'friends' and takes the plunge into matrimony. His step-sister, Sarah, who is fourteen years old was severely injured by the accident, and it is rumoured that James Allingham is her sole guardian. However, he has returned to his Knightsbridge house alone.

Grimacing with distaste Jenna put the paper down. So now she knew why James Allingham had left the auction so abruptly. She shivered slightly. No matter what she felt about him personally, she couldn't help but be torn by compassion for his step-sister. The speculatively coy tone of the article sickened her, with its covert intrusive curiosity and she pushed the paper on one side in disgust, getting up to call Lucy yet again.

Her niece appeared several seconds later, tousle-haired and still sulky, her answers to all Jenna's too-bright questions monosyllabic to the point of rudeness.

'I'm going now, Lucy.' Jenna made herself sound cheerfully unaware of Lucy's attitude. 'I'll be back about five.' On a sudden impulse she hesitated and added, 'Look, how would you like to go out to dinner tonight? Just the two of us, we'll go somewhere glamorous and —— '

'I'm eating at Janet's.'

Recognising that she had been snubbed, Jenna pressed her lips firmly together. 'Well, perhaps another time then,' she added brightly. 'Have a nice time.'

It was ridiculous that a woman who could run her

own business successfully should quail beneath the resentment of a fifteen-year-old, Jenna told herself wryly as she stepped outside. Even though she hated to admit it to herself, it would be a relief in a way when Lucy was back at school. At the moment having her in the house was like living with a time-bomb. But simply because Lucy was back at school didn't mean their problems had disappeared, Jenna reminded herself. Somehow, she and Lucy were going to have to find a common meeting ground. Without knowing why, she found herself thinking about James Allingham. How was he coping with his step-sister? Compared with him, her problems were minimal, Jenna told herself, but, then, no doubt man-like, he could hand over the care and comfort of his step-sister to others without any of the guilt she as a woman had to endure for abandoning her allotted female caring role.

On several occasions during the day Jenna found her thoughts returning to James Allingham. Each time she made a conscious effort to dismiss him from her mind, blaming his intrusiveness on the intense antipathy she had felt towards him. But now that antipathy was tempered with compassion, especially for his step-sister.

Jenna had been too young to remember anything about her own parents — her father had worked for one of the major oil companies and both he and her mother had been killed during a tribal uprising when he was working in a remote desert area. She had had to rely on Rachel's dim memories of their parents to form an impression of them. Her aunt had never spoken about them, grimly dissuading the two sisters from doing so as well. Jenna had grown up with the uncomfortable feeling that, for some reason, her aunt had disapproved of their parents. Although their father had been her sister's only child she had never talked to the girls about his childhood or his parents. If she hadn't had Rachel . . .

Abruptly, Jenna came to a full stop in the street, appalled to realise the parallels that could be drawn between her aunt's attitude and her own. But she would gladly have talked to Lucy about her parents if it had been possible . . .

But how was Lucy to know the reason why she was so evasive about her father? Shaking off the chilly sensation of despair running down her spine, Jenna straightened her shoulders and hurried on. It was pointless regretting her omissions of the past now. Lucy was far too vulnerable at the moment to accept the truth.

As she stepped into the building which housed her architects Jenna remembered Bill's suggestion that she marry and provide Lucy with a substitute father-figure. Her mouth compressed slightly, her body instinctively shrinking from the thought of the sexual intimacy marriage would bring. No matter how much she analysed her own emotions or how logically she tried to look at things, Jenna was forced to admit that what had happened to Rachel had left its scars on her too. In some way that went deeper than logic could she was frightened of committing herself to a sexual relationship with anyone. She had seen what had happened to her sister, and even though she knew quite well that all men were not rapists the effect of Rachel's death had been so traumatic that it had somehow frozen her ability to grow to full woman-hood. Inside she was still a frightened teenager, Jenna told herself as she stepped out of the lift, and the only way she could ever contemplate marriage would be if it were merely a business arrangement, excluding any form of physical contact.

She closed her eyes briefly in a surge of mental torment as she imagined the reaction of the men who knew her in her business life if they were ever to discover the truth. She would instantly lose all her credibility and be demoted to the role of 'frigid spinster'. That was the reason why she had always been at such pains to cultivate the glamorous sophisticated image she had been surprised to find herself labelled with when she first started working for John Howard. It made a very safe barrier to hide behind and she had played the part for so long now that it was almost second nature.

The receptionist behind the desk greeted her with a respectful smile and buzzed through on her intercom as Jenna sat down. She wasn't kept waiting long, and as she was shown through into the partners' office Jenna noted that it was Craig Manners, the senior partner, who held open the door for her and pulled out her chair.

'Jenna . . . what can we do for you?' he asked her once his secretary had poured their coffee.

'Not an awful lot on this occasion,' Jenna told him, crossing one slim leg over the other as she watched him quickly mask his disappointment. In the past, she had put several good contracts their way. Sometimes her clients wanted more than mere interior redecoration and once they started talking about structural alterations Jenna was always firm about insisting they sought qualified advice. She herself was no architect or builder and while design-wise she could often help her clients to crystallise their somewhat vague ideas, she was scrupulous about telling them that she had no qualifications in those other fields.

'I was hoping you might be able to supply me with the name of a good architect in Yorkshire,' she told him.

'Yorkshire — rather far afield for you, isn't it?'

Briefly she explained the situation to him.

'So you intend moving your business up there as well?' He frowned slightly. 'Are you sure that's a wise move in these recessionary times?'

'I will be keeping on an office and staff in London,' Jenna informed him, half resenting his almost paternalistic criticism.

'Well, you know best . . . ' His hurried backing-off made Jenna suppress a faint smile. 'And as to giving you the name of an architect, quite by coincidence an old friend of mine has a partnership in York.' He jotted down a name and address on his notepad and handed it to Jenna.

'They're a first-class firm, and they have a department specialising in restoration work. They should be able to find you a good builder — but if you have any problems . . . '

Jenna got up shaking her head. 'No . . . I . . . '

Craig got up too. 'Before you leave London, Jenna, we must have lunch together . . . or dinner,' he added speculatively.

'That would be lovely, but I doubt that I'll have the time, I'm afraid,' Jenna replied diplomatically, avoiding his eyes. She was always wary when male colleagues proffered dinner invitations, and had a rule that she always refused them unless they included other people.

Why was it that even the most domesticated of the male species could never seem to resist trying their luck? Was it male instinct to pursue almost every unattached female that crossed their path?

She had several more meetings that morning, culminating in lunch with her bank manager. This was the appointment she was most dreading. She could, with patience and charm, just about manage to persuade Harley and her accountants that she had sound business reasons for what she was doing, but Gordon Burns was another matter.

She had used the same bankers right from the start of her career, although it was only more latterly, since her business had been successful that her branch's most senior manager, Gordon Burns, had taken charge of her banking affairs.

He was a stooping, grizzled Scot, with an extremely shrewd mind and a dry sense of humour, which she enjoyed, and Jenna suspected he would prove far more difficult to convince than Harley had been. She had already endured one rather uncomfortable telephone call with Gordon Burns when she had had to increase the amount of her proposed loan. He hadn't turned her down, but Jenna had sensed a cautious note of censure in his voice when he reminded her of the heavy financial burden she would be taking on.

He greeted her warmly enough, taking her coat and smiling at her. In his late fifties with a wealth of banking experience behind him, he always treated her with an olde-worlde masculine courtesy that was something of an anachronism, and yet, strangely enough, out of all her male colleagues and advisers he was the only one, who, when it came down to business, treated her exactly as he might another man.

Once they were seated he got briskly down to business, shaking his head a little as he studied the computer figures spread out on his desk. 'Your turnover for the past couple of years,' he told Jenna indicating the figures to her, and shaking his head slightly. 'You don't need me to tell you just how finely you're cutting things, Jenna, and I won't mince matters with you, I don't like it.'

'But you still gave me the loan?'

He grimaced faintly. 'From the bank's point of view it's good business. The money's out on loan to you at an extremely profitable rate of interest to us, and it's well secured by the deeds on your London apartment and the old Hall itself. No, my concern isn't for the bank's money,' he told her rather grimly, 'but for your ability to repay it. You've taken on one hell of a burden. The interest repayments alone are going to amount to . . . ' He named a figure that made Jenna wince. 'I know you're doing very well at the moment, but what you're talking about doing now is virtually to start again and new ventures are notorious for swallowing up money — oh, I'm not saying you won't be successful in the North, only that you might find yourself with a cashflow problem and that's if you're lucky. If you're not lucky, you could lose the lot.'

It was no more than Jenna knew herself, but to hear it said out loud so pragmatically made her stomach clench and her throat close up.

'What monies are you likely to have coming in over the next six months?' He turned to some cashflow forecasts Harley had drawn up for her and studied them thoughtfully.

'Umm . . . not too bad, but I'd like to see at least a couple more large, guaranteed contracts.' He frowned, and tapped thoughtfully on his desk. 'I'll be honest with you, Jenna. On paper it looks viable but my banker's nose warns me against it.'

Jenna felt her heart sink. Bankers were notoriously cautious, she comforted herself a little later over lunch, and yet she knew that Gordon Burns had paid her the compliment of being honest with her, and that if she were wise she would listen to what he had to say. But she was committed now, she reminded herself. It was too late to change her mind, even had she wanted to do so. Just for a moment the image of James Allingham's grim face rose up before her. He would probably buy the house from . . . But no! She wasn't going to sell it. She didn't *want* to sell it, least of all to him!

By the time their lunch was over she had managed to persuade herself that the picture was not as black as Gordon Burns had painted it. True, financially she would be rather stretched . . . but she would survive. It was in a mood of optimism that she returned to the empty apartment later in the afternoon. Lucy was still out, and after making herself a pot of tea, Jenna settled herself at her desk and gave herself up to the pleasure of planning out the restoration to its former glory of the old Hall.

Because it had two wings it would easily adapt to the dual purpose she had in mind of business premises and home. The Georgian wing would be her business showcase, with the older part of the building restored and adapted as a home for herself and Lucy. Once she had started, enthusiasm gripped her, and it was the growing dusk that eventually made her stop, massaging her cramped fingers as she put down her pen.

She glanced at her watch. Nearly nine. Where was Lucy? Frowning slightly, Jenna went to the phone and looked up the number of her friend's parents, quickly dialling it.

It was several seconds before it was answered, a brief spasm of time during which Jenna tried hard not to dwell on how late Lucy was and all the dreadful fates that might have befallen her.

When the phone was answered and she spoke to Janet's mother she learned that both girls had gone to a party being held by the daughter of one of their neighbours.

'Didn't Lucy ring you?' Emily Harris asked. 'She said she was going to?'

'She may have tried to. I was out until four o'clock,' Jenna told her, thinking though that Lucy had not tried very hard to get in touch with her. Lucy was old enough to be aware of how much she worried about her, and Jenna wondered if Lucy was still deliberately trying to punish her. She sighed as she replaced the receiver, her earlier optimism banished. Her head had started to ache slightly and suddenly she was overwhelmed by a desire to breathe in the clean, cool air of the moors. Funny how, until now, she had never realised how much she missed the solitude and peace of Yorkshire.

Was she being entirely fair to Lucy in uprooting her? But she wasn't being completely uprooted, Jenna reminded herself. Many of her schoolfriends lived out of London; indeed they came from all parts of the country. Lucy could invited them to stay with her during the school holidays and could visit them in turn. Jenna had always been scrupulous about not being over-possessive with Lucy, encouraging her to make friends and spend time with them, worried that as an only child she might grow up lonely and introverted without company of her own age.

And yet now, as far as Lucy was concerned, nothing she could do was right. Her head really aching now, Jenna wandered into the kitchen to make herself a drink, suddenly aware of a deep sense of depression.

What was she going to do to put things right between herself and Lucy? Perhaps it was just as well that Lucy was returning to school on Sunday, although Jenna was loath to part from her in her present mood. Maybe it would do them both good to be away from one another for a while?

CHAPTER FOUR

'You're early.'

Jenna grimaced at Maggie Chadwick, her secretary, and gestured to the large pile of mail already on her desk. 'With good reason so it seems.'

'Mmm. Things did rather mount up while you were away.'

Maggie was an excellent secretary and had been with the company for the last three years. Watching her frown, Jenna wondered if something was troubling her. She knew that she was deeply involved in an affair with a foreign news correspondent for one of the national papers and also that their relationship was an extremely stormy one. Thinking perhaps that her secretary's lack of good spirits might be the result of a quarrel, she enquired gently, 'Maggie, is something wrong?'

Almost immediately the other woman's forehead cleared. 'Well, I know it's none of my business,' she began, 'but we do seem to be having problems with cashflow at the moment. Some of our clients are being very slow to pay.' She gnawed worriedly at her bottom lip. 'I know I don't have any right to say this, but —'

'But what Maggie?' Anxiety sharpened Jenna's voice, her conversation with Gordon Burns still very fresh in her mind. There were always clients in this business who jibbed at paying their bills: some of them, those with the reputation and standing to do so, even got away without paying them at all, but they were in a minority and Jenna was meticulous about investigating the reliability of those clients with whom she took on large contracts. Only the previous month she had turned down a contract from a Greek millionaire to revamp his huge London apartment because she had discovered by discreet enquiry that he was not over-zealous about meeting his bills.

She saw the apprehension darken her secretary's eyes and realised that she had probably sounded more brusque than she had intended, but then, Maggie didn't know how concerned she was about the loan she had taken on to buy the Hall.

'I'm sorry,' Jenna apologised, smiling at her. 'I know I sounded snappy but it wasn't intended for you. I'm having problems with Lucy at the moment.'

The admission was made before she could stop it, leaving Jenna surprised at herself. She never discussed her personal life with any of her staff, not even Harley, and although she liked Maggie and considered her as much a friend as an employee, it would never normally have occurred to her to confide in her. She had grown so used to making her own decisions and relying on herself that she never sought the advice or help of others on a personal basis. In her heart of hearts much as she liked Maggie, she also faintly despised her.

Maggie was a very attractive girl, who was held fast in the throes of a relationship which, as far as Jenna could see, had no advantages for her at all. Rick Forbes was well known to have a roving eye, and Jenna doubted very much if he remained faithful to stay-at-home Maggie when he was away covering stories for his paper, and yet Maggie put up with his fickleness. The flat they lived in was Maggie's bought with some money she had inherited from her grand-parents; she washed, cooked and cleaned for both of them, and if she was lucky, in return for all that, Rick took her out for the odd meal whenever he returned to London. Maggie excused him on the grounds that when he did return home he was too tired to want to do anything other than mooch around the flat, sleeping and working.

Was it any wonder that men rode roughshod over the female sex when women were so weak with them? Well, no man would ever do that to her! If she ever married . . . Startled, Jenna stared unseeingly through her office window. *If* she married? But, of course, she wasn't going to! All that male pressure was beginning to get to her, she reflected, dismissing her thoughts and turning her attention back to Maggie.

'It's okay, I know you're under a lot of pressure at the moment,' her secretary smiled, accepting the apology. Many of her peers flatly refused to work for a woman boss, saying that they were far worse than men. Men could be coaxed and flattered into giving way if need be, women could not. They were notorious for refusing to give their own sex a hand up the career ladder, but Maggie had never once regretted her decision to come and work for Jenna. For one thing the work itself was fascinating, and Jenna often gave her the opportunity to exercise her own judgement, praising and encouraging her when she did so. It was unlike her to be snappy.

Maggie frowned and wished she could find a way to put her fears over to Jenna without making any direct accusations. Over the last few months she had seen how Richard Hollis had taken on contracts that were not always as financially sound as they might be. He was a very ambitious young man, though Jenna did not seem to see that, perhaps because in her presence he was always obsequious and obedient. Maggie, however, had seen a different side of him. When Jenna was away, Richard enjoyed ruling the roost. Short with mousy-brown hair, he was not the sort of man who made an impression at first sight, and perhaps because of that, Maggie sensed in him a driving ambition that he kept in check when Jenna was around.

Maggie was well aware of Jenna's contempt for and dislike of the male sex. There were men Jenna respected, businessmen, but for their professionalism, not their maleness. Maggie had heard one or two sneering remarks Richard had made behind Jenna's back which made her suspect that he wouldn't always be content merely to be Jenna's assistant. Not that there was anything wrong with that . . . but it was the way he hid his ambition and his feelings from Jenna, assuming a deference Maggie suspected he did not really feel, that alarmed her. Accounting was not Jenna's strong point, but surely in time she would realise that they were taking on more and more unprofitable contracts and would trace them back to Richard. Resolving that it was probably better to say nothing, Maggie picked up the diary.

'You haven't got any appointments today, but there's a cocktail party tonight at the Billingtons' — Margery Billington wants to show off her new décor.'

Jenna groaned. 'Dear God, that's all I need!' She chewed her bottom lip, thinking rapidly. Could she get out of the party? She certainly didn't want to go. She had promised herself that tonight she would talk to Lucy, but the Billington contract had been an extremely profitable one. Margery Billington was

American by birth with a wide circle of friends both her own and her second husband's. Vincent Billington was a well-known racing stable owner. An awful lot of influential and wealthy people had horses in training at the Billington stables and Jenna knew that she ought to attend the party.

She was just drinking her mid-morning cup of coffee when Richard walked into her office, doing a brief double-take when he saw her there.

'I thought you were working at home today?'

She remembered intimating to him that she might, and something in his manner puzzled her slightly. She sensed a certain tension about him as though, somehow, finding her in her office had thrown him a little.

'Well, I came in instead. Now that I've bought the Hall, I've got to make some money to pay for it.' She said it jokingly, but it was, of course, the truth, and saying it reminded her of something she wanted to discuss with him.

'Richard, there's a returned contract in my mail this morning from Victor James — I thought we agreed that we wouldn't do that one? You know the reputation he's got. He's parted company with three designers already.'

Richard shrugged. 'Well, he came on to me when you were away, virtually pleading with us to do it. The money's right . . . '

Jenna frowned slightly.

'Look, Jenna, you were away and a decision had to be made. I'm sorry if I made the wrong one but . . . '

Once again, she sensed a slight hostility in his tone, and then told herself that she was imagining it. No doubt he was on the defensive because she had queried his decision. Men hated their decisions being questioned by a woman, but she was the head of the company and if she had been here . . . But she could hardly blame Richard for her absence.

'Well, it's done now,' she agreed, forcing a smile, 'but no more contracts unless I've okayed them, mmm?'

'You're the boss. It's the Billington bash tonight, isn't it?' Richard added carelessly, 'Want me to go in your place?'

It wasn't unusual for him to stand in for her at various social functions, but even though ten minutes ago she had been thinking of asking him to do so at this one, for some reason she found herself shaking her head.

'No. I'll go myself. What did you want me for, by the way?'

'Oh . . . there's going to be an unforeseen delay with the carpet for the Holmes contract — you remember it had to be specially dyed . . . '

'How long a delay?' Jenna frowned. As she remembered it, that carpet had been ordered months ago. The Holmeses' daughter was getting married shortly, and when they had originally contacted Jenna some time ago, they had stressed that all the work must be finished in time for that event.

'Six weeks . . . maybe eight . . . '

Jenna thought rapidly. That was far too long a delay.

'Leave it with me,' she said crisply, Richard's presence all but forgotten, all her attention given to the new problem. 'Thanks, Richard,' she dismissed him briefly. I'll have to try and sort something out. I want to talk to you about the new contracts we're taking on, but I'll arrange something later.'

Once he had gone, she buzzed through to Maggie

and asked her to bring in the Holmeses' file.

As she studied it, frowning, she turned to her own original notes, jotted down after her initial visit to the Holmeses'. They had been remarkably clear about what they wanted. They had just moved into a large 1930's house in Wimbledon, previously owned by an Arab family, which in Helen Holmes's view needed completely redoing. A pleasantly plump ex-general's daughter in her mid-forties, she had know exactly what she wanted. Colefax & Fowler fabrics, Osborne & Little papers. In short, typically country-house furnishings, but her chief request had been for a carpet all through the house which would suit a variety of colours.

In the end she had settled on a very subtle shade of peachy-pink, which would have to be specially dyed, and aware of the delay which might arise, Jenna had put in hand immediate instructions for the order and dyeing of the carpet. Bierley's was a company that she used regularly: completely reliable and producing a first-class result. She closed her eyes, leaning back in her chair, aware of the beginnings of a tension headache in the base of her skull. She could already imagine Mrs Holmes's reaction when she learned that the carpet might not arrive in time for the wedding. She picked up the file again, looking for the original order note. Although it might not do much good, at least if she could point out to the company doing the dyeing that they were way, way over the time limit agreed, it might help her to get rid of some of her tension. It was rather late in the day to find someone else to do the job now — especially someone reliable. Dyeing carpets to an exact shade as delicate as the one the Holmeses had chosen was a skilled business . . .

She traced through the file, locating the memos she

had done putting various orders into effect, remembering briefly that she had been away for several days at the time the contract commenced, visiting a client in Spain who had just bought a villa there. A frown pleated her forehead as she looked at the date on her memo and then compared it with the date on the carpet order. Six weeks . . . why had there been that delay? It was a glaring error on their own part, and yet she could see no reason for it. Well, it was pointless crying over spilt milk, she reflected tensely, picking up her phone and asking Maggie to get the managing director of Bierley's for her.

He was sympathetic when she explained her position to him. Yes, of course he could see that her client would want her carpet down for her daughter's wedding, but, he explained, the delay was the usual one, the normal time-lapse between receiving an order and completion of it — three months, as it was in this case. However, he told Jenna much to her relief, because she was one of their better clients, and because they were presently just about to mix the dye for another large order which was not required urgently, he felt they might be able to reschedule things and get her carpet done in time. Thanking him Jenna hung up, and then frowning again she rang through to Richard's office. His secretary answered the phone and put her through to him. Quickly she told him about the delay in the original order. 'Obviously someone's slipped up somewhere,' she said crisply. 'We can't afford errors like that, Richard. Fortunately, the carpet will be ready in time after all, but its delay could have cost us the whole contract.'

There was a brief pause, and then he said heartily, 'Well, thank God you managed to get it all sorted out. I can't think what went wrong, although you know

I've never been keen on your method of sending out memos. You know, I feel that we should each take on certain contracts and see them through to the finish instead of splitting the responsibility as we do now.'

Jenna let him finish and then said, 'But if we did that, Richard, you would be my partner and not my assistant. People who use this firm as their designers are using it because of *my* reputation and have a right to expect me to be fully involved in what's going on.'

She let him digest her comments and then rang off, still frowning. Problems with Richard were the very last thing she needed right now. Her phone rang, and Maggie informed her that there was a call for her. Banishing Richard from her mind, Jenna got back to work.

The backlog on her desk was far greater than she had realised: at least a dozen telephone calls were outstanding and there had been a rash of minor problems with their existing contracts that took time to sort out. Of course they would all happen now, just when she needed life to run smoothly, she reflected grimly, suddenly remembering something else she had to do, and jotting a note down on her pad to call in at a shop she knew, which specialised in reproduction mouldings for ornamentation and also copied or made up brass and wood motifs to order. She wanted to talk to them about copying the Adam plasterwork at the Hall which was badly damaged and also to discuss brass doorplates for the mahogany doors to match the Adam décor. Adam, she knew, would often use a central motif all through his work, so that it was echoed in minute detail all through a room. She reflected fleetingly that it was a pity there was no record of Robert Adam's original designs for the new wing of the house, and then grimaced as the harsh purr of her phone broke into her thoughts.

It was gone six before she was free to leave her office. Everyone else had already gone, and as she stepped out on to the street, she realised that for the first time she had not paused to enjoy the thrill of pride the nameplate outside the main door gave her.

She was overtired, she told herself, and worried about Lucy, but she also knew that her heart was not in London. She was aching to get back to Yorkshire and the old Hall.

There was no Lucy to greet her when she got home. Instead, there was a message on the answerphone announcing that she was staying another night with her friend. The flat seemed empty and sterile and as she made herself a cup of coffee all her old guilts came flooding over her. What sort of a parent was she really to Lucy? There had been a hurtful degree of truth in the accusation that Lucy had thrown at her, but what was the alternative? How could she have kept Lucy without the financial means to support them both? She could have given her up for adoption, of course . . . Putting her coffee down, she prowled restlessly into the drawing-room, pacing up and down tensely. Would Lucy have been happier if she had? It was all very well telling herself that all teenagers were rebellious but there was a lack of communication between them that hurt as well as worried her. She knew its roots were in her refusal to talk to Lucy about her father. It was all very well for other people to be full of good advice, Bill, Nancy, James Allingham . . .

Her mouth hardened. Why on earth had she thought of him? A playboy millionaire who had inherited and not earned his wealth, a man who typified qualities of his sex she particularly disliked, rampantly male and arrogantly pleased by the fact, she thought unkindly, using his sexuality about as subtly as a caveman with a club. To denigrate him mentally released some of her tension and, she reflected sardonically as she headed for her bedroom to change for the evening, having a sick step-sister to care for would certainly cramp his style.

She showered quickly, putting on clean underwear before sitting down to do her make-up and hair. Her underwear was white and plain, pristinely immaculate, her taste quite different from Lucy's who tended to go for pretty pastel cottons with embroidery and bows. Jenna despised even the idea of dressing to please a man, of using her body to gain male favour. The male sex as a whole was worthy only of contempt, she thought as she applied her foundation, so vain and egotistical that it honestly believed all the tricks of the feminine repertoire were motivated by desire rather than necessity. It constantly amazed her how the shrewd business brain behind a successful business could genuinely believe that his pretty secretary flattered him because she found him sexually desirable. Men were past masters at deception — especially of themselves. Take James Allingham, for instance. No doubt in twenty years' time he would still be believing that it was his body and not his money that drew beautiful women to his side. Maybe now that was the truth, but like so many other men before him he would never be able to admit that he was ageing, less attractive. Women, unfortunately, were not able to be so self-deluding.

She got up and opened her wardrobe. What should she wear? She had several elegant formal dresses especially bought for these sort of dos and eventually selected a plain black silk skirt topped with a white silk jacket. The jacket had wide revers and a fitted waist. The skirt was straight with a discreet pleat at the back. To go with it, she chose very fine silk tights. She styled her hair in an elegant French pleat and then stood back to study her reflection with approval. Elegant and businesslike. No one looking at her to-night would mistake her for someone's wife — or someone's mistress.

The invitation had been for eight-thirty and it was just gone nine when she rang the doorbell of the Billingtons' apartment.

Margery Billington greeted her, hugging her theatri-cally. 'Jenna, darling. I'm so glad you're here! Every-one adores your décor.'

Jenna smile diplomatically and followed her hostess into the drawing-room. It was full of dinner-suited males and designer-clad women. Margery had speci-fied something eye-catching and different that also looked expensive and Jenna had done her best to oblige. The walls had been dragged in a soft aqua greeny-blue effect and then veined in gold to produce a delicate shimmer almost like a translucent pearled marble.

The carpet echoed the base colour of the walls; the furniture a matt off-white — to Jenna's critical eye the scheme was rather theatrical but Margery had loved it. As she acknowledged several people she knew, she edged her way over to the fireplace to study the huge giltwood mirror she had commissioned from a young student at the Royal College of Art. He had done an excellent job, she noted approvingly, seeing that the cherubs holding the frame had Margery's features. The mirror had been expensive, but . . .

'Jenna, I absolutely adore it. You must do some-thing similar for me.'

She turned away from her contemplation of the mirror to talk to the woman who had come to join her. She was the owner of an extremely successful New York-based boutique which sold British designs at a horrendous mark-up.

'I'm thinking of buying a *pied-à-terre* over here . . . Just something small to use while I'm here on buying trips.'

They chatted for a while, Jenna making a mental note to follow up their talk.

'Jenna, I'm so thrilled,' effused Margery. '*Maison* want to do a feature on the apartment. One of the directors has a filly with us, and they're contemplating a horse-racing issue — You know . . . noted trainers and their lifestyle, owners, races, that sort of thing, and he wants to feature us.'

Jenna knew the magazine, an upmarket glossy which would do her no harm to be seen in.

'It would be fantastic advertising for you,' Margery pressed. She looked sly as she added. 'We're thinking of redoing the cottage. I'd like you to do it for us, but you know what men are . . . he's kicking a bit over the cost. With the business that will come your way from the *Maison* feature I'm sure you could see your way to, well . . . compromising a little.'

Jenna didn't let any reaction show on her face. The Billingtons were multi-millionaires and could well afford a designer four or five times as costly as herself, but she had no wish to offend Margery, and she thought wryly that there were ways and means of offering a discount that was not always what it seemed. She never had, and never would, seek to make outrageous profits, and charged what she considered to be a reasonable fee for her services. That way she believed she was preserving both her integrity and her reputation, but people like the Billingtons were so used to being ripped off that it probably never occurred to them that she wasn't jumping on the bandwagon.

'I'm sure we can work something out,' she agreed with a smile. 'Why don't we get together after the *Maison* feature is finalised?'

A subtle way of letting Margery know that she hadn't been born yesterday: no feature, no discount!

She came up against a good many Margery Billingtons in her work and had learned to accept that to succeed she often needed to employ a degree of subtlety.

There were quite a lot of people at the party whom she knew. In the dining-room, hired staff were serving a buffet — the fashionably *de rigueur* wholefood-cum-*nouvelle-cuisine* type, Jenna noticed, accepting a glass of wine from a passing waiter. She had nothing against wholefood *per se*, and indeed was extremely particular about what she and Lucy ate, but most of the people at the party had probably dined well at lunchtime and would go on to consume another hearty meal later. Gluttony for food was like gluttony for sex, she thought distastefully, wondering as she did so why it was she who always seemed to stand apart from the rest of the human race.

Bill and Nancy were the only people she was really close to, and she kept even them at a distance. Sometimes she suspected from the sharp looks that Nancy gave her when she was particularly scathing about the male sex, that the older woman was about to take her to task. There was no one with whom she could share her innermost thoughts and fears — no one at all. She frowned, wondering why she should have such a depressive thought. Her lack of intimate relationships had never bothered her before, in fact she had deliberately cultivated it. The crowd round the buffet table thinned and her frown deepened as she caught sight of a familiar dark head. James Allingham — *here*?

She was just about to dismiss her suspicion as the product of an overworked imagination when he turned round and she realised she was right. He was looking straight across at her, and she flushed, knowing that to ignore his pointed scrutiny as she wanted would be both rude and gauche. There was a girl with him, a tiny blonde, with a carefully tousled mane of blonde hair, and the sort of immaculate make-up that shrieked model. She might have guessed he would go for that type, Jenna reflected, allowing herself a cool smile before letting her eyes slide away. However, she was not allowed to escape quite so easily. As she made for the drawing-room, Margery came up to her with James and his pocket Venus in tow.

'Jenna, darling, let me introduce you . . . James . . . '

'Jenna and I have already met.'

Jenna was aware of the hard speculation in the blonde's eyes and grimaced inwardly. The girl had nothing to fear from Jenna, if she did but know it.

'James has a horse with us, darling. He's just moved into a new apartment. James . . . ' she turned towards him, 'you simply must get Jenna to decorate it for you.'

Jenna saw the look in his eyes as they studied the drawing-room, and seethed inwardly, recognising it. How dare he sit in judgement on her? Didn't he realise that a good interior designer always took note of the client's own taste? She had never sought to impose her own taste on anyone and never would.

'Jay, darling, there's Naomi . . . do let's go over and talk to her.' The blonde's pointed determination to ignore her only amused Jenna, as did her affected, breathy way of speaking. As she watched them go, it gave her quite a degree of pleasure to be able to reflect scathingly on James Allingham's taste in women. Somehow it reduced him to the ranks of other members of his sex whom she also despised, making her feel . . . safer. Safer? What possible danger could he be to her? It was probably a hang-over from her fear of losing the Hall to him, she reflected, sipping her wine slowly.

At ten-thirty she was ready to go. Cocktail parties bored her in the main. She recalled that Nancy had been shocked to hear her say so. 'You're getting too high-falutin' ideas about yourself, my girl,' she had told Jenna bluntly. 'You're only human like the rest of us, you know.'

Even Bill had remonstrated gently with her, reminding her that she was a member of the human race. 'You can't always remain aloof from life, Jenna,' he had told her quietly.

But Jenna had learned the hard way that by remaining aloof she remained safe. If Rachel had been more aloof . . . less naïve . . .

'Ah, there you are, Jenna . . . ' It was too late to escape, being thoroughly embraced by the man bearing down on her, although Jenna held herself rigid beneath his embrace, turning her face so that his kiss landed on her cheek instead of her mouth.

'Roger . . . ' Her eyes and voice were cool, but he appeared not to register that fact. Roger Bennett, supermarket entrepreneur *extraordinaire* was probably too used to riding roughshod over people to be put off by anything less subtle than a sledgehammer, Jenna thought, asking sweetly, 'Maria not with you?'

Maria was his long-suffering wife, to whom he was

constantly unfaithful with a parade of starlets and
pseudo-débutantes. Jenna detested him, loathing his
arrogance and the way he had of reducing every
member of her sex under forty to a sex object. Roger
Bennett had never respected any woman in his life
and would have laughed himself sick if anyone had
suggested that he should. He was everything Jenna
most disliked in a man, and her mouth curled disparagingly as he said, 'Saw you talking to James
Allingham. Now there's a pretty piece he had with
him. I bet she keeps him warm in bed at night.'

'I'm sure.' Jenna's voice was cold. 'Excuse me,
Roger, but . . . '

'No, don't go yet, I want to talk to you. I'm moving
into the property market — apartments abroad — upmarket stuff, and I could be in a position to put some
business your way. Why don't we go into the study
and talk about it?'

Little though she wanted to, Jenna felt she had
to agree. A contract like that was something she
couldn't afford to turn down right now. Since her
talk with Gordon Burns, the burden of the loan she
had taken out to buy the Hall was weighing heavily
upon her.

She glanced at her watch and said coolly, 'Well, I
was just about to leave, but I can manage half an
hour.'

Men like Roger were impossible to deal with once
you let them get the upper hand. Jenna had had to
learn to deal with many Rogers during the course of
her career and she had found that a schoolmistressy
bossiness was the best answer. For some reason it always de-sexed her in their eyes and once that had
happened they became far less of a nuisance. She preferred to work for married couples and even then with

the woman, but one couldn't always choose one's contracts.

The study was decorated in the traditional manner complete with a mock fireplace. Roger went to stand by it, one foot on the fender, his arm on the mantelpiece. Jenna stayed several feet away from him as she listened to him talking about the proposed contract. It sounded extremely promising, and whether because of that, or because her mind was still on the burden of the loan hanging over her, she failed to notice that Roger had moved, until she felt his arm slide round her.

'Of course, if you get this contract, it will mean us working closely together . . . going out to Spain to view the properties. You're a very attractive woman, Jenna . . . I've always thought so . . .'

Sensing that he was about to proposition her, Jenna stiffened. Her immediate instinct was to wrench free of him and tell him in no uncertain terms exactly what she thought of him, but caution prevailed. Gently easing herself away from him, she began, 'Roger . . .' breaking off in relief as the study door opened.

Roger had his back to the door and didn't realise they were no longer alone until James Allingham said coolly, 'Am I interrupting? I thought I might find Vincent in here . . .'

'Roger and I were just having a business discussion,' Jenna told him coldly. Dear God, of all the people to find her in such an embarrassing position it would have to be him.

His raised eyebrows conveyed a polite disinclination to put any real belief in her excuse, and all her relief at being interrupted was overtaken by a fierce surge of anger against him. For the second time this evening he was trying to disparage her.

'Roger. Ah, there you are . . . ' said Margery, appearing in the doorway. 'I've been looking everywhere for you, I want you to come and tell Phil Edgerton all about this new development of yours.'

As Margery led Roger away, Jenna was acutely conscious of the silence left behind. James Allingham stood between her and the door, and for some reason that fact alarmed her.

'I'll leave you to wait for Vincent,' she said, striving to appear calm, and heading for the door. He didn't move and in order to get past him she would have to come within inches of his body. The thought made her cringe inwardly and then mentally berate herself angrily for her reaction to him. What on earth was getting into her? He was a man like any other, shallow, vain, impossibly egotistical, and with an uncomfortable habit of catching her off-guard and unprepared, she acknowledged.

'I see you're taking my advice,' he drawled as she drew level with him.

His remark made her look frowningly at him.

'About providing Lucy with a father.' One eyebrow rose. 'I wouldn't recommend that you try to secure Mr Bennett for the post, though. He's hoping for a peerage and most unlikely to divorce Maria . . . '

For a second she was too stunned to speak, and then the mockery in his eyes was like a burning torch applied to gunpowder, anger exploding so intensely inside her that it totally overwhelmed everything else. Too wrought up even to think of finding the words to release her fury Jenna reacted in the only way she could, all the anger and contempt she felt towards him behind the force of her open palm against his face.

The violence of it made her palm tingle and gave her a glorious, dizzying sense of release so heady that she was barely aware of his reaction until she felt his fingers snap round her wrists.

Fury glittered in her eyes, the trappings of civilisation stripped from her expression as she let him see the loathing in their depths, using all her strength to resist the pressure he was exerting to drag her into his arms.

She expected him to release her and he did, but only to force her hands behind her back and manacle them there, imprisoning her against his body with his other hand. Shock darkened her green eyes to emerald. No man had ever dared to handle her in this way before! She was too angry to feel fear, only an all-consuming rage that he should dare to touch her as he was. Through her suit she could feel the hardness of his body and the rapid thud of his heart. Arching back she glared up into his eyes. They were like ice water, glittering with a rage to match her own. In his jaw a pulse thudded erratically just below the dark red marks of her hand.

'So, there is life beneath that controlled façade, after all.' He bared his teeth in a parody of a smile. 'What a pity your friend isn't here to observe the real Jenna. I'm sure he'd find it most illuminating.'

'Roger Bennett is no friend of mine,' Jenna spat at him furiously. 'We came in here to discuss business, but like all your sex, he believes he has a God-given appeal to women that none of us can resist.'

James Allingham's eyes narrowed on Jenna's face as she spoke, the anger dying out of them to be replaced by cool speculation.

'A feminist, I see. Well, my dear, you'll have to castrate the entire male sex to convert the world to believing as you do.'

'With the greatest of pleasure.' She had grated out

the words before she could stop herself, twisting desperately to break free of him as she saw his expression change.

'I see. Then I shall know how to exact retribution for this, shan't I?' he drawled nastily, briefly releasing her to touch the scarlet marks against his skin.

Jenna tried to use her momentary advantage to escape, bucking fiercely against his punishing grip on her wrists, driven wild by fury when she felt the soundless laugh that shook his body, and then his hand was at the nape of her neck, his fingers sliding up into her hair in a taunting parody of tenderness, the pressure of his body against hers forcing her back until she felt her muscles clench against the pressure. She tried to kick him and was rewarded by the hard pressure of his leg trapping hers, forcing her between his thighs.

Stubbornly, she refused to give in to the pressure of his hand splayed against her head, and to the agonising pain she felt when his fingers tightened punishingly into her hair, dislodging the pins in her French pleat. He was hurting her deliberately, and enjoying it, damn him!

'No one should be allowed to inflict pain without accepting the risk of getting it back,' he told her softly, his eyes on hers.

'Is that how you get your kicks?' Her own glared back at him. 'By hurting women?'

'*Are* you a woman?' His mocking smile was derisive. 'I haven't seen anything to convince me of that — yet!'

Jenna struggled harder, driven to fury by his behaviour. 'Damn you! Let me go!' She arched against him, trying to break free, tensing suddenly when his glance fell to her breasts, moving in uneven agitation beneath her jacket.

For a moment, she thought he meant to touch her and a wave of hostile rejection gripped her body.

'Don't worry,' he told her laconically. 'I find you about as sexy as a Barbie doll and nearly as plastic.'

Just for a second his contempt pierced through her, hurting her in a way she had never thought to be hurt but then the pain was gone superseded by sheer animal rage. 'Then why don't you let me go and get back to your little blonde playmate?' she shot at him. 'I'm sure she's everything a man like you could ever need.'

Her mouth twisted cynically over the word 'man'. He let her finish and then said silkily, 'You asked for this.'

She couldn't even free her hands to beat at his shoulders as his mouth ground down on hers. Her attempt to twist away at the last moment was foiled by the fierce pressure of his fingers in her hair, tugging back her head until she thought her neck might break, his mouth grinding her lips back against her teeth, a savage display of male anger and contempt, of male desire to subdue and physically destroy the female. It asked for and got no response. It was not designed to. It was inflicted upon her purely as punishment.

When he eventually released her, her mouth felt bruised and sore. She could taste blood on her lips, and wiped her hand across her mouth distastefully, hating him with a ferocity that almost matched her hatred of Lucy's father. But then, of course, he too was a member of that accursed family. No wonder he had behaved as he had. It must be in the Deveril blood, this desire to humiliate and degrade women.

'If you're trying to frighten me into giving the Hall

to you, I can tell you now, you won't succeed,' she told him scathingly.

He smiled then, very coldly, with eyes like ice. 'I wasn't, but don't think I've given up, it will be mine.'

'Over my dead body.'

He laughed then, and drawled tauntingly, 'All things are possible.'

She was still blindingly angry when she got home. She had managed to leave the apartment via the back entrance, without anyone seeing her, and when she got home had been so appalled by her own appearance that she was thankful no one had. Her hair hung down her back in untidy strands, her eyes glittered febrilely, hot colour staining her cheekbones. And, dear God, her mouth! She touched its swollen outline, wincing at its soreness. Her bottom lip was split and still bleeding slightly.

When he had been grinding his mouth down against hers she had almost bitten him; the temptation had been overwhelming but she had been aware that to give in to it was to allow him even more opportunity to hurt her. Even now she felt acutely sick at the thought of the loathsome intimacies he might have forced on her had he been able to get beyond the gritted barrier of her teeth. Vile, arrogant animal! She shuddered, stripping off her clothes and going into her bathroom. She even felt as though she smelled of him. She was too wrought up for sleep and decided instead to do some work. Pulling a comfortable old bathrobe over her nude body she went through into her small study.

CHAPTER FIVE

SHE had been working for over an hour when she heard her doorbell ring. Thinking that Lucy must, after all, have decided to return home she padded into the hall, releasing the safety catch and opening the door.

It wasn't Lucy who stood outside, but James Allingham. It was too late to bar the door to him, but to her surprise he made no attempt to push his way inside, merely stretching out one long arm to display her jacket, held lightly in his hand.

'You forgot this.' He said it softly, the smile in his eyes totally derisory as he added tauntingly, 'I wonder why?'

Every instinct she had screamed at her to snatch the cloth from his fingers and slam the door in his face, but the lesson he had already forced upon her lingered, and she was reluctant to do anything that would bring her into contact with him, no matter how briefly. It infuriated her that he should have had such a powerful effect upon her instincts. She had never gone in fear of any man, and it goaded her to the point where her temper was ready to explode that this man should engender it in her.

'Margery noticed it when we were leaving, so I volunteered to deliver it for you, since I had to drive past.'

'Thank you, but you really needn't have bothered.'

Margery thrived on gossip and wasn't above doing

102

a little extra embroidery of her own, and there was no limit to the fairy tale she would be able to concoct out of his simple offer. She was always questioning Jenna about the lack of men in her life. Her eyes narrowed as something rather odd struck her. 'How did you know my address?' she demanded flatly.

The dark eyebrows rose in mockery. 'Isn't there a saying — know one's enemy? Through circumstances beyond my control, I might have been obliged to drop out of the auction and allow you to gain possession of the old Hall, but the game isn't over yet.'

'Why are you so anxious to possess it?'

Jenna bit her lip in vexation the moment the question was asked, angry with herself for being betrayed into showing any interest in anything about him.

'It *is* my ancestral home.'

Jenna could not deny that, but she sensed that something stronger than a mere yearning to possess the house that belonged to his ancestors drove him. Compulsive determination to reach a specific goal was no stranger to her — perhaps that was why she recognised it so clearly in someone else.

'Why were *you* so determined to possess it?'

'I fell in love with it.' She offered him a tight smile to accompany the words, which were, after all, true, if only part of the whole truth.

'You know, I find that an extremely intriguing admission. You don't strike me as a woman who knows the meaning of the word,' he told her brutally.

For one crazy moment she wanted to strike him, to hit out at him violently in her own pain, but she withstood the fierce drive to retaliate, remembering how he had reacted to her before.

'I mustn't keep you waiting.' She stretched out her fingers, trembling slightly as they curled round the fabric of her jacket and he allowed it to slip from his own, without making any attempt to restrain her.

His glance slid lazily over her body as she stepped back from it, making an openly sexual inventory of her that made her tense with raw rage.

'Your friend will be wondering what's happened to you,' she added with pointed curtness.

'I doubt it.' His teeth gleamed white in a brief smile. 'I dropped her off on the way here.'

Jenna felt her stomach lurch, without quite knowing why it should. She took another step backwards, starting to close the door, tensing when long male fingers curled round the wood just above her own.

'Before you do, I have a small favour to ask you.'

Jenna watched him warily.

'I have some family documents and diaries relating to the old Hall, including descriptions of some of the rooms as they originally were when my ancestor left England — I didn't have them with me when I went round the place before the auction and I was wondering if you would allow me to go round again. Just out of interest, of course.'

He was challenging her, Jenna knew that, telling her that he knew she feared him, and mocking her for it, letting her know that he already anticipated her refusal. But if he was speaking the truth and he did have some records, they would be an invaluable source of information for her in her desire to refurbish the house as closely as she could to the original. Thinking quickly she said, 'I think that could be arranged, but only if you are willing to allow me to look at these records: they could be of interest to me in my renovation work.'

'That sounds fine.' His expression was hidden from her by the fall of dark lashes guarding his eyes.

'I'll give you a call later in the week and we can fix something up. No doubt you'll want to be in attendance when I visit — just to make sure I don't steal the place away brick by brick. When you've got the time to go up there, let me know and we'll go together.'

That wasn't what Jenna had had in mind at all, but she knew there was no way she could refuse his suggestion without betraying her fear of him. She clenched her fists angrily, wishing her desire to see the documents he had described had not led her into agreeing to his visit, but it was too late to back out now.

She stepped back again, her expression firm as she made to close the door, relieved that this time he made no attempt to stop her. Only when it was firmly locked and the safety chain in place did she feel she could actually relax. Her mood for work was gone now and instead she went through into her bedroom. Her own reflection caught her eye as she drew level with a mirror. Her thin robe outlined the curves of her body, the shape and fullness of her breasts clearly visible beneath it. A wave of hot colour beat up under her skin as she remembered James Allingham's leisurely scrutiny of her. Her fingers curled into angry claws. How she detested the man! She wished she had never agreed to allow him to look round the house. He meant to try and take it away from her, she knew that, but she would never let him have it . . . never!

Jenna had a very disturbed night. When she eventually managed to get to sleep, her rest was punctuated by vivid dreams so realistic that when she woke up just before dawn, she was trembling, still half convinced that if she opened her eyes she would find herself not in her own bed, but in a walnut four-poster in a room at the Hall. But, far worse than that, if she turned her head, she would discover beside her the man who had just seduced her — the dark, cynical-eyed Regency buck from the portrait that hung above the stairs at the old Hall.

Shuddering, she tried to dismiss the dream, but it refused to go away. Every time she closed her eyes, it came flooding back, and she saw herself dressed in a flimsy, gauzy muslin dress, adorned with fluttering ribbons, the fabric so fine that when she moved it swirled like mist round her body, provocatively revealing more than it concealed.

Tonight marked the occasion of her betrothal ball. All that she and her aunt had worked so determinedly towards during the London season had now come to fruition. As the only daughter of an immensely wealthy tradesman, if it had not been for her family connections on her mother's side, she would have been denied any entrée into aristocratic society. Its doors were closed to tradesmen and their offspring no matter how wealthy. At twenty-six she was old for a débutante, but during his lifetime her father had never allowed her to mix in society. She had been sent to school in Bath and there had suffered innumerable snubs and slights from the daughters of the poverty-stricken upper class who also boarded there. Mrs Hartwell had taken her as a boarder only because her father had paid her well to do so, and she had grown up hating those other little girls, who had every social advantage denied to her and were all too eager to make her conscious of that fact.

Now with her aunt's connivance and backing she

had finally breached the walls of aristocratic contempt. Her aunt's connections and her own wealth had secured for her an invitation to one of the most exclusive balls of the season. It was there that she had met Viscount Deveril.

The viscount and his father were on the look-out for a rich bride, or so the gossips said. Their Yorkshire estates were deeply in debt, and the viscount himself, although only thirty-five, had already gambled away a fortune like his father before him. Physically, he had little appeal to her. But she craved the social position being his wife would give her, and so, deliberately and subtly, using the bait of her wealth, she had set out to snare him.

Now she had succeeded and it was the evening of their betrothal ball, which was being held at his ancestral home in Yorkshire. By the end of the week they would be married — her husband-to-be's debts would not allow a long delay, and since her father-in-law was a widower, she would have full control of the household. Although Francis did not know it yet, she intended to keep an extremely tight hand on the purse-strings once they were wed. She liked Sir George even less than she liked his eldest son, but she was still determined to go through with the match. She knew that people talked about her behind her back, mocking her single-minded determination to get herself a titled husband, but she did not care. As the viscount's wife, she would be in a position to turn the tables fully on those stuck-up misses who had made her school-days such a misery.

Francis, for his part, made no secret of his reasons for marrying her. He despised her for her low birth but he wanted her wealth — his father wanted her wealth and Francis did not have the strength of mind to withstand his domineering parent. She did not like Sir George. There were disturbing tales about the death of his wife, stories that he had mistreated her in some way. However, that need not concern her. Once she had provided Francis with an heir they could go their own separate ways in life, their marriage merely one of mutual convenience.

Eyeing her reflection in one of the long mirrors on the wall she frowned, not seeing herself but the man standing behind her, Francis's younger brother. Unlike her husband-to-be he did not favour foppish, dandified clothes, but was clad from head to foot in black, apart from the contrasting white of his cambric shirt. She felt the rage shimmering inside her boil to the surface as she watched him.

She had seen him once or twice in London, his expression always cynical and mocking. Like Francis he had no money, and if Francis did not marry and produce an heir he would be the one to inherit — providing always, of course, that he outlived Francis. He had a reputation for embroiling himself in duels and living dangerously, as well as a predilection for other men's wives, which suggested that his life expectancy would not be a long one. And that was not all. Rumour had it that he was not really Sir George's son . . . that Sir George's wife had played her husband false and that his second son had been fathered by the lady's lover. She had no idea whether the gossip was true, but it was a fact that James Deveril did not favour either his father or his brother, and he certainly did not live in accord with either of them. She had seen that much for herself.

The first time she saw him she had been conscious of a powerful magnetism emanating from him; he constantly taunted her, reminding her in a thousand subtle ways of who she was — and how lowly her birth compared with his own. She detested him and once she and Francis were wed, she would see to it that he was no longer made welcome at Deveril Hall. She had heard that Stuart blood ran in his veins, and while his dark arrogance attested to this gossip, she herself was not inclined to believe it. She did not *want* to believe it.

She and Francis opened the ball, dancing together, his hand felt cold and clammy in her own and she deliberately closed her mind to the fact that within the week he would be entitled to do far more than merely touch her hand. She would have what she wanted, and she could endure the price to be paid for it. Pray God she conceived quickly.

'This dance, I think, is mine.'

She watched him approach, his hair as black as his clothes, his eyes the same colour as the sapphires in her betrothal ring, wishing she could simply turn away and ignore him, but knowing that she could not, that they were being watched. He had a reputation with women that made many members of her sex find him additionally exciting — and there was no denying that the way he moved suggested that, beneath his evening clothes, his body was hard and firm unlike that of his brother.

They danced in silence, and she was so intent on holding herself away from him and maintaining her frigid distance that she was not aware that he was carefully manoeuvring her into the shadows and out of sight of the other guests until, abruptly, he stopped. He had taken her from the ballroom into a small salon off it where a buffet meal was laid out in readiness for later in the evening. When she turned away from him he grasped her wrist. Shock waves of tension burned her skin. No gentleman touched a lady — especially an unmarried lady — with such familiarity.

'You still intend to go through with this marriage?'

Her eyes hardened as they met the sapphire blue of his. 'Yes.' She snapped the word out at him, daring him to challenge her determination.

'So brave,' he mocked, laughing at her. 'My brother is no expert lover, madam. I hope you realise the price you will have to pay for the title of viscountess.'

'I care nothing for lovers, my lord,' she returned curtly. 'As a tradesman's daughter, I am more used to dealing in realities than fictions.'

'And you barter your father's wealth for my brother's title? You will breed him strong sons to displace me from my hopes of inheriting from him.'

'By all accounts you are not justified in entertaining such hopes, sir,' she challenged recklessly, wishing she had held her tongue when she saw the black rage sweep down over his face.

'By my troth, madam, you will pay for that,' he told her thickly, watching her.

She knew she was treading dangerously but was too incensed to stop herself, her whole body going rigid as she felt him sweep her up into his arms. She cried out to him to put her down, but her protests were ignored as he strode from the room and up an ancient flight of narrow stairs.

She was as yet unused to her new home. It was a hotch-potch of styles and passages, each generation apparently having added to the original whole but her abductor seemed to know his way through the warren of passages and narrow flights of stairs, for he never once checked until he stood outside a stout oaken door in what she assumed must be the older part of the house — as yet unexplored by her.

Securing her with one arm, he ignored the fists she was hammering against his shoulder, to open the door and drag her inside, locking it behind them and tossing the key on to a tallboy.

A fire was the room's only illumination, and she felt her stomach muscles clench as she recognised the room's entirely male ambience. On a chair before the fire she could see a ruffled shirt, thrown carelessly down as though its owner had disrobed in haste.

'Unlike Francis, I cannot run to the expense of my own valet,' she was told by a mocking voice. 'But tonight I am in luck, for you may perform that service for me.'

At first, she had been too angry at his effrontery in dragging her away from the ball to register her own danger, but now, suddenly, it overwhelmed her. Just to be found in a gentleman's company unchaperoned meant the complete destruction of an unmarried female's reputation. To be found alone with him in his bedchamber . . ! She shuddered and ran despairingly to the door, even though she knew it was locked, hammering on it with protesting fists, crying out for aid.

'You waste your breath — no one will hear you. My father's impecunious state means that what servants we have are all employed on duties connected with tonight's ball.'

'Why?' she demanded, turning to face him, her back pressed against the door. 'Why are you doing this?'

'Oh, there are any number of reasons.'

She watched in horrified fascination as he removed his coat and set about unlacing the ties of his shirt. His skin beneath the fine white lawn was brown, his chest covered in fine dark hair. Jenna had never in her life seen a man without his clothes, apart from servants, who did not count, of course, and even though caution warned her to drag her gaze away it was as though he had bewitched her and she could not.

'You are a very proud and arrogant young woman,' he told Jenna mockingly. 'And, moreover, by your meddling determination to buy yourself my brother's title, you have upset all my own plans. Before your arrival in my life, it was odds on that my charming brother would either drink himself to hell or be despatched there by one of his gaming cronies.

'My father has been most anxious to encourage Francis to take you to wife. Should Francis die without legitimate issue, his title and therefore my father's would eventually come to me, something my revered parent is at great pains to prevent. And shall I tell you why?' His voice had dropped to a soft, almost mesmeric whisper that she was powerless to deny even had she wanted to. 'It is because I am not my father's son, merely my mother's.' His mouth twisted bitterly. 'Having made my mother's life so miserable that she willed herself to death in order to escape from him, he would now like to see me destroyed also.'

He stopped and laughed harshly. 'I realise now that there is nothing I can do to stop this marriage. You are plainly set on it. Had you been of a different nature there was always the possibility that I might be able to persuade you to transfer your affections from Francis's title to my person.' He sneered openly as he looked at her. 'But you are not woman enough to fall for such a ploy. Therefore, it came to me that if I could not rely on inheriting my brother's glories for myself, I could secure them for my son . . . For I am sure that you, unlike my poor mother, would never betray by whom your child was fathered.'

'*Your* son, but . . .'

'Come, madam, you are not really so naïve as not to understand what I mean.'

In that second, with the sapphire eyes fixed implacably on her own, she did, and the knowledge galvanised her into frenzied action. She flung herself away from the door and towards the window, thinking it might offer a means of escape, but he was there before her, barring her way, laughing deep in his chest as he picked her up and tossed her easily on to the fourposter bed. The brooding look she had seen in his eyes when he spoke of his mother was gone, and in its place was one of devilish determination.

'Surely, madam, you do not mean me to believe that death is preferable to enduring my embraces? I assure you you will take a deal more pleasure in them than in those of my brother, and the result in the end is all the same, is it not? What matters it to you which of us fathers your child, so long as you are secure as my brother's wife?'

'I will be missed!' she burst out frenziedly, struggling to disentangle shuddering limbs from her skirts and escape from him. 'Francis will —— '

'Francis will be too drunk to know where you are, and if he asks you will tell him you had a headache and retired to your room. Of course, you could always tell him the truth, but do you think that he will wed you if he believes you might bear my bastard child?'

What he was saying was all too grimly true, but she had something of her father's determined spirit and would not give up so easily.

'Stop!' she warned him, backing away as he advanced towards the bed. His shirt was open to the waist now, the wristbands untied to display dark sinewy arms.

'If you let me go I shall pay you well,' she told him,

panting slightly in mingled fear and outrage, 'and, moreover, I shall say nothing to — to Francis of what has passed between us.'

When he threw back his head and laughed she longed to tear her nails down the olive mockery of his face, to destroy for ever that cynical male beauty and to give vent to her anger.

'I think I already have the better deal,' he told her softly. 'It will give me great pleasure to see your belly swell with my child and to know that he will inherit this estate from my foolish brother. A fine idea, think you not, madam?'

She moved blindly, instinctively warned by the soft menace in his voice, but she was too late. The bed subsided beneath his weight, her attempt to escape foiled by the smothering weight of his body over her own, her wild, twisting, thrashing of limbs and torso, succeeding only in tangling her in a web of bed-clothes.

He plucked her from them as easily as though she were only a child, staring down at her trapped body in its flimsy muslin gown, his legs pinning her to the bed, his fingers cruel bands of steel that tightened round her wrists as she tried in vain to lift her hand to push him off. She could see the faint shadow darkening his jaw, and the heat of their struggle had raised tiny beads of sweat along his chest. He smelt male and alien, and she gave a despairing cry as she tensed her body and tried to thrust him off.

'Be still! Remember, it is no different from what you might expect to endure on your wedding night at my brother's . . . at my half-brother's hands,' he told her harshly, underlining the real relationship which exist-ed between Francis and himself, as though doing so gave him some additional measure of pleasure. 'And you were ready enough to accept that,' he added curtly.

'Because Francis would have that right as my husband,' she managed to spit bitterly. 'You have no rights! You are a vile seducer!'

He laughed then — so heartily that she wanted to kill him — plainly not the slightest bit put out at her insult.

'You prick my ego, madam! I assure you there are many who would give a great deal to be where you are this night.'

That she knew from gossip that he spoke the truth only infuriated her the more.

'Well, I am not one of them, sir,' she stormed back at him. 'You flatter yourself indeed if you think I will ever pant after your favours like a bitch on heat.'

She knew she had made a mistake the moment the insulting words left her lips. Without a word he stared down at her until she felt as though his eyes bored into her very skull, and laid bare every single thought that was there.

'Say you so, madam?' he said silkily at last. 'That being the case there is no need for me to waste my poor talents on convincing you otherwise, and the deed might as well be done with all despatch possible.'

'It cannot be over soon enough for me,' she responded bitterly, knowing now that there was no escape, and that no matter how she railed or argued she could not shake him from his purpose. She would, after all, endure no more than she might expect to endure with Francis. Wives could expect little consideration from their husbands after all. And if she did conceive . . . She grimaced inwardly. She had no love for Francis; it mattered little to her whose child she carried as long as Francis accepted it as his own.

Afterwards, once she was safely married to Francis, she would find a means of dealing with his arrogant half-brother.

'Well, then,' her tormentor said softly, 'let us to work.'

His hands gripped the top of her gown, his wrists twisting deftly as he rent it from top to hem, leaving her clad only in her silk stockings and garters. Her overriding instinct to cover herself from him was thwarted by the strong grip of his fingers round her wrists, forcing her arms above her head. She was fashionably slender with narrow hips and a well-formed bosom, but had never thought particularly about the appeal of her shape to the male eye until now.

As a tradesman's daughter, no one had ever thought to protect her from the realities of sex as they might a true young lady. She knew all about the physical coupling of a man and a woman, and had lately endured several lectures from her aunt about the correct behaviour of a young bride, who ought not to question the wishes of a husband but simply accede to them. She had thought herself strong enough to do so, to be able to separate her mind from her body and simply blot out that which was unacceptable to her, but it seemed now that she had overestimated her own powers of self-control and a shudder racked through her helpless body as her tormentor continued his slow scrutiny of her.

'A prize delectable enough to tempt any man.' The words were drawled in a mocking tone, but she noticed the glitter darkening his eyes as they roamed her body for a second time, and she tensed automatically, sensing something outside her own experience.

The dark head bent towards her, his torso arching

over her, her arms ached from being imprisoned. She longed to twist despairingly away but sensed that he would enjoy subduing her if she did, and so she stared as steadily as she could into his eyes until there was nothing but their vivid blueness. She felt his breath caress her skin and, in spite of her determination, shivered at the intimacy of it, waiting until the last moment to turn her mouth away from his, her body stiff and tense as she felt his soundless laughter.

'By all means, if that is the way you wish to play it,' he whispered softly into her ear, biting the tender flesh with sharp teeth, making her wince. 'I merely thought to make it more pleasurable for you.'

He moved and she closed her eyes, gritting her teeth, shocked by the sudden sensation of his torso touching her own, her breasts pressed flat against hard muscle, his weight constricting her breathing so that she had to pant. His mouth touched her shoulder and moved slowly along it, her tension increasing with every breath she took. She hated him for drawing out her torment, willing him to get the deed over and done with. This was a greater torture than if he had simply taken her and gone, and she sensed that he meant to punish her for her earlier challenging words.

His mouth burned her throat, his teeth sharp against the delicate skin. She wanted to move beneath him, to writhe away from the too-close contact with his body. Her skin felt hot where his mouth had touched it, and she was conscious of a strange dizziness, which she put down to the pain in her arms. His mouth moved tormentingly over her skin, and against her closed eyelids danced mental impressions of his dark head against her body. He moved, easing his weight off her slightly, and she drew in a much-needed breath, expelling it on a sharp, high cry of shock as she felt his mouth against her breast.

This time it was impossible to stop her body's bitter writhing to break free, but her hands were firmly pinioned and his mouth retained possession of the deep rose centre of her breast firmly sucking on it until she felt a totally unfamiliar sensation flower into life inside her. That her tormentor knew of it too was shamingly obvious when he slowly released her wrists, lifting his head from her breasts and then cupping them both in his hands. She found she was trembling as though held in the grip of a fierce fever, her body shaking with an ague, which she told herself came purely from the pain of the blood returning to her aching arms. Too weak as yet to thrust her tormentor off, she willed them to recover from their imprisonment, closing her eyes the better to martial her concentration.

Her breasts ached and throbbed with a pain that was wholly unfamiliar and she jerked protestingly against the tormentingly intimate caresses being inflicted on them. When her arms finally stopped tingling she lifted her hands to his shoulders, trying to push him away from her, but he merely laughed, his mouth once again caressing her breasts, moving slowly from one to the other until in the fireglow cast over the bed she could see that her nipples had grown a rosily dark red and that, unlike her mind, they seemed to have no objection to her attacker's continued ravishment of them, seeming rather to enjoy the moist attention of his lips and tongue.

Her fingers curled into his shoulders, one part of her mind registering with surprise how warm and pleasant his skin felt beneath them. How tempting it was to allow her hands to drift over the mystery of hard bones clothed in satin skin, and she reined in her thoughts swiftly, drawing her nails sharply over his skin, glorying in inflicting on him some measure of pain in payment for his humiliation of her.

Retaliation was swift and shocking. His teeth caught against the delicate flesh of her nipple making her cry out and shudder in torment. She seemed to be falling into some black abyss when instinct, and instinct alone, made her cling for safety to the warmth of his body, locking her arms round his neck, her body shivering in waves of shocked pain. Her fingers encountered something warm and sticky. She opened her eyes and saw the rowelling scratch marks against the darkness of his skin. Two of them oozed blood from her nails and her body tensed in shock that she had inflicted them.

Against her will her eyes were drawn to his. They glittered feverishly, bright with rage. He was breathing harshly, his voice thick and low as he demanded savagely, 'Lick them, it will staunch the bleeding. The only blood I would have on my sheets this night, will be yours, madam,' he added ruthlessly. 'Unless, which I doubt, someone else has already had your maidenhead. You are fortunate my brother is always so befuddled with drink, and will not know the difference. Lick them, I say,' he demanded again, grasping her neck with one hand, sliding his fingers into her hair until her scalp ached, forcing her against his skin. It was impossible to resist, to defy his will. She could sense that he intended to make her bow to it, and she would be the one to suffer if she did not. Her tongue brushed against the first scratch, recoiling from the salty-iron taste of his blood. She could feel the differing textures of his skin where it was smooth and where it was torn. He moved against her, pressing his skin against her mouth. Her tongue touched it tentatively again; she felt his mouth against her throat, his hand on her breast and a shuddering weakness possessed her. It seemed an age before she had cleansed his wound to his satisfaction, the movements of his heavy body against her own intensely disturbing.

When at last he released her, his eyes were dark, almost black, and they glittered hotly over her skin. 'It seems you are not the cold creature I had assumed,' he told her throatily. 'Perhaps after all there will be pleasure in what goes forward — for both of us!'

'No!' She cried out her denial, hating him for even daring to suggest that she might find his embrace anything other than loathsome, but he ignored it, laughing at her, pulling her into his arms and savaging her body with his mouth and hands until she could no longer resist him, or the dark force he seemed to conjure up at will inside her. When his mouth finally stopped tormenting her skin, she opened her eyes to discover that she was still clasping him, her hands inside his shirt, gripping the firm muscles of his upper arms. He was breathing as fast as she was herself, and as he looked down at her, an aching weakness took possession of her lower body. Simply by looking at her he was turning her bones to water, making her yearn for . . . Helplessly, her glance slid over his body, noting its arousal and tension. His head bent towards her and this time she did not avoid it. His mouth touched hers, brushing it lightly and then fiercely until she was clinging helplessly to him, gripped by a need that seemed to drive out all rational thought.

When he moved away from her to strip off his clothes, she made no attempt to get up and escape. Wordlessly, she watched him, drinking in the masculine perfection of him in the light from the fire. He came to her, bending over her to remove her garters and then roll down her silk stockings. His mouth brushed the instep of her foot and she quivered in mute response, shuddering as his mouth moved lazily upwards, over her skin. Torn between the need to escape the intimate intrusion of his touch and the even stronger need to prolong it, her body tensed and then arched as though in obedience to some unspoken commands. His tongue teased the silken flesh of her thigh and she cried out his name, denying with words what she invited with actions.

As he knelt over her she could see the ridged muscles of his back, the taut flatness of his buttocks. She struggled to sit up and ran her fingers slowly down his spine, tracing each indentation, wondering at the satin smoothness of his skin, so delicate in comparison to the hard bone beneath. He shuddered beneath her touch, muttered something against her skin and drew her down beneath him so that he could lie between her thighs.

She felt the heat and maleness of him hard against her and reacted instinctively to its intrusion. His mouth on hers silenced her protests, muffling her cries of denial, frustrating her attempts to cry out against what he was doing. With her mind she hated the maleness of him and all that it represented but her body . . . how it ached and longed for his penetration and possession!

Muzzily, Jenna sat up and switched on her bedside lamp. Her mouth was dry, her whole body gripped in fierce tension. She often had dreams, but never one like this, never one so real that she could actually feel the ache of deprivation deep in the pit of her stomach. She felt acutely sick, shocked by the intensely physical nature of her dream and its undeniable reality. How could her mind so clearly have conjured up the image of that long-dead man? And to dream in such a way of him!

Acute self-disgust gripped her. Rape in any of its many forms was totally abhorrent to her, and yet she had just dreamed . . . Or had her mind merely provided her with an acceptable cloak for a desire to which she did not want to admit? Had she dreamed of being forced to endure caresses that she could not admit that she actively desired? Her mind rejected the thought instinctively. Her dream was just a result of becoming so intensely involved with the house. She had been struck by the portrait right from the moment she first saw it. But to imbue a portrait with all the attributes of a living, breathing man! Her stomach twisted into aching knots, her body tense. Forget it, she told herself determinedly. She must just dismiss the whole thing as some sort of mental aberration.

But as dawn broke and sleep continued to evade her, she found her dream wasn't quite as easy to dismiss as she had hoped. It was the most erotic and flagrantly sexual experience she could ever remember having, and even now she could not shake the heavy lassitude from her body. When she closed her eyes she could still conjure up the swift surge of excitement her dream lover's touch had aroused within her; she could still see those sapphire eyes . . . still feel the warmth of him in her bed. Angry with herself, she pushed aside the bedclothes and swung her feet to the floor. Since she could not sleep she might as well use the time to work. She had enough to do.

Showering quickly and then dressing she went to her small study, but it was difficult to work. She

managed to push the dream out of her mind but she
was uneasily conscious of her promise to allow James
Allingham to look round the Hall. She closed her eyes
for a moment, leaning back in her chair, hoping to
ease the tension from her muscles, but instead James
Allingham's arrogant features immediately formed in
her mind's eye. Swiftly she tried to banish it, but the
image refused to disappear. Instead, subtly and,
frighteningly, it altered imperceptibly, until the face
she saw was that of the portrait: the hair still as darkly
thick as James Allingham's but longer and tied back in
a queue, the eyes the same, just as vividly blue, the
mouth curled in the sardonic expression of amusement she had seen so recently on James Allingham's
mouth.

'No!' Unaware of having spoken aloud Jenna got up
and paced restlessly, trying to get a grip on her shattered self-control.

Things like this simply did not happen to her. She
had never had a dream like the one she experienced
last night. She loathed James Allingham and all he
represented. She had dreamed about the man in the
portrait and not him. It was just a trick of her mind
that somehow made them one and the same person.

After an exhausting ten minutes' pacing, she felt
slightly calmer. As she sat down at her desk again, she
had managed to convince herself that she had banished the dream successfully and everything to do
with it to the remotest corner of her mind and that
never again would it be resurrected. She had no logical explanation for what she had experienced but it
was over now and best forgotten.

She opened her diary briskly and started to go
through it. If she was to go to Yorkshire she would
have some rearranging to do. On Sunday she was

taking Lucy back to school. Monday she had several appointments; the rest of the week was busy, but she could clear one day if she had to by juggling other engagements. It would be interesting to see the papers James Allingham claimed to have, but if he thought he was going to oust her from possession of the old Hall, then he was going to be sadly disappointed. She must just pray that luck was with her and that her business would run smoothly and profitably, she told herself firmly, banishing the small warning voice that reminded her that life had a way of handing out unexpected shocks. It still unnerved her to realise how finely balanced her financial affairs were. If for any reason she should suffer a financial setback and had to sell the Hall, James Allingham would be first in line to take it from her. But she would never allow that to happen, she thought passionately. Never! Never!

CHAPTER SIX

'LUCY, do I have to remind you again that you're going back to school this afternoon, and you still haven't packed?' Jenna said briskly over the breakfast table.

Lucy had been sullen and withdrawn ever since her return from her friends, and Jenna had barely been able to get a word out of her. When she asked how they had spent their time, Lucy had said bitterly, 'Why do you want to know? You don't really care, as long as I'm out of your way. My *father* wouldn't treat me like you do . . . ' and Jenna had had to bite her lip to stop herself from saying waspishly that she was fortunate in not knowing her father, if she did but realise it.

Lucy was reading the Sunday papers and didn't even bother to lift her head in response to Jenna's nagging reminder. Sprawled out on the sitting-room floor, she looked every inch the gawky teenager that she was, but in her thin, colt-like limbs there was a suggestion of the elegance to come. She really was unbearably like Rachel, Jenna thought achingly. Thank God, she could discern no trace of her father in her at all, although she did have James Allingham's jet-black hair. The thought crept unbidden into her mind, causing her to tense and frown.

'You didn't tell me you'd been dating James Allingham?' Lucy's angry accusation shocked her out of her thoughts.

'I haven't,' Jenna denied, her frown deepening.

'Well, that's not what it says here.' Lucy waved the

paper she was reading in front of her. 'It says the two of you were at a party together and that you both disappeared for quite a long time!'

'We met by chance at Margery's,' Jenna told her, angry at the way the gossip columnist had totally misinterpreted their relationship. 'That was all.'

Lucy looked sulky. 'I like him,' she complained to Jenna. 'I bet if he was my father life would be a lot more fun than it is with you.'

'Well, he isn't,' Jenna snapped sharply, unaware of the sudden speculation in Lucy's eyes as she poured herself a second cup of coffee.

'Do go and start your packing, Lucy, I'll come and help you when I've finished my coffee.'

Surprisingly, this time Lucy obeyed her without argument. Once she had closed the door behind her, Jenna found herself unable to resist picking up the paper the girl had been reading and scanning it. The insinuation that she and James Allingham were lovers was very thinly concealed and she threw the paper down in disgust. The rubbish that these rags printed! And all on the very thinnest information. No doubt she had Margery and her gossip to thank for that piece! Well, it wouldn't be the first time her name had been linked with some man's, nor would it be the last, but it goaded her that in this instance the man in question should be James Allingham, until she realised that he was as unlikely to be pleased as she was herself. As sexy as a Barbie doll was how he had scathingly described her . . . She smiled a little grimly to herself. Let the gossip press print what it wanted. It didn't really affect her.

Finishing her coffee she got up and went after Lucy. She desperately wanted to get closer to her, but every time she tried, Lucy put up invincible barricades. Had she really actually thought that James Allingham might be her father? Jenna chewed worriedly on her bottom lip. Was Lucy so desperate to know her father that she was ready to imagine every man she came in contact with might be he?

When Jenna knocked and then walked into Lucy's room the younger girl hurriedly put down the address book she had been writing in. Her half-packed cases were still open on the bedroom floor, the clothes that Maureen, their daily, had had cleaned and laundered still in neat piles on the chair.

'Come on, I'll give you a hand,' Jenna said briskly, removing the untidy piles of clothes Lucy had heaped in the cases and setting about restoring some sense of order. Earlier in the week she had prepared a list for Lucy, and now she asked her to find it, quickly ticking off everything as it was packed.

'I hate school and I don't want to go back,' Lucy announced mutinously when Jenna had finished.

Although her heart ached with sympathy for her, Jenna felt she had to be firm.

'I didn't like it myself, darling,' she admitted, 'but a good education is so important — as you'll discover once you leave school, especially these days.'

'Important? Why?' Lucy demanded bitterly. 'So that I can be a career woman like you? That isn't what I want from life. I want to get married, have a family . . .'

Trying not to let herself be hurt by Lucy's obvious contempt for her own achievements, Jenna said patiently, 'Of course you do, Lucy, but life isn't a fairy story; there may come a time when for whatever reason you need to earn your own living. Marriage, for one thing, isn't always for ever, Lucy.'

'But at least I intend to get married,' Lucy returned acidly. 'I won't let my children grow up not knowing who their father is. Wouldn't he marry you? Didn't he love you enough?'

Jenna knew that Lucy was deliberately trying to hurt her, and she fought hard not to give in to the temptation to tell her the truth — or at least some of it. In her own mind Lucy had made Jenna the villain of the piece, imbuing her unknown father with all the virtues he had in reality never possessed.

'Will you be seeing James again?'

Lucy asked the question as she settled herself next to Jenna in the car.

Hiding her shock at the question Jenna tried to appear calm. 'I shouldn't think so. That item in the paper was just gossip-column stuff, Lucy — I've already told you, we only met at the party by the merest chance.'

'I wanted to go and see him when we heard about the accident,' Lucy blurted out. 'I like him.'

'Well, I don't,' Jenna snapped. 'Now, will you please stop talking about the man.'

Lucy lapsed into a sulky silence, and the miles sped past. They stopped for lunch at a small hotel that Jenna had patronised before. The head waiter remembered her, and they were shown to a small private table.

The conversation between them was stilted, Lucy making only monosyllabic responses to Jenna's questions.

'I'll ring you on Wednesday to see how you're getting on, and if you've forgotten anything,' Jenna suggested when they headed back to the car after lunch. She quickly checked herself to amend, 'No, not Wednesday, I forgot. That's the day I think I'll be going to Yorkshire with James Allingham ... It will have to be —— '

'You're going to Yorkshire with James? You said you didn't like him,' Lucy accused.

'I don't. This is a business matter. He has some documents relating to the old Hall. He wants to look over the house again and I've agreed. In return he's going to let me see certain papers and diaries relating to the original decoration of the house.'

'Business!' Lucy said bitterly, curling her upper lip, but there was a speculative look in her eye that warned Jenna that Lucy did not entirely believe her explanation. Teenage girls were so prone to romantic daydreams — she had been herself in the days before Rachel's death.

'Janet's mother got married again at Christmas,' Lucy supplied thoughtfully after a small silence. 'Janet really likes her step-father, she says he's great. He's going to buy her a car for her seventeenth birthday and he's taking them all to America for their holidays this year ... '

Jenna's mouth thinned slightly. Was Lucy seriously suggesting that she wanted a step-father? A feeling of guilt attacked her. Was it so strange that she should? After all, Bill and Nancy had both warned her that Lucy needed a man in her life to whom she could relate. It seemed the whole world was determined to get her married off, Jenna reflected grimly, as the miles passed, if not for financial reasons then for emotional ones. Was she being selfish in depriving Lucy of a father-figure? But who was there in her life who could fulfil that role? Most of the men she knew were business acquaintances, mainly ambitious, artistic types, far too vain to want to play father to a teenage girl.

They arrived at the school in the middle of the afternoon. The car park was already quite busy with parents' cars.

As an older girl Lucy shared a very pretty room with a classmate. The school, although strict, did not believe in an austere regime; the food was good and healthy, the girls were encouraged to develop their own individuality, and there were many opportunities to pursue art and sport leisure interests. The school also had an excellent reputation and the headmistress was a woman who was genuinely caring about the girls under her authority, but still Lucy was not happy.

They said goodbye awkwardly, Lucy turning away as Jenna bent to kiss her. This aversion to being touched by her was something painfully new and hurtful, but Jenna refused to let Lucy see her chagrin.

She was just heading back to her car when the Headmistress's secretary caught up with her.

'Ms Stevens, Mrs Goodman would like to have a word with you if you can spare the time.'

'Of course.'

Norma Goodman was a tall, elegant woman in her mid-fifties. Her grey hair was fashionably styled, her make-up and clothes immaculate. Nothing about her was remotely headmistressy, and she greeted Jenna warmly, offering a glass of sherry.

'I'd better not, I'm driving back, and I have the lowest alcohol tolerance of anyone I know,' Jenna admitted wryly.

They exchanged pleasantries for several minutes, Norma Goodman expressing her admiration of a colour scheme Jenna had recently organised for a mutual acquaintance.

Then, with the barest hesitation in her manner, she

walked over to the window that looked out on to the front of the school. After pausing for a few seconds, she turned to face Jenna, and what Jenna saw in her face made her heart sink.

'It's Lucy, isn't it?' she asked tensely.

'Yes ... I'm afraid so. She's an extremely intelligent girl you know, one of the brightest we have — definitely Oxbridge material. But she can't settle here, and because of that she isn't able to give her best attention to her work. In our pre-enlightenment days she would have been described as a bad influence on the rest of the class, but now we know that these pupils, who seem determined to disrupt their classes and flout authority continuously, are normally suffering from some deep-seated emotional problem. In Lucy's case, and from the talks I've had with her, there can be no doubt that she resents being a boarder ... '

'And she resents me,' Jenna supplied tiredly. 'I know. Just lately we don't seem to be able to get on at all. She seems to be obsessed with the fact that she doesn't know the identity of her father.'

'Surely not entirely unusual in a girl of her age,' Norma Goodman suggested gently. 'I think it's a natural human desire to know one's antecedents. Lucy is undeniably one of those girls who responds best to masculine authority. She isn't alone in that, of course.' She looked gravely at Jenna and added, 'I wonder if you realise fully just what that could mean. In a very short space of time she will be eighteen and adult, at least according to the laws of this country — that means free of all parental control — free to vote, and also free to marry. Far too often I've seen what happens to a girl of eighteen who marries for a parental substitute — as I've just said Lucy is an extremely intelligent girl. Of course, like most girls of her age a career is the last thing on her mind. It's almost impossible for them to visualise being forty, and alone with a couple of children to bring up, but regrettably that is what happens to a good many women.

'Here at Chalmhurst we don't teach our girls to despise marriage and motherhood, but neither do we advocate it as an escape from reality and responsibility. We like to think we teach our pupils to be self-sufficient, whether as a wife and mother or as a single woman. We try to make them understand that leaning on emotional crutches and other people is false security and that the only real security in life comes from being self-reliant.

'In Lucy's case, I suspect she is deliberately shutting her ears to what we have to say. I know all teenage girls dream of marriage and motherhood, but with Lucy I'm afraid it's more than that. Her lack of a father seems to have given rise to an almost obsessive desire to form her own family unit. She'll leave here . . . and marry within twelve months, almost certainly to a man old enough to be her father. Ordinarily, I wouldn't dream of imposing my personal views on the life of my pupils — for some girls such a marriage could work, but not for Lucy. I suspect by the time she's in her mid-twenties, she'd feel trapped; her independence and intelligence would reassert themselves, but by then it would be too late. She'd be trapped in a little-girl relationship with an immature father-figure — probably with a couple of children dependent on her — and my view is that because of her own background she will stick by the marriage for the sake of those children.'

The picture she was painting was not a pleasant one, but it was all too possible.

'Is it really not possible to tell Lucy the identity of her father?' Norma Goodman pressed gently. 'It would give her someone to relate to if nothing else.'

Numbly, Jenna shook her head, and then taking a deep breath quickly explained the truth.

For a moment the headmistress was silent. 'No . . . I quite see that that is impossible,' she said at last. Then added, 'My dear, I am so sorry . . . I had no idea.'

'Bill and Nancy . . . the couple who took Lucy and me in when Rachel died, both want me to tell Lucy the truth — I wish now that I had done so years ago when she was young enough to accept it, but she's so resentful and bitter towards me now that I feel if I did tell her it would alienate her completely.'

'Yes. I can quite see your point.' Norma Goodman paused and then said delicately, 'I suppose there's no chance of you yourself getting married . . ?'

'To provide Lucy with a substitute father? You aren't the first person to suggest it,' Jenna admitted wryly, 'but . . . ' She shrugged, unable to bring herself to explain to the older woman her own aversion to the male sex.

'Well, we'll keep Lucy here for another term and see what develops,' Norma Goodman suggested, 'but if she still can't settle down, I'm going to have to suggest that she leaves. Not as a form of punishment,' she hastened to add, 'nothing like that, but simply because I don't believe in keeping a pupil at a school where she is plainly so unhappy.'

Lucy was on Jenna's mind during the long drive back to London. Norma Goodman had done no more than voice her own fears for Lucy's future, but what was the answer? Once she was based in Yorkshire,

Lucy could attend a day school there: since Jenna would be working from home she would be on hand much more to supervise Lucy and to spend time with her, but Lucy herself had said that she did not want to move to Yorkshire.

Jenna felt that until she could come up with some rational reason for keeping the identity of Lucy's father from her, Lucy would not respond to her. Sometimes she felt as though the girl hated her and it hurt Jenna bitterly when she thought of her own relationship with Rachel. It was almost as though she had let her sister down, as though Lucy would have been happier had she been adopted at birth and brought up in the security of the family environment she craved. It was a problem to which there seemed to be no realistic solution.

Despite her late night on the Sunday, Jenna was at her desk by eight on Monday morning. When Maggie arrived, she found that Jenna had already been through the post and was frowning over two letters.

'Problems?' Maggie enquired with concern, noting her frown.

'A complaint from Lady Farnham — she isn't happy with the silk wall hangings in her drawing-room. Apparently they've started to fade rather badly. Richard was in charge of that contract, wasn't he? I'll have to talk to him about it.'

'And?' Maggie prompted, glancing at the other letter Jenna was reading.

'Oh, that one's good — confirmation from Bierley's that they'll be able to supply the Holmeses' carpet on time.

'Maggie, I'd love a cup of coffee, and if Richard's arrived, I'd like to see him.'

'You wanted me?' Richard grinned cheerfully at her as he walked into her office.

'Umm . . . ' Jenna motioned to him to sit down and then showed him the letter.

'Damn,' he swore quietly. 'What do you suggest we do?'

'The silk shouldn't have faded,' Jenna told him. 'Dewharts who supply it use the very best quality fabrics and dyes and we've never had any trouble with them before. I'll pass on the complaint to them, I think, and see what they have to say.'

'Ah!' Richard sat back in his chair and grimaced boyishly. 'I'm afraid for that contract we didn't use Dewharts.'

Jenna frowned. 'But we always use them. You know how tricky silk wall hangings can be, especially red, and Lady Farnham did specify red for her dining-room as I remember it.'

'Yes, well, it was about the time when you were talking about making economies. I found this firm who could supply the silk at almost half the cost of Dewharts, and so I took a chance and bought from them.'

Jenna felt her heart sink. She made it a rule never to use products that she could not completely rely on and she thought that Richard had understood this.

She looked at him blankly for a few seconds, struggling to contain her rising temper. Far from looking apologetic he was watching her with a bland self-confidence that suddenly she found immensely irritating.

'You did specify economies,' he reminded her quietly.

'And this firm you bought from . . . '

'Well . . . ' Now he did look apologetically sheepish.

'I'm afraid they've gone bust . . . It seemed they were selling too cheaply and . . . '

'And we have no chance of recouping anything from them.' Jenna finished for him with a calm she was far from feeling. 'You do realise what this means, don't you, Richard? We shall have to redo the walls completely — at our own expense and using the right fabric.'

He shrugged. 'Surely you're covered for these things under your insurance?'

In a voice that splintered with icy rage Jenna told him bitingly, 'No insurance policy offers cover for errors of judgement, Richard — instead of saving us money, what you've actually done is cost us money.'

'I am sorry, but I acted in the best of faith.' He stood up and glanced at his watch. 'Look, Jenna, I must run, I've got an appointment with Fergie Longton at ten: he wants to discuss a contract for the show apartment in a new block he's building.'

'Fergie Longton?' A sharp frown creased her forehead, 'but he's notorious for cutting corners and costs. We don't want his sort of image, Richard. Please don't accept a contract from him. In fact,' she looked at him squarely, 'I've decided that from now on I shall sign all contracts myself.'

Anger flashed in the pale blue eyes, but he had himself under control quickly. 'If that's what you want,' he told her, 'after all, you're the boss.'

There had been a faintly jeering note in the way he said the last few words that jarred on Jenna, but before she had time to dwell on it Maggie was ringing through to tell her that James Allingham had called and arranged to go to Yorkshire on Wednesday.

There was more than a hint of speculation in Maggie's voice as she relayed this information and acting on a sudden impulse Jenna searched her diary for the number of the York architects. Quickly dialling it herself, she drummed impatient fingers on her desk. She would soon scotch any ideas that there was a romance brewing between James and herself.

She got through quite quickly and asked to speak to the partner she had been recommended to use. When she explained to him that she was travelling to Yorkshire on Wednesday and that she would appreciate his advice on certain aspects of her proposed alterations to the Hall, he quickly agreed to meet her there.

She wasn't sure yet what architectural changes she wished to make; so long as the property was structurally sound she would be content to leave the rooms as they were. The warren of passages and tiny rooms that formed the kitchens would need attention of course, and there would be the perennial problem of central heating. More damage had been done to many ancient buildings by the installation of central heating than anything else, but she knew an excellent firm who could be relied upon to devise a system that would provide heat without being either obtrusive or damaging.

She made several phone calls, and by lunchtime she was ready to leave the office to go and visit several of the craftsmen she had rung that morning. In particular she wanted to call on a young couple who specialised in traditional wood gilding.

The drawing-room and ballroom at the old Hall both had ornate marble fireplaces, which originally would have had specially designed decorated mirrors above them, and Jenna wanted the couple to design and produce authentic-looking period mirrors for those rooms.

They lived and worked in a small mews house in

Chelsea. Vanessa Hargreaves opened the door to Jenna, embracing her warmly. A tiny, vivacious brunette with a cloud of pre-Raphaelite hair, her gamine features were ruefully expressive as she glanced from Jenna's immaculate tailored suit to her own faded blouse and stained jeans.

'Jenna, you always make me feel like a typical scruffy arty type,' she complained. 'Come on up to the studio. Alan's out at the moment but he shouldn't be long. I'll make us a cup of coffee while we wait for him.'

The studio was at the top of the house, a light airy room with an easel in one window and the traditional gilder's tools on a bench in another.

Briefly, Jenna explained what she was looking for while they waited for Alan to return.

'Sounds exciting — quite a challenge. It's a pity you don't have any sketches of the original room. Of course, there are plenty of examples of Adam's work we can use for inspiration but if you want total authenticity . . .'

'Well, there might be.' Jenna explained about James Allingham.

'Allingham?' Vanessa rubbed her nose thoughtfully, and then grinned. 'Now, that name has a familiar ring to it,' she teased Jenna. 'I wonder why?'

Fortunately Alan came in before Vanessa could question her further, and once again Jenna explained what she was looking for.

'The best thing we can do is to get up there and take a look around,' Alan commented. 'Take some measurements, see exactly what's involved. Then we could produce some outline ideas, see how they take your fancy. Where's the diary, Van?' He found it underneath a pile of papers on the floor, and commented wryly, 'Great filing system we have here.'

'At least it's all in one place,' Vanessa countered defensively.

'Umm. The first day we could spare to go up there is the eighteenth of next month,' Alan told Jenna. 'How would that suit you?'

She checked her own diary and nodded her head. 'By then I should have more idea of exactly what if any reconstruction work is going to be needed, so that should be fine.'

There were other people she had to see in connection with work she already had in hand as well as the renovation of the Hall and, all too soon, it was Wednesday morning.

Jenna woke up earlier than usual and lay in bed, trying to quell the unusual rush of butterflies in her stomach. Was she afraid of meeting James Allingham? Ridiculous, why should she be? She disliked and despised the man.

Knowing how filthy and uncared-for the old Hall was, she dressed casually in jeans and a loose sweat-shirt top over a fine cotton blouse, pulling soft boots on to her feet. She pulled her hair off her face with a silk scarf. There, she thought, studying her reflection in her bedroom mirror. There would be no question of James Allingham thinking that she had dressed to catch his attention. As she hurried into her kitchen she was unaware that the jeans emphasised the length and slenderness of her legs, the huge sweatshirt giving her an air of fragile femininity. She was also unaware that the casual style of her hair made her look closer to twenty than thirty.

James had made arrangements via Maggie to pick her up and even though she still resented his high-

handed assumption of control, she had decided not to
object too forcefully to it. Indifference was her best
weapon where a man like James Allingham was concerned, and as she gathered together notebooks, pens,
a measuring tape and a camera it never occurred to
her to wonder why she should feel in need of such
protection.

He arrived promptly on the dot of eight-thirty, his
eyebrows lifting slightly in surprise as he registered
her casual appearance, but Jenna refused to acknowledge it.

'Ready?'

'Yes,' she confirmed crisply.

'Mmm . . . pity, I was hoping I might be offered a
cup of coffee before we set off. I missed mine this
morning.'

'What a shame,' Jenna smiled acidly at him. 'Next
time, choose a bedmate who can cook.'

'Sharp, but wrong,' he told her crisply. 'I've got my
step-sister living with me at the moment, and she was
due to go into hospital this morning. I wanted to take
her myself. She's still suffering from the emotional
shock of losing her parents, and she tends to be unhappy in the presence of strangers.'

Jenna knew she was flushing in a mixture of guilt
and chagrin. It wasn't entirely her fault she had leapt
to the wrong conclusion, she told herself as she locked
the front door behind her and joined him by the lift.
Knowing his lifestyle it had been a perfectly natural
assumption to make. But she would have been wiser
not to have voiced it, an inner voice told her. In her
desire to put him down, she had only succeeded in
making herself look crassly thoughtless.

His car was parked outside the apartments, and
Jenna was surprised when he walked round to the

passenger door and opened it for her, handing her into the car before returning to the driver's side. She was unused to such old-fashioned male courtesies from anyone other than Bill and had even begun to believe they had ceased to exist.

The city centre traffic was heavy and Jenna leaned back in her seat closing her eyes, leaving James to concentrate on driving. He was a good driver, she recognised unwillingly, neither impatient nor a dawdler.

'Tired?'

His question startled her.

'A little,' she admitted. 'It's been a hectic week.' Only yesterday afternoon she had had a phone call from Gordon Burns complaining that the business account overdraft was too high. There were monies outstanding to her company and Jenna had promised herself once she returned from Yorkshire she would get down to collecting them. Even so, the telephone call had disturbed her. It seemed suddenly as though fate had turned completely against her, and that everything in her life was going wrong. She had the Hall though, she reminded herself comfortingly, closing her eyes as a signal to James Allingham that she had no desire to talk.

A little to her surprise he respected it. She was aware of them turning on to the motorway and then nothing until she felt him shaking her awake. Stunned, she opened her eyes, her mind still muzzy with sleep. 'Are we there already?'

'No. I thought it was time I had a break.' His hand was still on her shoulder, his nails clean and neatly cut, his fingers lean and strong. A strange quiver of sensation coiled through her stomach and unnervingly she was reminded of other hands on her body . . . of her dream . . . Swiftly shutting the memory away, she struggled to sit upright.

'You look more like Lucy's sister than her mother in that get up,' James told her softly. 'Did you know you sleep with your mouth open?'

'Doesn't everyone?' Jenna returned shortly. His voice was seductively teasing, deepening the enclosed intimacy of the car. She could smell the faint tang of his cologne, elegant and masculine. Like her he was wearing jeans, old and faded, the soft fabric clinging to the muscles of his thighs. The leather blouson jacket he had been wearing was lying on the back seat. He had taken it off before getting in the car and the fine wool checked shirt he had on underneath it was open at the throat.

A curious constriction seemed to grip her own throat muscles as he leaned over her. A panicky desire to push him away from her tensed her muscles as she fought against it. To react to his proximity in such an adolescent way would be totally humiliating. She knew quite well that he was deliberately taunting her with his sexuality, knowing that she was unnerved by it, but she also knew there was no real reason for her fear; he was not going to attack her as Charles had attacked Rachel.

That kiss he had forced upon her in Margery's study had been an act of retaliation, not one of undeserved aggression, but even so his closeness ignited all her repressed feelings of anger for and fear of his sex.

'You have the most lovely hair.' He raised his hand to touch her head and instantly Jenna jerked away, fear suddenly far stronger than logic, panic flaring briefly in her eyes as she froze.

His hand dropped, his eyes narrowing disbelievingly. 'What are you so afraid of?'

Her mouth had gone dry, her heart thudding erratically. It was worse than all her most terrifying nightmares: she was always so careful about hiding her
inner fears, and yet here she was betraying them to
the one man she would most hate to recognise them.

'Nothing.' Even to her own ears her voice sounded
husky and unfamiliar.

'Liar.' His hand lifted to her face and then dropped
away again as she was unable to stop herself from
cringing. His mouth compressed and Jenna could see
the anger in his eyes. She felt sick with inner disgust.

'Come on,' he said abruptly, 'let's go and get that
coffee. It seems that we both need it.'

He had stopped off the motorway at a small country
hotel. They had the comfortable coffee lounge completely to themselves. A smiling waitress brought
them a pot of coffee, and even though Jenna had not
particularly wanted a drink its aromatic fragrance
tempted her tastebuds.

'Black for me,' James told her, as she picked up the
pot.

Lounging opposite her in a deep armchair he was
completely at ease. Conversely, she was perched tensely on the edge of hers. Biting her lip Jenna tried to
relax. She hadn't wanted to share the journey north
with him and now it seemed as though she had had
good reason not to.

'Lucy safely back at school?' he asked, picking up
his coffee.

In anyone else the question would merely have
been a civil attempt to make conversation, but remembering his criticisms of her as a mother Jenna flushed
angrily.

'Yes, she is,' she told him curtly. She kept her attention on her coffee-cup until good manners prompted

her to say hesitantly, 'It must have been a dreadful shock to you to lose your father and step-mother . . . I hope your step-sister is soon better.'

He shrugged before replacing his coffee-cup. 'I was always closer to my mother than my father, but yes, it's always painful to come to terms with the loss of a parent. Sarah — my step-sister — is finding it particularly hard. She was in the car with them when it happened and was trapped there for several hours before they could free her. Since then she hasn't moved — the doctors tell me that physically there's nothing wrong with her, that the paralysis is psychosomatic, probably a result of shock and fear. She had to lie completely still while they cut her free, in case she injured herself. At the moment I feel she's too cut off from other people to make a speedy recovery, but she refuses to see anyone other than myself and her nurse. She's convinced the scratches she received on her face will make her hideous for life. At the moment the scars do look bad, but the doctors assure me that they will fade and eventually disappear completely. She's always been rather shy and withdrawn.

'As soon as she's free of hospital tests I intend to buy a house away from London —— ' He frowned suddenly, checking himself. 'However, I'm sure you don't really want to hear any of this.'

His sardonic comment increased her feeling of guilt. It was plain from what he said that he cared deeply about his step-sister, and that he was prepared to make changes in his own life, sacrifices, in fact, for her benefit. Was she being selfish in insisting on moving to the old Hall?

'How is Lucy?'

His question startled her, and she looked directly at him for the first time that day. The startling blue of his eyes shocked her, bringing back memories she had thought successfully submerged. Her skin grew hot as she fought them down again. James might bear some resemblance to the ancestor she had dreamed about, but they were not one and the same person.

'Not too happy, I'm afraid,' she admitted unwillingly. 'Her headmistress is concerned about her too. She's worried that Lucy might ruin her life by rushing into marriage — looking for a father-figure.'

'So . . . why not provide her with one yourself? Either tell her about her real father, or marry and provide her with a substitute one.'

'It isn't as easy as that.'

'Isn't it? Or are you just telling yourself that to ease your own conscience.'

'Of course I'm not.' He had goaded her into real anger now. 'Would you marry just to provide your step-sister with a substitute mother?'

'I might . . . if I thought I had sufficient grounds for doing so.'

His answer stunned her and he shrugged briefly, his eyes thoughtful as he registered her surprise.

'I don't entirely support the modern view that marriage should be a relationship founded on true love — for one thing love is an extremely difficult emotion to define. Most of us make the mistake of confusing it with sexual desire — a pretty potent force to resist, I admit, but no basis for a lifelong relationship. Marriage demands mutual respect and a lot of hard work, a willingness to compromise on both sides and an understanding of what makes the other person tick. It demands acceptance of them too . . . compassion and a lack of desire to completely transform their character.

'It's my view that no marriage is far, far better than a

bad marriage, and good ones are very hard to find. We're all taught these days to expect perfection in a relationship and it doesn't exist, so the moment things don't work out, we get disappointed and angry and fall out of love. If people took a more realistic view of marriage and what they can expect of it, it would last a lot longer.'

'And yet believing all that, you can still advocate that I marry purely to provide Lucy with a substitute father?'

He shrugged again. 'It's all a matter of priorities —a question of what you put first: Lucy's happiness or . . . '

'My own?' Jenna enquired sweetly.

Instead of replying James glanced at his watch. 'Time we were on our way,' he told her calmly.

They made good time, but even so Jenna was stiff and tired when he eventually stopped the car outside the Hall just before midday.

Jenna had arranged for the architect to meet her at two, and when James suggested lunch, she said coolly that she would only require a snack and, moreover, that she had an appointment.

'Suits me fine,' was James's laconic response. 'I'll have a wander round and meet you outside at one. We can get a quick snack in the hotel in the village.'

Jenna forbore to comment. She had intended to tell him that she was lunching with Bill and Nancy, but he hadn't given her time to make the excuse.

They went inside the house together, James wandering off into the older wing, leaving Jenna alone to make a careful tour of the Georgian rooms.

Without the initial excitement of her purchase to buoy her up she could see that she was going to have a far harder job on her hands than she had at first visualised. In her imagination she clothed the rooms as she wanted to see them, but she could not deny that it would take a long time to get them like that. Using her camera to record details of the plasterwork that needed repairing and the motif on the mahogany doors, she made detailed notes. Tattered brocade curtains hung at the library windows, the once elegant room dingy and drab. She knew a firm that specialised in traditional fabric patterns; they were expensive, but very good. She itched to see James's sketches, but he had not mentioned them to her as yet and she was not going to ask.

Her tour of the downstairs completed, she retraced her steps into the hall. The staircase curved elegantly upwards, or at least it would be elegant once it was repaired. Sighing faintly, she stepped over a pile of rubbish on the floor and mounted the stairs. Immediately in front of her was the portrait. She tensed as she looked up at it, licking her lips, her muscles suddenly locking. To look into those mocking blue eyes was to remember in vivid detail the acutely sexual nature of her dream. The portrait at once fascinated and revolted her. She stepped backwards, stifling a shocked scream as she felt hands grasp her shoulders.

'It's okay, it's only me,' James said easily from behind her. 'Sorry if I startled you.' He released her immediately, moving away from her but as she turned to face him Jenna was struck by his likeness to the portrait. It shuddered through her flooding her mind with confused mental pictures.

'My scapegrace ancestor,' James commented wryly. 'I'm surprised Sir Alan kept the portrait hanging there.'

'People get so used to what's around them that they cease to notice it in the end,' Jenna said huskily. She felt curiously weak and faint, and told herself it was because she was hungry.

'It's getting on for one,' James informed her. 'If you've finished down here, how about going for lunch now?'

There was no reason for her to refuse. She knew the hotel in the village quite well, and although the owner was justifiably proud of his carvery lunch, Jenna found she was barely able to touch her plateful of food, despite her earlier conviction that she was hungry.

James on the other hand cleaned his plate.

He was a very complex man, she reflected, eyeing him briefly as she drank her coffee. Despite his assertion to her that he meant to gain possession of the Hall, he had not betrayed that intention today by so much as a word or gesture. What really went on inside that hard masculine skull, she wondered, watching him. He glanced up and smiled mockingly. 'Normally when a woman looks at a man like that she's wondering what he's like in bed,' he drawled tormentingly.

'Well, I'm not!' Anger made the colour leave her face, her eyes glittering furiously into his.

'Pity! I would have enjoyed showing you.'

His blatant masculine arrogance took her breath away. It stunned her to realise that he meant it too; that despite the fact that he didn't particularly like her, and he certainly knew how much she loathed him, he could still talk about making love to her and see it as a viable proposition. But, then, men did not have to be emotionally involved to enjoy sex . . . quite the contrary, she thought grimly, draining her coffee-cup and standing up.

'I'll walk back to the old Hall,' she told him coolly, picking up her large shoulder-bag.

For a moment she thought he meant to protest, but apart from a warning gleam in his eyes he seemed indifferent to her decision.

It didn't take her long, and the June day was warm enough to make the walk a pleasant one. She got to the end of the drive at the same time as a small estate car turned into it. The driver stopped and she walked over to him.

'Peter Clifford,' he introduced himself. 'You wouldn't by any chance be my prospective client?'

When Jenna agreed that she was, he offered her a lift up to the house.

'It's a real architectural hotch-potch,' he commented to Jenna when they got out of the car. 'What exactly do you have in mind for it?'

Briefly she told him.

'The restoration work might prove difficult, especially if you're after authentic reproduction, but let's go in and see what it's like inside.'

His comment depressed Jenna slightly. She had been hoping that he might be able to give her introductions to firms of the same standard as those she used in London. She had no doubt that they did exist, but finding them would take time; in the meantime she would have to use those she knew in London, which would mean extra expense.

They had just reached the Tudor part of the building when she heard James's car drive up. She heard him walking over the bare floorboards as he came in search of them, and she also saw the speculation in the architect's eyes when James finally appeared.

Almost immediately, instead of addressing his comments to Jenna he addressed them to James. His automatic assumption that James was the one he would be working for infuriated her, but she refused to allow her anger to appear.

'Of course, when it comes to the décor, no doubt you'll have your own ideas,' he commented, turning to Jenna at last, his expression slightly condescending. 'Women have their own views on these things,' he added to James.

'They do indeed, don't they, darling?' The endearment and the casual arm James placed round her shoulders stunned Jenna into complete silence. When the architect's back was turned she glared at him, and tried to pull away, but his arm simply tightened round her. While she tried to struggle, the architect kept talking to James. It was plain that he thought them a couple and Jenna gritted her teeth, thinking of the biting remarks she would be making to him when she told him the truth.

And James. For what possible reason could he be reinforcing the architect's error? Sheer devilment, she suspected, giving up trying to move away from him, and instead, simply turning her head away and refusing to acknowledge his presence in any way.

It took the better part of the afternoon to go through the house, at the end of which Jenna's temper had reached exploding point.

As she watched the architect drive away she turned to James and demanded bitterly, 'Just what the hell do you think you were doing? Giving him the idea that —— '

'That we were lovers?' His eyebrows rose and he shrugged. 'It was obvious that he thought it anyway, it would only have embarrassed him to discover the truth.'

'So you decided to embarrass me instead, is that it?'

Jenna seethed. 'As a mere woman my embarrassment doesn't matter?'

James blinked and said laconically, 'As the unmarried mother of a teenage child, I find it hard to understand why the thought of having a lover should embarrass you.'

Goaded beyond her endurance but unable to retaliate Jenna snapped her teeth shut, gritting them together.

'You have some sketches to show me,' she reminded him curtly.

'Yes, but I don't have them with me. Some of them are very fragile, and I didn't want to risk getting them damaged. I'll show them to you when we get back.'

Grimly, Jenna said nothing. She had no desire to go back to James's apartment with him, but it seemed she had little choice. She only hoped that his precious sketches, once she got to see them, would prove to be worth the trouble.

They stopped once on the way back for a brief snack and a cup of tea, but James seemed disinclined to make idle conversation for which she was grateful. It was gone ten when they reached the outskirts of London and in the dimness of the car Jenna studied him covertly. The resemblance to the portrait on the stairs was less obvious now; it was only when one looked at him full face that he could have passed for the double of his ancestor.

Heredity was a funny thing . . . One of the reasons she had been so reluctant to tell Lucy about her father was her fear that Lucy might grow up always looking for the Deveril strain in herself. If anything, however, Jenna felt that Lucy shared her own temperament rather than that of either of her parents, although her features were Rachel's. Once again her eyes were drawn to James's profile: he was an exceedingly physically attractive male, there was no doubt about that, but unlike most of her sex she found his masculine perfection repellent rather than attractive.

'Taking an inventory?'

He had turned to smile mockingly at her. Furiously determined to prove to him that her scrutiny of him had no personal basis, Jenna retorted tightly, 'No one could ever question that Deveril blood runs in your veins.'

Incredibly his face went white, his fingers tensing on the steering-wheel. 'Just what in hell do you mean by that?' he demanded harshly, stunning her with the intensity of his anger. She had thought him a man without an Achilles' heel and yet, incredibly, it seemed she was wrong. She had no idea why he should be so bitterly resentful of his Deveril blood, but it excited her to know that he was not as invulnerable as she had supposed.

She managed a light shrug, longing to probe into the reason for his furious response but knowing that this was not the time.

'The portrait on the stairs,' she told him simply. 'Surely you must have seen the resemblance?'

Amazingly, his anger was gone, leaving in its place a lazy amusement. 'Ah yes . . . the family black sheep. My revered ancestor . . . Yes, there is a similarity. Apparently it crops up in every so many generations,' he added carelessly, 'but I'm afraid I have to tell you that he was no Deveril.'

Jenna stared at him. 'But of course he was . . . you said yourself . . . '

'I know what I said, but what I didn't tell you was that it was rumoured at the time and later confirmed by his mother on her deathbed that he was not her husband's child, but her lover's. Hence the reason his supposed "father" was so eager to get rid of him. Hence also the reason why he had no compunction about taking his wife's family name, I suspect,' James added musingly. 'I have in my possession his grand-daughter's diary; the whole story is written down there. It wasn't exactly an uncommon occurrence, in those days!'

So James wasn't a Deveril! Jenna's head was whirl-ing. All of a sudden she remembered her vivid dream and her seducer's shocking revelation that he was not his father's son, merely his mother's. But she had be-lieved that to be just the imaginings of her dream . . . She abruptly brought herself back to the present. Why, she wondered, had James been so furious when she had commented on his Deveril blood? And why, when his connection with the family was so vague, was he so determined to possess the old Hall?

In view of his recent disclosures she felt that the latter question was one she could quite reasonably put to him.

He looked at her briefly before replying, his mouth grim. 'Let us just say that I do have my reasons — more valid and justifiable than yours, I suspect,' he added, his glance flicking dispassionately over her half-averted face.

In other words, he wasn't going to tell her, Jenna thought wryly. Well, it was scarcely any of her busi-ness, but she was still curious to know. You know what curiosity did to the cat, she reminded herself, and James Allingham did not strike her as a man who would deal lightly with anyone trying to pry into his personal life.

CHAPTER SEVEN

JAMES didn't speak again until he turned off the main
road and into a private entrance leading to an under-
ground car park. Sensing her tension he said easily, 'I
thought you might care to look over the sketches and
other documents while the layout of the Hall is still
fresh in your mind.'

It was true that she did want to see the papers —after
all, wasn't that the whole purpose in agreeing
to allow him to accompany her today? Stop being so
stupid, she told herself, as he stopped the car. All right,
so he had kissed her once, in anger, as a form of punishment and not an expression of desire. It was hardly
likely to happen again. Despite the taunts she had
thrown at him, she knew quite well that James was not a
man who would ever need to go short of feminine companionship — and certainly never to the extent that he
would need to force himself on any woman. She might
not like him herself, might even have to admit to a faint
trace of fear of him, but that didn't totally obliterate her
common sense, which told her quite plainly that James
was no Charles Deveril.

'Stiff?'

He got out of the car and opened her door for her,
leaning across her to release her seat-belt. The gesture
was no more than common politeness on his part, she
suspected, because he performed the small service easily and quickly, but she was all too conscious of the bulk
and maleness of him as he leaned across her, his body

154

blocking out both light and air. She could see the con-
formation of the muscles in his arms as he released the
seat-belt catch, and the beginnings of his beard along
his jaw.

As he moved away from her his arm brushed against
her breasts. Instantly she recoiled, her pupils dilating in
shocked recognition of the unexpected contact.

'Are you all right?' He was frowning as he put out a
hand to help her from the car. No doubt he wasn't used
to her sex withdrawing from his touch, Jenna thought
acidly, ignoring his hand and determinedly stepping
past him.

'I'm fine.' She gave him a brilliant, but totally false,
smile as he locked the car and led the way to a small
private lift.

The atmosphere inside it to Jenna was almost claus-
trophobic. She hated the enforced intimacy of having to
be so close to him, and it brought back all the old night-
time terrors she had suffered after Rachel's death.

Often in those early days she had dreamed of her sister . . . dreamed she heard her screams and cries for
help, but that in going to her aid was attacked herself,
smothering in a blanket of fear and revulsion as Charles
Deveril turned from Rachel to her. Over the years those
dreams had faded, but they had left their scars, and
now, enclosed in the small space with James, Jenna was
vividly reminded of them.

She could feel the tension building up inside her, and
for one crazy moment was tempted to throw herself at
the closed door and hammer it open. As she fought to
get control of herself the lift stopped and the doors
opened. She gulped in air, her body bathed in perspira-
tion.

'Are you okay?'

There was concern and puzzlement in James's eyes

as he touched her elbow. 'You almost look as though you're about to faint.'

'I'm fine,' she managed a tight smile, spoiling her impression of total control as she jerked nervously away from him. 'I just don't like lifts,' she lied.

His apartment surprised her. As she followed him inside the drawing-room and saw the elegant shape of the windows, she realised it was in one of the Regency terraces fronting on to the park. Beyond the window she could see a wrought-iron balcony, and, more surprising still, the drawing-room was furnished with the comfortable shabbiness that spoke of a home rather than the living quarters of a bachelor.

A richly hued nineteenth-century Persian carpet covered the floor and Jenna bent instinctively to touch the silky fibres. Bookcases flanked an ornate marble fireplace. She studied the room slowly, admiring the elegant, inlaid-marquetry Regency card table. The room was quite sparsely furnished, but all the pieces apart from the huge leather chesterfield were antiques.

When she eventually remembered the purpose of her visit she turned and looked at her host, and found that he was studying her with raised eyebrows.

'Does it pass the expert's tests?' he mocked lightly.

'It's very comfortable and homely.' She couldn't quite keep the surprise out of her voice, but if he recognised it he was not going to comment.

'The antiques and the carpet came from the house I inherited from my grandfather on St Justine — it's one of the Virgin Islands,' he added.

'Is that where you're developing the new holiday complex?'

His eyebrows lifted again, and Jenna defended herself quickly. 'I read about it in the papers.'

She was annoyed with herself for betraying that she knew anything about him. He was vain enough to think now that she was actually interested in him.

'Yes, it is. The development's coming along quite nicely. I'm due to go out there soon to check up on progress.' He frowned. 'It's going to be quite a problem, I can't take Sarah with me, and I'm not too happy about leaving her here alone. A nurse, no matter how skilled and well-trained, is no substitute for a family. It's at times like these that I regret our mutual lack of relatives.'

'Perhaps *you* should get married,' Jenna told him idly. 'That way you could leave her in the care of your wife.'

She had intended the comment as a mild form of mockery, but to her surprise, his expression became extremely thoughtful.

'The papers,' she reminded him hastily. She wanted to get away from him and the warm ambience of his flat that reminded her all too uncomfortably of the lack of male companionship in her own life.

'Yes. I'll get them for you, and you can browse through them while I make us some coffee. Can I offer you anything to eat?'

Jenna wasn't particularly hungry and she shook her head, following him over to a beautiful Sheraton lady's writing desk.

'This belonged to the wife of the man in your portrait,' he told her, opening it and removing a folder.

'These are photocopies of the originals, but I think you'll find them interesting. Do you have any plans for what you're going to do to the old Hall?'

This was ground on which she felt relatively safe, and Jenna explained to him that she wanted all her restoration work to be as authentic as possible. 'I want to be able to use the house as a display-case for our work.' She broke off, laughing rather self-consciously. 'I'm afraid I tend to get rather carried away when I'm talking about my work!' She made a small face. 'I must be boring you.'

'Not at all. It makes quite a change to get more than half a dozen reluctant words from you. The Hall means an awful lot to you, doesn't it?' he asked quietly.

When she would have denied it, he added, 'Listening to you then I could hear it in your voice, see it in your face. You look quite different when you're animated . . . softer . . . younger. It's very intriguing, a woman of hidden passions . . . '

Jenna tensed and looked away from him, picking up the folder. For a moment she had almost felt relaxed, but he had spoiled it all by that blatantly sexist remark.

'I'll go and make the coffee.'

She opened the folder and started to look through it, and was soon lost in its contents. There were photocopied extracts from the diary of the granddaughter of the man in her portrait, fine, delicate sketches she had made from her grandfather's memories of his English home. It seemed that he had talked to her about it a great deal in his last years and Jenna was thrilled and amazed by the accuracy of his memory. The drawings and sketches of the rooms were remarkably accurate when she thought that the artist had never seen them, and she read on, excited by references to particular pieces of furniture and colours.

The French drawing-room, as the diary called it, had been decorated in that shade between blue and green so popular during the Regency. The ceiling had been painted in what Jenna suspected from the description in the diary had been an allegorical theme in a *trompe l'oeil* effect. She had wondered if this might be the case from her knowledge of the period, but it was intensely exciting to see down on paper a description of the original painting. Judging from what she read, Jenna suspected that the ceiling had been decorated with the astrological signs of the family — a popular theme at the time — combined with the artist's impression of the Deveril crest. She was very familiar with this type of work and knew a brilliant young artist who was making a name for himself in restoration and reproduction work in the field.

As for the green silk hung on the wall panels and used to cover the chairs and Egyptian sofa, that would have to come from a firm who specialised in reproducing traditional patterns and dyes.

The original carpet would probably have been to a design specified by Robert Adam, almost certainly with a background of the same green as the silk, bordered in that subtle browny-pink he had been so fond of using, and decorated with shell and other motifs to match the ceiling in a soft cream. Lost in mentally viewing the room as it had once been and would be again she jumped when she heard James's voice.

He was holding a mug of coffee which he handed to her. 'Any good?' He looked at the papers spread out on the desk in front of her.

'Marvellous.' She was far too excited to dissemble. Her cheeks glowed with it, her eyes sparkling a deep and clear green. 'It's fascinating how she managed to reproduce the rooms so accurately without seeing them.' She hesitated for a second. 'Would it be possible for me to have copies of these papers?'

There was no reason on earth why he should help her. After all, hadn't he already made it clear that he resented her ownership of the Hall and that he intended to take it from her? The only reason she was being allowed to see these papers now was because of the trade-off they had agreed.

'I don't see why not.' His mouth curled in a teasing smile. 'At a price, of course.'

Instantly her excitement dimmed, washed out by the apprehension crawling along her spine. She stood up, moving jerkily, tensing as he reached out an arm to steady her. Instinctively she jerked back from him, her eyes dilating as fear swamped her. He was standing far too close to her — she could hardly breathe. She closed her eyes and tried to steady herself, and immediately a vision of the man in the portrait filled the darkness — not looking as he did in the portrait, but as he had in her dream: the lawn shirt open to the waist, the blue eyes dark with a mixture of anger and desire. Jenna shuddered deeply forcing her eyes open.

'My God, you *are* frightened of me, aren't you?' She heard James mutter disbelievingly. 'What . . ?' He reached out to touch her arm and a totally uncontrollable sense of oppression and terror blotted out reason completely. She heard herself scream and then she was falling into an endless black void, terrorised by some nightmare fear she could not subdue.

Consciousness returned slowly. She was aware of having fainted and now of lying on something firm and comfortable, of a sense of weakness, but most overpoweringly of all she was left with a vivid memory of those seconds before she had fainted: of seeing in her mind's eye the face and figure of the man she had dreamed of as a lover, suddenly transferred to the man who had been standing opposite. It had been a shatteringly unnerving sensation, but one she was over now. She struggled to sit up, opening her eyes, to discover James crouching down beside her, his forehead creased in a frown.

'What the hell's going on?' he demanded bitingly.

'You reacted to me then as though you feared I was about to rape you.'

The strong note of distaste in his voice warned her that she wasn't going to escape without explanation. She could hardly tell him the truth — Jenna felt her skin grow hot just at the mere thought of telling anyone about that intensely disturbing dream.

Thinking quickly she went instinctively into the attack. 'It would hardly be surprising if I did after the way you . . . kissed me the other night.'

His eyes locked cynically on hers. 'Possibly, if you were an adolescent virgin on the verge of womanhood I might just buy that, but you're not . . . You're an adult woman with a teenage daughter.'

'And because of that I can be mauled and abused as your sex pleases, is that it?' Jenna flung at him, bitterly furious.

'I kissed you because it was either that or hit you,' James told her bluntly. 'And you know it. It was a ploy your sex has been known to use when they want a man's attention,' he told her mockingly, watching her shocked reaction with eyes that comprehended the tiny movement of her throat as she registered her revulsion. 'All right, I acquit you of that!'

Jenna managed to regain control of herself sufficiently to say rustily, 'Well, thanks very much . . . '

Just that effort was enough to drain her of energy and she let her head fall back on to the cushions of the leather chesterfield, closing her eyes for a moment.

She heard James's soft laugh, and sensed that he had moved, but she was too exhausted to open her eyes until she felt his hand on her neck.

As his fingers slid into her hair, pinning her head, her eyes flew open.

'If it *was* my kiss that frightened you so much,

perhaps I'd better do something about it.'

He was going to kiss her and there was nothing she could do about it. Her body tensed as he bent his head, her eyes staring blankly into his, her mouth compressed in rigid rejection of his intent. His breath sighed lightly against her skin, sensitising the tiny delicate hairs and making her shiver. His mouth touched her eyes forcing her to blink and then close them. His body wasn't touching hers in any way at all, and yet she was acutely conscious of him. She wanted to raise her hands to push him away but she was frightened of the contact with his maleness.

His mouth touched hers, lightly, delicately, caressing the corners. His hand released its hold of her head and slid round to cup her jaw. Apprehension crawled along her spine as the soft pad of his thumb slowly caressed her bottom lip. Her mouth felt dry. She wanted to open it and touch her lips with her tongue. She fought the impulse shuddering with shock as she felt the warmth of James's mouth caressing her own. His teeth tugged gently on her bottom lip and then his tongue ran lightly over its swelling contours, softly probing for entrance.

Another deep shudder racked her and Jenna knew she could not endure any more, raising her palms to his chest she pushed hard, opening her mouth to say fiercely, 'No!'

The sound was silenced beneath the smothering heat of James's kiss. His tongue stroked and cajoled her own, the shock of the unexpected intimacy of what he was doing to her causing the strength to drain out of her arms as they dropped from his chest. Against her mouth, James made a softly sensual murmur of protest. His fingers grasped her wrist and then slid to entwine with hers, lifting her palm back to his body, and holding it there. The pressure of his mouth on hers was slowly increasing, deepening.

In stunned shock she felt him move her hand, so that it was resting against bare skin instead of his shirt front. His body felt hot, alien and intensely masculine. She wanted to draw away from him and yet the movement of his mouth against her own was inducing a mind-drugging languor that felt like falling into warm cotton wool. She wanted to protest, to resist, but she felt unable to drag her mouth away from his.

When she tried his teeth nipped sharply at her skin, bruising her mouth as he refused to let her go. Fear clawed at her stomach and suddenly she was trembling wildly, reality sliding into fantasy so that it was not James who held and kissed her but that other —— Fear and panic mingled sickeningly inside her, and then totally unexpectedly she was free. She blinked in dazed stupefaction as James drew away from her, conscious of a strange ringing in her ears.

'Some people choose the damnedest times to phone,' James commented wryly standing up. He was looking at her in a way that disturbed her, and she shivered, wondering if he had known that she was so lost in his kiss that she hadn't even heard the phone.

As he went to answer it reality came back. If she stayed now he might well take it that she was tacitly inviting him to make love to her. Shivering, she got up; he had his back to her. She found her bag and headed for the door, closing it softly behind her. As she ran through the hall and out to the lift she prayed that he would not come after her. By luck she managed to find a cruising taxi right outside the apartment. Clambering into it she gave the driver her address.

When she eventually got home she was still shaking.

What had possessed her, she wondered as she unlocked her front door. Why had she allowed James to kiss her, to touch her at all? As she stepped inside, the phone rang. She didn't answer it and when it stopped she took the receiver off the hook. In all probability James would not ring her; she had made her position plain enough by leaving, but she was not taking any chances. James did not really desire her, she knew that . . . but something about him disturbed her, and she didn't as yet know what it was.

She was appalled by how easily the image in her mind had become transferred to the man holding her in his arms. She knew quite well that it was just some trick of her imagination that had transformed James into her dream lover, but it made her face burn and her mind writhe in humiliated anguish. Unable to stop shaking she sat down in a chair and closed her eyes. It was a mistake: a jumble of pictures flashed past her eyes, memories of the sensations aroused by the caresses of the man in the portrait confused with the reality of James's kiss.

Had her dream really been a subconscious urge to experience his love-making?

'No!' She screamed the denial out loud, her hands over her ears as though somehow she could block out her own soundless thoughts.

Too keyed up for sleep she tried to control her tormenting thoughts. She found some relief in trying to concentrate on the ideas she had been carrying round in her head for work on the house. Perhaps the artist she intended to commission to do the ceiling could incorporate a heron somewhere in the design; if so that would add an individual touch that was hers and hers alone. It pleased her to think of leaving her own individual stamp on the house. She made a note to contact him, and to arrange for him to visit the Hall. Biting her lip she put down her pen and stared pensively at the wall. Organising all the work needing to be done on the old Hall from London was going to prove more difficult than she had envisaged, and yet she needed her London contacts. It seemed as though she would be spending weeks driving to Yorkshire and back.

Concentrating, she tried to work out a timetable. A great deal depended on the surveyor's report she had commissioned from the architect. He had told James that he believed the house was sound. Angrily Jenna threw down her pen. It had annoyed her that the architect had assumed that they were together, that James owned the Hall. But there was nothing she could do about it, and it was pointless working herself up into a lather. The next time he saw her — alone — no doubt he would realise the truth, she thought rather grimly, reapplying herself to her work.

'There's someone here to see you.'

Jenna frowned, looking up from her overflowing desk as Maggie walked into her office. She glanced at her diary. 'I don't have any appointments.'

'No, I know. It's —— ' Maggie glanced over her shoulder as the office door opened and James walked in. Jenna's eyes widened fractionally before hardening on his face. How dare he assume the right to walk into her office? She stood up to face him, her eyes and mouth cold.

'James, I'm afraid I'm rather busy . . . ' she began, but he overruled her, making her blood boil with his masculinely arrogant assumption of command.

'It won't take long. I just called in to drop these photocopies off. You mentioned that you wanted them last night — at my flat,' he goaded softly.

Jenna stiffened, conscious of Maggie's curious scrutiny. Despite herself she felt her skin burn and cursed its betraying fairness. She had never learned to control her give-away tendency to blush — ridiculous in a woman of twenty-nine.

'Yes, thank you, you're very kind,' she managed to say disjointedly.

The outer office phone rang and Maggie went to answer it before Jenna could ask her to show her uninvited guest out.

'How about lunch?' James asked.

'Why?' Jenna eyed him challengingly. 'We don't have anything to say to one another.'

'You think not?' He smiled, and then his bantering manner dropped from him as he said quietly, 'Jenna, I'd like you to reconsider about selling the Hall to me. Don't you think you might have bitten off more than you can chew?' he asked her, watching her with eyes that registered every single fluctuating emotion that stormed her. 'It's no great secret in the city that financially your firm's none too secure at the moment.'

Jenna felt herself sway. She wanted to deny his quiet, assertive comment, to demand to know how he had come by such information, but pride would not let her.

'It's just a temporary cashflow problem,' she told him through gritted teeth, 'and no, no way would I ever sell the Hall to you.'

Her eyes defied him to press her further. At that moment she felt all her original loathing and distrust of him come racing back. Was that why he had kissed her last night? Had he hoped to use his sexual mastery to get her to agree to sell him the old Hall? The mere thought drove her into a frenzied temper.

'Never. Never will I sell the Hall to you, James

Allingham,' she told him fiercely. 'Now, please leave my office.'

A little to her surprise, he did. When Maggie came in ten minutes later, Jenna could see that she was curious, but she was too well trained to pry. However, she did comment lightly, 'That will be more fodder for the gossip press if he was seen. I take it there is nothing in the rumour currently circulating that the pair of you are an interesting item?'

'Nothing whatsoever,' Jenna told her shortly.

She was too wrought up and angry to worry about the gossip press. What did concern her was how James had found out about her financial position.

Stop being so naïve, she told herself grimly. Men like James always had ways of discovering what they wanted to know. And owning what they wanted to possess, a tiny inner voice warned her, but she shut it away refusing to listen to it. This time he would learn different. There was no way he was going to get the old Hall, no way at all.

His visit seemed to have set the seal on her week, and it went from bad to worse. Two prospective clients telephoned to cancel contracts she had thought secure and had proved strangely reluctant to tell her why. She also discovered that one of her clients had defaulted on payment and, according to his accountants, had left the country and could not be contacted.

All in all she was glad when Friday came, even though her daily paper did carry an item in the gossip column commenting on her visit to Yorkshire with James. It also mentioned James's connection with the Hall and went on to suggest that marriage might be in the air. There was even allusion to a supposed long-ago romance between them, so ridiculously far-fetched that Jenna threw the paper down in disgust.

She was still uneasy about Lucy, who had been truculent and unforthcoming the night she rang her. Suddenly it seemed as though her life was becoming unravelled, falling apart around her, and it all seemed to date from the time she met James Allingham.

She could hardly blame him for Lucy's behaviour, she told herself wryly. In fact, the only thing she could think of that pleased her was that she had had no more dreams featuring Regency rakes — or their modern-day equivalents — and her painter, after going up to Yorkshire, had reported to her that he would be delighted to take on the commission and had produced some initial sketches that looked extremely promising.

She was just about to clear her desk when Richard knocked on her half-open office door and walked in.

'Jenna, I've got something to tell you,' he announced, sitting down without waiting for her to invite him to do so.

When she looked at him, his eyes slid away from her own, and apprehension started to curl through her stomach. Whatever Richard had to say, it obviously was not going to be good. Please God, don't let us have lost another contract, Jenna thought despairingly, enough things had gone wrong this week already.

'Yes?'

'I'm leaving,' Richard said flatly. 'I've had an offer from . . . from someone to set me up on my own.'

For a moment Jenna was too stunned to take in what he was saying. Richard was a good assistant, but he lacked individual flair, and as far as she knew had never had any ambition to set up in business on his own. And then, as she absorbed what he was saying to her, various things began to click into place.

'And you're taking with you some of our clients?' she accused, getting up and walking over to her window.

She saw him colour uncomfortably, his voice faintly aggressive as he demanded, 'Why shouldn't I? They were contracts I got in the first place. If they choose to come with me . . . '

'Did they?' Jenna asked coldly. 'Or were they bribed — my designs used, but at a lower price? Oh come on, Richard, I'm not that naïve, I know it's done,' she said heatedly, 'but have you thought what's going to happen when they discover you're incapable of any innovative work of your own, excellent copyist though you might be?'

Jenna could see from the expression on his face that she had now totally alienated him.

'God, typical of a woman,' he exclaimed, jumping up out of his chair. 'You damn career types, you all think you're so wonderful! Success doesn't keep you warm in bed at night though, does it?' Richard sneered, looking at her in a way that made Jenna long to strike him.

And then suddenly it hit her. Richard had mentioned an offer from someone else to help set him up — that could only mean an offer of financial assistance. Her body felt hot and light, and yet at the same time she was shivering. James must have offered him the money. James must have done this to her because he knew that without those contracts, without Richard's assistance, she simply could not continue her business and hold on to the old Hall as well. The office seemed to recede and swing dizzily round her. She must not faint now, she must not, not in front of Richard. Somehow, she found the concentration to tell him to go. He looked sulky but triumphant, she noticed absently. James would have to be prepared to lose whatever money it was costing him to back Richard, she reflected in unexpectedly vicious delight, because ultimately Richard would not be a success. What she had said to him was true: he was an excellent copyist but no innovator. James had done this to her.

She was overwhelmed by a need to cry, but she couldn't let herself. Thank God Maggie had asked to leave early and there was no one to see her like this. She managed to make her way to her small private shower-room and once there, stared in mute disbelief at her white face and huge eyes. She looked at least ten years older. She started to shake, the movements of her body, normally so graceful, jerky and unco-ordinated.

What was she going to do? The bank would not lend her any more money — she knew that. Slowly she made her way back to her office and dialled Harley's number. He had been away on holiday since she bought the Hall but he was due back today, and would be in the office this morning.

He answered on the fourth ring. Tensely, Jenna explained to him what had happened. He was silent for a moment and then whistled tunelessly. 'You'll have to sell the Hall, Jenna,' he told her quietly at last. 'If you don't, it's going to pull everything else down around you. I warned you not to buy it.'

'I won't sell it.' She hadn't told him of her suspicions about James primarily because she had known that his answer would be to sell him the house and get rid of it, but she wasn't going to part with the Hall no matter what James did.

She spent all Friday night lying awake, desperately searching for a solution to her problems but none was forthcoming. She had virtually no assets to mortgage. With Richard leaving and taking contracts with him the work she had in hand scarcely merited the bank loan she already had. There must be some way, she thought exhaustedly just before sleep finally claimed her, her final thought being that surely nothing else bad could happen this week — it would be impossible to top this latest blow.

On Saturday she discovered that she was wrong. She was reading her paper, her attention caught by a photograph of James entering the hospital where his stepsister had been receiving treatment, and a few brief lines saying that he was arriving to take her home. There was then a hint of speculation as to how he intended to look after her, the implication being that perhaps marriage might be the answer. Once again her own name was mentioned, but Jenna ignored it. Let the gossip columnists write what they wanted; she had far more important things to worry about.

The phone rang and she put the paper down, frowning as she picked up the receiver. The last person she expected to hear on the other end of the line was Norma Goodman.

Her normally calm voice was fractured with anxiety as she told Jenna that Lucy was missing from school.

'We can't pinpoint an exact time, but we believe she left during games yesterday afternoon. She hasn't taken her clothes. I've talked to all the girls in her set and none of them knows anything about it. At first I thought she might just have been playing truant, but she's been missing for three hours now and I thought I ought to let you know.'

Jenna swallowed. 'Have the police . . . ?'

'I haven't informed them yet,' Mrs Goodman told her, anticipating her query. 'I wasn't sure whether you'd want me to.'

Jenna thought bleakly of all the pitfalls waiting for a young girl on her own and said huskily, 'Please do. Of course, I'm hoping that she intends to come home — I blame myself for what's happened. I knew she wasn't happy at school.'

Visions of Lucy alone in London, vulnerable to a variety of unpleasant fates, tormented her mind agonisingly. Lucy would not come home, Jenna was sure of that.

But why had she run away from school? There had been no quarrel with anyone, no criticisms on the part of a teacher which might have precipitated her departure. She had been withdrawn and quiet, Norma Goodman told Jenna, but then that was not unusual for Lucy.

'I'll contact the police at this end,' suggested Mrs Goodman. 'It will probably be easier for them to institute enquiries. No doubt they'll be in touch with you.'

'I'll stay by the phone until they do,' Jenna confirmed.

When she had replaced the receiver she sat, simply staring into space, her head in her hands. Dear God, Lucy . . . How could she have failed Rachel's child to this extent? Her whole body ached with weariness and misery.

Had she really been so unapproachable that Lucy had been driven to running away? Jenna could see no chance of the proud, stubborn teenager voluntarily getting in touch with her. Where would she go?

She got up and rushed into Lucy's bedroom. What was the surname of her friend? Lucy had, of course, taken her address book with her. Jenna remembered seeing her writing in it just before they left. Tears scalded her throat and eyes as she thought back to that occasion. Dear God, please keep her safe, she found herself praying as she searched feverishly through her memory and finally came up with the family's surname.

Fortunately, Jenna knew where they lived, and with that information it was relatively easy to find their number. It seemed an eternity before the phone was answered, and she knew instantly from the surprise in

Emily Harris's voice that Lucy was not there.

There was no place in her life for pride now. Quickly she explained to Emily Harris what had happened. She was so instantly and overwhelmingly sympathetic that Jenna — who never cried — found herself close to tears again.

'Janet's just come in,' Emily told her. 'Let me talk to her and then I'll ring you back. Look,' she added suddenly, 'don't think me interfering, but would you like me to come round? I can't do anything, but it must be hell to be alone with something like this.'

Jenna knew instinctively that the offer was made through genuine concern, but she was still amazed to hear herself accepting. She had never leaned on anyone, not even Bill and Nancy. Even when Rachel had died she had stood on her own two feet.

'I'll be round as soon as I've spoken to Janet. Try not to worry too much. You know what teenagers are like, it's probably all blown up over a row with a boyfriend or a squabble at school. God preserve me from ever being fifteen again!'

As she replaced the receiver, Jenna wondered feverishly if Lucy could have gone to Bill and Nancy. She professed not to like Yorkshire, but up until recently she had been fond of the older couple.

Nervously she dialled the Yorkshire number. Nancy answered the phone. Barely able to articulate Jenna poured out her story.

'Well, she's not here,' Nancy told her. 'But try not to worry. I'll get Bill to drive to York and wait at the station in case she arrives. She'll be all right, Jenna,' she said reassuringly, but Jenna knew they were both frightened that she might not. Horrific stories of children being assaulted and murdered stormed her mind — and Lucy was still only a child, for all her fifteen years. If only she had tried to explain to her about her parents. If only she had not ignored her demands to know more. This was all her fault, all of it . . . Rachel, how can you forgive me? Tears blocked her throat, but she was too overwrought to weep.

The sound of the doorbell brought her back to reality. She went to open it and admit Emily Harris. Jenna had met her only once before briefly, but now they were united in a bond that all parents share.

'Come and sit down and I'll make us a cup of tea. Has there been any news yet?'

As she spoke the phone rang, and Jenna tensed instinctively, staring at it, unable to pick it up. In the end Emily did it for her, holding the receiver out to her.

It was Mrs Goodman on the phone.

'The police have just been on to me,' she told Jenna. 'Apparently Lucy was picked up by a woman from whom she hitched a lift a couple of miles from the school. She told her that she was on her way home for the weekend and asked to be dropped at the station in Bath.'

Lucy hitchhiking! Jenna's heart started to thud rapidly. How many times had she warned her? She bit her lip, gripped with foreboding and despair.

'Unfortunately, no one can remember issuing her with a ticket, although the police suspect it's a safe bet that she'll go to London.'

To London, but not to me, Jenna reflected bitterly.

'They'll be getting in touch with you, Jenna, to talk to you about Lucy. Of course they'll do a check on the stations, but it might already be too late, she's had ample time to get to London now.'

Too late. The most mournful and poignant words in the English language, Jenna reflected hollowly as she put down the phone.

Emily tried to coax her to eat, and sat with her, listening sympathetically while Jenna talked about Lucy. She got out the photograph album and showed her photos of Lucy as a baby, a toddler . . . always smiling in those simpler sunnier days.

Where had it all gone — the love that had once existed between them? Had she been too busy trying to establish a good standard of living for them? Had she been guilty of neglecting Lucy? Maybe, but surely not of loving her too little? It all came back to her reluctance to discuss Lucy's father with her, Jenna knew, and bit her lip anticipating the questions the police would ask her. They would have to know the truth of course.

Emily stayed with her while they interviewed her. The WPC and the sergeant with her were not unsympathetic, but with every question asked Jenna felt her guilt increase.

It was gone four in the afternoon when they left. Pulling herself together she managed a wan smile for Emily who was watching her with concern. 'I can't forgive myself for not telling Lucy something about her father.'

'In the circumstances I can see why you didn't,' Emily sympathised. She glanced at her watch. 'I'm afraid I'll have to go now. But I could come back?'

Jenna shook her head. 'No. You've done more than enough as it is.'

'Ring me as soon as you hear anything,' Emily said to Jenna as she left, and both of them knew that she had carefully avoided saying, 'if you hear anything'.

With every hour that slipped by, Jenna knew the chances of finding Lucy grew slimmer. London was a big city and one teenage girl could disappear in it all too quickly.

At first it was the commonplace things that tormented her: had she any money? Where would she sleep?

Would she eat properly? And then her thoughts became darker and more despairing, thoughts of drugs and prostitution filled her tormented mind, thoughts far too horrible to contemplate.

It was then that Jenna cried, weeping all the tears she had suppressed over the long years since Rachel's death. She felt as alone and frightened now as she had done then, longing for someone to turn to and share her burdens with.

At first she didn't even hear the doorbell and then eventually it penetrated her misery. Hope flared inside her and she rushed to answer it, stepping back in mute shock as she saw James standing outside.

He followed her in and closed the door behind him. His face looked dark and forbidding, and Jenna was suddenly conscious of her bedraggled appearance. He would know that she had been crying.

'Jenna, it's all right. Lucy's with me.'

She couldn't believe it. She stared at him in total stunned disbelief and then a bitter tidal wave of anger flooded over her.

She flew at him, hitting him with her fists, anguished tears pouring down her face as she cried bitterly. 'How could you do this to me? How . . ?'

'Hush. Come on, it's all right.'

His calm, even voice penetrated her shock. She tensed and then shuddered as his arms came round her, drawing her against the warmth of his body, his hand pressing her head into the curve of his shoulder.

'She only arrived an hour ago, and at first I didn't realise she'd run away from school. I would have come sooner, but I had to calm her down and get her settled. I've left her with Sarah — they seem to have hit it off . . . '

For some reason she could not stop shaking; she

could feel James's body absorbing the frantic tremors of hers. His hand was stroking her hair, and he was talking to her, but she was totally unaware of what was being said. Lucy had gone to James. She was still trying to assimilate it.

'I must go to her.'

'No.' He said it gently but firmly. 'You're both too overwrought at the moment. Let her stay with me tonight. She'll be perfectly safe.'

'Why are you doing this to me?' Jenna cried out despairingly, suddenly hating him. 'Wasn't it enough that you've ruined my business to get the old Hall? Did you have to do this too?'

She felt him tense and then he was turning her face up so that he could look down at her. She could see the anger glittering in his eyes and flinched from it.

'Do you honestly think that's true? Any of it?' he demanded bitingly. 'I don't know what all this about your business is, but I can assure you if it's ruined, then it's not because of anything I've done. And where Lucy's concerned . . . ' His mouth compressed. 'Come and sit down.'

He led her over to the sofa and pushed her down on to it gently.

'It seems she's got some bee in her bonnet about my being her father. Don't ask me why, something to do with all this nonsense in the papers, probably. She came to see me to ask me if I was. That was why she came to see me.'

Jenna stared at him. 'Lucy thinks you're her father?' She couldn't take it in. Later she would be relieved and grateful that her niece was safe, but now she was so battered by shock and fear herself that she could barely function.

'That's what I said,' James agreed with fine irony.

'Look it's no business of mine, but wouldn't it be better to tell her the truth?'

Jenna went white. 'I can't,' she told him wildly. 'You don't understand . . . ' To her horror she started to cry again. She tried to stop, and found she could not.

'Hush . . . it's all right,' James murmured, his arms enfolding her again. 'It's only reaction and shock . . . it will soon pass . . . '

'I've got to ring Norma Goodman, and the police and Nancy . . . ' Jenna muttered hectically. 'I — '

'I'll do that in a minute.'

It was wrong to let him take control like this, but how heavenly it was to have the burdens shifted off her shoulders even if it was only momentarily.

Even now she could not believe that Lucy had actually thought James was her father, and her heart ached for her niece.

'I have a proposition to put to you,' James told her quietly. 'Maybe now isn't the time . . . '

She pulled away from him, searching for a tissue to dry her face. God, she must look dreadful, eyes all blotchy, hair untidy . . .

'If it's another offer to buy the Hall, then the answer's no,' she told him tautly.

'Not exactly.' His voice was carefully neutral. 'What I actually had in mind was that you and I get married.'

CHAPTER EIGHT

'MARRIED!' Jenna stared disbelievingly at him, and then said bitterly, 'Just what sort of a joke is this?'

'No joke,' James assured her coolly. 'I've been giving the matter a good deal of thought lately. You weren't far off the mark when you said I needed a wife. A London apartment is no place for Sarah at the moment; she needs the type of care and attention that being part of a family unit can provide.'

'And for your step-sister's sake you're proposing to me?' Jenna thought she must be hearing things.

'Not entirely.' He looked at her thoughtfully and then said, 'I take it you never intend to tell Lucy the identity of her father?'

Jenna shook her head. 'I can't . . . and I can't tell you either.'

He shrugged powerful shoulders. 'Well, frankly it's none of my business, but it has occurred to me that since Lucy is so desperately in need of a father-figure to relate to and since she seems to have already cast me in that role, it would do no harm to allow her to continue to think so.'

What he was suggesting was ridiculous. Jenna frowned. 'Haven't you told her you're not her father?'

'Not in so many words,' he admitted. And then added wryly, betraying an odd hint of vulnerability, 'Would you like to tell an emotional adolescent who's just cast herself on your chest crying "Daddy!" that she's got the wrong man? I'm not suggesting that we allow her to believe I'm her father for ever, but certainly until she's over this present emotional trauma. I believe that given a secure family background for a few years, she'll find it easier to accept the truth than she would now.'

From Lucy's point of view what he was saying made good sense, but from her own . . . She swallowed hard.

'And you?' she questioned him. 'What would you gain from this act of gallantry?'

His eyebrows rose. 'Why the old Hall, of course,' he responded silkily. 'Did you need to ask?'

But of course. She ought to have guessed.

'Think about it,' he told her, standing up. 'I'll come and collect you in the morning and take you back to my apartment to see Lucy. I'm perfectly serious about this, Jenna. It's obvious that you won't sell the Hall to me and if your business is in as fragile a state as I suspect, the bank could go over your head and re-auction it. I've got several commitments abroad at the moment and it would be just my luck to lose out again — I don't want that happening. A marriage between us seems to me to be the obvious solution.'

'You would think that with your ancestry,' Jenna flung at him bitterly, remembering the story he had told them about the man in the portrait.

'The benefits wouldn't be all on my side, Jenna,' he reminded her coolly. 'If you can't think of any yourself, then think of Lucy. You can't have it all ways. Either you tell her who her father is, or you allow her the luxury of inventing a substitute. If you don't the kid's going to destroy herself.'

Jenna couldn't deny his accusation.

She pressed tired fingers to her head. 'I'll . . . I'll have to think about it,' she told him huskily, too disturbed and overwrought to be aware that she had not, as she had first intended, turned his proposal down flat. She felt so muddled and confused; she had already endured more than enough emotional turmoil for one short day.

'Give me those phone numbers,' James told her. 'I'll make the calls while you get ready for bed.'

He saw her expression and lifted his eyebrows and, although she wanted to demur, strangely she found it impossible. She showed him the pad where she had written the numbers and heard him pick up the receiver and start dialling as she left the room.

She had thought she would be far too upset to sleep, but with the low, confident murmur of James's voice reaching her from the sitting-room she found herself quickly drifting off.

He came in to her room before he left and stood at the foot of the bed.

'You'll be all right on your own?'

'Yes.' What would he do if she said no, Jenna wondered wildly — volunteer to stay with her? She shivered at the sensation her thoughts produced.

'I'll come round at ten to pick you up. And I'd like you to have an answer for me by then, Jenna.'

She wanted to protest that he was rushing her, that she couldn't think straight right now, when all her emotional responses were so drained and flat. It was an effort merely to say yes or no, never mind make a commitment for her entire future.

But would it be for the future? What kind of marriage did James have in mind? A temporary arrangement meant to last until Sarah was better and Lucy was adult? Or perhaps just until he found a way of taking the Hall away from her.

Tension flared along her nerve paths. She sat up in bed, suddenly restless, shivering in the night air.

She was being selfish again, Jenna told herself, putting herself first and not Lucy. Perhaps James was right.

Perhaps it was time she started making some sacrifices for Lucy's sake. She would have to tell James that it would not be a real marriage, that physically they could not be man and wife, but that should hardly bother him. She had little doubt that even married he had no intention of remaining faithful. It would after all be primarily a business arrangement. She would have to find a way of making sure he could not take the old Hall from her, though.

Frowning, she lay down again and tried to go to sleep. Time enough to worry about that in the morning. After all, she hadn't made her mind up yet, but as she drifted into sleep Jenna acknowledged that she had precious little alternative. She had been given a second chance to put things right with Lucy . . . and if she threw it away, how long would it be before Lucy ran away from school again? Or from home? She couldn't watch her all the time. It was wrong to allow Lucy to believe that James was her father, but the deception would be far more acceptable than the truth.

The decision tormented her, even in sleep, disturbing dreams full of unseen stalking fears. One moment her dreams were full of James telling her equably that marriage could be a business arrangement, a logical partnership between two people with something to give each other. The next he had changed into the man in the portrait, determined to subdue her both in mind and body.

She woke up shivering, wondering if her brain was trying to tell her something — if there was perhaps more of his ancestor in James than she had yet recognised. But even she could not see James forcing himself on a woman: he was too suave, too coolly controlled, too cynically convinced that sex was an appetite easily fed by the act of possession to feel any strong desire to

possess one specific woman, which surely made it all
the more strange that he was so determined to possess
the Hall.

Outwardly, James was a cynical, controlled man who
treated life with a lazy self-assurance that Jenna found
intensely irritating. He gave the impression of never
having had to try very hard to get anything; he was the
only son of an extremely wealthy man, and wealthy in
his own right too. Although he had taken on the responsibility of his step-sister, Jenna had never heard him
express any anguish at the loss of his father and step-
mother. But, then, why should he to her?

She sat up in bed, wrapping her arms around her
knees, her hair falling over her shoulder in a red-gold
swathe. In the eyes of the world she would be very fortunate in securing a husband like James, of course, and
from every viewpoint she took, there was really little
logical alternative other than to accept his proposal. But
inwardly she didn't want to. Buried under all her hostility and dislike of him was a sharply cutting fear that she
could neither analyse nor understand. Originally she
could have dismissed it as a result of his connection
with the Deveril family, but now that was not possible — he wasn't connected with them by blood at all.

Jenna got up reluctantly and showered. How would
Lucy react to seeing her? It had hurt to know that her
niece had gone to James, and where on earth had she
got the idea that James was her father? It was too late to
worry about that now, Jenna thought, putting on clean
plain underwear and opening her wardrobe doors.

Most of her clothes were geared for work and she
pulled out some toning separates — a peach skirt in a
fine wool gaberdine mixture, and a soft figured silk
shirt two shades lighter.

The outfit was new and she hadn't worn it yet. It had a

beautifully cut top coat in the same fabric and shade as the shirt to go with it, and while it was elegant it was also slightly more feminine than the clothes she normally chose.

Would Lucy be glad to see her, or would she reject her? Jenna worried over how Lucy would receive her while she played with her breakfast. If she married James Lucy would be pleased, Jenna knew that; she had been drawn to him, even before she had convinced herself that he was her father.

The phone rang just as she was finishing her coffee and she picked up the receiver, pleased to hear Nancy's down-to-earth Yorkshire tones.

'James rang us last night to tell us that Lucy was with him, but I thought I'd give you a call this morning to see how you are.'

'Bewildered,' Jenna admitted honestly. 'Did James tell you that she's decided that he is her father?'

'Yes. Not that you can blame her,' Nancy added caustically, 'with all this nonsense that they've been printing in the papers lately. What are you going to do about it?'

Jenna hesitated and then said slowly. 'James has asked me to marry him, Nancy — oh, it isn't a romance, don't think that. He still wants the old Hall and he knows there's no way I'd part with it. If we married he claims that we'd both gain something from the marriage — for him there'd be the old Hall, and someone to help him share the responsibility of his step-sister, and for me there'd be help with the financial problems I've got at the moment, and more important, a father-figure for Lucy. James hasn't told her yet that he isn't her father. He says he's quite prepared to take on the role.'

'So what's your problem?' Nancy asked her drily. 'You've left it too late to tell the lass the truth, Jenna, and you know it. There's not many men who would offer to do what James has done.'

'The advantages aren't all on my side, Nancy,' Jenna reminded her, her spirits lowered still further by Nancy's obvious approval of James's proposal. 'James will stand to gain as well.'

'Aye, I'm not denying that, I'm just saying there's not many men who would be willing to take on the responsibility of another man's child, to the extent that he would be doing.'

'I can see I'm not going to get any sympathy from you,' Jenna interrupted, adding on a suddenly panicky note, 'Nancy, it's such a dangerous step to take — like walking off the top of a high building and praying there's someone down there to catch you. You know I've never wanted to marry. You know —— ' She broke off. 'I know that logically I should agree but —— '

'No buts,' Nancy told her firmly. 'Tell him yes!'

She was ready half an hour before James arrived, pacing the floor nervously — not so much at the thought of seeing James but because of coming face to face with Lucy. Would she still be as sulkily cold towards her as she had been over the past few months?

Even though she had been waiting for it, the sound of the bell ringing made her jump.

When she opened the door to James, she felt illogically annoyed that he could look so calm and at ease, when she was torn about by nervous qualms.

'Ready?'

'I'll just get my coat.'

She put it on in the hall and walked towards him, stopping when she saw the way he was regarding her.

'Very nice,' he said calmly, his thorough inspection over.

He had judged her as coolly and critically as though

she were a piece of bloodstock he was considering buying and it infuriated her, goading her into saying, 'I'm not your possession yet, James, and I don't need your approval — for anything.'

He smiled and further infuriated her by saying lightly, 'Don't worry. I think Lucy is just as nervous of seeing you as you are of seeing her. I had a long talk with her last night, and she knows quite well that I don't approve of what she's done.'

'And of course because you don't approve, she'll be duly chastened,' Jenna spat at him bitterly.

It was childish to resent him because of what had happened, but she did. She was jealous of the fact that Lucy seemed to have transferred her affections from her to James, and even though she knew she was being ridiculous she couldn't stop herself from flinging the angry accusation at him.

'Perhaps.' Something glinted in his eyes as he stopped her by his car, his hand on her arm. Jenna withdrew immediately, her face tight with rage and misery. 'At the moment, as far as Lucy's concerned, I'm a novelty — the realisation of her dreams of finding her father, but I can assure you that won't last. I predict that by the time we've been married six months or so, she'll be complaining to you that I'm too strict with her.'

'I haven't agreed that we will be married yet,' Jenna reminded him sharply.

'I hope you're adult enough not to allow a temporary fit of jealousy to blind you to reason, Jenna,' was his calm reply. 'I can't make you marry me, of course . . . '

'No, you can't,' Jenna agreed, climbing into the car, and closing the door before he could help her.

She sat in silence while he drove them to his apartment, butterflies storming the pit of her stomach. What if Lucy refused to see her . . . or speak to her . . . and what about James's step-sister? What if she didn't like her?

'Lucy is having an extremely beneficial effect upon Sarah,' James commented as they got into the lift. 'I actually heard her laughing this morning.' He grimaced faintly. 'It hasn't been easy for her, of course, losing her parents, and then being transported to a country where she knows virtually no one.'

'She had you.'

'Mmm. You're not the only one who has generation-gap problems, you know. I'd only seen Sarah on a few brief occasions before the accident. I was already an adult when she arrived on the scene. My father re-married when I was fifteen, and I left home shortly afterwards.'

He saw her expression. 'No, I didn't run away, but it was felt in the family that my father and his new wife would have an easier life without the presence of a teenage boy. I went to live with my grandfather on St Justine.'

'Did you mind?'

It was almost the first personal question she had asked him, and even now she half wished she had not done so. She didn't want to know anything about him that would make him seem human and vulnerable: she wanted to keep him at a distance and preserve a wall of silence between them.

'At first, but I got on very well with my grandfather, and on balance I think I was far better off as a much-wanted grandson than I would have been as a reluctant-ly accepted step-son.'

Was he saying that his step-mother had not wanted him?

As they had reached the door of his apartment Jenna could not ask. The tension inside her was appalling as she waited for him to open the door. To have to follow him into the empty drawing-room was a painful let-down.

'Lucy's probably with Sarah in her room. She's in a wheelchair now, although the doctors are still convinced that the paralysis is hysterical and will eventually go. I'll go and get Lucy. Would you like a cup of coffee?'

Jenna nodded numbly. Her mouth felt dry, her head ready to burst with pain.

She stood in front of the window overlooking the park, one remote corner of her mind admiring the delicacy of the wrought-iron balcony while the rest of it was seized by crippling tension.

'Hello!'

She turned round at the sound of Lucy's voice. Her niece stood just inside the door, and there was no sign of James. Lucy looked tired and pale. There was an open anxiety in her eyes and all the resentment and bitterness Jenna had felt on learning that she had gone to James dissolved. Automatically she opened her arms, unsure which of them it was who sobbed first as Lucy ran into them.

'I'm sorry . . . so sorry,' Lucy whispered tearfully hugging her with fierce intensity. 'I didn't mean to hurt and upset you. It's just that I've been so desperate to know about my father, it's almost been like being ill. I can't explain it to you, but . . .'

'It's all right, I do understand.'

Of course she did, and it was almost worth all the pain and trauma of the last twenty-four hours to see Lucy transformed like this and once again the loving, affectionate girl she had previously been.

'James was furious with me when he found out that I'd run away from school. He said I was the most thoughtless, selfish brat he'd ever met.'

Tears glimmered in the brown eyes, but unbelievably Lucy was grinning. 'I think that's what convinced me more than anything else that he is my father . . . he sounded so much like a parent!'

Jenna felt her throat constrict. The difference in Lucy was unbelievable. Did she have the right to destroy her very evident happiness by telling her the truth?

'James?' she questioned, raising her eyebrows a little.

'Well, somehow it doesn't seem right calling him "daddy"!' Lucy pulled a wry face. 'He's far too macho to be a parent.' She giggled. 'I think if he wasn't my father, I could almost fall for him myself! Sarah calls him James too.'

'She *is* his sister,' Jenna pointed out.

'Umm. I wonder what that will make us when you and James are married? We'll be step-sisters, but she'll also be my aunt, won't she?'

Jenna was stunned. Shock followed by a swift burst of anger. James had had no right to tell Lucy they were getting married. He had out-manoeuvred her very neatly, knowing quite well that she could hardly turn round and tell Lucy they weren't.

'Wasn't it a coincidence,' Lucy was chattering on happily, 'the two of you bumping into one another like that after all these years? James told me that you met when you first came to London, and that he had to go away when his grandfather became ill and that when he came back you'd disappeared.' Lucy looked reproachful. 'Why didn't you let him know you were expecting me?'

'Because, my dear daughter, your mother is far too proud to attempt what she no doubt saw as a form of moral blackmail,' James drawled, coming into the room carrying a tray of coffee. 'In fact it was a mix-up all round. When she didn't reply to my letters, I naturally assumed that she no longer wanted to have anything to do with me. I had no idea that . . . '

'She was expecting me,' Lucy concluded for him, dancing over to him and relieving him of the tray. 'I was just telling Ma that you're so sexy that if you weren't my father I could quite easily fall for you myself!' she told James cheekily, putting the tray on the table and turning back to hug him.

Watching his easy acceptance of her exuberant affection, Jenna saw that she had been wrong in thinking that he would make a poor parent. He seemed to know instinctively how to handle Lucy: he was firm with her yet understanding.

'When's the wedding going to be?' Lucy was perched on the arm of a chair, nibbling biscuits and looking at Jenna.

'Just as soon as we can arrange it,' James answered for her. 'In fact, I'm planning to take your mother out to dinner tonight so that we can discuss it.'

He turned to Jenna. 'Come and meet Sarah.'

With Lucy trilling away happily at her side about the wedding and how exciting and thrilling it all was there was nothing Jenna could say. She followed James into an inner corridor with several doors off it.

He opened one of them and stood back so that Lucy and Jenna could precede him.

Jenna's first feeling when she saw the slight blonde-haired girl in the wheelchair was one of intense compassion. Sarah lifted her head and smiled rather hesitantly at her, while James performed the introductions. Sarah was much shyer than Lucy and very withdrawn, not just with her, Jenna noted, but with James as well. She treated him like a distant acquaintance rather than a brother, and when he bent down to help her manoeuvre her wheelchair she snapped bitterly at him.

'For God's sake, leave me alone. I can do it myself.'

It wasn't a completely unexpected reaction from a pretty teenage girl who must resent being tied to a chair however temporarily, but Jenna sensed there was more to Sarah's hostility than mere frustration over her physical disabilities.

'If we have an early lunch there should just be time this afternoon to run you back to school, young lady,' James told Lucy, glancing at his watch.

Although Lucy gave a brief pout, Jenna noticed that she didn't argue with him and, once again, she was aware of an irrational feeling of jealousy, although this went quickly enough when Lucy turned to her and asked uncertainly, 'What did they say, at school, I mean? What will happen when I go back?'

'Nothing,' Jenna assured her gently. She wanted to have a long talk with Lucy about her dislike of the school, to try and find out what Lucy really wanted, but once again it seemed that James had beaten her to it.

'James says I may not need to go to boarding school once we all move to the old Hall. He says Sarah and I could both attend day school.'

'I thought you didn't want to move to Yorkshire,' Jenna reminded her.

Lucy shrugged. 'That was before . . . before I knew about you and James. I mean, it will be different now. We'll be a proper family.'

If only Lucy knew!

'You're going to invite Bill and Nancy to the wedding, aren't you?' Lucy asked. 'Where will it be?'

Jenna had not thought that far ahead yet. She was still trying to come to terms with the way James had forced her into a corner.

'Since this is to be a first marriage for both of us, I think a church ceremony,' James supplied.

Over Lucy's head, Jenna stared at James.

'I hope you don't expect me to appear in a veil and a long white dress?' she questioned him sarcastically.

His smile, a blend of tenderness and whimsicality, momentarily silenced her. He came towards her and took her hand in his, lifting it to his mouth. She could feel the warmth of his breath against her fingers, tiny shivers of sensation tingling over her skin. His eyes seemed to mesmerise her into standing quite still, even her breath suspended when he turned her hand palm upwards, and brushed a light kiss against the sensitive skin.

'Whatever you wear, you'll look radiant,' he assured her.

Jenna longed to rail and scream at him that she would not take part in the subterfuge he had thrust them both into, that she would not play the role of lovers that he seemed to have cast for them both, but before she could get the breath to do so the sound of a crash from Sarah's bedroom riveted her attention.

Both she and James moved at the same time, James's longer legs ensuring that he covered the distance before her. Even so, Jenna was right behind him as he thrust open the bedroom door.

The wheelchair lay on its side, wheels spinning, while its occupant lay sprawled on the floor, sobbing noisily. As James bent over her Sarah raised her head from the floor and screamed, 'Don't touch me! Don't come near me! I hate you! Why couldn't you be the one to die? Go away from me.'

For the first time Jenna saw him look undecided about what to do, and instinctively she took charge.

Crouching down on the floor beside the weeping girl she slid one arm beneath her to support her head, and stroked the blonde hair with her free hand.

'I think you'd better go,' she told James quietly. 'Should she have a doctor to check that she's all right?'

'I'll see to it.'

As the door closed behind him Sarah sobbed bitterly, 'I hate him! And I hate living here! I want to go home.'

Smoothing Sarah's hair back off her hot forehead, Jenna sighed. 'Sarah, I understand how you feel and so does James, but he can't bring back your parents for you, and you know he can't let you live alone in America.'

'My folks would never have wanted me to live with James. He and my mother never got along. He was horrible to her when she first met Daddy.'

Without knowing why she should feel the need to defend him, Jenna found herself saying, 'Sarah, wasn't James very much the same age you are now when his father married your mother? Try to imagine how you would have felt if that had happened to you, if your mother had died and your father was going to marry someone else. It isn't always easy to behave the way we know we should, is it?'

'You mean James was jealous of my mother?'

She had stopped crying now and the fever heat was beginning to leave her skin. Jenna was glad because she had been afraid that Sarah might work herself up to near hysteria.

'It would only have been natural if he was, wouldn't it? Perhaps he might even have felt that he was betraying his own mother by trying to like yours. And might your mother not have been a little bit jealous of him too? All of us feel insecure when we form a new and important relationship,' she went on, before Sarah could leap to her mother's defence. 'I know if I was marrying someone who had a child or children from a previous marriage, I would be a little bit nervous about how they were going to react to me: would they be comparing me to their own mother? Would they make things awkward for me and my new husband? Just because we're "grown-up" it doesn't mean our feelings completely change, you know.

'In fact, you should be able to understand exactly how James felt. Like you he had to go and live far away from his friends and his father . . . '

'He went to live with his grandfather,' Sarah told her, 'but I always thought that was because he wanted to go.'

'Maybe he did because he felt that he wasn't welcome in his father's new marriage,' Jenna said as gently as she could. 'Everyone has their pride, you know, Sarah, and we all try to hide it from others when we're hurt, sometimes even to the extent of pretending we don't care at all.'

'I know, I pretend that I don't mind about being in this chair but I do, and I hate it when the doctor says that there's nothing wrong with me. If there wasn't I'd be able to walk, wouldn't I?'

'And so you will,' Jenna soothed her. 'When the doctor says there's nothing wrong, he means nothing wrong physically, but our minds exert a tremendous power over our bodies, you know. You were involved in a dreadful accident, and now your mind is telling your body not to move because when it moved it got hurt. But some day when your mind stops being frightened it won't tell your body that any more.'

'And then I'll be able to walk again.' She pulled a wry face. 'I have to have physiotherapy twice a week and I hate it.' She looked away from Jenna and started plaiting the fringed hem on her jumper.

'What will happen to me when you and James get married and you move to Yorkshire?'

'Oh, Sarah, you'll come with us of course. Surely you didn't think . . ?' She saw the tears glistening in the blue eyes and tugged Sarah's hair gently. 'James cares an awful lot about you, you know. One of the reasons he wants to get married is because he wants you to have a secure family background again.'

It would do no harm to tell her the truth and might even help to break down her antipathy towards her step-brother, although quite why she should want to do anything to help James, Jenna could not understand. Because it sprang from her own innate sense of fair play. He had helped her with Lucy, so she should help him in turn.

'I didn't even know you and Lucy existed until yesterday,' Sarah whispered, having digested her comment.

'Well, it all happened a long time ago and I never thought that . . .'

'That you would fall in love all over again. It's just like a movie.'

Jenna couldn't help but laugh, even though she was thinking privately how shocked both Lucy and Sarah would be if they knew the truth.

'Doctor's here.' Lucy pushed open the door and came in, her eyes anxious. 'Are you okay, Sarah?'

'I think so. I just get so impatient with myself when I can't do things.'

'Don't worry,' Lucy comforted her, 'you'll soon be out of that thing and until you are, I'll chauffeur it around for you. We'll have to do plenty of shopping before we move to Yorkshire, Ma,' she told Jenna. 'Nearly everything Sarah's got is too short for her now, and there are no decent shops in York. I'm dreading it,' she groaned theatrically to Sarah. 'No Top Shop, no Oxford Street . . .'

'No eternal requests for advances on your allowance,'

Jenna chimed in, standing up as James and the doctor walked in.

'I'll go and wait outside,' she offered, but Sarah clutched her arm. 'Please stay with me,' she begged.

Across the small space that separated them Jenna's eyes met James. The expression in his was wryly enigmatic and Jenna wondered what he read in her own. Compassion for Sarah . . . . but did he also know that some of that compassion was for him too? Talking to Sarah she had experienced a tiny surge of fellow-feeling for him, when she realised that he wasn't as totally removed from the nagging problems of life as she had first imagined.

'Well, now, young lady, let's have a look at you.'

Jenna waited while the doctor examined Sarah, relieved when he pronounced that no damage had been done.

'Can't run before we can walk, can we?' he tut-tutted when he had finished his examination.

Sarah grimaced. 'Just walking would be enough for me right now.'

'It will come in time, never fret.'

'James tells me wedding bells are in the offing,' he said to Jenna as she escorted him back to the drawing-room.

Her mouth compressed a little. James was being remarkably talkative about their marriage, especially in view of the fact that she had not yet agreed to it.

When they dropped Lucy off at her school later on that afternoon Jenna thought her niece looked happier than she had for a long time. During the long drive she had chattered to both Jenna and James impartially, bouncing about excitedly in the back seat whenever she talked about the wedding, plaguing James to tell her when it was going to be, but all he would say was that she would be the first to know once they had decided.

'And this time, stay put. Is that understood?' he demanded sternly as Lucy threw her arms round his neck to kiss him goodbye.

'Don't worry, I'll be the perfect pupil.' She hugged Jenna tightly. 'Sorry for being such an obnoxious toad lately, Mum . . . but you do understand, don't you?'

'Yes.' There were tears in Jenna's throat. In one way she resented the fact that James was the one who had restored her loving, affectionate daughter to her, and yet she knew she ought to feel gratitude, but then, when had the human heart ever been able to be schooled in what it should and should not feel?

'I thought we might stop for dinner and a talk on the way back,' James suggested, as they drove away. 'Sarah will be all right for a few hours with my house-keeper.'

'What exactly is there left to talk about?' Jenna asked sarcastically. 'It seems you've anticipated my accep-tance of your proposal. You've even decided where we're going to be married!'

'I didn't tell Lucy deliberately, if that's what you're hinting,' James returned evenly.

Jenna compressed her lips. James had never struck her as a man who would let himself be pushed into saying or doing anything he did not wish.

'What did she do?' Her voice was dripping with acid. 'Apply thumbscrews?'

'Not in a physical sense. She asked me if she could spend part of her school holidays with me, and if I would talk to you about her visiting me in London. She was working herself up into quite a state and so I told her that I'd proposed to you.'

'But not that I had not accepted.'

Jenna was aware of him looking at her, his glance

sharp and objective. 'You could always have told her that yourself.'

Jenna mentally visualised Lucy's reaction if she had done so and remained silent.

'You don't need to give me dinner,' she said after a few minutes.

'Maybe not, but it will provide a relaxing background for us to talk in — and on neutral territory. There's a place a couple of miles down the road from here. I sometimes call in on the way to my godmother's. Which reminds me, I must take you down to meet her soon. I'd thought of asking her to take charge of the girls while we're away.'

'Away?' Jenna frowned. 'Away where?'

'Where do newly-married couples normally go? On honeymoon, of course.'

'No! There's absolutely no reason for anything like that!'

'On the contrary, there are several excellent reasons,' James argued silkily. 'None of them the ones that usually apply I'll admit, but excellent none the less. For a start I have business in the Caribbean that needs attending to. The holiday complex I'm involved in has reached the stage where discussions are due —as a matter of fact I want to pick your professional brain over some aspects of the décor of the luxury suites, so it won't exactly be a holiday for you either. And then there's the fact that we are going to be living with two extremely sharp-eyed young women and I think a brief break away on our own, so that we can get used to one another and feel more at ease with one another, is essential.'

Jenna took a deep breath. 'Before you go any further, I want to make it plain to you that if I marry you, it will be a marriage in name only — without sex,' she added baldly.

'Unusual . . . but not impossible. Am I allowed to ask why?'

For a moment she was too startled by his calm reaction to speak. 'I don't love you.'

She saw his eyebrows lift and could have sworn his mouth twitched in faint amusement. 'Is that necessary?'

He was making her feel like a gauche seventeen-year-old. 'For me, yes,' she said firmly. 'Since you've put me in a position where I can't really refuse to marry you, I will, but only if I have your guarantee that you'll never . . . '

'Force my unwanted attentions on you?' He sounded more amused than put out. 'Very well. You have it. Tell me, though, does this guarantee *me* to live life as a celibate?'

'Would that be possible?' She said it drily, and was disturbed by the sudden glint of anger in his eyes.

'Maybe not, but obviously it is for you unless you're trying to tell me that you have a lover.'

Jenna's mouth went dry, but she knew he meant to get an answer to his question.

'No . . . no, I don't,' she admitted at length, her voice a cracked, hoarse sound in the silence of the car, leaving her with the feeling that she had betrayed far more to him than she had intended.

'So. No lover and no sex. Why?'

'Why not? Not everyone centres their life on the gratification of their sexual desires.'

'No, but very few people exclude them from their lives entirely, which is, I assume, what you're saying you do?'

He had turned off the main road now, and Jenna cursed his mental dexterity which enabled him to continue driving and questioning her at the same time.

'Am I permitted to ask if this aversion is of a recent or long-standing nature?'

'Does it really matter?' Suddenly Jenna felt tired and defeated. 'If you still want to marry me then you know my terms, James. It's up to you.'

They were driving past stone pillars embellished with spread-winged eagles, attractive flares illuminating their path.

'This hotel is renowned for the excellence of its suites,' James told her wryly, as he stopped the car. 'If it wasn't for your embargo on sex, I might have suggested that we stay the night and sample one — all in the course of business, naturally,' he added in an indolent drawl.

Jenna refused to be affected by his mockery. 'I'm sure there'll be other times — and other companions, James,' she said to him crisply.

His questioning about her reasons for wanting a no-sex marriage had left her nerves raw and edgy. The last thing she wanted to do now was sit down and dine with him as he discussed their forthcoming marriage, but as on so many occasions since he came into her life, it seemed she had no choice.

'Shall we go in?'

Jenna joined him reluctantly, pausing briefly to admire the clever lighting that made the most of the hotel's creeper-clad exterior. Architecturally it had no particular beauty and was, she suspected, Edwardian originally.

Unusually, the entrance of the hotel was via a conservatory. A huge vine covered most of its roof and walls, the greenery massed in the background high-lighting the black and white lozenge-tiled floor.

The area behind the reception desk was mirrored and cleverly lit, the whole effect striking and original.

'The restaurant is through here,' James touched her arm indicating an archway to their right.

A thick carpet in a rich blue-grey muffled their footsteps up the shallow flight of half a dozen stairs leading to a wider archway with the restaurant beyond.

An aura of intimacy had been created by the deft use of deep, upholstered sofas instead of the regulation chairs, the tables set at angles to one another so that they were not directly overlooked.

The same blue-grey carpet in the corridor covered the floor, a peachy-toned wallpaper in a ragged effect adding a note of warmth. Very traditional blue-grey velvet curtains hung at the windows, their matching pelmets edged in the same peach as the paper, as were the tiebacks.

The sofas were upholstered in a peach-on-blue fabric in some instances, with the colourway reversed to blue on peach in others, contrasting cushions adding a definitive note. The tablecloths were white damask, the cutlery a very traditional silver-plate. There was a soothing murmur of conversation all around them — no single voice particularly discernible, just a pleasant background sound like waves on a beach.

The head waiter greeted James by name and personally escorted them to a discreetly sheltered table.

In an effort to maintain some control of the evening Jenna made a show of studying the menu she was handed. She had never felt less like eating but having allowed the printed words on the card held in her hand to dance illegibly in front of her for several minutes she put it down as though having made her choice.

James was still studying his menu, his concentration providing Jenna with a rare opportunity to study him at close quarters without him being aware of it. His hair was dark and thick, shining with health and good grooming. She wondered rather absently if it would feel as silky as it looked and then checked the thought, her eyes widening in faint shock at herself just as he put down his menu and looked up at her.

'Something wrong?'

Jenna shook her head. She was astounded by the direction of her own thoughts.

'Ready to order?'

A waiter was hovering and she told him what she wanted. A little to her surprise, when the wine waiter arrived James consulted her about her own preferences. Jenna rarely drank. The teachings of her Calvinistic great-aunt still clung, and had been reinforced during her teens by the stark realisation that too much to drink meant a corresponding lessening of self-control.

She had ordered *petits éclairs de saumon ou truite.*
fumée, for her first course — tiny éclairs filled with smoked fish mousse and served with a fresh cucumber and dill sauce — and James had ordered pâté. Jenna had also ordered a fish dish for her main course, sole *bonne femme,* whereas James had chosen duck with a rich accompanying sauce.

'I don't really have any preference,' Jenna told him. 'Something white and fairly dry.'

She watched as James consulted the list and then conversed with the hovering wine waiter.

When he had gone James said to her, 'Well, I hope you approve of my choice — it can be as difficult to choose a wine for someone else's palate as it can be to buy perfume for a woman one doesn't know well.'

Jenna shrugged indifferently. 'It really doesn't matter what it is. I don't drink much.'

James's eyebrows went up. 'What *do* you do?' he jibed softly. 'It seems to me that for a beautiful woman you're remarkably unappreciative of many of the more sensual pleasures in life. Even your clothes suggest a certain lack of —— '

'Femininity?' Jenna supplied icily. 'I'm sorry if my appearance doesn't match your high standards.' Her eyes flashed dark storm warnings.

To her surprise James laughed. 'No, you're not,' he contradicted her calmly. 'If ever a woman was given to making and then reinforcing the statement that she doesn't give a damn what any member of the male sex thinks about her, then that woman is you. What I want to know is why?'

His perception made Jenna feel uncomfortable. She felt as though somehow she had been trapped. As though he was deliberately leading their conversation in the direction he wanted it to go, and she had unwittingly allowed him to do so.

'Does there have to be a reason?' She took refuge in the brittle deflective reply, shrugging her shoulders, relieved that the arrival of their first course prevented James from continuing to press her.

However, he was more determined than she had thought. Immediately the waiter left he said, 'Yes, I think there does. Something connected with Lucy's father perhaps?'

Jenna dropped her fork, shock a painful spiking pain twisting inside her. What could James possibly know about Lucy's father? The thought that he might know anything made her feel so ill that she couldn't touch her food, and she pushed away the plate. Her throat felt extremely dry and she drank quickly from her glass. The wine was light and delicate, cleanly cold against her tongue and rather pleasant. As it slid down her throat it cooled and calmed her strained nerves, settling her stomach.

James continued to eat quite calmly, as though

unaware of her perturbation, but once their plates had been removed and their main course put in front of them, he said smoothly, 'I'm right, aren't I, Jenna? Is it because he left you alone and carrying his child?'

She was so relieved she started to tremble as the tension flooded out of her. Of course James had no idea who Lucy's real father was. She was being a fool to fear even for a minute that he might. Male-like her lack of interest in his sex had piqued his curiosity and he was applying what, to his masculine-tuned mind, was the most logical explanation for her attitude.

'Think what you like,' she told him coolly, applying herself to her sole, her appetite almost miraculously restored. The relief of knowing that he wasn't some all-powerful being, capable of probing her deepest secrets was a heady release. She drank more wine, enjoying its subtle flavour, allowing their waiter to refill her glass.

A little to her surprise James did not press the issue, turning instead to ask her how long she expected it to be before she would be ready to move into the Hall.

'It all depends.' Her response was guarded. 'If it is sound structurally, as I believe it will be, I had intended to move in almost immediately so that I can supervise the work as it takes place.' She frowned, a thought suddenly striking her. 'How will you be able to conduct your business affairs away from London?'

'In exactly the same way as I do when I'm in the Caribbean or the States,' he told her drily. 'In these days of advanced electronics and computers, distance is no bar.'

'But you won't want to work among all the chaos of alterations and refurbishment surely?' Jenna suggested. Unadmitted as yet — but there in her mind all the same — had been the conviction that once they were married she would be able to escape from James on the very valid excuse of being needed on site to check that all was progressing as it should be.

'On the contrary,' came his laconic drawl, 'I'm quite looking forward to it — it should prove extremely interesting.'

'But what about Sarah? Surely it would be unwise to move her at the moment? There's her visit to hospital and —— '

'York has an excellent hospital equally well-equipped to deal with her condition,' James told her coolly. 'I've already checked.' His eyes held hers as he said softly, 'Stop wriggling, Jenna. You've laid down your conditions for this marriage; now it's my turn to lay down mine. Providing there are no structural problems with the old Hall, we shall be married at the end of the month — I'm already due to fly out to the Caribbean that week, and undue comment expressed by the Press about the suddenness of our marriage can be logically explained away by the fact that I want to combine an existing business trip with a honeymoon — extremely unromantic but less likely to give rise to speculation than a rushed ceremony and then an abrupt departure for Yorkshire, don't you think?'

Jenna was forced to agree, fighting down an increasing sense of panic and unreality as James continued. 'Once we return from the Caribbean I'm hoping that we'll be able to move North almost straight away. From what you've told me and I've seen myself, the renovation of the old Hall isn't going to be accomplished overnight, so my suggestion is that we move into the older part for the present, while they're working on the Georgian wing, and then transfer over to that once it's been finished to allow them to work on the rest of the house. Some of the rooms are reasonably habitable, and if you think you're going to have any problems organising a suite to accommodate ourselves plus Sarah and Lucy, then let me know and I'll see what I can do.'

His arrogant assumption that he could achieve more than she could infuriated Jenna. Her chin lifted and tilted firmly. She looked him in the eye and said coolly, 'That won't be necessary. I can manage.'

Just too late she saw the triumphant gleam shimmer in his eyes, and realised that he had challenged her deliberately, baiting the trap so cleverly that she had fallen into it without even being aware that it was there — not just fallen, but rushed headlong to meet it, Jenna admitted ruefully, willing herself not to give vent to the anger she could feel building up inside her.

'Once we're settled, I think it would be a good idea to find a local school for Lucy,' James continued, apparently oblivious to her rising fury. 'She isn't happy at her present school, and since one of the reasons we're getting married is for her sake, it seems only reasonable that she should be there to benefit from our relationship.'

Jenna waited until he had finished, and then, drawing a calming breath, enquired sweetly, 'Anything else?'

To her surprise James laughed. 'Ah . . . so that red hair is indicative of a temper after all! I *was* beginning to wonder.' He saw her confusion and said softly, 'Has no one ever teased you before, Jenna?'

Teased her? She stared at him in bewilderment. Yes . . . once long ago, Rachel . . . Tears blurred her vision, a terrible aching pain flooding over her as the memory of the agony of the loss of her sister swept over her. For a moment James was forgotten and she was back in the past, sharing jokes with her sister, sharing the warmth of their close relationship.

'Jenna . . . '

His voice was an alien intrusion in her private world and she wanted to shut it out, but it was too late. Blinking rapidly she banished the tears threatening to fall. She had finished her meal and she pushed back her chair slightly saying, 'I think it's time we left, James. With all that I've got to accomplish between now and the end of the month, I'm going to need an early start in the morning.' She judged it best to ignore his last comment and her own reaction to it. He was a dangerously perceptive man, and she wished with all her heart she was not going to have to marry him, but he wouldn't let her escape now. He wanted the Hall too much for that.

CHAPTER NINE

'YES... structurally it's fine ...' Jenna cradled the tele-phone receiver against her shoulder as she listened to the surveyor's report on the old Hall, scribbling down notes with her free hand.

Maggie came in, grinning from ear to ear as she de-posited a typed message on Jenna's desk. Jenna frowned as her eyes flicked over it.

'Lunch at 1 p.m. with James,' Maggie had written.

Damn, she had already planned to work through lunch today. There was an awful lot to do if the Hall was going to be ready for them to move into in the time James had stipulated. She could, of course, tell him that what he wanted was impossible, but Jenna had the un-pleasant feeling that if she did, somehow he would find a way of proving her wrong.

Picking up the note, she scribbled across it, 'Okay', and handed it back to Maggie.

Ten minutes later, when she had finished on the phone and her secretary had come back into the office, Maggie enquired lightly, 'Dare I ask if this is more than merely a business meeting, or will I get my head bitten off?'

Without lifting her head from the papers on her desk Jenna said calmly, 'James and I are getting married.'

For a moment there was silence, and then Maggie said weakly, 'Tell me if I'm hearing things. You and James Allingham are getting married?'

'That's right.' Jenna stood up and walked briskly

over to a filing cabinet, pulling open a drawer. 'Yes, that's right . . . At the end of the month.'

'But, Jenna . . .' Maggie swallowed with visible effort, and asked helplessly, 'Where have I gone wrong? Why doesn't some gorgeous-looking millionaire sweep me off my feet and ask me to marry him?'

Jenna could have told her, but instead she smiled rather grimly, and wondered what Maggie would say if she told her she was welcome to James and his millions just as long as she was allowed to keep the old Hall.

'The end of the month? Rather a rush.'

'James has business in the Caribbean, and he thought we might as well combine it with a honeymoon,' Jenna told her, grudgingly appreciating James's wisdom in suggesting his Caribbean trip as a good excuse for their haste.

'Lucky you. He's involved in a holiday complex development out there, isn't he?' Maggie asked, wrinkling her forehead. 'Wow! Isn't Richard going to be sick! Is there any chance of us getting any business from the complex?'

'James is talking about using us as consultants for the more luxurious part of it,' Jenna told her. 'From what little he's told me about the complex, I think most of it's already completed.'

'Richard *will* be sick,' Maggie claimed positively with another grin. 'This will beat the Spanish contract he's got from Harry Waters into a cocked hat.'

'If the contract actually comes off with Harry Waters,' Jenna agreed. 'You know what he's like for wriggling.'

'Mmm, but word on the grapevine is that he's one of Richard's backers.'

So much for her accusation to James, Jenna thought wryly. She should have guessed that Harry Waters might have a hand in Richard's defection. He had complained bitterly about her charges on more than one occasion in the past, and no doubt this was his way of getting back at her. She had sensed on the last occasion when she rebuffed him that she had made an enemy of him.

At ten to one she was suddenly attacked by a swarm of butterflies busily fluttering in her stomach. At first she dismissed the reason for their presence and then when work became impossible she got up and walked tensely over to her window. There was no reason for her to feel in the least nervous. She and James had struck a bargain and that was all there was to it.

By one o'clock she had managed to gain control of herself. When Maggie knocked softly on her door she was seated behind her desk, studying some papers.

'James is here,' her secretary told her, standing to one side so that he could walk into the room.

He walked easily towards her, and by the time Jenna's stunned mind had assimilated the fact that he did not intend to stop on the other side of her desk, he was already sweeping her up out of her chair.

'Ready for lunch?'

The question was innocuous enough in itself, but murmured against her mouth it had a totally overwhelming effect on her. Because of his grip on her arms it was impossible to step back from James as she wished, neither could she berate him for his outrageous behaviour with Maggie standing by, an avid spectator of what was going on.

'I don't think I'm very hungry.' She said it stiffly, her body tense with rejection and anger. How dare he walk in here and treat her like this, when he knew what they had agreed?

His laughter further infuriated her. She shot him a

bitterly corrosive glare and tensed still further.

'No, neither do I,' he agreed wickedly, looking at her in a way that brought a wave of angrily disbelieving colour to her skin. How dare he look at her like that — as though he were already visualising her naked and in his bed, and in full view of Maggie too, when he knew quite well what they had agreed?

For a moment, Jenna was so caught up in her own anger that she was completely unaware of anything else, including Maggie's muffled, 'Er . . . I think I hear the phone,' and the hasty closing of her office door.

The moment it did close James released her. Startled to be free she stepped back from him and almost immediately overbalanced as her heel struck the foot of her chair. As James reached for her she struck him away, her face hard with anger.

'You know what we agreed,' she seethed, backing away from him. 'You —— '

'I remember.' His voice unlike hers was perfectly controlled. 'However, I don't remember either of us agreeing that we would make the true nature of our marriage an open secret.'

He was right, of course, but Jenna was beyond acknowledging that.

'Oh, I see,' she jeered, 'the great James Allingham doesn't want anyone to know that at least one woman doesn't find him irresistible.'

Imperceptibly his expression changed, hardened, anger and a certain degree of icy contempt killing the amusement that had been in his eyes.

'What makes you so sure it will be *my* sexual appeal that will be held in doubt,' he taunted softly. 'Remember, you're the one with the hang-ups about sex. It isn't exactly a secret, how you feel about the male sex, Jenna. You're going to have to be careful. If it becomes common knowledge that physically you can't bear me anywhere near you, people are going to start to talk.' He shrugged, watching her like a cat at a mousehole. 'No one's ever been in doubt about my sexual proclivities, but yours . . . No doubt there are quite a few unattractive motives the less charitable among the gutter-press writers could attribute to your agreement to marry me — they won't hurt me, Jenna, but they could hurt you.'

It was no less than the truth, but, God, how she hated him for bringing it home to her. She wanted to lash out at him physically, to destroy, to cause him the same anguish he had just caused her. And then the full meaning of what he had just intimated burst upon her and she cringed, physically and mentally. She had never been attracted to any member of her own sex, and his blunt suggestion that there might be those who would say publicly any different made her feel ill with inner anger. Why should anyone's private life become a matter for public speculation? She knew reporters . . . once they thought there might be the slightest suggestion of any scandal in her life, they would start digging and they would not stop until . . . until they disinterred her sister.

'Jenna!'

James's voice cut sharply through her tumultuous thoughts. 'Dear God, that's not —— You aren't —— '

Oddly enough he looked as pale and shaken as she felt.

'No.' She forced the denial from an aching throat, tense with pain and fear.

She reached behind her chair for the jacket to the suit she was wearing, her back to him as she reaffirmed it. 'No. There's nothing like that.'

He took her jacket from her and she suffered his

helping her into it. 'Where are we going for lunch?'

'Wait and see.'

With an ease that she resented privately he managed to find a cruising taxi the moment they stepped outside. Since Jenna got in first she didn't catch what he said to the driver, but frowned in bewilderment when the cab stopped, not outside a restaurant, but instead outside Garrard's, the Crown jewellers.

'Come on.' James helped her out, guiding her towards the main door. The commissionaire opened it for them and James murmured something to him.

The commissionaire disappeared, and Jenna gazed at her surroundings, awestruck by such opulent magnificence. Before she had time to speak the commissionaire was back, another man behind him.

'Mr Allingham,' he greeted James with a courteous smile, 'and this, of course, must be your fiancée?'

Jenna forced a rather stilted smile.

'If you'll both come this way.'

A private room had been put at their disposal. Jenna sat down in a deep, buttoned velvet chair still trying to get her breath as a velvet tray bearing a selection of rings was presented for her consideration. Nearly all of them comprised diamonds and emeralds, and the reason for this was explained when James told her, 'I specified emeralds this morning when I made the appointment, because of your eyes, but if you have some other preference . . . '

Jenna had not, mainly because she had never given any thought to her choice of an engagement ring — not even since James had put his proposition to her. For some reason it had never struck her that he would give her an engagement ring. Her throat closed tightly in a mixture of pain and anguish as she stared at the exquisite rings presented for her consideration. She wanted to tell James that she had no need of an engagement ring, but she sensed that he would overrule her. To judge from the size and quality of the stones just one of those rings would cost far more than she needed to overcome her present cashflow problems, and a shaft of bitterness pierced her. Perhaps she should choose the most expensive-looking of them all, and then pawn it. Just for a moment she dwelt on James's reaction to discovering she had managed to evade his trap by pawning the engagement ring he had bought her. It was frightening enough to make her shiver slightly.

The gems in front of her shimmered and danced, cold green and white lights sparkling from them. They were all beautiful, but cold and empty — like her marriage would be. Suddenly, she knew she could not wear any of them. She turned impulsively to James shaking her head. 'They're all lovely . . . but . . . '

James was frowning. The man on the other side of the small antique desk staring as though unable to believe his ears. If she refused a ring James would feel humiliated, Jenna realised suddenly. She had within her grasp the perfect weapon for hurting and humiliating him as he had done her on far too many occasions already. The words hovered in her mind, but instead she heard herself saying huskily, 'James, I've always wanted to have an antique engagement ring. I . . . '

It was almost funny how both male faces cleared as if by magic. 'Of course,' James was actually smiling at her. 'I should have thought of that. My fiancée is an interior designer, with a special love of the Georgian period,' he informed the other man.

While Jenna was wondering how on earth James knew of her love of that particular period the sales assistant was beaming. 'We have a beautiful Georgian ring in at the moment, sir. A client has asked us to dispose of it on his behalf. If you would give me a moment.'

He wasn't gone very long, returning with a shabby leather box which he opened and then put down on the table. Jenna caught her breath and then held it. Tears smarted weakly in her eyes, burning the back of her throat as she stared at the smooth circle of gold. An intricate and delicate setting had been woven in gold to display the ring's one beautiful emerald. Although it was nothing like the modern stones she had seen with their sparkling diamond surrounds, Jenna sensed none the less that the stone she was looking at surpassed those others in its perfection. It had a depth and purity of colour that fascinated her, drew her, until she felt almost as though she could drown in its green depths. Its effect was almost mesmeric and she had to blink before she could tear her glance away.

'It's beautiful.' She was whispering without knowing why she should do so.

'And extremely rare,' the salesman told her with a smile. 'It's been handed down through the same family since the days of Elizabeth I — at least the stone has: it was placed in its present setting during George III's reign as a betrothal gift from the then owner to his fiancée. The present owner has no immediate family to hand it on to — by tradition it has been the betrothal ring of his family since Georgian times. He lost his fiancée during the last war and has remained alone since then.'

Jenna looked at the ring again and shook her head regretfully. 'It must be terribly expensive . . . ' She was using the words as an excuse and a defence. What really prevented her from sliding the ring on to her finger was the feeling that up until now it had always been given and worn with love, and somehow she could not tarnish all that the ring represented by allowing James to give it to her to seal what was only a business arrangement. Out of the corner of her eye she saw James shake his head at the other man.

'I think we'll leave it for now,' she heard James saying easily as he stood up.

As Jenna turned towards the door, James paused to say something to the sales assistant but Jenna wasn't listening. She felt a curious numbness envelop her and she knew that if she had to wear an engagement ring, that was the one she wanted. Already she was half regretting her emotional decision, but as James took her arm and escorted her out into the main foyer of the jewellers', she knew it was too late to tell him she had changed her mind.

'I'm sorry to be so difficult to please.' She made the apology in a stilted voice.

'Don't worry about it.' James sounded quite relaxed and unworried. 'If anything, it's my fault, I should have given you more warning.' He glanced at his watch and then indicated a wine bar a short distance away. 'Would a quick lunch here be okay with you? I'm afraid I don't have much time left.'

'Fine.'

They were lucky enough to find a double booth which was quite private. James had behaved so well over her reluctance to select a ring that Jenna was feeling almost guilty.

'Will that fierce feminine pride of yours object if I tell you that I've made arrangements for us to visit my godmother this weekend?' he questioned once they had their food. 'I would have consulted you first, but when I rang this morning Maggie said you were busy. My godmother is getting on in years — she was very good to me when my mother first died and I know she would be hurt if I let her find out about us through the press. I also wanted to ask her if she would have Sarah while we're away. She doesn't live too far away from Lucy's school, so if we can get all the arrangements for the wedding fixed up by the weekend, I thought we might possibly take Lucy out of school on Saturday afternoon, so that she can meet my godmother, and we can tell her about the arrangements for the wedding.'

It all sounded so reasonable that Jenna felt she could hardly object.

'The surveyor rang this morning and confirmed that there's no real structural work necessary on the Hall,' she told James when she had signified her agreement. 'I had thought of going up there this week to earmark living accommodation for us while the contractors are working on the Georgian wing. What exactly will you need?'

'A bedroom, of course . . . ' He glanced wryly at her. 'I am assuming that I won't be sharing yours, but if I could make the suggestion that they at least adjoin in some way so that it doesn't give rise to too much speculation?' Without waiting for her agreement he went on, 'A sitting-room-cum-office . . . '

'And somewhere for your computers, I expect.'

'Well, I was thinking one of the cellars could quite easily be converted into a computer room. I had a look at them the last time we were there and they seem perfectly dry. I'll need to go up there and have another look, but I can't fit that in this week. Maybe next. Sarah will need a ground-floor bedroom, if that can be organised, and I think it might be a good idea if we had some sort of communal sitting-room — Lucy will expect to come home for the odd weekend, and for both hers and Sarah's sake, I want to give our relationship as normal an air as possible.'

Jenna could not see any problems with the accommodation requirements he was outlining — they were very much in line with her own thoughts on the subject. There was a very old-fashioned kitchen in the older wing which Sir Alan's staff had obviously used, and a small breakfast-room off it. They could not move into the rooms in their present state, but Jenna believed with a little money and a lot of imagination she could turn what were at present very drab and offputting rooms into warm and pleasant living accommodation. In fact, she could already feel herself responding to the challenge of doing so, and with a small start she realised that this was the first time she had actually anticipated with pleasure the thought of designing a background for a family unit which included herself. Forgetting her animosity towards James, she burst out impulsively, 'There are several large cellars, maybe one of them could be converted into some sort of gym area for Sarah to help her exercise her legs?'

'Good idea. In fact I'd already wondered about having an indoor pool built — a properly organised exercise room off it might not be a bad idea. When I'm in London I try to visit my gym twice a week at least.'

He saw her expression and said coolly, 'No, not out of vanity, I assure you. I happen to believe that it is the responsibility of every individual to maintain their own health and fitness . . . a certain amount of exercise is necessary to do that. No doubt in man's cavemen days he got enough exercise to keep his body in good condition simply trying to exist; these days it's rather different. Like most businessmen I tend to exercise my brain at the expense of my body, so I find a bi-weekly workout of double benefit — as well as keeping me physically fit, it helps to get rid of any aggression too. You should try it,' he added suavely.

Jenna fought down an urge to make a snappy retort

and said equably instead, 'You don't have to convert me, I already agree with everything you've said.' She made a wry face. 'I try to get to a gym twice a week or so myself, but like all good intentions . . . '

Her mind tracked back to the Hall. 'I agree with what you say about a pool, but mightn't it be rather difficult for Sarah to reach a separate pool and gym area in her wheelchair, especially once we get into winter?'

She wasn't sure what he planned but suspected he was talking about building a self-contained pool and exercise unit somewhere in the grounds. To her surprise, he shook his head and explained.

'What I'd got in mind was to have a conservatory built on to the house at the back of the Georgian wing — something along the lines of the traditional orangeries that were so fashionable at that time. The pool would be sunk into the floor of the conservatory: the warmth of the water and the moisture from it would make it an ideal place to grow semi-tropical creepers and the like. I think it would make a very attractive spot to relax in on a cold, wintry day.'

Jenna could only agree with him, a picture of the pool house conservatory already unfolding in her mind's eye. It would have a traditional black and white tiled floor, and white cane furniture, perhaps with green and white patterned cotton covers.

'Come back!' James mocked lightly, indicating her as yet untouched glass of wine. 'I suppose I should be flattered that you find my idea so appealing. In the meantime, I agree with you that it would be a good idea to provide a small gym area for Sarah.' He frowned, and pushed his plate away. 'I'm concerned about her, Jenna. She ought to be making at least some recovery by now. The doctors assure me that there's nothing physically wrong with her. I know how she feels about her parent's death but to keep on punishing herself because of it . . . '

'Perhaps it isn't herself she's punishing,' Jenna said, 'but you.'

James looked at her blankly and then comprehension darkened his eyes with pain. 'Of course . . . yes . . . that makes much more sense,' he said wryly. 'I wonder why I didn't think of it first.'

'You're probably standing too close to the situation to see it as clearly as someone on the outside. You know that Sarah feels that you disliked her mother?'

'Yes.' He was silent for a moment and then said curtly. 'The whole situation is extremely complicated, I can't —— ' He broke off as a man walked past their table and then did a double-take.

'Well, well!' Shrewd blue eyes went from Jenna to James and then back again. 'What have we here? Two lovebirds, perhaps, hatching a little secret?'

Jenna recognised him now, a well-known gossip columnist. She heard James swear under his breath and then he said coolly, 'You may as well be the first to know, Lyons. Jenna and I are getting married at the end of this month.'

As she listened to him saying the words, Jenna knew that now there was no escape. A tight feeling of panic coiled up inside her, and then, unbelievably, it started to ebb away as James touched her hand. She blinked, totally unable to believe that his touch could have relaxed and reassured her to such an extent.

'Come on, it's time we left,' he told her, helping her to her feet, and into her jacket.

For the first time she did not flinch beneath his touch, saying only as he guided her towards the exit, 'But what about your godmother?'

'I told her we were getting engaged, but what I said

about wanting you to meet her still stands.' He paused, frowned and then added, 'I was hoping you would agree to our marriage taking place in her village church — it can be arranged, I've already checked.'

Jenna's first instinct was to refuse, and then she checked the impulse. Whether she liked it or not she and James were going to be married, and it would be in her own best interests to get along with him as best she could. It was really of little importance to her where they got married, and what was the point in childishly antagonising him now for no purpose?

'If that's what you want.'

As they stepped outside into the June sunshine, Jenna caught the glimmer of amusement in his eyes.

'You're unusually docile,' he mocked, watching her reaction. 'I wonder why?'

'No reason. It's a matter of indifference to me where we get married.'

James had a business appointment at two-thirty but he put Jenna in a taxi to take her back to her own office. She was glad of the mountain of work Richard's abrupt and unexpected departure had brought to her desk. It stopped her from dwelling too much on what lay ahead. She had committed herself to marriage with James now and there was no escape — not without hurting Lucy, and possibly Sarah too. Jenna sensed that James's stepsister needed someone to confide in and turn to, and she had genuinely felt compassion for the young girl. It was a devastating experience to lose the people you loved most in life — Jenna knew that from her own life. Sarah already had a maturity that Lucy lacked, and Jenna knew that maturity came solely from experiencing emotional pain.

How strange were the threads that linked and drew lives together. How could she have known that day standing outside the old Hall that soon she would be facing the reality of marriage to the man she had seen then and instantly disliked and despised? She had already learned how foolishly unperceptive she had been in despising him. Would her dislike prove to be as unfounded as her contempt? What a strange thought for her to have, thought Jenna, putting down her pen and walking agitatedly over to her office window. She always stood there when she was disturbed: it was as though looking out of it held a magical power to soothe her in some strange way. But why should the thought of losing her dislike of James upset her so much? Surely it could only be beneficial if they could co-exist in harmony? But it did upset her and, more than that, it alarmed her in some intangible intuitive way, as though by losing her dislike of him she might in some way be making herself vulnerable.

Shrugging the thought aside she returned to her desk. She had a lot to get through this week, especially if she was going to fit in a visit to Yorkshire. In her mind's eye she saw the older part of the house and earmarked the room they could use. Sarah could have the downstairs study which had French windows out on to the gardens. There was an attractive sunken garden just outside them with a paved sitting area and an old-fashioned rose arbour. James could occupy the bedroom that had been Sir Alan's. She shuddered in distaste at the thought of using it herself. As she remembered it there was a dressing-room off it and a private bathroom. She would have the bedroom next door, which, if she remembered correctly, also had access to the dressing-room and had possibly been Sir Alan's wife's bedroom. If either of the girls queried their having separate rooms she would make some excuse that she was a poor sleeper — it was, after all, quite true.

Suddenly and all too vividly she remembered her dream, hurriedly shutting away the mental images as quickly as they formed, trying to deny their force and power. That dream had been a complete mental aberration conjured up by she knew not what — a never-to-be-repeated folly, which she preferred not to think about.

That evening Lucy rang from school sounding chirpy and bright — and obviously very excited about the wedding. Without meaning to, Jenna found herself telling her about the weekend and before Lucy rang off she had extracted a promise from Jenna that they would most definitely take her out of school on the Saturday afternoon. When she replaced the receiver Jenna admitted rather sadly that Lucy's present happiness was directly as a result of James's presence in their lives, and while that thought was in her mind on impulse she dialled the private number James had given her. He answered on the third ring, his voice so calm and easily recognisable that Jenna could not understand why on earth her heart was beating so fast.

'I rang to have a chat with Sarah,' she told him a little breathlessly. 'I thought she might be feeling a little bit lonely — even having second thoughts about getting a step-sister-in-law.'

'That's very thoughtful of you. She is a bit down tonight — nothing to do with you. She just has these bouts of depression from time to time. Hang on a sec . . . '

The line went dead, and then within seconds Jenna was talking to Sarah, noting the faint listlessness of the young girl's voice, which gradually disappeared as they chatted.

'I'd better go now,' Jenna said after a while. 'I need an early night after all the excitement of this weekend.'

'I'll put you back to James, then,' Sarah told her, doing just that before Jenna could protest.

'Sarah put me back on to you before I could tell her not to.' Why did she sound so defensive? He already knew quite well that she had no desire to speak to him.

'No doubt she thinks that neither of us will sleep without saying good night to one another,' James said with irony. 'Teenagers are like that, or don't you remember?'

Her throat closed up and she could not respond. She could remember her own teenage dreams all too well, before reality had smashed and destroyed them beyond any kind of repair.

'Jenna?'

'Yes . . . yes, I'm still here.' She could hear the sharp edge of irritation under his voice. 'I'm tired, James. I'll say good night and let you get on with whatever you were doing before I interrupted you.'

'Scrutinising contracts for various franchises connected with the Caribbean complex,' he told her drily. 'Very exciting stuff.'

Jenna did not speak to or see James until much later in the week. An item had appeared in the gossip press about them, announcing their engagement, the day after they had been spotted in the wine bar by the reporter, but since James had already sent a formal announcement to *The Times* it caused very little stir in Jenna's life, apart from bringing Richard storming into her office one afternoon, to accuse her of out-manoeuvring him and deliberately encouraging Harry Waters to entice him away so that she would have the business to herself.

'No doubt Allingham will put plenty of fat contracts

your way,' Richard sneered. Then added viciously, 'What's he got that the rest of us don't possess, Jenna? It must be something pretty special to thaw out a cold bitch like you!'

There was more in the same vein, vituperative and distasteful, but, strangely enough, none of it really touched her, and Jenna's only emotion when Richard finally ran out of steam and stormed out of her office was one of empty tiredness coupled with a faint relief that she was no longer connected, if only professionally, with such a petty and grubby-minded individual. His comments about her own lack of sexual appeal hadn't touched her. How could they? She knew they were true, but they had little power to hurt. All that did amaze her was that Richard should actually think that she and James were lovers, when he so obviously held an extremely low opinion of her sexual attractiveness.

Only his last few words had struck home and even then not for the reasons he might have supposed.

'Just you wait,' he had jeered on finally leaving, 'he'll grow tired of you, once he realises what you're really like. A cold bitch like you will never hold a man like him, and I'm really going to enjoy being around to see you fall to pieces when he walks out on you, Jenna . . . because a man like that doesn't give anything for nothing, and when he realises how little you've got to offer him as a woman you can be sure he'll make you pay for his favours in some other way. I shouldn't be surprised if he takes this whole business that you're so passionately attached to from you in lieu . . .'

She wasn't worried that James would do as Richard was suggesting, but what did concern her was the truth in Richard's unspoken suggestion that James was a man with a keenly honed sexual appetite. She didn't expect him to remain celibate; after all, she hardly had the right, but there was bound to come a time when his relationships outside marriage would catch the public eye and how would that affect Lucy? Already her niece had put him on a pedestal, and not just because she thought of him as her father. She would have to worry about that bridge when the time came to cross it, Jenna decided wearily, managing a reassuring smile for Maggie who came into her office in the wake of Richard's exit, wide-eyed with anxiety and concern.

'He pushed past me before I could stop him and then the phone rang.'

'Don't worry about it,' Jenna assured her. 'Who was on the phone?'

'The bank. I said you'd call them back.'

As Jenna had suspected Gordon Burns was delighted to hear that she was marrying James. 'I suppose *now* if I ask you for credit . . ?'

'The criteria remain the same,' he told her firmly. But added with a smile in his voice, 'However, of course with your husband's guarantee . . . '

Jenna let the matter go, but in her own heart of hearts she knew she had come to a crossroad in her professional life. Originally when she bought the Hall, it had been her intention to keep the London end of the business going with Richard standing in her place. Now, with James's financial backing behind her, she could afford to take on a fully qualified partner and do exactly that, but the problems she had recently experienced had soured her. If she was totally honest with herself she had preferred her business when it was small and newly emerging and when she herself was responsible for every aspect of a contract. She enjoyed talking to suppliers, buying, spending time combing antique shops for just the right item. She still wanted to specialise as she had planned when she originally bought the old

Hall, but possibly on a much smaller scale.

As James's wife she had no need to work for a living. He had told her as much, insisting that he intended to make her a generous personal allowance, even when she had told him she did not want it. Now she was beginning to accept that there would be a change of pace and direction to her life: she would need time to spend with Sarah, to spend on the house, to spend, too, with Lucy if she did transfer to a local school. The driving force that had motivated so much of her life — the need to earn sufficient to support Lucy and herself — was gone. She could still work but at a far less intense level. For some reason she had become acutely conscious of all that she had missed from life — all that she *was* missing. During the week she had spent a day at the old Hall as she had planned to, and she had found the slower pace of life the house itself enforced upon her strangely delightful.

Up until she and James married she would be very busy, but once they returned from the Caribbean she intended to reassess the situation *vis-à-vis* her business. Most of her existing contracts were nearing completion and there was no reason really for her to keep the London end of the business running. Even Maggie had mentioned that she fancied a change and that her sister in the States had asked her out there for a visit.

She was conscious of being carried by an unstoppable tide towards a new life, and instead of fighting against that current, she seemed to be allowing herself to be carried by it.

For Lucy's sake she had no real option, she told herself, no alternative at all.

The day Jenna went to the Hall it rained. She called in briefly on Nancy and Bill in the morning. Both of them were openly thrilled about her engagement, although

Nancy clucked over her lack of a ring. She stopped just long enough to have a cup of coffee and then hurried on to the Hall. By lunchtime she had surveyed the rooms she intended to turn into their living quarters, and had made an inventory of what furniture was there that they could use and what would need to be bought.

The rooms were in the Tudor part of the building and still retained their original panelling and parquet block floors. By the time she left for York later in the afternoon Jenna had a clear picture in her mind of how she intended their temporary apartment to look when they moved in. Although the accommodation there would only be temporary, she wanted to make it look as attractive and homelike as possible. Fortunately, because it was summer, the lack of central heating would not be too much of a problem. New bathrooms would have to be installed, but once again she could see no major difficulty since the room she had selected for Sarah's bedroom was immediately under James's room, and could share the drainage already in existence for the ancient bathroom off that room.

Her head buzzing with ideas, she parked her car in York, and hurried towards the architects' office to drop off some specifications for the central heating in the Georgian wing that they had sent her, and to return some detailed plans they had submitted for the new larger kitchen and the attractive morning-room off it.

The partner Jenna had dealt with was not available, but she left the papers with his assistant, enquiring on impulse if he could direct her to a local antique dealer with a good reputation. What she wanted were some pieces of Jacobean oak furniture to supplement the odd bits she had already found scattered around the house. None of what she had found were particularly good pieces but they did have the virtue of being authentic. A rather battered Queen Anne bachelor chest had caught her eye, although the walnut veneer which had been laid on top of the oak from which the chest was made, was in need of some attention.

Armed with the information she had requested, Jenna set out in the direction she had been told. The antique shop she was looking for was tucked away down one of York's many attractive narrow alleyways — or wynds as they were called locally. She was just about to push open the door when a man emerged, almost knocking her over as he stepped backwards out of the shop. The moment he was aware of what he had done he began to apologise. Laughter lines crinkled the corners of his eyes, plain ordinary hazel eyes, Jenna noticed, but kind eyes for all that. She guessed he was somewhere around forty, tall, with a lanky, lean frame and the kind of soft brown hair that flopped over his forehead. His smile was wry and very sincere and he had, she reflected, a certain boyish charm that had its own appeal.

'Are you looking for something special, or just browsing?' he asked Jenna when she had assured him that she was unhurt.

'Jacobean furniture,' she told him coolly. 'In particular a bookcase and a gateleg table.'

'Well, I don't have anything like that in at the moment.' He frowned, obviously deep in thought which gave Jenna time to study him with renewed interest. She had not realised when he first bumped into her that he was the owner of the shop. He would be quite successful, she conceded, watching him. He had the sort of manner that was reassuring to old ladies and young children.

'I think I know where I might be able to get the gateleg table. The bookcase is something else. We do get

them, but they don't come cheap. What do you want it
for?'

Jenna explained briefly.

'You've bought the old Hall? Lucky you,' he told her
enviously. 'It's a magnificent house.'

'Yes, and my fiancé wants us to move in in just under
two months' time, so I'm trying to get a small apartment
sorted out as quickly as I can.' She went on to explain to
him that they would only be living in it on a temporary
basis while the Georgian wing was renovated.

'Well, I'll certainly keep my eyes open for a bookcase.
Would you care to see the table?'

Jenna followed him back inside and studied the table
he showed her. It was a reasonable example of what she
wanted, and quite reasonably priced as well. She paid
him for it, and arranged that he would keep it for her
until she was ready to have it delivered.

By the time she was ready to leave she had the
address of a man who he assured her would bring the
dull linenfold panelling back to life and the names of
several other local antique dealers of repute who might
be able to help her in her quest for a bookcase.

It was too late for her to visit them all now, but Jenna
decided to give them a ring from London.

She got back late, just in time to hear the dying rings
of her telephone as she raced to pick up the receiver.
Knowing that it had probably only been James who had
said that he would ring her that evening she was surprised by her own feeling of disappointment. No doubt
it was because she was buoyed up about her plans for
the house, Jenna told herself as she prepared for bed. It
was only natural that in her excitement she would want
to share them with someone.

By the end of the next day she had organised curtains
for all the rooms: bedhangings for the four-poster in

what would be James's room and fabric to re-cover the
window seats in hers and James's bedroom and the
downstairs sitting-room. She had also bought carpets
for all the rooms — James had told her to spare no
expense in preparing their temporary apartment but
Jenna had been cautious about spending money, choosing carefully. The Persian rugs she had selected were
soft and silky, brilliantly hued in rich reds and blues
which would set off the heavy oak and the linenfold.
Only on James's four-poster had she been what she herself considered outrageously extravagant ordering a
very traditional and very expensive heavy brocade in a
fleur de lis pattern which had been very much in vogue
in the Stuart period.

The brocade was hand-embroidered in the traditional manner, gold thread gleaming against a soft
cream background. She had brought all the measurements back with her, plus photographs, and the firm
she was using was one entrusted with work by the
National Trust on many of their historic properties. A
small footstool and a comfortable winged chair were to
be covered in the same fabric and Jenna had selected
plain, cream silk curtains in exactly the same shade as
the brocade.

There was also a four-poster in her room although
not as large as the one in James's; for that she had selected a less expensive brocade, again in cream, but this
time with a design worked on it in blues and greens.
She had chosen a toning blue silk for the lining of the
bedhangings and the trim of the bedcover — the ones
in James's room would be lined in a dull, rich gold and
would have a truly masculine ambience, while hers was
brighter, more feminine.

Three new bathrooms would have to be installed,
one for James, one downstairs for Sarah, and a further

one upstairs connecting with Jenna's room that Lucy could use as well when she was home from school.

Jenna had selected plain, Victorian-styled traditional sanitaryware judging it the most acceptable choice to complement the décor.

By the time Friday afternoon came round, Jenna was conscious of a satisfied tiredness. The week had been an exhausting one and she was very pleased with what she had accomplished. That keeping herself so busy had a secondary and almost more important purpose — in keeping her mind off her looming marriage — was something she preferred not to think about.

James had already telephoned and arranged to pick her up at her apartment at six. They were taking Sarah down to his godmother's with them, and would have dinner when they reached their destination.

For the first time in as long as she could remember since she had had the money to spend on herself Jenna was perplexed about what to wear. Nearly all her clothes were geared towards her life as a business-woman — neat, immaculate suits chosen for their conservatism; a good cashmere coat in dark navy, elegant silk shirts and fine cashmere sweaters in neutral colours.

What did she have in her wardrobe that was suitable garb for a new fiancée meeting someone important in her husband-to-be's life for the first time?

The answer was she would have to wear one of her normal business outfits, but as she dressed in a tailored, beige, linen summer suit with a soft, coffee-brown toning shirt, for the first time Jenna did not feel comfortable in her clothes. Although she was unaware of it she wore her clothes well, her movements economic but co-ordinated in a way that drew attention to the slim length of her thigh beneath the fine fabric of her skirt.

Because she had spent so much time dithering about

what to wear and pack she was running late. In her suitcase were her jeans and a couple of casual tops, a plain
black dinner dress and another tailored suit.

She was just about to loop her hair up into a chignon
when she heard the bell. Impatience made her fingers
clumsy, and in the end she had to leave her hair loose
while she went to let James in.

He surveyed her outfit thoughtfully, a tiny frown
pleating his forehead.

'Rather formal, isn't it?' he drawled finally, his scrutiny completed. 'My godmother won't know if it's my
fiancée she's meeting or a new member of the board!'

Despite, or perhaps because of, her own reservations
Jenna instantly fired up, her skin tinting angry pink as
she spun round and said fiercely, 'I'm sorry if my taste
in clothes doesn't appeal to you, James, but it isn't too
late for you to change your mind and find someone else
to marry you!'

She knew she was goading him, but his comment,
coming on top of her own doubts about the suitability of
her clothes prickled her. Jenna could still remember the
days after Lucy's birth and later when money had been
scarce and she had been desperately conscious of her
shabby appearance and how detrimental it was to the
image she had wanted to project. Clothes might not
make the man or woman, but they certainly helped to
create a visual impression and they were important.

'It would be much easier simply to change your clothes,' he retorted softly. 'Why did you choose that outfit,
Jenna? To remind me of my promise not to touch? I've
never seen you wearing anything feminine yet.'

'Not all women like frills and bows,' Jenna snapped
back, disliking him more with every second that passed.

'No, but *you* are an extremely feminine woman,
whether you're prepared to admit it or not, and yet for

some reason you deliberately try to deny that femininity. Why?'

'I have to go and do my hair,' Jenna hurried towards
the door. 'I won't be long.'

She had thought by refusing to acknowledge James's
question that she had outsmarted him, but he reached
the door before her, leaning broad shoulders against it,
effectively blocking her exit unless she physically
pushed past him, and to do that would mean reaching
out and touching that powerful masculine frame. Jenna
shuddered in mute recognition of her own inability to
do any such thing, barely listening as he said, 'If doing
your hair means scraping it back off your face, then
don't bother, I prefer it the way it is.'

His arrogant assumption that his views held any
sway with her made Jenna livid.

'Well, *I* don't,' she told him grittily. 'Now if you will
let me pass . . . '

'Jenna.' There was a warning in the way he said her
name that made her hesitate. 'Tonight I am going to
introduce you to my godmother as my wife-to-be. She's
an old lady who means a great deal to me, and if the
only way I can convince her that there's more to this
marriage between us than a mere business arrangement
is by physically *making* you leave your hair loose, then
believe me I will.'

Jenna did believe him, but even so her face remained
stubbornly set. Deep down inside herself she knew she
was being stubborn to no good cause. What did it matter
which way she left her hair? But she was determined not
to let James get the better of her, and tell her what to do.

'Scrape it back if that's what you wish,' he told her
coolly, 'but I promise you when you walk into my godmother's house it will be loose.'

'That, of course, being the term that best describes

your normal choice of woman,' Jenna said acidly, knowing that physically she could not best him, but determined not to be totally vanquished.

To her amazement he laughed.

'Now there's an old-fashioned turn of phrase,' he mocked when he had finally quelled his amusement. 'My godmother knows I appreciate beauty, whether it be beauty in a woman or in an inanimate object,' he told her. 'As I said, she's an old lady who's been nagging me to get married for at least the past ten years. Don't try to hurt me through her, Jenna,' he warned, 'or I promise you you'll wish you'd never been born. Where's your case?' he asked, indicating that as far as he was concerned the subject was closed.

'There.' Jenna had placed it by the door, and James picked it up. It was on the tip of her tongue to tell him that she was not going to go with him after all, but what would that achieve? All the pleasure she had felt earlier in the work she had accomplished during the week was gone. Now she felt drained and, worse, irritated with herself as well as with him.

Some of her irritation vanished when she greeted Sarah. She was propped up in the back of the car and welcomed Jenna with obvious pleasure.

As he set the car in motion Jenna refused to look at James. She couldn't bear to see the satisfaction in his eyes when he looked at her flowing hair.

He was a good driver and the Beethoven tape playing through the car's cassette speakers was pleasantly soothing. It was very tempting to lie back and close her eyes.

'Go to sleep if you feel like it.'

His ability to follow the direction of her thoughts was something that Jenna found distinctly disturbing. She wasn't used to other people anticipating her wishes for her. In truth, she wasn't used to the sort of intimacy her relationship with James was forcing upon her. Unlike her, he seemed to have adapted to the role of her fiancé with comparative ease, whereas she felt acutely uncomfortable in it. She jumped every time he came too close to her, and she knew he was aware of it. She was tense nearly all the time she was in his company, and yet there was no reason for her to be; he had given her his word that he would respect her wishes in regard to the physical side of their marriage, and anyway, it was hardly likely that he should have more than a passing interest in her. Not when there were so many other far more attractive and sensual women only too willing to share their beds with him. She shrugged the thought away, her face burning hotly as she had an unwanted mental image of James's body entwined with that of another woman, his skin dark and virile against her paler slenderness.

'Too hot?' He bent to adjust the heater and Jenna turned away from him, thanking providence that he didn't really possess the ability to read her thoughts.

A second later she was wondering if she had misjudged him. 'My godmother is old-fashioned,' he told her calmly, 'and there will be no question of her giving us a shared bedroom, or indeed considering us to be lovers, but in general, friends and acquaintances will find it extremely odd that you jump ten miles in the air and freeze every time I come near you.'

'Sarah . . .' Jenna began desperately, her face burning again.

'She's asleep,' James told her. 'Is this reaction reserved solely for me, Jenna, or for mankind in general?'

She opened her mouth to speak, but he forestalled her by adding coolly, 'I know you're about to damn me to eternal hell for daring to ask, but if we're going to establish any kind of working relationship there must be at least some degree of honesty between us — and trust.' He glanced across at her, his eyes inimical as they held hers. 'I have already given you my word that I'll make no unwanted sexual advances to you, but if you're going to continue flinching away from me as though I'm Bluebeard you're going to make life unnecessarily difficult for both of us.'

Jenna knew that he was right, and that it would be foolish to allow her dislike of his probing to lead to open warfare between them. That was not how she wanted to live, it would not be good for Lucy and Sarah, and ultimately she suspected that James would, in any case, weather it far better than she.

'It isn't just you,' she managed to say with a creditable degree of openness. 'I don't like being pawed ... touched ... ' she amended quickly on seeing the look he gave her, 'by any man.'

'But you must have liked it, or at least acceded to it at least once,' he pointed out.

'Lucy ... ' he added enlighteningly, his grim expression suddenly darkening, his mouth tightening even further as he said quietly, 'unless of course she was the result of an act of violence, such as rape.'

Jenna went white, jerking involuntarily against her seat-belt her eyes wide with terror.

She heard James curse, the car slowed down and then stopped. He glanced in his driving mirror to check that Sarah was still asleep Jenna guessed, and then said slowly, 'Is that it, Jenna? Were you raped?'

She had never been more relieved to be able to say with all honesty, 'No, no, I wasn't.' She knew her words held an unmistakable echo of truth, and although James's grim look did not totally disappear he seemed to relax slightly.

Jenna was just about to draw a shaky sigh of relief when he pressed, 'Then why? Were your first sexual experiences bad ones? Have you had some sort of unpleasant sexual experience?'

Once again she was able to say quite truthfully, 'No.'

'Then this abhorrence of the male sex springs from the fact that your lover deserted you and left you alone to carry Lucy, is that it?'

He was persistent, Jenna had to give him that. She moved restlessly in her seat and forced herself to face him. Now that the immediate danger was over, now that she was safely past that hated word 'rape,' she could do so with at least some degree of equanimity. 'I don't want to discuss what happened in the past with you, James. It has no bearing on our relationship today.'

'No.' His eyes were bleak and cold. 'How can you say that to me, Jenna, when you flinch every time I come within touching distance of you? I should say completely the opposite, that the past has every bearing on the present, but since I can't force you to confide in me we'll let it lie, but I promise you one thing. I have no intention of becoming the object of speculation and curiosity among my friends and acquaintances because of your obvious abhorrence of me. We're engaged, Jenna, and that in today's terms means we're lovers. If you can't find a way to accept my touch in public with at least indifference, then I'll have to find a way to teach you, and believe me I will.'

She did believe him, and even while she hated him for what he was saying, one part of her brain acknowledged that he had some grounds for his comments. Even so something goaded her to say childishly, 'What's the matter — are you afraid that if I don't cling adoringly to your arm you'll lose your macho image?'

His mouth tightened as he restarted the car.

'Let's just cut out the childish comments, shall we, Jenna? And while we're on the subject — ' his glance swept her suited figure with derogatory thoroughness, 'if your wardrobe is full of look-alikes of that, you're going to need some new clothes.' He saw the angry rejection trembling on her lips and continued smoothly, 'As my wife there will be certain functions you'll be expected to attend with me, certain duties you'll be expected to perform.' Something glinted momentarily in his eyes as he finished with silky menace. 'If you won't help me in this respect, Jenna, I'm perfectly capable of choosing you a new wardrobe without that help.'

For once rage overcame caution, and she spat at him bitterly, 'Go ahead then, because I'm perfectly happy with the clothes I already own.'

It was a lie as she had already proved to herself once tonight, but she was not going to have him reordering her life to his requirements.

'If you don't like it, you know what you can do,' she added tauntingly. 'We aren't married yet.'

'But we will be.' There was a certain savage satisfaction in the way he said it, but she was too furious to register it properly.

'Yes, because you can't bear to lose the Hall,' Jenna agreed bitingly.

'That's one consideration. Lucy is another, or have you forgotten her?'

Jenna was silent, hating herself for allowing her own fears and insecurities to take precedence over Lucy's happiness. She *had* forgotten Lucy, if only momentarily, and it galled her to be reminded of her niece's claims on her by James.

'Sarah's waking up,' James warned her quietly. Jenna turned round and saw that Sarah was rubbing her eyes as she opened them.

'How much longer?' she asked James tiredly.

'Only another half an hour or so.'

His estimate proved to be accurate; within forty minutes they were turning down a country lane, the dying sun disappearing beyond the rise of the hills and bathing everything in rich gold. Gloucestershire was a lovely county, Jenna reflected, trying to imbue something into herself of the peace of the surrounding countryside.

Up ahead of them a signpost indicated an hotel. 'My godmother sold the family home when she was widowed and it's now an hotel,' James enlightened her. 'She retained the lodge for her own use and is far more comfortable there. She has a live-in housekeeper-cum-companion who has been with her for the past twenty years. You can see the lodge now, if you look to the right.'

Jenna peered in the direction he indicated but all she could see was a moss-green roof, and then, as they turned a bend in the road, the lodge was there. Long and low, hugging the ground, the weathered stone lichened in places and dripping with the pink blossoms of a rambling rose.

Tiny mullioned windows painted white and framed with stone peered out from behind the trellis of rose and clematis. Too large to be described as a mere cottage, and yet not stately enough to merit the term house, the lodge looked as though it had been specifically designed for a calendar rather than as genuine habitation.

There was even a true cottage garden in front of it, complete with grassy path and a white picket fence.

'I'll have to drive round the back,' James told Jenna. 'There's nowhere to leave the car here at the front.'

Another lane meandered to the rear of the building with a five-barred gate leading into a cobbled yard enclosed on two sides by the house and on the third by the road. Beyond the cobbled area lay more gardens, and Jenna was aghast when James drove through the gate and parked his car on the pretty cobbles.

'Sacrilege, I know,' he agreed, smiling at her, 'but there's no alternative. My godmother only has one garage,' he indicated a single-storey building which formed one side of the L-shaped yard, 'and it houses all her gardening tools plus her extremely ancient and temperamental Bentley.'

A heavy, wooden, studded back door opened, and a small round woman hurried out.

'Jessie, my godmother's companion,' James explained as he opened his door and got out.

While James responded to Jessie's warm greeting Jenna got out of the car, and simply stood for a moment breathing in the clear, sweet country air. It was softer here than the air at home, but it still carried the familiar country scents. At this time of the year a combination of hay and sun, mixed with those indefinable smells that only those who know the country can accurately dissect, and then she remembered Sarah and hurried to the rear of the car. James was there before her, lifting his step-sister out. Held in his arms Sarah looked so fragile that Jenna felt her throat lock. Her problems seemed minimal when she compared them with the burdens Sarah had to carry.

'Come on in, and get the lassie settled somewhere comfortable,' Jessie instructed. Her voice still held the faint burr of her native Scotland and Jenna wondered if she ever longed for the stark beauty of the highlands, here in the lush, chocolate-box prettiness of the South.

The back door led directly into the kitchen, a large, comfortable room with an Aga, and a quantity of sensible, plain, wooden-fronted cupboards. Quarry tiles shone on the floor, and in the centre of it stood an old-fashioned, bleached pine table. The mouthwatering smell of something cooking filled the room, and Jenna felt hungry.

'We're a little short on bedrooms, so we've put the lassie and yourself in the one room,' Jessie explained to Jenna opening a door into a narrow hall.

'That's fine,' Jenna assured her easily, 'especially if Sarah finds she needs anything during the night. I'll be on hand then without having to disturb anyone else.'

As she spoke she was conscious of Jessie studying her, and when she had finished the Scotswoman nodded her head. 'Aye,' was all she said but Jenna felt somehow as though she had just passed some test she hadn't even known she was about to sit.

James confirmed her thoughts as he murmured against her ear, 'Jessie approves of you!' Jenna turned to look at him and just caught the twinkle in his eye as he added in a voice so low that only she could hear it, 'And that's certainly a first — like you, she has no brief for loose women!'

Jenna let James precede her up the stairs, following at a more leisurely pace as she paused to admire their sturdy oak construction. Although plain, the staircase had its own beauty. The wood had mellowed with age, the treads and banister worn smooth by many feet and hands. When Jenna touched the wood it felt warm and alive, and she paused to daydream for a few seconds, wondering how many other hands had touched the same spot, how many generations of people had lived, laughed and loved beneath this ancient roof. Unlike the old Hall, this house had a very definite aura of having been filled with busy people, of being used to bustle and hustle. It was a family home, Jenna thought reflectively. She could see them in it: the lodgekeeper with his brood of children and his rosy-cheeked wife. The girls would go in service to the big house, the boys on the land . . .

'Jenna.' She looked up, shocked out of her trance by the sound of James's voice. He was standing at the top of the stairs looking down at her.

'You were miles away,' he told her. 'I wonder where?'

'Here,' Jenna told him. 'Thinking about the people who must have lived here . . . '

'Mmm, it has a much more robust aura than the Hall, doesn't it? One gets a far clearer feeling of people having lived here, rather than merely existed.'

His thoughts mirrored her own so clearly that Jenna found it impossible to speak. It was uncanny how he managed to read her mind — and it would have to stop. She had to have some defences against him, some private part of herself that would always be inviolate and protected.

'I'll go up to Sarah,' she said, disconcerted to find herself slightly breathless. James stood to one side as she reached the top of the stairs but because of the narrowness of the landing, Jenna had to squeeze past him. For some reason she half stumbled, falling heavily against him. James steadied her, grabbing her waist, his fingers biting deep into her skin.

'Are you okay?'

His voice reverberated through her body, and she heard it inwardly rather than outwardly. She felt dizzy and faintly sick. Too long without food, she told herself, remembering her skipped lunch and the long drive.

'Faint from lack of food,' she told him, forcing a brief smile.

She could feel her own heart racing, hear its agitated thump. James was still holding her, although less fiercely. Her eyes were on a level with his throat. She lifted them to his face, a curious spasm of sensation curling through her as he smiled down at her.

'Now then, you two, that's enough of that!' Jessie's briskly firm tones broke them apart, Jenna too bemused to be upset by her assumption and James merely laughing at the older woman as he said teasingly: 'Jessie, you must remember we've only just got engaged!'

'Aye, well, in my day engaged meant engaged and not married, and we'll have no carryings on under this roof, her ladyship wouldn't like it!'

'Her ladyship?' Jenna stared hard at James, but he refused to respond.

'You go and check up on Sarah, then, my love,' was all he said, 'and then we'll go downstairs. Knock when you're ready. That's my door.' He indicated a stout wooden door opposite from the one Jessie was holding open.

'You won't have your own bathroom I'm afraid, miss,' she told Jenna as she ushered her into her bedroom. 'We don't run to that here.'

Jenna smiled reassuringly, her smile deepening as she viewed her room. It was comfortably large with three small, dormer, leaded windows that immediately overlooked the courtyard and then the countryside beyond it. A pretty rosebud-decorated wallpaper covered the walls. Flounced white muslin curtains hung at the windows, the same fabric being used on the two single beds. The floor was bare, polished boards, with a deep, rich shine, a rag rug in soft faded pinks in between the two beds. Although she and Sarah had no private bathroom the room had a basin set into an attractive vanity unit.

'It's pretty, isn't it?' Sarah was lying on one of the beds, and although she smiled, Jenna sensed that she was tired and in some degree of pain.

'Very,' she agreed, 'typically English cottagey. You look tired. I don't know what time we're going to eat.'

She turned enquiringly to Jessie who told her, 'Her ladyship said to have dinner ready when you arrived — it's only home-made soup, cold game pie and salad, so if the young lady would like something on a tray . . ?'

'Would you like that, Sarah?' Jenna questioned, sitting down on her own bed and taking one of Sarah's hands between her own. She didn't want to give Sarah the impression that she and James did not want her company. She knew how sensitive she was and was anxious not to hurt her.

'I think so, if you don't mind.'

'Not at all. A tray would be lovely,' she told Jessie with a smile. 'What would you like to drink, Sarah? Milk? Tea?'

'Or there's home-made lemonade,' Jessie supplied.

'Milk, I think.'

When Jessie bustled off, Jenna enquired tactfully if Sarah wished to use the bathroom. Watching her colour slightly, Jenna felt a wave of sympathy for her. 'I can manage by myself at the flat. I've got my chair. But here . . . '

'Don't worry. James will bring your chair up. You know that he intends to ask his godmother if you and Lucy can stay here while we're away. How do you feel about that, Sarah?'

'I think I shall quite like it if Lucy is here too.'

Her response was obviously genuine and Jenna felt relieved.

'You look to me as though you're suffering some discomfort,' she told Sarah bluntly. 'Do you have something you can take?'

'Yes, some painkillers. They're in my bag.'

Jenna got them for her and gave her a glass of water.

'My back started aching in the car, but I didn't want to take them then. They make me so sleepy. Sometimes I feel as though I'm sleeping my whole life away.' Frustration edged her voice and Jenna felt compassion ache inside her. 'Maybe that's the best thing I can do,' Sarah added dolefully, 'sleep myself into oblivion.'

'Nonsense,' Jenna retorted crisply. 'You *will* get better, Sarah, and in fact, I think that your back aching is a good sign. You're obviously getting some sensation returning.'

She could see that Sarah had not thought of that aspect of her pain, her face brightening slightly. 'Do you really think so?'

'Yes, I do.' Jenna mentally crossed her fingers that she was right. 'We must mention it on your next hospital appointment.' She grimaced faintly and got off her own bed. 'I'd better go downstairs. James will be wondering what I'm doing. I hadn't realised his godmother was titled.'

'Yes, she and James's mother were cousins.'

In the end she had no need to go and knock on James's door. He came into her room with Jessie when she brought Sarah's tray. He talked to his step-sister for a few minutes while Jenna combed her hair, and then said calmly when she had finished, 'Ready to go down?'

Almost automatically Jenna bent to deposit a light kiss on Sarah's forehead before leaving the room. The younger girl flushed, but Jenna could tell that she was pleased. If nothing else was achieved by this marriage, if it helped Lucy and Sarah, that alone would be worthwhile.

She hadn't realised how tense she was as they went downstairs, until James murmured against her hair, 'Don't worry, my godmother won't eat you!'

'You mean *her ladyship* won't eat me,' Jenna responded drily. 'Why didn't you tell me . . ?'

'Because I didn't consider it to be important,' came the equally dry response and then James was opening the door into the lodge's small drawing-room and there was no opportunity for further conversation.

A tiny elegant woman rose from the sofa and came towards them.

'James!'

She had a pleasing, warm-timbred voice, the way she said his name conveying a depth of emotion far more poignant than any multitude of gratuitous endearments.

Jenna watched as James hugged his godmother. She was dressed in a pale lilac silk dress with a high neck and a tiny ruffled collar, rather Edwardian in appearance, silver-grey hair framing a face that Jenna could see had once been extremely beautiful and still was, although its beauty was that of the purity of its bone structure rather than of the flesh. Cool grey eyes surveyed Jenna thoughtfully as James stood back.

'Jenna, my godmother, Lady Lucille Carmichael. Lucille, allow me to introduce Jenna to you.' James pulled Jenna gently forwards, and for once she did not flinch as he kept her within the curve of his arm. There was something about this sharp-eyed old lady that made her feel every omission in her character was written on her forehead in large characters.

'She isn't one of your usual empty-headed beauties, James.'

Jenna felt the beginnings of anger mingle with her apprehension. Her mouth tightened slightly. She didn't enjoy being discussed as though she were an inanimate object.

Surprisingly, Lady Carmichael smiled — really smiled — at her, her grey eyes twinkling as she laughed softly. She turned to James and told him, 'She has a temper, James, I like that. It will do you good. I'm glad you're not another of his adoring, feeble-minded girls, my dear,' she told Jenna, extending a hand towards her. 'Come and sit down here beside me and tell me all about yourself. James, you can go and find Jessie and ask her to bring us all a drink. You can tell her we'll be ready to eat in half an hour. I don't want to rush you,' she added to Jenna with another smile, 'but the Aga can be temperamental!'

'Go along, James,' she reiterated firmly, 'you may stop hovering like an expectant father. I promise you I will not eat your young lady!'

It amused Jenna to see James treated like a small boy, but she was not deceived by the by-play between the two of them. She could tell quite easily that Lady Carmichael adored her godson, and she suspected that despite her polite exterior, her hostess intended to make very sure that she discovered as much as she could about the woman who was going to marry into her family.

She grilled Jenna thoroughly but diplomatically, and in spite of everything Jenna discovered that she liked her. She made no bones about the fact that she cared very deeply for James, and Jenna sensed that she was not a woman who placed false values on social position or wealth, but who judged her fellow man on the merits of their personality.

'James tells me that you have a daughter,' she said at length, when Jenna had told her about her childhood, omitting any mention of Rachel from her tale.

'Yes.' Jenna held her head up proudly. 'Lucy is fifteen.'

'Mmm, I see that the gutter press are hinting that my godson is her father.'

'I'm afraid so. The subject of her father is something I cannot discuss with Lucy for . . . very private reasons. I'm afraid she, too, has convinced herself that James is her father. He does not intend to disillusion her, and in fact one of the reasons we are marrying is ——— '

'For her sake,' Lady Carmichael supplied shrewdly, adding when Jenna coloured a little, 'oh, you need not be embarrassed. I had already suspected it was not what in my day was called a love-match. So . . . you gain a father for your daughter from the marriage. What does James gain?'

'Someone to help him with Sarah and a share in the Hall — I bought it some weeks ago.'

'The Hall. I see . . .' Lady Carmichael suddenly looked older. Troubled shadows darkened her eyes. 'I thought he had put all that behind him, poor boy. I'll be honest with you,' she told Jenna. 'When James first told me about this marriage I was very disappointed. I've been wanting him to marry for a long time but not ——— '

'To an unmarried mother with a fifteen-year-old daughter and a rather unstable business to support,' Jenna supplied grimly. 'Well, I . . . '

'You misunderstand me,' Lady Carmichael interrupted firmly. 'But not, I was going to say, to one of the young women he has sometimes brought down here with him — young women far more interested in themselves than any man, young women who look on marriage as a pleasant interlude in their lives, which can be terminated as soon as they grow bored with it. In my day a couple did not divorce simply because they had fallen out of love, because in most cases they did not fall in love in the first place. They married with due regard to the wishes of their family, and entered that marriage as a lifelong commitment. You, I can see, are not a

young woman who would enter any commitment
lightly. You have had to work hard to support yourself
and your daughter, so James tells me. He admires you a
great deal.'

He did! That was news to Jenna, but she supposed it
was only natural that James should want to paint a flattering picture of her for his godmother's scrutiny.

'I am glad you have been honest with me,' she added
with a smile. 'I like you, Jenna, and I think we shall
get on very well together. James will not make an easy
husband, but, of course, you must already know this.
His mother's death and the subsequent scandal have
left their mark on him. I can't deny that I was beginning
to despair of ever seeing him marry. I can't like
this . . . obsession he has about the old Hall, of course.'
She saw Jenna's expression and said sharply, 'Hasn't he
told you about his mother?'

Jenna shook her head, and was just about to ask what
Lady Carmichael meant when the door opened and
James came in.

'Ah, James. You see your lovely wife-to-be is still in
one piece!'

'Which doesn't mean to say that you haven't very
cleverly dissected her and put the pieces neatly together
again,' James drawled but his eyes were not on his godmother, they were on Jenna, and she could almost
believe there was a hint of anxiety in them, as though he
were truly concerned that Lady Carmichael might have
upset her. It set up a tremulous reaction in the pit of her
stomach, a kind of achy, nervous weakness she wasn't
at all used to.

'I see that Jenna has no engagement ring,' Lady
Carmichael commented in a disapproving voice.

Jenna was just about to tell her that she hadn't
wanted one when James forestalled her. 'An omission I

intended to rectify this weekend, but you've pre-empt-
ed me somewhat.' He reached into his pocket and withdrew a small jeweller's box with one hand, taking hold
of Jenna's with his other. Her fingers trembled slightly
beneath the warm contact with his and for some strange
reason when her eyes met his, she couldn't look away.

She heard the tiny snap of the box being opened, and
then felt the cool slide of metal on to her finger.

'You can look now!' James sounded faintly amused,
and that amusement broke the spell holding her in
thrall. She looked down at her left hand, went cold and
then hot, and couldn't prevent the small gasp of pleasure leaving her lips as the ornate gold setting and green
fire of the Regency betrothal ring glowed back at her.

'James! You shouldn't have!' she protested huskily. 'It
was so expensive!'

She heard Lady Carmichael snort derisively and mutter. 'What's that to say to anything? God knows, he's
rich enough to cover you from head to foot in diamonds
without breaking the bank. Let me look.' She studied
Jenna's trembling hand and said, "Mmm, very attractive. You have excellent taste, child. It's very pretty.'

To describe the priceless antique she was wearing on
her finger as 'very pretty', struck Jenna as achingly
funny. She wanted to laugh very badly. Hysteria, she
recognised wryly, and no wonder.

'James . . . ' She wanted to tell him the ring was far
too valuable for her to wear, but he had moved closer to
her than she realised and when she turned her head her
face brushed the cool silk of his shirt. The warm male
smell of his body engulfed her, promoting an aura of
intimacy between them that provoked the strangest reaction in the pit of her stomach. She started to move
away, but James's hand against her throat stopped her.
His thumb lifted her chin so that she was forced to meet

his eyes. He bent his head towards her; wicked lights dancing blatantly in his eyes. 'I'm glad you like it.' He whispered the words against her mouth, the sensation of his breath stroking her lips, making the sensitive skin quiver faintly.

His thumb left her chin and pressed lightly on her bottom lip. Instinctively she opened her mouth slightly and was stunned by the heart-jerking swiftness with which the warmth of James's mouth covered her own.

It was only the lightest of kisses, brief and quickly over, but long after he had stepped back from her, her lips tingled in memory of the heat of his against them. Even without closing her eyes she could far too easily sense the firm pressure of his thumb against her lower lip. He had not kissed her with any force or passion but the memory of the feeling of his mouth against her own stirred feelings inside her she found it hard to dismiss or even rationalise. All she did know was that they caused her alarm and apprehension, a feathering sensation of panic coiling along her nerves more frightening because for the first time she was experiencing the fear without the adrenalin-surging boost of anger.

The main topic of conversation over dinner was the wedding. James had arranged for them both to see the vicar in the morning and Jenna had an irrational impulse to tell him that things were moving too fast, that she wasn't ready yet to commit herself so totally. What did she want? An old-fashioned courtship? Hardly! After all, there was nothing personal between them. Their marriage was to be a business arrangement and one from which she had already gained in the material sense. Her bank manager was highly delighted about it; the suppliers she had ordered from since the news of the engagement had broken had offered her very generous credit terms without her even having to ask. Jenna was no fool; she was fully aware that being James's wife would bring an added lustre to her reputation, and that any number of rich and thrusting social climbers would be only too pleased to pay for the privilege of boasting that James Allingham's wife had done their décor — and they would be prompt payers. With a little hardheaded shrewdness she could use James's reputation and her own standing as his wife to treble her business at least, but she had little desire to do so. The business world had lost its savour for her some time ago, she admitted to herself as she listened to James and his godmother talking. The impetus had been gone for some time.

'So that's settled then! Lovely.'

Jenna came out of her reverie at the tail end of the conversation, not quite sure what had been said until Lady Carmichael said to her, 'James is leaving you behind when he goes to collect Lucy tomorrow, Jenna. We'll be able to have a long chat.'

'I thought another long car ride might be too much for Sarah,' he explained to Jenna. 'When she and Lucy come down here to stay I'll make arrangements for a private nurse to attend her daily, but for this weekend . . .'

'I'm quite happy to look after her, James,' Jenna told him quietly. She remembered Sarah's complaints about her back and a gleam of excitement illuminated her eyes. 'I forgot to tell you,' without realising what she was doing Jenna curled her fingers into the fine wool of his suit jacket, 'Sarah was complaining of some discomfort in her back this evening. Surely that must mean she has some feeling there?'

For a moment he didn't respond. Beneath her fingers his arm felt curiously tense and as she looked up at him Jenna realised he wasn't looking at her, but at her hand on his arm. The curious rigidity she could sense in his body increased, and then as he looked up and found her watching him, subsided. He looked different, but she could not have said why exactly.

'James?'

He caught the uncertainty in her voice and said levelly, 'Yes, I think you could well be right.'

'I thought you might mention it at the hospital on her next visit.'

'Yes, yes I shall.' He spoke with his usual cool decisiveness, but Jenna had the strangest feeling that his mind was on something else. Lady Carmichael asked a question about the accident — James replied, and the strange moment was gone.

After dinner they had coffee and at ten-thirty Lady Carmichael announced that she was going to bed. 'I think I'll go up too.' Jenna stood up to follow her from the room. James opened the door for them, and as she walked past him she thought for a moment that he looked almost . . . lonely. But she dismissed the notion as being ridiculous. Men like James were never lonely — they might be solitary upon occasion by choice, but lonely? Never!

'Ah, there you are, my dear. Do you mind if I join you?' asked Lady Carmichael. Jenna was lazing beneath a shady tree in the lodge garden, the book she was supposed to be reading open across her lap. James had left just after lunch to collect Lucy, and Sarah had gone upstairs for her afternoon rest. A bee hummed soothingly among the tall hollyhocks and the beneficent warmth of the June sun lulled her into a pleasant state of drowsiness.

'Not at all. After all, it is your garden. It's lovely,' Jenna praised. 'You must spend an awful lot of time on it.'

'I did, but now I find my rheumatism puts anything more arduous than a little gentle weeding out of my scope. We're lucky enough to have a devoted gardener who comes round three times a week. James was telling me that the gardens at the old Hall need a good deal of attention.

'Yes, they do,' Jenna agreed. 'The whole place does.'

'Has James told you anything about why the old Hall is so important to him?'

'He did say that an ancestor of his had originally lived there.' Briefly, Jenna thought of the face in the portrait and a tiny shiver raised goosebumps on her skin. In her mind's eye that dark face bent towards her, the indolent, aristocratic hand lifting to her face, touching her mouth as James had done last night. Stop it, stop it, she cautioned herself, trying instead to concentrate on what her hostess was telling her.

'Well, that *is* part of it,' Lady Carmichael conceded, 'although to be competely accurate James's ancestor was never really a member of the Deveril family. His mother was married to one of them, but his father was not her husband. There was a suggestion at the time that his father had Stuart blood in his veins and certainly, there is a degree of resemblance, but that, of course, is all mere speculation. However, that is not what really motivates James in his desire to acquire the old Hall.

'Has he told you anything about his mother?'

Jenna shook her head. 'Very little. I know that she committed suicide.'

'Yes, it was tragic. She was my cousin, you know, much younger than me, of course, the youngest in the family, in fact, and I'm afraid quite spoiled in the way that pretty little girls are. Her parents were comfortably off, but nothing like as wealthy as James's father's family. David fell madly in love with her the moment he saw her. It was during the war and he was posted over here. Christine liked him and was flattered by his obvious love for her, but I'm afraid she never really loved him in that same intense, devouring way.

It was really her parents who persuaded her to marry him. They were concerned about her safety if she stayed in England — during those early days of the war, the outcome wasn't certain and they thought she'd be far safer in America. She was only nineteen when they married — and a very young nineteen at that. James was born in 1949. I remember how thrilled her parents were when they heard the news. They went over to the States to see them. They were killed in an aircrash on the way back.' She paused and Jenna waited, understanding, knowing that her hostess was back among old ghosts, reluctant to let them go.

She sighed faintly. 'Where was I? Oh, yes. I heard from Christine rather sporadically after that. Christmas and birthday cards, that sort of thing, the odd letter, and then David had to come to England on business. Christine and James came with him. We saw quite a lot of them that first summer. James was an enchanting child. Very sturdy and male, very sweet-natured too. He adored his mother — in fact, most men did. She was that sort of woman,' Lady Carmichael told Jenna wryly.

'David had to go from London to Paris for some business discussions and it was during that time that Christine must have met Alan Deveril.'

For the first time Jenna tensed. Her eyes widened fractionally, and as though sensing her concentrated interest her hostess asked, 'Did you ever meet him? You came from his part of the world originally, of course.'

'I knew him,' Jenna said in a clipped voice, 'but not socially if that's what you mean. My great-aunt was not from the sort of social background that made her welcome in Sir Alan Deveril's drawing-room.'

'Yes, he was the most unmitigated snob,' Lady Carmichael agreed. 'I met him once with Christine. I bumped into them in the Ritz and she introduced him to me. I didn't like him.

'Of course, it didn't take long for the gossip to start — David was busy in Paris, and Christine always had been headstrong. Alan seemed to exercise a kind of fascination for her that I've never been able to understand. After all, she had everything a woman could possibly want: an adoring husband, a delightful son, a very comfortable lifestyle . . . '

'Everything but excitement,' Jenna suggested.

Lady Carmichael's glance acknowledged her shrewdness. 'There was that, of course. Deveril did possess a certain reptilian brand of charm, I suppose. He certainly had an extremely bad reputation. He was married, of course. No one ever saw his wife. He kept her away from society at the Hall. It was commonly rumoured that he married her for her money, but that wasn't all that uncommon. However, Christine wasn't his first affair during his marriage. There had been talk of a young daughter of an acquaintance, hurriedly packed off abroad, hints of other relationships, but never anything as flamboyant as this affair with Christine.

'She, poor fool, was besotted with him. God knows why, she was convinced that he intended to divorce his wife and marry her. She told me as much and the gossip press was full of hints and speculation. Of course, in those days divorce was much more shocking than it is today. I had my doubts even then. Lovely though she was, Christine had no money of her own, and he was a man notorious for his expensive tastes: gambling, drink, and the old Hall. God, how he loved that house.

He could bore on for hours about it. It was almost an obsession with him, how it had been in the family for centuries.

'Of course, when David came back from Paris the scandal finally broke. He confronted Christine about her affair — she told me this herself — and she told him she wanted a divorce and that Deveril and she intended to marry. David begged her to reconsider, but she refused.

'She went to Deveril that night — to his London flat. When she told him what she had done — that she had left David — he went crazy with her, told her he had never had any intention of marrying her, that for one thing if he did he would probably lose the Hall because he would not have access to his wife's money if they were divorced. Poor Christine could not believe him. She asked him if he honestly expected her to believe that a mere house was more important than their love. Their love . . . He laughed at her, she said . . . told her that like all women she was a fool, that nothing mattered more to him than keeping the Hall, that it was the only reason he had married his wife in the first place. He would kill to keep it if he had to, he told her.

'She couldn't go back to David — not then. So she came to me and was too distraught to conceal anything from me. She told me everything.

'Eventually, I persuaded her to go back to her husband. He still wanted her and was prepared to make a fresh start.' She sighed again. 'I sometimes wish I had not done that. It didn't work, it couldn't. She wasn't the same person. She was like a broken mechanical toy, completely unable to function. She and David had only been back in the States a matter of weeks when she committed suicide. James found her.' For a long time there was silence and then Lady Carmichael said emotionally, 'Now, perhaps, you can understand why this obsessive desire of his to possess the old Hall so distresses me.'

'Perhaps now that he does possess it, he will be able to put the past behind him,' Jenna suggested quietly.

'Maybe. Certainly he's strong enough to do so if he wishes . . . but *does* he wish? I sometimes think it's just as well there are no Deverils left alive, because if there were . . . .'

There was a roaring noise in Jenna's ears, a feeling of weakness sapping her strength but she fought it back. Lucy, Lucy, she thought achingly, as wronged by the Deverils as James himself and yet at the same time part of them.

Knowing this should make her feel closer to him, but it merely increased her fear of him. He had an unnerving talent for burying his deepest feelings very thoroughly, but they were there and they were strong enough to motivate him to pursue a course relentlessly until it got him what he wanted. But thankfully he did not want her, she reminded herself. She had nothing to fear. The Hall was what he wanted. The Hall, that was all.

CHAPTER TEN

'WITH my body I thee worship . . . '

Tiny frissons of sensation ran down Jenna's spine. It was cool in the small Norman church and the scent of the roses decorating it almost overpowered her. She still could not believe that this was her, actually marrying James. But it was. And now the vicar was turning to her, telling her that she and James were man and wife.

There was a tense expectant pause, a waiting silence from the others in the church with them that stirred fingers of apprehension along her spine. Instinctively, she started to move away from her new husband, tensing in shock as James's fingers curled round her wrist and he drew her towards him.

His head bent and before she could define his intentions, his breath, cool and fresh stroked her skin, his mouth unexpectedly warm as it touched hers. A curious tension gripped her, pain coiling achingly through her stomach. It was nerves, just nerves, she told herself as she jerked tensely away, and James released her. Only the wedding breakfast to get through now. She mustn't let herself think about that unanticipated and unwanted kiss. All it had been was a gesture, a sop to convention, something she mustn't even think about now. James surely wouldn't be.

The wedding breakfast was being held at the hotel that had once been Lucille Carmichael's home. Bill and Nancy were staying there courtesy of James. They had a room with a four-poster bed, Nancy had told Jenna only that morning, as she helped her to dress.

Her dress! Jenna stared down at it, closing her mind to the excited babble of their guests. She had found the dress in a small shop in South Molton Street, after an exhausting search. She had not wanted to wear white, in fact she had not known what to wear. A church ceremony seemed to call for something more than a simple suit, however expensive. In the end she had settled on a cream lace blouse with a high neck, delicately tucked and flounced, very Edwardian in appearance with long sleeves and deep cuffs also tucked and frilled. The matching skirt was full length and faintly A line in design, again with an unmistakable Edwardian flavour about it. It had a deep waistband which had had to be taken in — Jenna had lost weight in the weeks before the wedding from all the work she had had to do, not to mention the endless succession of sleepless nights. The skirt was plain apart from the decorative waistband and the deep, pin-tucked and lace-trimmed flounce at the hem.

Maggie who had gone with her to buy it had raved over it. Jenna herself had felt a little uncertain about wearing something so different from her normal style.

Instead of the traditional veil she had opted for a frivolous cream hat that perched precariously on her hair and had a tiny spotted net veil which covered the upper part of her face.

James made no attempt to remove it when he kissed her for which she was sincerely grateful for she was terrified that it might fall off at the lightest touch.

For Jenna, the wedding breakfast passed in a blur of voices and faces. James had invited several business colleagues and their wives, plus some of his own staff — executives whom she had already met at a dinner party, held by James's accountant's wife two weeks before the wedding. They all seemed pleasant enough, although Jenna had the sense to know that at the moment she was being treated with the reserve naturally accorded to the chairman's wife.

As well as Bill and Nancy, she had invited Harley, who once he got over his petulance about not being informed ahead of anyone else of her plans had been pleased about the match, Gordon Burns and his wife, Maggie and her boyfriend, and one or two others.

Now she was aching with tiredness and reaction, and the thought of the long flight out to the Caribbean the following morning appalled her.

They were each staying in their respective apartments tonight, James having made the suggestion that it would make their departure easier. Jenna had been a little surprised, but his suggestion made sense. It was pointless moving all her clothes into James's apartment only to have to move them out again the moment they came back from St Justine.

They would be away for two weekends in all, and Lucy was going to spend them here with Lady Carmichael and Sarah. James had organised everything meticulously, Jenna acknowledged, wondering why that fact should irritate her so much. It had struck her only the previous day that everything was running on oiled wheels and almost too perfectly. Sarah's consultant had confirmed that a degree of sensation was returning to her paralysed body. Lucy seemed much happier and more settled. Everything was ready for them at the Hall. Jenna had supervised the final hanging of the curtains and other drapes only that week. James had not seen their quarters yet. Would he like them? Did it really matter? she asked herself wryly. She was surprised to find that it did, but then, of course, as an interior designer she was used to hoping that her

clients approved of her work, and this was only a carry-
through from that feeling.

James! All the time at the back of her mind was the
information Lady Carmichael had given her about his
mother. About her affair with Sir Alan and her subsequent death. Every time she thought about it, Jenna
experienced a tiny thrill of apprehension. It disturbed
her immeasurably that James should be so good at hiding his real feelings. Unless, of course, he had overcome
his hatred of Sir Alan. But in that case, why did he want
the old Hall so desperately? Oh yes, Jenna could understand how he wanted it. She could even sympathise
with him, and if she were not committed to marriage to
him no doubt she could have experienced a good deal
more fellow feeling towards him.

'Ready to leave?'

He was at her side, his hand on her arm, drawing her
away from the laughing well-wishers.

'In a minute. I've just got to say goodbye to Lucy and
Sarah and then I'll go and change.'

It was late afternoon when they finally drove away
from the village. James stopped just outside it to remove
the slogans from the paintwork.

'It all seemed to go off pretty well,' he commented.

'Yes.'

She felt him looking at her, and leaned back in her
seat closing her eyes.

'Tired?'

'A little . . . I didn't manage to get back from Yorkshire until two in the morning the other night.'

'I know.'

She opened her eyes. He was watching her closely,
the blue eyes were scrutinising her keenly.

'I know, I rang you both at the apartment and at the
Hall, about ten and then again at one.'

'It took longer than I expected to hang the curtains.'

'You must have paid the makers an awful lot of over-time if they were prepared to stay so late to get the job done.'

Jenna felt herself flush. 'They finished at eight,' she told him shortly. 'I went out for something to eat with someone afterwards.'

'An old friend?'

Jenna felt her nerve endings prickle warningly at the silky menace wrapped round the words.

'No,' she told him shortly. 'An antique dealer I met several weeks ago when I was looking for a Jacobean bookcase for the sitting-room.'

'Ah, I see, he'd found you one.'

Jenna didn't ask how James knew that the antique dealer in question was a man. 'No, no, he hadn't, but he had found some dining chairs he thought I might be interested in.'

'Obviously a useful contact to have.'

James didn't say anything else but Jenna was conscious of wishing she had not needed to tell him about dining with Graham Wilde. He had rung her during the afternoon to tell her about the chairs, and when he had suggested dinner that evening she had demurred at first, but then, realising how late she would have to work, had changed her mind. She had enjoyed his company. He was very knowledgeable about antiques without forcing his views on her, and the time had gone past very quickly.

She knew that Graham was very attracted to her, but he knew that she was on the point of getting mar-ried and so she felt that the friendship between them was a safe one. An unusual experience for her, which was probably why she had been able to relax with him so much without wondering how she was going to get rid of him at the end of the evening.

It was still light when James stopped his car outside her apartment at nine o'clock. Jenna didn't ask him in, she intended to go straight to bed, since she had to be up so early in the morning for their eight o'clock flight.

'I'll pick you up at quarter to seven,' James reminded her as he leaned over to close the door. 'Sleep well.'

Her luggage was already at his apartment: all she had to do now was get ready for bed and then sleep. Sleep . . . how she ached for it Jenna thought tiredly as she locked her front door behind her. A tiny smile curled her mouth as she wondered how many brides had spent their wedding night apart from their husbands like this. Not very many.

She showered and then went to bed, lying there reliving the events of the day for several minutes. There had been no doubt about Lucy's and Sarah's pleasure in the marriage. Lucy was a changed girl. It was amazing how uninvolved emotionally Jenna felt in what had happened — she could almost have been a bystander at the wedding and not a major participant in it. She didn't feel married. She didn't feel anything, she acknowledged sleepily, she was far too tired.

Jenna groaned as the alarm went off. Struggling against sleep she had a momentary but vivid memory of her dreams. In one she had been trapped in the arms of her fantasy lover from the portrait and then disturbingly his face had become James's, his hands . . . Jenna pushed the memory firmly aside and got out of bed. Less than an hour to get ready in before James arrived.

She showered quickly putting on new cool cotton underwear, in readiness for the heat of the Caribbean. James had suggested that she wear something comfortable to travel in and she had picked out a new cotton skirt in a pale, soft yellow, with a matching slightly off the shoulder tee-shirt in yellow and white. As a precaution against the air-conditioning in the plane she had with her her fleecy-lined summer jacket. Low-heeled white canvas shoes completed her outfit. Her hair was still damp from the shower. If she left it it would dry with a natural curl and save her time.

She made some filter coffee and removed the grapefruit she had prepared for herself from the fridge. The sharp, tangy taste set her teeth slightly on edge, but she preferred it like that without added sugar.

She was just pouring her second cup of coffee when she heard the bell. She glanced at her watch, the same rather old and tatty one she had been wearing since she first started working, and reflected wryly that it was high time she bought a new one. James was five minutes early.

She went to let him in and saw that he was dressed as casually as she was herself in cream canvas jeans and a soft blue and cream striped short-sleeved shirt. Unlike her he was already tanned. She would look awful on the beach, Jenna reflected wryly, her skin tanned very slowly and she had stuffed her cosmetics case full of sun filters and expensive protective creams.

'Coffee?'

'Please.' He pulled out a stool and sat down at her breakfast bar while Jenna poured it for him. They could have been any married couple Jenna thought as the sunlight glinted on the new gold of her wedding ring.

'By the way, I forgot to give you this yesterday.' James was carrying a canvas jacket that matched his jeans and he pulled a small long package out of it and tossed it over to her.

'A wedding gift,' he said when she frowned slightly. Instantly, Jenna flushed. 'James, you shouldn't have bought me anything,' she told him. 'I never thought to buy something for you.'

'Does a gift always have to be repaid with a corresponding present? Open it,' he told her.

She did, momentarily stunned by what she found in the jeweller's box. It was one of the most beautiful watches she had ever seen, the delicate oval face framed in gold and set with diamonds and emeralds. It had a gold bracelet strap and was so delicate that Jenna felt almost afraid to wear it.

'I should leave it behind on this trip if I were you,' James suggested. 'It isn't exactly beachwear!'

'No, I'd hate to dive into the pool and find I was still wearing it.' Jenna shuddered at the very thought.

'It wouldn't be the end of the world. It's insured!'

'Yes, but . . . ' Jenna stopped, realising how foolish she would sound if she said it wasn't so much the value of the gift that concerned her although she had little doubt that it was expensive, it was more the thought of destroying her wedding gift actually on her honeymoon. Of course, that would sound ridiculously sentimental to James, and no wonder. No doubt to him the watch was just something he had noticed she needed, and he had bought it for her because it was the thing to do. There was no sentiment attached to it as far as he was concerned. Nor any where she was concerned either, she was quick to tell herself, but then she looked up and he was watching her, the look on his face so close to the one she had seen that night in her dreams that her whole body went tight with shock and fear.

James seemed not to notice. He glanced at his own watch and said briskly, 'Time we were leaving. I'll wash these while —— '

'No, you can leave them,' Jenna told him. 'Maureen will be coming round later to clean everywhere up.'

Jenna intended to sub-let her apartment and had already found someone to take over the lease from her but they would not be moving in until after she and James were back from the Caribbean.

'It's okay, we're airborne, you can relax now.'

Flushing angrily Jenna detached her fingers from the warmth of James's. She had always loathed flying although she hadn't told him this and in that stomach-lurching second when she felt the plane start to lift off the ground she had reacted automatically, burying her head in his shoulder and clinging tightly to his hand.

His obvious amusement to her reaction only served to increase her own feeling of embarrassment. 'Would you like a drink?'

Jenna nodded her head. 'Perrier water, please.' They were travelling first class, and now that her nervous dread had subsided she was able to take stock of their surroundings for the first time as the stewardesses moved calmly among the passengers.

A little to her surprise James too ordered Perrier. 'I never drink alcohol in flight,' he told her. 'It only increases the effect of jet lag, especially on a long flight like this one.'

Six hours at least, Jenna reflected, and then an inter-island flight from St Lucia to their final destination. She sat back in her seat and closed her eyes.

She was unaware that James had bent towards her until she felt his breath feather against her ear. 'If you want to use my shoulder as a pillow, please feel free,' he murmured.

Jenna felt her mouth tighten slightly. She would rather die than touch him she thought ungratefully. His amusement over her terrified reaction when they took off still rankled.

Apart from its length the flight was uneventful, Jenna dozed most of the morning without really being able to sleep. The lunch they were served was appetising, but she wasn't really hungry. Later she watched the film, but again without much interest. James had brought some work with him connected with the holiday complex, and he studied that after lunch.

Jenna had not missed the curious and appreciative looks the cabin stewardesses gave him. No doubt they were thinking she was very lucky to be his wife, she thought to herself. Never in a thousand years would they be able to appreciate her true feelings. She knew she had no reason to be so tense and nervy when she was with him, but she was . . . It was almost as though her deeply based feminine instincts knew something her logical mind did not. Or perhaps she was simply suffering from an excess of woman's very natural fear of man.

It was dusk when they landed at St Lucia, night falling with unexpected swiftness, the sun a blood-orange ball against a purple-black backdrop.

'Impressive, but you'll get used to it,' James told her as she came to a halt on the runway tarmac to gaze at the sunset.

St Lucia's airport facilities were almost primitive in comparison to those in the European places Jenna had visited, and the thought of yet another hour's flight was totally unappealing.

When she asked James if ultimately it would be possible to fly direct to the island he told her that there was a site where an international airport could be constructed, but that so far he had been against this as the island was promoting the image of a luxury holiday retreat and that once direct flights with Europe were established it might lose it.

'Great care has been taken to ensure that the complex we've been building blends into the landscape. It's only three storeys high and I don't intend to allow the island to be spoiled by row upon row of high-rise buildings.'

When Jenna saw the plane that would take them out to St Justine she quailed inwardly.

'Don't worry, they're very safe,' James told her. 'See this one's got floats as well, so that if there is an emergency we can land on the water.'

That did reassure her, and this time when they taxied down the runway she dug her nails into her palms, determined at all costs not to reach for James.

Even so, she could not stop herself from closing her eyes when they finally started to lift, and although she could never have admitted it to anyone, when James's hand covered hers, his thumb stroking soothingly over her bunched knuckles, it was the most reassuring feeling she had ever known.

The landing facilities at St Justine surprised her. Despite the single runway the arrivals lounge was air-conditioned and pleasantly furnished, the staff helpful and smartly uniformed, and James told her that he and the other members of the consortium responsible for the development of the island had insisted that the airport facilities echoed the first-class, luxury image they wished to give the island.

'People will be arriving tired and irritable after a long flight and we want to make them feel comfortable and relaxed from the moment they leave the plane.'

Several taxis waited outside the airport buildings, but James ignored them and instead directed the porter with their luggage towards a parked Mercedes.

'This is one of the cars we put at the use of hotel guests. Normally it's chauffeur-driven, but on this occasion I said I would drive myself.'

He produced a set of keys and unlocked the door so that Jenna could get in. The porter loaded their luggage and then James started the car. The blast of cool air from the air-conditioning was blessedly welcome. Although it was nine o'clock at night it was stiflingly hot outside, an oppressive moist heat that Jenna's system hadn't acclimatised to yet.

It took half an hour to drive to the hotel complex. As James had said, it was a long, low, rambling building, painted white, set among informal gardens and reached by a curving drive illuminated with coloured torches. In the light streaming out of the hotel and illuminating the front of it Jenna could see the bushes and palm trees dotted throughout the gardens. To the rear of the hotel were three pools, more gardens, tennis courts, and open-air cinema and various other facilities, plus the beach.

'We intend later on to construct bungalows in the grounds themselves, but at the moment the only accommodation offered is in the hotel.' Jenna was a little surprised when they walked into its cool marble-walled and tiled foyer to discover how busy the hotel already was. 'Friends and family of the people who have worked on the place,' James told her. 'We thought it was a good way of making sure the hotel staff get plenty of experience before we open formally.'

Jenna was perplexed. 'But you said that you wanted my advice about the décor for some of the suites.'

'The suites, yes. Apart from mine they're not ready yet, but the main bedrooms and the rest of the hotel are. The suites are at the far end of the hotel; they have their own pool area . . . but you can see all that tomorrow. Wait here a second.' He went over to the desk, said something to a beaming, coffee-coloured girl, and was handed a set of keys.

'The suite's ready for us. I thought we'd eat there tonight. After the flight I didn't think either of us would be
up to eating in the restaurant.'

Jenna said nothing. In fact she was too tired to do
more than follow James down a long marble corridor.

A lift took them up to their suite, which James told her
was actually on ground level, because at this point the
level of the land rose and the hotel had been built into
the hillside itself.

He unlocked the door and allowed her to precede him
inside. Someone had already switched on the lamps
and Jenna's first impression was of a blessedly cool and
welcoming room decorated in soothing creams with
brilliant splashes of green provided by displays of tropi-
cal plants and flowers.

As in the foyer the floor was covered in pink-veined,
cream marble tiles. Two sofas upholstered in a pretty
pink and green floral fabric on a cream background, and
made of a dark-mahogany-toned cane faced one another across a cream marble coffee-table. The plants,
Jenna noticed, were standing in cream marble tubs, and
there was even set into one wall, an open fireplace with
a brass surround. Flanking the chimney-breast were
two mirrored alcoves with bookshelves. Some pretty,
pinky-beige, shaggy cotton rugs covered the marble
tiles in places and the shades on the brass light-fittings
and lamps were in distinctive art deco style. As she bent
closer to one of the lamps to study the pink, green and
cream glass Jenna realised that the lamp portrayed an
island scene.

She glanced up queryingly and James told her, 'I had
them made to my own design in London.'

'By Carla Meadows,' Jenna said for him, wondering
momentarily if his relationship with the provocative
and talented designer had been merely a business one.

A minute later she was chiding herself for the thought. What business of hers was it what sort of relationship James had had with Carla . . . or might continue to have, for that matter?

'I recognise her style,' she told James. 'She's very good.'

'Would you like to see the rest of the suite while we wait for our dinner? I ordered it in advance,' he told her forestalling her question.

Large, sliding windows looked out on to the velvet darkness of the Caribbean night, and Jenna gestured towards them. 'What's outside?'

'Come and have a look.' James walked over to the windows and touched a switch. Immediately, lights sprang on outside, subtly illuminating a delightful private patio area, with raised, mellowed-brick plant containers and a high brick wall on one side, which James explained separated them from the next suite. Set into the wall was a bench and further along a barbecue. When Jenna marvelled over the detail that had gone into the patio's construction James explained to her that they had designed the suites so that anyone taking one could either use the facilities of the hotel or could remain independent of it and prepare their own meals.

'Couples who have staff to wait on them at home, sometimes prefer to cook for themselves on holiday. Each suite has its own small kitchen. So far mine is the only one to be completed and furnished. Of course, if you want to make any changes to it . . .'

'Who chose the décor?' Jenna asked him curiously, reluctantly turning her back on the patio to study the sitting-room once more. It was a very attractive room. Cool and yet welcoming, with attention paid to detail, right down to the prints of scenes of the island set against the same dusky pink background found in the upholstery fabric, and framed in matt white.

'I did,' James told her, surprising her. Of course a lot of the top interior designers were men, but somehow she had never imagined that James might possess this talent.

'The room's perfect,' she told him generously.

A strange expression crossed his face, but before Jenna had had time to evaluate it, he said drily, 'Anything can be had at a price — even good taste!'

'You're wrong,' Jenna corrected him, 'believe me.' She shuddered to think of the things she had been asked to do, and the tact she had sometimes had to exercise to prevent some of her clients from giving in to their more bizarre impulses.

'Come and see the rest of it.'

Beyond the sitting-room was a small dining-room which also opened out on to the patio. The furniture was constructed of the same wood as that in the sitting-room. He had seen it used a good deal in Spain and the Canary Islands, James told her, and had liked the effect of its dark richness against the pastel backgrounds. Both the sitting-room and dining-room walls were painted a soft pinky-beige, which was both warm and relaxing.

The kitchen was small but well equipped, making use of the same dark wood.

'With air-conditioning we don't need to worry about the wood rotting or warping in the moist heat, which is one blessing. 'The bedrooms are this way.'

A door led out of the kitchen into a corridor with two doors off it.

'Two double bedrooms,' James told her, each with its own bathroom. The first bedroom was plainly decorated in the same shades as the sitting-room. Two single beds with dark wood headboards, and cream, pink and green cotton covers were the room's only furniture other than a traditional rocking chair, but Jenna realised why when she walked further into the room and saw the long wall of mirrored wardrobes with a well-designed dressing-table in between. At the end of the wall was a door, which she discovered opened into the bathroom. Here, again, marble had been used, but this time it was pink rather than beige, the pink exactly matching the colour of the sanitaryware.

'And this is the master bedroom,' James continued when Jenna rejoined him in the corridor.

It was larger than the previous room and possessed a double bed. It was also, and this surprised Jenna, distinctly feminine. Above the top of the bed set into the ceiling was a pale, bluey-green, marbled corona embellished with carved shells, a pearl set between each one. Jenna recognised it instantly as the work of Catherine Palmer and acknowledged that it was beautiful. Gauzy silk-fine cotton muslin curtains in the same shade of bluey-green fell from the corner to drape the top of the bed caught by shell clasps attached to the wall before falling to the floor.

The headboard itself was also shaped like a shell, and had been painted and veined in the most delicate colours so that it shimmered in a stunning mother-of-pearl effect.

The valance, and what she could see of the sheets and pillowcases, was the same soft bluey-green as the cotton curtains, and the bedspread was a work of art in itself; pale cream heavy satin appliquéd with self-coloured satin shells the edges of each one worked in a combination of delicate peach and bluey-green.

Here, too, the floor was marble tiled, not cream or pink, but deep turquoise so that it was like walking on water. Even the walls repeated the colour motif although in a much paler tone, and they, too, had been marbled.

A cornice in a soft cream shell design, which Jenna knew must have been specially designed, separated the walls from the ceiling, which in turn picked up the colour of the floor.

'I . . . I've never seen anything like it,' she told James truthfully. 'It's stunning.'

'I'm glad you like it. It was designed with you in mind.' He saw her face and explained lightly, 'The colour is a perfect foil for your hair.'

It was, but Jenna could scarcely credit that James had specifically designed this room because of that. 'But . . . but you couldn't have had time to organise all this?'

Everything in the room had been done by someone who was an expert in his or her field. Catherine Palmer alone had a four-month order book, Jenna knew that much for a fact.

'But I did,' James told her gently.

It seemed almost too fantastic to believe. And why should he have had this room designed for her in any case? He was an extremely rich man she reminded herself and rich men could afford to indulge their whims, no matter how fantastic. It was an uncharitable thought and Jenna knew it, but it made her feel slightly uncomfortable and uneasy in some way to think of this room being designed especially for her. It was a beautiful woman's room, and not just that it was a room that whispered a sensuous message, that suggested a woman who was proud of and enjoyed her own sexuality — a woman as different from her as it would be possible to be.

Shaking the thought out of her mind she went across to study the wall of wardrobes. These were not mirrored but had been painted with the same marble finish as the walls and blended perfectly with them.

She opened the only other door in the room and stepped into the bathroom stunned by what she saw. She had expected something similar to the bedroom, but it was anything but . . . The bathroom possessed an opulence and extravagance fit for the most free-spending of Arab princes. Everything in it . . . the walls, floor, sanitaryware, everything, was constructed from a dark green-gold veined substance, which Jenna recognised as malachite, even though she had never seen it in such vast quantities before. In the mirrors lining one wall she caught sight of her own reflection and thought how out of place she looked in her creased cotton skirt and thin blouse amid all this opulence. She touched a gold tap wonderingly. It ought to have looked overpowering and out of place but instead it conveyed a sensuous richness that she could almost feel like heat against her skin.

She backed out and closed the door and then turned to James. 'I've never seen anything like it in my life,' she told him truthfully.

His mouth twitched and he smiled at her. 'It is somewhat startling, isn't it?' he agreed. 'But what sold me on it was the artist's impression of it the designer showed me. He had sketched a woman standing in the shower. He had only drawn the back view but what caught my eye was her hair. It was exactly the same colour as yours.'

A frisson of sensation ran shockingly down Jenna's spine. She wanted to speak but found she couldn't, and then before either of them could say anything the intercom crackled and a sing-song voice announced that their cases had arrived.

James went to let her porter in, and before Jenna could say anything the man had wheeled both sets of luggage through into the master bedroom. She shrugged mentally as James tipped the man. They could sort it all out later. Right now she was feeling very tired. She wondered how long their dinner would be. She would probably feel better if she at least showered and changed, she decided, but when she went to open the cases she discovered that apart from her cosmetics case, hers seemed to be missing. She studied the tag on one unfamiliar navy case, and frowned over it, checking one of the Gucci bags she knew belonged to James. The handwriting was the same in both cases, but the blue bags were definitely not hers.

'Having problems?' James stood by the open doorway watching her.

'These cases . . . ' Jenna waved a hand towards them. 'You seem to have written the labels for them but they aren't mine.'

'They are now. Here are the keys.' He threw a small set of keys towards her which she caught with a clumsy reflex action, her forehead pleated in a small frown as she struggled to understand.

'Remember what I said to you about your clothes?' James told her. 'I decided to take steps to make sure that you didn't ignore me.'

Enlightenment dawned. Jenna's eyes widened, first in shock and then in anger. Grasping the keys she unlocked the first case and threw back the lid.

It was full of filmy silk and cotton underwear. Colouring hotly she slammed down the lid again, inwardly fuming. How dare James do this? The very thought of his high-handedness in arbitrarily deciding and planning his course of action brought her anger to seething, bubbling, boiling point.

She opened another case and discovered that it seemed to be full of cotton beach and casual wear, most of it in either pink or the soft greeny-turquoise colour he seemed to like so much. The label on a pair of shorts caught her eye and her mouth hardened. She recognised it, having seen it when she had been shopping for clothes to bring away with her, and though the American designed resort clothes had appealed to her immensely she had dismissed them as being far too expensive and had gone for chain-store clothes instead.

Gritting her teeth she opened the third and final case. This one was packed with evening and more formal wear, and shoes. She pulled out one dress of finely pleated multi-shaded pink silk. The dress itself was no more than a tube of the delicate material with what appeared to be a dangerously low back.

Closing the case she turned to James. She wanted to scream and rage at him, to take the cases and dump the entire contents in the hotel pool, but even as the longing to do so possessed her, she knew it would be sheer folly. The very last thing she wanted was to be marooned in their suite with nothing but what she was standing up in.

'I did warn you,' James told her mildly.

Anger seethed through Jenna. 'I bought new clothes,' she told him through gritted teeth.

'Yes. Chain-store beachwear that Lucy told me was dull and boring, and a couple of cotton dresses from last season's range that had been marked down.'

'So why should that bother you?' Jenna stormed at him. 'Just because I'm your wife, it doesn't give you the right to tell me how to dress!'

'But you *are* my wife and others will judge you accordingly. It would start an immediate panic in the City if you were seen on honeymoon wearing sale-bought clothes,' he told her mockingly. 'I couldn't let you do it. I have my financial reputation to think of.'

Jenna knew he was mocking her. 'Like hell,' she flung at him bitterly.

James ignored her comment and glanced at his watch. 'You've got half an hour to shower and dress in before dinner. If you're not ready when it is then, I warn you, Jenna, I'll shower and dress you myself!' He saw her expression and laughed shortly. 'Hardly a flattering reaction, but still if it accomplishes what I require . . . ' He paused in the doorway before striding over to the bed and picking up one of his own cases. 'I'll leave you to it,' he told her as he left. 'And remember, Jenna, you've got half an hour. No more.'

'More wine?'

Recklessly, Jenna nodded her head and then immediately wished she had not done so when the room started to whirl round her. She had already drunk far more than she was used to. James had ordered a bottle of champagne which they had drunk before their meal and this was her third glass of wine. The meal had been delicious — the hotel employed a *nouvelle cuisine* chef, James told her, and their meal had been produced by him.

Jenna had enjoyed every mouthful but now she felt exhausted. It was almost one o'clock in the morning British time, and the effects of the long flight were beginning to catch up with her.

'Would you prefer to have your coffee in the sitting-room?'

This time she didn't nod her head, but she noticed rather absently that it was difficult for her to frame the word yes, but somehow that didn't have the power to concern her greatly.

James stood up and went to the back of her chair, pulling it away from the table for her. Forewarned by her woozy head Jenna stood up slowly and carefully. She wasn't sure, but as she turned round she thought she caught sight of an amused grin just disappearing from James's mouth.

Unlike her he must have a hard head, she thought muzzily, he certainly wasn't exhibiting any of the unsteadiness she herself was experiencing.

She made it to the sitting-room by walking with exaggerated caution. James followed on behind carrying a tray with the coffee things on it and their glasses.

Jenna notice as he put them down that hers had been topped up.

'I'll never finish all that,' she protested, but James merely smiled. 'Drink it up,' he told her, 'it will help you sleep — the first few nights out here can be disturbed by trying to get accustomed to the time difference.'

For once Jenna was not inclined to argue with him. She drank her wine slowly, alternating it with sips of the deliciously hot, fragrant coffee James had poured for her.

James had opened the glass doors to the patio area and Jenna watched as he walked out on to it. Unfamiliar night sounds filled the air. She wanted to get up and join him, a heady excitement suddenly gripping her as she realised she was actually here in the Caribbean. Unsteadily she got to her feet, following him outside. She was still carrying her wine glass and he took it from her, laughing soundlessly as he looked at her.

'Why are you laughing at me?' Her forehead wrinkled, her voice huskily uncertain.

'Not at you.' He reached out and slid his arms round her waist pulling her gently against his body, and steadying her there as she swayed slightly. Jenna knew that she ought to object, but somehow it hardly seemed worthwhile. To tell the truth, it was much pleasanter to lean against James than to try to stand upright.

'What were you laughing at then?' She sounded petulant and she knew it, but she didn't like the thought of his laughing at her.

'Your attempts to walk in a straight line. I had no idea you had such a low tolerance of alcohol!'

Later, Jenna would remember those words, but now she merely frowned again, and pronounced slowly, 'I thought I told you . . . '

'If you did, you certainly did not volunteer the information.' His voice was very dry — so much so that she leaned back against his supporting arm to look up at him and see what caused it.

Dizzily she managed to focus her eyes on his. 'I've never seen anyone with such blue eyes.' Jenna frowned. Had she really said that? Another smile curled James's mouth. 'Except of course the portrait . . . on the stairs at the old Hall.'

'Ah, yes, my disreputable ancestor. Do you realise how little I know about you?' he murmured quietly. 'About the real *you*, I mean. You keep yourself guarded and hidden away like a miser with his gold, Jenna.'

She wasn't sure she liked the simile: it made her sound more mean than cautious which was what she had always thought she was. She didn't like the thought of being considered mean.

'What do you want to know?' she asked him gravely.

'Oh, all sorts of things.'

'Like what?'

'Like why you're so afraid of sex?'

Jenna stiffened, the softly spoken words penetrating the tipsy mist clouding her brain. She started to struggle, but James refused to let her go. 'You *are* frightened of it, aren't you, Jenna?'

'Of course not. Why should I be? I just don't care very much for it, that's all . . .

She stopped trying to fight him and his grip slackened enough for her to put a little more distance between their bodies. All her enjoyment of the night air and their surroundings had gone. She still felt distinctly dizzy and woozy, but now fear had chased away her earlier euphoria.

'I'm tired,' she announced childishly. 'I want to go to bed.'

'Mmm. It is rather late. Can you walk, or do you need help?'

'I can walk, of course.'

His arms fell away and she took a few tottering steps. She heard James move, and then she was being lifted in his arms as he said wyrly against her ear. 'So you can — after a fashion, but I think this will be much quicker, and safer, too, don't you?'

Quicker maybe, but safer . . . Never. There was no way she could ever feel safe in any man's arms, never mind this man's.

'Put me down,' she commanded breathlessly, but he refused to listen to her, carrying her through the suite and into her bedroom. She had left one of the lamps on when she got changed for dinner. Her suitcases were still open and unpacked because James had told her to leave them. The maid would attend to them in the morning, he had said.

The dress she was wearing was a soft, fragile confection in silk; a swirling skirt comprising several layers of differing shades of pink silk with a 'twenties-style top in slanting stripes of pink and grey on a white background, with tiny mother-of-pearl buttons all the way up the back and a sash that tied in a bow on one hip. She had fallen in love with it the minute she saw it, even though she had resented the fact that James had bought it for her. As he dumped her on the bed, one of her high-heeled, pink satin evening slippers fell off. She made a faint protest in the back of her throat, but it went un-heeded, as James merely glanced down at her bare foot, and then deliberately tugged off the other shoe letting it fall on to the floor to join its mate.

Underneath the evening two-piece, she was wearing a matching bra and panty set in palest grey silk satin, sheer hold-up stockings in cobwebby grey adorning her legs.

'How do you get out of this thing? Ah yes, I see.' James's fingers were investigating the buttons on her top as he pushed her over on to her front slightly.

Jenna let out a yelp of protest as she felt him undoing the top button. 'I can manage by myself . . . ' she ex-claimed icily, spoiling the effect of her cool rejection of his assistance by trying to glare over her shoulder at him and immediately losing her balance.

By the time James reached the final button she was becoming seriously afraid. She was still under the effect of the alcohol she had consumed, still unable to co-ordi-nate her body properly, but mentally she was com-pletely aware of what was happening.

'James . . . ' Her voice sounded only a degree steadier than it had done before, but at least now he was stop-ping what he was doing and standing back so that she could pull herself up into a sitting position and look at him.

'I can manage by myself now,' she told him bravely. 'Please go . . . ' The fine silk slithered off her shoulder and she made a desperate attempt to catch it and cover herself up.

'There is such a thing as taking modesty to a ridicu-lous length,' James told her in a light drawl. 'I'm hardly likely to start foaming at the mouth with passion just because I've caught a glimpse of your naked shoulder.'

The mockery in his voice made her colour up. 'It isn't that . . . '

'Then what is it?' He reached out easily and tugged the neckline of her top up to cover her bare skin. His fingers just brushed the bones in her shoulder barely touching them, but Jenna quivered uncontrollably.

He sat down on the bed, and took both her hands in his. 'What is it you're so afraid of, Jenna?' he asked quietly. 'Surely not me?'

'No . . . but . . . '

'No buts,' he told her softly. 'I don't know what it is about the sexual act that makes you so full of fear, but I do know that it's time you let those fears go. What sort of example are you going to set Lucy and Sarah if you cringe away like a whipped puppy every time I come within a yard of you? Surely you want them both to grow up into normal healthy young women fully able to appreciate and enjoy their very natural sexuality?'

'Yes . . . ' Of course she did. 'But . . . ' How could she explain to James that it wasn't as simple as that? That she seemed unable to let the past and her fears go. She couldn't tell him the truth and even if she could she didn't really believe that telling him, or anyone else, would free her from her own fear.

'I don't think talking about it will achieve anything, James,' she said tiredly at length.

To her astonishment he agreed with her. 'Neither do I . . . at least not at this stage.'

She was genuinely puzzled. 'Then what are you suggesting?' she asked him.

'This.' His mouth touched hers, lightly but so deliberately caressing that Jenna knew instantly what he meant. She drew away, her eyes darkened by fear and anger.

'But you promised me! You gave me your word that —— '

'That I would not force anything sexual on you that you did not want . . . and I mean to keep that promise. But Jenna,' he told her softly, 'I'm not convinced yet that you do not want my love-making . . . '

Jenna was astounded. She couldn't believe what she was hearing. He had trapped her, cheated her . . . 'If you do this to me now, it will be rape,' she told him fiercely.

'Rape is an act of aggression and violence. I promise there will be nothing of either of those emotions in my love-making.'

'But why? Why? You don't want me . . . You . . . '

He bent towards her, curving his palm round her throat, his thumb stroking the smooth firmness of her chin as he tilted her face upwards.

'Of course I do,' he told her softly. 'I wanted you the moment I set eyes on you . . . '

CHAPTER ELEVEN

JENNA knew that she cried out, she could hear the echo of that tormented sound dying away in the close confines of the bedroom as she struggled desperately away from James. He let her get as far as the edge of the bed, before hauling her back with humiliating ease.

Furious with him, too angry to be frightened, Jenna pounded his chest with her fists. Unbelievably she could feel the vibrations of his silent laughter shaking his chest. He grasped her wrists in one hand, holding her slightly away from him, his other hand tangling in her hair, forcing her back so that he could look into her eyes.

'When you're angry they burn like green fire,' he murmured softly. 'I wonder what it will take to make them glow with the heat of desire.'

'You can wonder as much as you like,' Jenna grated back, 'but you'll never know.'

'I think I will. I think that beneath this fear you've walled yourself up behind, there's an extremely sensuous, warm woman.'

Rage curled her fingers into talons but James was imprisoning her wrists too tightly for her to break free. Even so, he was not hurting her. His thumb brushed her wrist bone in light circular caresses almost as though he were stroking a cat, she thought fancifully. Hurriedly she clamped down on any thought that did not help to focus and strengthen her anger. Already she was becoming aware of ambivalent feelings about what was happening. She didn't want James to touch her, to make love to her, and yet his admission that he desired her was something she found disturbingly flattering, for a woman who claimed she was totally indifferent to male desire.

'I think we can quite happily do without these.'

'These' were her skirt and top, and Jenna fought furiously against his skilled removal of both garments until she realised that all she was doing was exhausting herself. Fear was creeping through her alongside anger now, but it was a muted fear, a tiny thread of sensation rather than a full torrent. It must be the wine, numbing her, subduing her ability to function properly.

She ought to cry out, to scream, Jenna thought stupidly. That would stop him, but almost as though he read her thoughts James covered her mouth with his own, smothering any sound she might have made.

There was no way she could respond to him and no way she wanted to but the slow movement of his mouth against her own was dangerously seductive. Against her will she felt her lips soften slightly as though they were aware of some ancient magic she did not recognise that urged them to cling softly to James's. Angered by what she considered their betrayal she tensed her body, forcing her lips to reject the subtle seduction of James's kiss.

'It won't work, Jenna,' he whispered softly against her mouth. 'Sooner or later, I'm going to break down all those barriers.'

'Never!'

He laughed with lazy amusement but there was nothing lazy or amused about the look in his eyes. They were glittering brilliantly with something that Jenna dimly recognised as intense male desire.

She wanted to cry out against the unfairness of what

was happening. To remind him of his promise to her, but pride would not let her. Instead, she strained mutely against the iron band of his fingers gripping her wrists, tugging away from him.

James was watching her, scrutinising every inch of her body, now so inadequately concealed in the delicate silk undies he had bought for her. He took his time, his total concentration on her body something she could almost feel, like searing heat against her skin. The very thought of the physical desire which motivated his scrutiny made her shudder on a thrust of real fear, strong enough to pierce the alcohol-induced clouds that had so far anaesthetised her.

James bent his head and she shuddered again, turning her face away. She felt his laughter brush her skin as his lips touched and then caressed the sensitive curve between her throat and shoulder. His lips moved upward, moistly caressing her skin, lingering over each tiny caress until the tension within her was so great that she felt she might break apart under it.

His teeth tugged gently on her ear lobe, his tongue-tip delicately exploring the crevice of her ear.

Jenna gave a short, agonised, 'Don't!' so filled with loathing and despair that she half expected him to mock her for it. Instead, she felt him withdraw slightly, and then he cupped her face, turning her head so that he could look at her.

'What is it that frightens you so much?'

'I can't tell you . . . ' How could she explain to him her deep-rooted fear of any kind of involvement or commitment with a member of his sex? It wasn't something she could analyse fully even to herself. She only knew that where he was concerned her fear was intensified by some deep inner knowledge that he made her feel acutely vulnerable . . . that she mustn't let him get close to her either physically or mentally.

'Jenna, I promise I'm not going to hurt you.'

His words were enough to unleash an avalanche of intense dread. Her deepest and most agonising fears were those connected with Rachel and the pain she had suffered; the hurt that had been inflicted on her and James's words were enough to destroy her rigid self control, her body shivering in a mixture of primitive fear and protective anger as his mouth once more touched hers.

Helpless tears of rage and fear trickled from her eyes as she lay tense and unmoving still imprisoned by James's grip on her wrists. She had refused to close her eyes when he kissed her or to move so much as a muscle in any way, and now she was forced to have her vision filled with the sight of his skin, brown and smooth, his eyelashes dark fans across his cheeks, flickering slightly as his mouth moved more possessively over her own. He murmured a small sound of satisfaction as his probing tongue finally defeated the barrier of her primly closed lips to stroke tormentingly against their inner sensitivity.

Unable to stem her tears she tried to pull away, but his hand on her nape stopped her. The crystal drops ran down on to his skin. He opened his eyes and Jenna saw that the pupils were hugely dilated, the outer rings a dense sapphire-blue. They seemed to blaze into her with a heat that made her flinch.

'Jenna . . .'

He murmured her name against her mouth so that her lips could feel the vibrations of the sound, and then he dropped back against the bed, so that he was lying full length on it. His hand on her nape forced her to bend towards him, although she managed to remain kneeling upright. Jenna felt as though her back would break under the strain he was imposing on her muscles, but she was not going to let him force her to lie down beside him. The very thought of his muscular, masculine body pressed close to her made her shake with . . . with fear and disgust. Fresh tears fell on to his skin. James opened his eyes and stared into hers. His tongue touched the crystal drops dampening her skin and Jenna shivered convulsively beneath the softly abrasive rasp of his tongue against her flesh.

'The next time you cry in my arms, Jenna, it will be with pleasure and satisfaction,' he murmured against her mouth.

'It won't!' She fairly shrieked the denial at him. 'And I won't let you do this to me. Let me go! Let me go!' Blind hysteria possessed her now; she didn't know what she feared the most, James or herself. Just for a moment then with his mouth feathering her own she had felt the oddest reaction flare up inside herself; quite what it was she could not have said, she only knew it had made her heartbeat quicken and her resolve weaken. As she hurled her defiant rejection at him she knew it was going to take every ounce of will-power she possessed to reject him. She ought not to fight, an inner voice warned her. She should remain cold and unmoving. Fighting only led to . . . Unbidden memories of her dream lover flooded her mind. To banish them she closed her eyes. James's mouth caressed hers with moist heat, and suddenly, terrifyingly, the face in the mental image changed and it was not James who was kissing her but her dream lover . . . and her mouth was softening . . . flowering beneath the coaxing pressure caressing it and it was too late to stop it.

Confused mental images flashed behind Jenna's closed eyelids. She saw the man from the portrait as he had appeared to her in her dream. She felt his hands on her skin, and was powerless to stop the sweetly savage flood of answering desire rising up inside her, even though she knew it was James who held her; James who caressed the trembling uncertainty of her lips until they clung moistly to his and parted at his command. James whose hands swept downwards over her body, skimming the soft outline of her breasts, expelling his breath with ragged unevenness into her mouth as he cupped his palms round their fullness. James . . . James . . . James . . . and no one else, but the images persisted, zigzagging through her brain until dream and reality became a tangled blur, and all she was really aware of was that the harshly fast breathing she could hear signalled a male desire that her body, with a primitive force she had not known it possessed, was already responding to.

When she felt James's fingers on the clasp of her bra, she recovered enough to cry numbly, 'No!'

For a moment his hands tensed on her skin and then he breathed hoarsely, 'Yes,' and he had released the catch before she could protest again.

Her bra fell away, the straps entangling her arms as she lifted her hands to cover her breasts. James's hands still rested on her back. He lay simply looking up at her, and although she wanted to look away Jenna found she could not. Totally unable to move she trembled violently as his hands slid round to cover her own, brown and masculine against the smaller, feminine ones.

'Let go . . . '

If anything his whispered command made her tense even more, and she had to fight down fresh tears of humiliation as James swiftly prised her hands free of her breasts and then tugged her arms down so that the upper half of her body was completely revealed to him.

He took his time in studying her, the drift of his attention from her eyes down over her throat and shoulders, and finally to her breasts so slow and deliberate that it felt like a refined form of torture.

When his fingers eventually freed her wrists, and stroked slowly upwards over her rib cage she tensed, closing her eyes against the unwanted sight of them caressing her breasts, but instead they gripped her upper arms, pulling her down over him. Jenna stiffened her spine against him, but it was useless, slowly he arched her body over his own.

When she opened her eyes Jenna saw that he was looking at her mouth. Traitorously, the sensitive skin tingled slightly in anticipation of his kiss. Hating herself for what she was feeling Jenna averted her head and then tensed warily as she heard him chuckle.

'All right, Jenna . . . if that's what you want.' He sounded so good-humoured that she was immediately on the defensive.

'Your skin is like alabaster . . . do you know that? But alabaster is cold, and you feel warm.'

She gasped in shock as she felt his lips brush the valley between her breasts, and knew then why he had been amused by her. In her dream her lover had touched and kissed her intimately, but he had not been gentle like James; he had been fierce and demanding, compelling from her a response that . . . Aghast at the direction of her thoughts Jenna raised her hands to James's chest to push him away. She could feel the even thud of his heart beneath his shirt, and for some reason it was oddly disturbing.

'Mmm . . . '

She winced beneath the appreciative sound of pleasure James made against her breast. Unexpectedly, his hands covered hers and he murmured against her skin. 'I like your touching me, Jenna, but I'd like it much more if I wasn't wearing this shirt. Help me take it off . . . '

Help him! Jenna ground her teeth, and once again she was conscious of laughter rumbling in his chest. His mouth was still exploring her breast, a delicate, thorough exploration which was having the oddest effect on her body. Tiny flutters of sensation unfurled themselves within her. Shockingly and unexpectedly her nipples peaked and hardened, her humiliation intensified when James noted their arousal with a soft masculine murmur of appreciation.

Like someone transfixed, Jenna was held in helpless thrall by the sensations his mouth against her sensitive skin was arousing inside her. It must be the drink, she thought wildly, when a shudder of pure primitive arousal convulsed her body, and then all thought was suspended as James's lips and tongue caressed the tight buds of her nipples, coaxing them to swell and flower until Jenna was possessed by a sweet, mindless ache of need so powerfully intense that it obliterated every other thought from her mind.

Willingly now she arched against James's caressing mouth, her rigid throat muscles stifling the betraying sounds of pleasure his touch induced.

When he released her to sit up and remove his clothes, she was too bewitched even to think of trying to escape. In the lamplight his skin glowed amber and gold, transporting her back once again to her dream.

Mindlessly she reached out and touched him, knowing already how his skin would feel beneath her fingertips, knowing the male scent of him and the power that those silk-sheathed muscles held. She could feel the pounding of his heart, sense the primeval force of his desire, and inexplicably, it thrilled and excited her. When his mouth moved hungrily on her own she responded to it, opening to the savage thrust of his tongue, welcoming the heat and weight of his body against hers as they fell across the bed.

His hands touched, stroked and explored every satin inch of her, quickly followed by the moist heat of his mouth, the sensations it aroused inside her causing Jenna to abandon herself totally to the fierce tongues of pleasure licking heatedly at her skin.

In her mind already she knew James's touch and her body welcomed the familiarity of it. In her dreams James already was her lover and her body felt none of the fear that had always so tormented her mind. It responded to James's touch as though it had been designed specifically to do so, inciting, encouraging him to the point where Jenna could hear the savage harshness of his breathing like a litany of desire against her skin.

Her stomach quivered as he knelt over her and stroked it with his fingers moving slowly downwards to where her body pulsed with desire for him. Neither of them spoke, but Jenna watched him with eyes dark with passionate need as he sat back and slowly removed her silk pants, running his hands upwards over her ankles and calves, the backs of her knees and then her thighs, deliberately spreading her legs apart, without using any urgency or force.

Desire quickened inside her, the same desire she had experienced in her dreams, hot and fierce, a ragingly urgent sensation that eclipsed any other she had ever known.

James reached the top of her thighs and she started to shiver and tremble wildly. His fingers stroked intimately into her body, releasing inside her a sheeting wild torrent of sensation that made her catch her breath and cry out loud. She wanted to resist the intimacy of what he was doing to her, what he was making her feel, but already her body was writhing sinuously beneath his touch, welcoming it, demanding and getting more.

Mounting waves of feeling built up inside her, each one moving her closer and closer to the brink of some sensation that lured and tantalised until she was driven crazy with the need to experience it.

When James moved between her thighs her body welcomed the male heat of him, her fingers clutching on to his shoulders as he kissed her deeply, his tongue thrusting into her mouth, his hands cupping the aching weight of her breasts. Her nipples were deeply pink and throbbed when he touched them.

She could feel the hard tension of his arousal against her body and ached to experience it more intimately. In her dream, she had not experienced beyond this point and now she ached to do so with a savage compulsiveness that overwhelmed her. Her body arched demandingly against his and she felt his corresponding tension. He released her mouth to expel a fierce deep breath and then she could feel the slow thrust of his body inside her.

Panic clawed briefly inside her, reality breaking through her desire-induced daze. Her body tensed, recoiling in anticipation of pain and against her ear James murmured soothing words of comfort.

'It's all right . . . I know it's been a long time . . . I promise I won't hurt you,' Jenna heard him say, and, astonishingly, it was enough to make her relax and allow the flood tide of desire to roll back inside her so that apart from a brief momentary pain her body welcomed the fierce surge of his within it. He paused and as though in answer to some unspoken command Jenna arched against him, rubbing her breasts against the dark hairs covering his chest.

James's breathing became fiercely harsh, tremors racking his body. He thrust deeper within her, unleashing a molten heat inside her that made her hips lift and writhe tormentedly against him, her slim legs gripping him to her as she felt him move rhythmically deep inside her until her body pulsed with aching tension that wanted only one release.

She was conscious of crying out his name, of burying her mouth against the flesh of his shoulder and wildly tasting the salt tang of his skin.

Waves of pleasure beat against her breaking over her in faster and fiercer tumult, the only sound in the room that of their mutually agonised breathing. She felt the waves break over her, submerging her, drowning her in pleasure and cried out in release, feeling the final powerful thrust of James's body within her own and then his swift release, his mouth locking on hers, draining all the sweetness from it as their breathing and heartbeats slowly returned to normal.

Now, when it was too late, she was assailed by a flood of guilt and self-hatred so intense that her body ached with it. The fulfilment of her driving need for release had brought her a momentary physical satisfaction, but it had also brought her an intensity of self-loathing and disgust that blotted out everything else as successfully as her desire had done earlier.

'Jenna . . . ' She felt James reach out towards her and curl her into the curve of his body, but she pulled away, revolted to the point of nausea by the thought of any physical contact with him.

'Come on . . . it's a little late for that now,' he told her sardonically. 'You wanted me, Jenna, and ——— '

'Only because you made me want you,' she spat at him. 'And I hate you for it, James . . . do you hear? I hate you.'

She moved as close to the edge of the bed as she could, waiting only until she heard the deeply even rise and fall of his breathing to slip out of it and into the bathroom where she scoured her skin until it glowed, hating the ripe fullness of her breasts and the soft satiny sheen on her skin because it betrayed the fact that James had spoken the truth. She had wanted him. But only because of her dream, she told herself fiercely. She had confused James with her dream lover and that was why.

James. Her mouth curled in disgust. He hadn't even realised that she was a virgin. Was? Had been, she reminded herself bitterly. She almost wished now that he had physically forced her and that her body bore the bruises to prove it; at least that way she would have something with which to quiet her conscience. As it was . . . Suddenly, she was so tired that she could have fallen asleep where she was in the bath. Getting out she dried herself lethargically and, wrapped in a clean towel, made her way back to bed. It was too much of an effort to hunt round for a nightdress now. All she wanted to do was to sleep — for ever if that could possibly be arranged.

As she fell asleep the last memory she had was of James telling her he wanted her. He had hidden that want very skilfully from her before their marriage.

Towards dawn she started to dream, shatteringly erotic dreams in which the man in the portrait and James became inexplicably one person. She tried to escape, to deny the potent immediacy of the desire conjured from her flesh and felt as though she were trapped, sinking into quicksands that refused to let her free.

She woke briefly, immediately conscious of James's arm beneath her breasts. He was lying on his side facing her, still deeply asleep, but even in sleep he refused to let her go, she thought bitterly. God, how she hated herself now! Her flesh crawled with self-disgust. How could she have wanted him? And with such a mindless intensity that even now it appalled her to contemplate its power.

Gradually she drifted back to sleep, waking again much later, immediately conscious of being alone in the bed. Somehow, she knew that James was not even in the suite and she let her mind toy wearily with that knowledge, wondering how she had come by it, how he managed to weave himself so intimately into her senses that already they were acutely aware of his absence.

She felt lethargic and drained. Her head ached appallingly and she was thirsty. Memories came surging back and she remembered the champagne and wine she had drunk. That knowledge was reassuring. It helped to banish at least some of her inner self-loathing. She was not totally responsible for her abandoned response to James's love-making. It made her writhe in tortured humiliation to think of how she had responded to him, how she . . . She pressed her fingertips to her aching temples and then reached for the phone. She knew quite well that she had no aspirins with her, but perhaps room service might be able to send some up.

The liquid sound of English spoken with a Caribbean accent soothed her tightly stretched nerves. She ordered coffee and Perrier water and asked if it would be possible for her to have some headache tablets.

The girl apologised profusely that they were not allowed to supply any form of medication however mild, adding that there was a chemist's concession within the shopping complex on the ground floor. Jenna expelled her breath on a faintly weary sigh. She felt too exhausted to get dressed and go downstairs.

Rather hesitantly the girl paused and then continued, 'Many people suffer from tension brought on by jet lag, if I might make a suggestion, the beauty shop provides an aromatherapy massage which is very relaxing and soothing.'

It sounded bliss, but as Jenna tiredly pointed out, she did not have the energy to make it down to the ground floor beauty salon.

Oh, but there was no need for that, the girl assured her. If she rang down to the beauty salon they would send a girl up to her room.

It was a tempting thought. Jenna had had an aromatherapy massage once before at The Sanctuary, an exclusive London health club, and it had been a most relaxing and pleasant experience. Before she could change her mind she dialled the beauty shop number and was answered by another liquid-voiced Caribbean girl.

Rather hesitantly she explained about her headache, adding that room service had suggested a massage might be beneficial to her. The girl on the other end of the line was instantly enthusiastic, offering to send their aromatherapy specialist up immediately.

As luck would have it, the girl arrived at the same time as the waiter with Jenna's coffee and Perrier.

As Jenna let her in and motioned to the waiter to put the tray down the girl smiled at her, shaking her head ruefully over the hot drink but approving the water. She was a pale-coffee-coloured, beautifully featured girl with a pronounced American accent, her trim pale green robe embroidered with the name of the hotel. She was carrying a wicker basket packed tight with bottles.

'Belle told me that you have a headache.' She indicated her basket and said with a smile, 'I have brought several oils with me which have a beneficial effect on tension.'

They went through into the bedroom where Jenna

pulled back the exquisite silk cover not wanting it to be marked by the oil.

'A towel would be a good idea, I think,' the masseuse commented. 'Shall I get one?'

Jenna thanked her and sat on her bed while she walked into the bathroom.

'This is a lovely suite. The only private one in the hotel.'

'Yes, my husband owned the land on which the complex was built,' Jenna told her. It gave her a funny feeling to describe James as her husband and to know that this was now the truth in all contexts. Where was he? Did she really care? She had expected to wake up this morning ready to do battle with him and tell him how much she resented what he had done to her, but what she actually felt was a growing reluctance to see him at all.

How could she present him with an angry, contemptuous resentment of what he had done, when she was unpleasantly aware of how easily he could retaliate, simply by reminding her that in the end she had gone more than willingly to him? She didn't credit him with the sensitivity to understand how she must be feeling this morning though. He could not have left her alone for her sake. Her mouth tightened. Where had he gone? Had the desire he claimed to feel for her been extinguished already? Had the discovery that she was a virgin — and she was sure he must have realised now he had had time to think about it, because there had been no mistaking that deliberate pause once his body had penetrated hers — perhaps shocked him?

Jenna bit her lip. Dear God, how could she have overlooked that! He must know that Lucy was not her child. The pain in her head increased as she automatically tensed her body, and it took the brief touch of the masseuse's hand on her arm to disperse her unhappy thoughts.

'Please call me Layla,' the girl invited when she had spread a large bathsheet on the bed. 'If you will please lie down . . .

'I think I will use a rose essence mixed with lavender,' she told Jenna. 'This is very soothing, very relaxing, very, very good for tension.'

Jenna lay face down on the bed, her forehead pillowed on her hands. She heard Layla mixing the oil and closed her eyes willing her tense muscles to relax. It was clear that they had not done so as she jumped when Layla gently touched her foot, and then started to massage it firmly.

The scent of roses and lavender wafted round the bed, and Jenna drank it in. As Layla expertly massaged her way up over the backs of her legs, Jenna could feel the tension easing from her.

Nearly an hour later when she was finally massaging the tension spots beneath her shoulders and at the top of her spine Jenna felt as though she were slowly dissolving into the mattress, her body so light and relaxed she could almost have floated upwards off the bed.

'If you would like to turn over, I . . . '

Slowly, Jenna shook her head. 'I'm too relaxed now to even think of moving,' she told her with a smile. 'If you don't mind, Layla, I think I'll just have half an hour's sleep.'

She smiled as the girl nodded her head, and picked up her basket. 'I can let myself out,' she assured Jenna. 'I am so glad you are feeling better. You were very tense.'

Yes, and it hadn't all been caused by jet lag, Jenna thought sleepily as she heard the main door to the suite close behind Layla. Heavens, she couldn't remember when she had last felt so relaxed . . . so good about herself. She stretched experimentally, feeling her muscles move in perfect fluid symmetry beneath her skin. She stretched again like a small cat and then yawned succumbing to the waves of sleep.

Something touched her spine. Something teasing and yet pleasurable making her want to arch and stretch, sending tiny shivers of delight racing over her skin. She murmured in her sleep, torn between clinging to sleep and the tantalising invitation of that light rippling touch.

'You smell good . . . what have you been doing?'

She knew the voice, and she stretched sensuously at the sound of it, still keeping her eyes closed.

The ripples of delight tormenting her spine continued, and she felt sleep receding abandoned to the need to explore a little further the delicious sensation building up inside her. Something pleasantly warm touched her bottom, caressing one gently rounded cheek, stroking the soft skin. She sighed in luxurious contentment, curling her toes like a cat kneading its paws before it starts purring.

'Well, well, here's a change!'

There was a hint of laughter in the familiar voice now and it made her frown slightly, and open her eyes as she rolled on to her side.

"Hello, James . . . '

He had obviously just showered. She could smell the clean piney scent of his soap and his hair was still wet. In the deep vee of the white towelling robe he had on she could see the honey-burnished sheen of his skin.

'Where have you been?' Jenna asked sleepily.

'Swimming. Have you missed me?'

He was watching her closely, but Jenna felt too relaxed and pleasantly floaty to heed the voice of warning urging her to remember all sorts of things she would

rather forget. The oils Layla used on her body seemed to
have done more than simply relax her body; they had
relaxed her mind as well.

'Why should I?' She pouted up at him, the teasing
glint in her eyes darkening to shock as he leaned over
her mock menacingly, grasping her shoulder and drop-
lets of ice-cold water from his wet hair splashed down
on to her skin, raising immediate goosebumps and a
tiny shriek of anguish.

One fell against her breast and hung there like a tiny
diamond, suspended, trembling with the deep breath
she took.

James made a sound deep in his throat that her senses
immediately recognised and responded to. She closed
her eyes as he bent his head, her body totally supine
and obedient to his will. His mouth caught the tiny drop
of water, savouring the coolness of it against the heat of
her skin.

'You taste of roses and lavender,' he whispered huskily against her breast. 'Did you know that?'

In spite of herself, Jenna giggled.

'It's the massage oil,' she told him. 'I had a headache
when I woke up and instead of aspirin the girl on room
service recommended a massage . . . '

'Did she now . . . ' His eyes darkened, saying things
to hers that there was no need to put into words. She
was lying on her side and his hands stroked slowly up
from her bottom, absorbing the texture of her oil-
warmed skin.

When he touched her breasts with his oil-slick hands,
slowly massaging and caressing them, Jenna felt the
now familiar slide down into intense desire begin. She
was too relaxed even to think of resisting it. The bitter
thoughts she had had that morning might never have
been. It must be the oil, she thought hazily, it must

possess some magical aphrodisiac powers. Either that or the way James's eyes hypnotised her senses. Whatever it was, it was all-powerful, subduing every lesser emotion, lifting her breathlessly above the mundane and into a world bounded only by the limits of her emotions and feelings, by the knowledge that this slowly rising, whirling tide of feeling inside her was something James was experiencing as well. She felt her heart thud crazily in longing. Her breasts felt heavy, taut with the desire conjured by James's slowly deliberate caresses. Her nipples ached, burning a deep rose red against the paleness of her skin.

James brushed one with his thumb, watching it quiver and flood with dark, passionate colour.

'Beautiful.' Jenna's head arched back, her throat tight and raw with furious need as his tongue curled delicately round one rose-red tip, his fingers gently caressing the other.

The ache in the pit of Jenna's stomach grew too much to bear. She reached up and locked her hands behind James's head, drawing him down against her body, tiny shudders fluttering through her as her hands slid from his neck to his shoulders, investigating the warmth of his skin beneath his robe. It felt like silk, sleek and yet firm. All at once she wanted to know more of him, to see what she was touching. Her fingers sought and found the belt of his robe, inexpertly she tugged at the knot, a tiny sound of satisfaction escaping her throat as she worked it free.

James had stopped moving but she didn't register that fact. Her eyes were all over his body as she pushed back his robe from his shoulders, and it fell free of him. She wanted to absorb every tiny detail of him into herself . . .she wanted to see . . . to touch . . . to know, with every sense she possessed, everything about him. The desire to do so was a feverish urgency inside her, a racing tide of heat that flooded her body and blotted out everything else. She was panting slightly, drawing in short husky breaths.

Her fingers locked in his hair and slid down to his shoulders, her nails making deep imprints in his skin as the pressure of his mouth against her breasts bent her backwards until she felt her spine would crack.

Her body was aching for more than the delicate caress of his fingers. It seemed possessed by a raging frustration; wanting the deep thrust of him within her. Her mouth found the smooth flesh of his shoulder and bit deeply into the salt-flecked skin, her hands stroking feverishly downward, seeking and finding the hard core of maleness that throbbed maddeningly against her.

James groaned against her breast, releasing the quivering tip he had been suckling. His hands linked behind her back and round her rib cage slowly lowering her on to the bed, and Jenna acquiesced mindlessly content to let him do what he willed with her just so long as it ended in his possession of her body.

He was kneeling between her parted thighs, his hands still on her waist. Impotently Jenna stretched her arms out to him but could not reach. He bent over her, kissing her slowly, shuddering deeply as her hands stroked his skin, feverishly exploring the ridged arch of his ribs, the soft line of body hair that narrowed and then widened where it met his maleness. His body throbbed madly where she touched him, his mouth hardening on hers, and then he was pushing her slightly away from him, his hands running smoothly down over her body, stopping when they reached the top of her thighs, sliding beneath her to stroke and then lift her body. Desire, molten hot and sweet roared through her.

Jenna closed her eyes, aching for him to complete

their union, shocked into one stunned gasp of denial when she felt his mouth against the most intimate part of her, his tongue stroking, circling, pressing against her until she was convulsed by a wild trembling that made her cry out, caught between anguish and ecstasy, so that when James started to move slowly up over her body, kissing and caressing her, she felt she could hardly bear the exquisite torment of his touch and yet knew she would die if it was withdrawn.

She needed no encouragement to accept his body within her own, eagerly asking for it, openly demanding it, sighing in obvious pleasure at the first tormentingly slow thrust of it, and then matching the powerful surge of his body all the way; loving each demanding thrusting masculine movement until the pleasure built to such a pitch that there was no room even to experience the sensations convulsing her, only to live them.

The climax was explosively shattering, James's mouth on her own absorbing her cries of pleasure, and then sobbing against her throat his own delirious release.

They both lay still, too exhausted to move. Gradually, reality swung back into focus. Jenna was aware of her skin prickling with sweat, her body aching with a delicious lethargy, her mind vacant and empty, or at least it was until James propped his head up on one hand and said lazily.

'Can I look forward to being greeted like that every morning?'

All her earlier ambivalent feelings came sweeping back, bringing with them a return of her earlier self-disgust, this time heightened by the knowledge that at no point in their love-making just now had James forced a single thing on her. She had wanted him to make love to her. Acute nausea gripped her. Pushing herself away from James she spat harshly, 'Keep away from me, I hate you.'

For a moment he looked angry and then he mocked, 'I see you hate *me*, but you love my body . . . my love-making, is that it?'

Jenna went scarlet, unable to hide her humiliation from him.

'I'll never forgive you for that,' she told him furiously as she slid off the bed and grabbed his discarded robe. 'I never, ever, want you to touch me again.'

All at once his expression hardened. He reached for her and grabbed her wrist before she could move.

'Now, just a minute, Jenna,' he told her softly. 'Last night, this morning, okay I could have understood your being annoyed with me . . . but what we did just now was completely mutual . . . I don't know what it is in that head of yours that makes you so ashamed of enjoying sex, and unless you tell me I won't know. But what I do know is that whether you're prepared to admit it or not, you enjoyed what we just did together. Now you're telling me that you don't want me to touch you again. Lady, I've got news for you,' he told her on a deepening voice, 'you've just picked up a mighty sharp two-edged sword, and you'd better be careful you aren't the one that gets cut up on it. And I'll tell you one other thing. No man likes being put down the way you've just put me down, Jenna. It's just as humiliating for a man to be treated as a sex object instead of a human being — maybe even more so. So far from me pressing my unwanted attentions on you, my dear wife, you're going to have to be the one to do the asking in future, and my bet is that whatever you think right now, you will. You're a very passionate woman, Jenna. Too passionate to live your life as a celibate.'

'Maybe so.' The truth of what he was saying stung,

scouring her pride, hurting her so painfully that she just had to hurt back. 'But I'll see you in hell before I ever ask you to be my lover, James.'

He laughed mirthlessly. 'You think so? After what we just experienced?'

It came to her then . . . blindingly . . . powerfully . . .just how she could get her own back and silence him.

'Ah, but you see,' she smiled sweetly. 'That wasn't *you* I was making love with . . . '

'No . . . ' His mouth curled derisively. 'My body tells me a different story. Who in hell was it then?'

'Your ancestor,' Jenna told him with sweet complacency. She stared dreamily into space and said softly, 'I dreamed he was my lover the first night I saw his portrait. If I close my eyes and wish hard enough, James, it's easy to think that you're him.'

She heard the sound he made in his throat and saw the sick whiteness of his face with a savage sense of satisfaction. Let *him* see how he liked being humiliated and mocked. Firmly she pushed away the sense of guilt filling her. What she had said wasn't entirely true. She *had* dreamed of the man in the portrait, of course . . . but that dream had contained James too . . . and if she was truthful with herself she wasn't quite sure which one of them it was she had desired as her lover. Certainly, the man in her dreams had possessed many of James's characteristics. James deserved to be hurt she told herself, ruthlessly, silencing her thoughts . . . He deserved it.

CHAPTER TWELVE

'I'm leaving now, Jenna, I'll be back late Thursday.'

Without a word, Jenna nodded coolly, refusing to so much as lift her head from the accounts she was working on as James lingered for a moment by the study door.

Only when she was sure he had gone did she release a shaky pent-up breath. How much longer could she continue with her present way of life and keep up the rigid self-control she was imposing on herself?

It was two months now since they had returned from their honeymoon. Their honeymoon! Even now she shuddered at the travesty of what their stay in the Caribbean had been. Even now the knowledge of how insultingly easy James had found it to make good his boast that she would beg him to make love to her, scorched her with humiliation, burning a self-contempt so deep into her soul that she felt she would never be free of it.

When she thought about those weeks in the Caribbean — which she did as seldom as possible — she could still recall them in such vivid detail that they seemed more real than the life she was at present living.

For four days she had avoided James, glad of the work that kept him away from her side, and then on the fifth he had found her when she was sunbathing by the privacy of their pool. He had touched her skin briefly as he sat down beside her, and that had been all it took to bring to life within her a clamouring need that refused to be contained.

That night she had deliberately drunk more wine than usual with her evening meal, hoping it would douse the fires of desire burning through her body, but all it had done had been to relax her inhibitions and pride to such an extent that later . . . but no . . . she wasn't going to think about that now . . . about how she had gone to James and . . . Jenna could feel the deep tide of colour washing over her skin, her fingers curling tensely into her palms as she tried not to think about that and all the other nights since when James had reduced her to a wanton, eager creature she barely recognised as herself, as his love-making raised her to the heights.

Heights from which she swiftly tumbled back to reality each morning, Jenna reminded herself bitterly. God, how she hated and loathed herself!

Possibly more even than she hated James. While she could accept that it was perfectly feasible for a man to experience desire without love or respect, she found it almost impossible to come to terms with the fact that she could experience such an intensity of desire for a man she knew she hated.

James seemed to derive a good deal of amusement from the situation. How many times since that first night had he tormented her with her own words, demanding to know who she thought she was making love to — himself or his ancestor, and if she refused to give him the right answer . . . She put down her pen, shuddering with the memory of the punishment he could invoke.

Sexually he could exercise a control over her that both terrified and fascinated her. She continually fought against him, loathing the fact that it was possible for him to generate such an intense reaction within her, and yet helpless against the fiercely swift tides of desire that ran within her at his lightest touch.

This week he was spending a few days in London — something he had done on several occasions in the two months they had been living at the Hall. On each occasion, she told herself, she was glad to see him go, and on each occasion the very first night of his absence she lay wakeful and aching for the warm reality of him in bed beside her. They no longer even had separate rooms. James would not allow it.

Sighing faintly she closed her heart against the desolation creeping over her. Sometimes it seemed that the harder she fought against the sexual chemistry that existed between them the stronger it became. Unlike her, James seemed to suffer no shame or self-contempt in desiring her. And he *did* desire her — he had told her so with his tongue as well as with his body, in ways that it still made her shudder delicately to recall.

'Jenna . . . can I come in?'

She had been so engrossed in her own painful thoughts that she hadn't heard the tap of Sarah's crutches over the parquet floor. Her step-sister-in-law had progressed to them only the previous week, and Jenna had organised a special meal to celebrate the occasion.

'I'm only working on the accounts,' Jenna told her, pulling a wry face. 'I'm only too glad to be interrupted.'

'Has James gone?' Sarah carefully avoided looking at her as she manoeuvered herself down into a chair.

Jenna sighed faintly. Although he never betrayed it to anyone she knew that James was hurt by Sarah's continual avoidance of him. Against her will she felt slightly sorry for him, and as always when she suffered these ambivalent feelings towards him Jenna tried to push them aside. Why should she feel sorry for him? Perhaps because she knew that in this instance he was being condemned unfairly, her conscience suggested mildly.

That much was true. Jenna knew that Sarah still resented what she considered to be James's rejection of her own mother, and even though she was now well on the way to full recovery from the trauma of the accident, Jenna knew that she still retained a slight residue of irrational conviction that somehow James was to blame for what had happened to her parents.

'I've just come from the other wing,' Sarah told her. 'The ceiling in the hall is almost finished.' Her eyes glowed vividly in her small pale face. 'Jenna, it is just so beautiful.'

Jenna smiled. The same artist who was doing the ceiling in the ballroom had been commissioned to do a similar *trompe l'oeil* allegorical work on the vaulted hall ceiling, and Sarah spent part of every day in there watching him work, fascinated by the scene growing in front of her eyes.

She was a gifted artist herself, and Jenna had not missed the long and earnest conversations Sarah had with the young Royal Art College graduate whom Geoffrey Rust employed as his assistant.

She watched as Sarah looked down at her hands for several seconds. 'Jenna, I'd like to go to art school,' she burst out at last. 'Watching what's been done here has been so fascinating.'

'Well, you certainly do have the talent,' Jenna agreed, frowning slightly before choosing her next words, and then adding quietly, 'but, Sarah, have you thought about how arduous it will be?'

'Too arduous for me because I'm virtually a cripple?' Sarah queried bitterly.

'Now that just isn't true. You are making an excellent

recovery. The doctor said as much last month when we went to see him. By the time you're ready to go to art school you should be fully recovered . . . but it won't be easy, Sarah,' she added gently.

'No, and if it hadn't been for —— ' She broke off, her face flushing slightly.

'Go on,' Jenna urged her. 'If it hadn't been for what, Sarah? For your accident? For your parents' deaths? For James?'

She watched the younger girl colour darkly as she mentioned James's name.

'I can't help it, Jenna,' Sarah admitted, twisting her fingers together anxiously. 'I know that logically he wasn't to blame. How could he be? But deep down inside I still feel that he's glad about what happened, that my mother is dead. I know he never liked her.'

Jenna sighed faintly and glanced at her watch. In half an hour the retired schoolteacher they were employing to give Sarah private lessons until she was fit enough to go back to school would be arriving. She had every logical reason to avoid dealing with the issue that Sarah had just raised. She could quite reasonably simply pass the problem on to James to deal with, after all Sarah was *his* half-sister. She knew that she ought to feel pleased that Sarah felt this resentment against him, but oddly enough she could not, because she realised what damage it was doing to Sarah to carry such a heavy burden of guilt mixed with anger and resentment. Jenna turned her chair away from her desk, so that she could look at her step-sister-in-law.

'Sarah, I'm going to tell you something now about James that is extremely private.' Quickly she outlined the story of James's mother as Lady Carmichael had told it to her, finishing by saying, 'So you see that as the boy James was when your mother and his father married he must naturally have felt resentful on his own mother's behalf.'

'You've said as much to me before,' Sarah admitted, 'but then, I didn't want to listen. I didn't want to believe that James could possibly have felt as I do. I even resented the fact that he might have shared my feelings. I wanted them to be my own.'

'We all feel like that at some time in our lives,' Jenna comforted her. 'But I honestly believe, Sarah, that as he grew older James ceased to resent your mother's marriage to his father. He learned to get over the feelings he had as a teenager, because he realised how damaging they could be. Just as you must realise the same thing and try to get over it. I know it won't be easy. It never is easy to rid ourselves of our deepest convictions. They're part of us, and really, deep down, we don't want to part with them . . . '

As she said the words, it suddenly struck Jenna that they had a particular relevance to herself. She had always told herself that sex was something she could never enjoy, and now because she did she resented the man who had made her realise the truth. Ridiculous, she told herself angrily. There were other reasons why she resented James, reasons that had nothing to do with the wild hunger he knew how to build up inside her.

'Jenna, come back!' Sarah commanded teasingly, her smile fading as she added slowly, 'I think I understand what you're trying to say. I know you're probably right, but like you say, it isn't always that easy. Whenever I feel myself liking James I get angry with myself,' she admitted wryly. 'I don't suppose you can understand that . . . '

All too well, Jenna thought inwardly, far better than Sarah could ever know.

'I think so,' was all she said. 'You feel torn between a

very natural feeling of being drawn towards your step-brother, and an equally natural feeling of guilt because part of you feels that by liking him you are in some way betraying your mother. If you genuinely want to go to art school, you're going to have to spend so much time studying and getting well that there won't be time for you to worry so much about your other problems.'

She paused as the phone rang and picked up the receiver.

'Jenna, it's me, Graham, are you free for lunch by any chance?'

She could feel the warm colour moving swiftly up under her skin as she held the receiver. Graham Wilde had rung her several times since her return from honeymoon. On the first occasion he had found the bookcase she had wanted, and she had gone with him to see it, and then on to a celebratory lunch afterwards, from which she had returned, slightly light-headed, to be greeted by a coolly disapproving James.

Some reckless instinct she hadn't known she possessed had led her into agreeing to go out to dinner with Graham two nights later, when he had called to invite her out. Graham knew that she was married, she argued with herself. Therefore, he was hardly likely to mean anything other than a social pleasantry by the invitation. James hadn't been pleased, but he hadn't argued either. She liked Graham. She found his company soothing, and his obvious admiration of her flattering. She also knew that their friendship irritated James, and for some reason that made her all the keener to pursue it. She might be married to James, she told herself, but he wasn't going to lay the law down as far as her personal friends were concerned.

'Yes . . . yes I am . . . ' she confirmed. They made arrangements to meet at a local pub which had a deservedly good reputation for its food and then Jenna replaced the receiver. As she did so she saw that Sarah was frowning slightly, but the younger girl made no comment, merely picking up her crutches and saying that it was almost time for Mrs Holder to arrive.

'With a bit of luck by Christmas I should be fit enough to go to school with Lucy.'

'Well, we certainly hope so,' Jenna agreed.

Lucy's school had closed for the summer holidays the previous month. She had spent three weeks at the Hall with them, and Jenna had been thrilled by the new warmth in her relationship with her niece.

One thing that had surprised her though had been Lucy's relationship with James. She had expected her niece to cling a little to him; and in fact rather to revel in her new relationship with him, but although it was undeniable that they got on well together, Lucy did not call James dad preferring, as Sarah did, to use his Christian name, and although it was obvious that she enjoyed his company her relationship with him was more that of niece and favourite uncle, or even sister and much older brother rather than daughter and father. This had surprised Jenna a little in view of Lucy's determination to claim him as her father.

This week Lucy was in London, staying with her friend, and James would be bringing her back with him when he returned on Thursday.

It had already been arranged that at the start of the autumn term Lucy would attend a local private school with an excellent scholastic record.

Indeed, everything had worked out very well, Jenna reflected wryly, if she discounted her own feelings about her relationship with James. Sarah was slowly recovering, and, she hoped, coming to terms with her feelings about her step-brother. Lucy was far more settled and far, far happier. The work on the house was progressing well. James had been delighted with what she had done on their own temporary apartments and Jenna had even been approached by one or two of their neighbours with a view to doing some work for them. However, she had decided not to take on any work until the old Hall was finished. In fact, it surprised her how much she was enjoying this break from her career.

She loved the old Hall with an intensity that sometimes frightened her, but nothing frightened her as much as the desire that James could arouse inside her that was, truthfully, terrifying. It was in an effort to counteract his effect upon her that she accepted so many of Graham's invitations. She found his company restful and undemanding after James's. She knew that Graham desired her, and she had even gone as far as to wonder what it would be like to be kissed by him, whether his touch would have the same cataclysmic effect upon her as James's had. In some ways, she wished it might. She didn't want James to be the only person to affect her in that way. It made her feel too vulnerable.

In truth, James aroused inside her many emotions she found it hard to come to terms with. Her life seemed to be a constant state of conflict: days during which she genuinely managed to convince herself that she was capable of treating him with indifference and cool contempt, and then nights when he brought her so close to hating herself and the way he made her feel with his clever hands and mouth that she almost felt as though she would prefer not to wake up again in the morning. Sometimes she felt as though she were two completely different people; by day the cool, calm woman she had always been, but by night an unfamiliar wanton creature; a changeling who had somehow relinquished her

real self and who wanted . . . What? she asked herself
tiredly. What *did* she really want?

She got up from her desk, irritably pushing aside the
accounts she had been working on. Against her will her
thoughts winged their way after James. Did he ever feel
torn apart by the way they lived, like she did? Did he
regret their marriage? If so, he gave no sign of it to her.

Did he even know how much she hated and resented
him? How bitter was her gall at being forced to accept
him as her husband and lover? Before they had married
she had made herself a vow that she would never live
with him as his wife. He had broken that vow for her as
easily as he might have destroyed a child's toy.

A bitter, corrosive anger welled up inside her, bathing
her with raw heat, fuelling a restless energy that demanded some physical outlet. James was making her do
what he wished her to do, and how she hated him for
that. But not as much as she hated herself for letting
him.

On impulse she went outside, walking hurriedly
through the grounds in the direction of the small or-
namental lake. August had faded into September, and
today there was just a warning touch of autumn in the
air. Jenna shivered a little as she walked alongside the
lake. How much more of this life could she endure?

Perhaps once the alterations to the Georgian wing
were finished she would feel better. It was too cramped,
living as they did at the moment. The contractors had
promised her that they would be finished for Christmas. James had suggested that they hold a masked
party on New Year's Eve in the newly decorated ballroom. Where the house was concerned he was unstint-
ing in his praise of what she had achieved. He was a
very complex man; more complex that she had ever
dreamed, she acknowledged, shivering again as her

body forced her to recall how swiftly he could change from the mockingly urbane businessman who discussed finance and business deals over dinner, to the dark, demanding lover who possessed her body during the shadowy hours of the night. Who came to her and used his knowledge of her body and its weaknesses to break through her silent resistance, making her cry out with despair and delight.

An acute feeling of nausea suddenly gripped her and she stopped dead where she was. What if she should conceive his child? The thought of being even more tied to him was intensely intolerable, and yet she had taken no precautions against motherhood.

The practical side of Jenna could hardly believe her own folly and yet she knew inside why she had done nothing . . . it was because to do something would be to admit that she and James would continue as lovers . . . to admit that she wanted him, not just on the odd rare occasion, or in a moment of weakness brought on by too much champagne and emotion, but permanently . . . always . . . and that was a truth that as yet she was unable to face.

Slowly, she made her way back to the house. If she was going to meet Graham for lunch she would have to shower and get changed. She enjoyed these meetings with the antique dealer. Softer, gentler than James he treated her with an olde-worlde courtesy that she found soothing. But, best of all, Graham did not threaten her. He did not possess James's particular brand of aggressive masculinity.

She dressed carefully in a new outfit, a softly pleated skirt in pink, with a matching long-line jacket worn over a toning pink and cream short-sleeved sweater. The colour was very striking against her hair which nowadays she normally wore down. James liked her to leave it loose, but James did not like her lunching with Graham. Her mouth compressed slightly over what she considered to be his dog-in-the-manger attitude. He had no emotional interest in her himself and yet he resented any friendships she formed elsewhere. Well, she was not totally his possession, Jenna raged, only too glad to find some way in which she could rebel properly against him. In her heart she knew quite well that her determination to pursue her friendship with Graham Wilde came from her bitter and deep resentment of the sexual hunger James aroused within her, but she fought the knowledge down, telling herself that she had every right to make her own friends, her own life.

She went to check on Sarah before going out for lunch and found her step-sister-in-law, as she had expected, in the Georgian hallway, watching enraptured as the two men worked silently on the high ceiling.

Jenna paused for a moment to watch herself. The allegorical scene was now taking real shape, the painted sky with its white clouds so realistic that one almost wanted to believe in it.

'Don't forget you've got schoolwork to do this afternoon, young lady,' she chided Sarah gently, as she went to join her.

An easy, warm relationship had developed between them and Sarah pulled a slight face, which changed to a rather worried frown as she asked, 'Will you be long? Or is it just lunch?'

Had she imagined the tiny thread of disapproval interwoven into the question? Jenna frowned slightly herself. 'I'm not quite sure. Graham has been on the look-out for some chairs for me for the dining-room. What I've got in mind is a set of Chippendale rococo, but they're extremely rare.'

Sarah's expression lightened a little, but then she added cautiously, 'Is Mr Wilde the only antique dealer you deal with? You seem to see rather a lot of him.'

Telling herself that now was not the time to take umbrage at the faint hint of criticism in Sarah's voice, Jenna gave a brief shrug. 'Not the only one, no, but he has been very helpful, and he is very knowledgeable about the period I'm interested in, and about the houses around here.'

'Mmm. I think he's fallen for you,' Sarah told her baldly, flushing a little uncomfortably when Jenna said nothing.

Jenna was quite well aware that Graham was attracted to her, but she had dismissed the knowledge to the back of her mind, telling herself that Graham was perfectly safe. He had never behaved in anything other than a gentlemanly fashion towards her, but now it annoyed her that Sarah should have noticed his attraction and commented on it.

'He knows that I'm married,' she pointed out coolly.

She left the hall before Sarah could say anything else, angry because the girl had made her feel guilty, when after all there was nothing for her to feel guilty about. It was hardly her fault if Graham *was* attracted to her. She had, after all, done nothing to encourage him.

But she had not done anything to discourage him either, Jenna reflected idly a little later that afternoon when she and Graham finished lunch and were sitting companionably over their cups of coffee.

'Do you have to rush back?' he asked when he had called for their bill. 'Only I think I know where you might be able to get your chairs . . . '

He laughed when Jenna pushed her cup aside, excitement bringing a sparkle to her eyes. 'I swear you love that house more passionately than ——— '

He broke off and looked embarrassed and Jenna supplied drily for him, 'More passionately than I love my husband, were you going to say?'

For a moment their eyes met and clung and then Graham said quietly, 'And would I be right?'

A tiny pulse started thudding in Jenna's throat. She knew she ought to deny Graham's suggestion and change the subject, but a tiny flaring sense of excitement was born inside her, together with the knowledge as old as Eve that every woman experiences when she knows that a man desires her. Where once she would have backed off, and put Graham down with some coolly cutting remark, now she felt a small reckless voice urging her to . . . To what? To encourage him to believe that she was not happy with James? So it was true, wasn't it? that same reckless inner voice demanded. She was *not* happy with him. But to admit that to someone else, to a man, moreover, who she knew was already too attracted to her . . . A tiny thrill of fear trembled down her spine at her own thoughts. What was happening to her? Sometimes she scarcely recognised the woman she was becoming . . . the woman James was making her become, she told herself bitterly, grateful for the interruption of the waiter bringing their bill which meant that she need not answer.

After lunch he took her to see the chairs. She left her own car, which had shown signs of temperament on her earlier drive, in the pub car park and Graham drove her through the flat vale of York and up on to the moors to a thick stone-built house set in its own walled garden. The garden walls and those of the house itself were thick with ivy in places, the whole air of the place one of neglect. The house was old, nowhere near as old or as large as the Hall, but impressive in its own way. The sort of house a rich merchant adventurer who valued his money might have had built.

The house had recently passed into the hands of a young Australian couple, Graham told her as he drove through open, rusty gates and down the short drive. 'Lisa Fairchild inherited it from her great-grandmother and she and her husband want to make their home here. There's quite a bit of land with it, and Peter Fairchild's got a good idea of what he can and can't do with it, but the house itself, like the old Hall, has been badly neglected and needs a fair amount spending on it. Unlike your husband, however, Peter does not have unlimited funds at his disposal. I got to know him quite by chance through my solicitor, and he got in touch with me the other day to ask me to go and value the furniture they were left with the house. He's got a set of ten Chippendale chairs there and a table — just what you want, I think, but I might as well warn you, Jenna, he won't sell them cheaply. In fact, if they didn't need the money so desperately for the house itself I doubt they'd sell them at all, and I don't blame them, it's a beautiful set. One of the finest I've seen.'

As they got out of the car Jenna felt her senses quicken. She was absurdly excited about the thought of acquiring the Chippendale set. Far more excited than she had been to discover that Graham desired her, she admitted uncomfortably. What was the matter with her? Was it that she found it easier to love inanimate objects than she did flesh-and-blood people? But that was absurd . . . she loved Lucy . . . she had loved her sister, Bill and Nancy . . . she was coming to love Sarah . . . but none of those loves were as strong as the hatred and resentment she felt towards James, she acknowledged, shocking herself with that admission. Sometimes at night after they had made love and she was lying alone in the vastness of their four-poster bed, she wasn't sure which of them she hated the most, him or herself.

'Hey, come back, dreamer . . . ' The light touch of Graham's hand on her arm brought her out of her sombre thoughts. She flashed him a brilliant smile, which faded as she saw the dark colour rush up under his skin and sensed his strong sexual response to her. Before either of them could speak the front door to the house was opened and a pretty blonde woman came out.

'Graham!' she exclaimed, holding out her hand to him. 'What excellent timing, and you must be Mrs Allingham?' She turned to Jenna and shook her hand, her clasp firm and warm.

'Please do come in,' she invited. 'My husband will be here shortly. He's gone to see someone about some sheep. We own some moorland grazing,' she explained to Jenna as the three of them went inside, 'and Peter is hoping to introduce a new strain of ewe here — a mixture of a proven moorland breed and a strain we found very hardy at home in Australia, especially in less fertile terrain. Will you have tea while you're waiting?'

Jenna nodded her head, her professional instincts making her study her surroundings as they passed through a panelled hallway and into the drawing-room beyond. A well-proportioned room, it ran the width of the house with windows overlooking both the front and the rear, and smaller ones flanking the chimney-breast. Although it was furnished in a collection of styles and colours, Jenna could see how charming the room could be.

Mentally she stripped the cold blue paint from the walls and replaced it with a soft yellow; the ceiling with its sturdy plasterwork could be picked out in white and gold with a base colour of a slightly deeper yellow than the walls . . . a mid-blue carpet perhaps, and floral upholstery . . . she knew a yellow Colefax & Fowler chintz with a pretty design of flowers in mid-blues and white that would be just the thing . . .

'Jenna, come back!'

She coloured a little as she realised that their hostess had been speaking and the conversation had gone right over her head.

'I'm sorry,' she apologised. 'I ran an interior design service before I was married, and I was just —— ' She broke off, embarrassed by her own implied criticism of her hostess's drawing-room, but to her relief the Australian girl laughed.

'Yes, it's pretty ghastly at the moment, isn't it? This blue on the walls is far too cold, but we just don't have either the money or the time to do anything about it as yet. The whole house is crying out for renovation, but we only have so much money and it's desperately needed for restocking and re-equipping. I don't know how much Graham has told you about us, but I inherited this place from my great-grandmother. It's been in our family ever since it was built, and both Peter and I desperately want to keep it. There's enough land for us to be able to farm competitively and profitably, but only if we are able to start off on an efficient basis. Unfortunately, there was no money to come with the house and so . . . ' She spread her hands.

'Graham told us that you were looking for a Chippendale set similar to the one we have here. It breaks my heart to part with it, I have to admit, but unfortunately we do need the money for other things.' She glanced disparagingly and faintly despairingly round the drawing-room. 'I'd love to be able to do something with the house itself, but I'm afraid it comes pretty low on our list of priorities.' She patted her stomach wryly and added, 'With a baby on the way as well, we're going to have our hands pretty full in the next few months.'

She excused herself to go and make the tea, and while she did so, Jenna got up to study the view from the back of the house. An attractive shrubbed and lawned garden stretched down to a stream and then beyond it the land rose up to the moors. This would be a good place to bring up a child, she thought absently, a little disturbed by her immediate feeling of envy when their hostess came back into the room accompanied by her husband.

It was obvious that a very deep bond of love and caring existed between them. Jenna was aware of it immediately. It wasn't the sort of love she had grown to be wary of and faintly despise in her London days, the flashy, 'Oh darling' sort of thing that had seemed to her to be patently false, but rather a deeper more enduring caring that for some unknown reason brought a faint sting of tears to her eyes and made her heart ache for something intangible that she knew she would never have. Peter Fairchild was a solid, quiet, fair-haired man, who looked every inch the farmer, and yet when he took the tea-tray from his wife and gently pushed her down into a chair saying that she ought to try to rest, Jenna could see how much he loved his wife . . . how careful he was of both her and their coming child.

'Lisa has explained our financial position to you, I believe, Mrs Allingham,' he said to Jenna when they all had a cup of tea. 'Reluctant though we are to part with the Chippendale set, we don't really have any choice.'

'Please call me Jenna,' Jenna invited. She felt curiously drawn to this couple, which was unusual for her. She felt drawn to them and yet undeniably she envied them. She suppressed a small inner sigh. No doubt they were envying her, thinking how fortunate she was to have no financial problems. She could have told them that there were worse things to bear.

When they had their tea, they took her to see the Chippendale furniture. It was exquisite, and very well preserved. Jenna could see at a glance how much love and care had been bestowed upon it through the years. The rich mahogany glowed softly in the afternoon sunlight, and the matching table top although scratched was beautifully polished. The seats would need recovering, of course: she wanted them done in the same rich crimson silk damask that was to hang on the walls in the dining-room, but that would be no problem.

Sedately following Lisa back into the drawing-room, Jenna sat down and then asked the Fairchilds what price they were asking for the furniture. She saw the glance that passed between husband and wife, and it was left to Peter Fairchild to name a sum.

It was a lot of money, but no more than the furniture was worth, Jenna acknowledged fairly. She looked at Graham and then said quietly, 'Yes, I think that's a fair price, and I'm prepared to accept it.'

A mist of tears shimmered in Lisa Fairchild's eyes. She smiled wryly and apologised to Jenna. 'Please do excuse me, but I feel as though I'm selling old friends. I'd never seen the furniture before I inherited the house, but my grandmother and my mother told me about it . . . I know we have to sell it, but even so . . . '

On impulse Jenna paused as she stood up and suggested hesitantly. 'Please don't think me pushy, but how would it be if, in addition to the price we've agreed upon, I . . . I renovated this room for you . . . ' She saw the words of denial forming on Peter Fairchild's lips and said quickly before he could speak, 'No, please let me explain. As I told your wife I was an interior designer before my marriage — I had my own business in

London, and I'm hoping to re-establish myself up here, but the work on the Hall, my own home, is taking so long that I haven't had time for anything else. If you allowed me to do this, it would help me to keep my hand in. It would benefit me as well as you,' she continued briskly as she saw him wavering slightly. 'You're bound to do a certain amount of entertaining — contrary to popular superstition, people of means do live in the north of England. I could get several commissions from people who see your drawing-room and like it . . .'

'Well . . .'

'We accept,' Lisa said, firmly silencing her husband with a brief look.

Just before Jenna and Graham left, Lisa took Jenna's arm and whispered to her, 'Thanks very much. I can't tell you what it will mean to me to have at least one room decent! It's very kind of you.'

'Not at all,' Jenna countered evenly. 'We'll both benefit from it, I'm sure.'

It was only when they were in the car that Graham made any comment. 'That was a very generous thing you did, Jenna,' he told her softly. 'Despite everything you might say, you know very well they could never have afforded to hire a designer of your calibre. And before you say another word, I know quite well that you've turned down several commissions locally already.'

It was true. Jenna had been approached by several people who wanted her to do some work for them, but the urge to work seemed to have left her. She was content simply to live . . . or at least she had been, until this afternoon. Something about that poor unloved drawing-room had called out to her, and she had welcomed that call as signalling a return to her normal self.

Perhaps if she was more occupied with work she would have less time to worry about her reaction to James.

'How about having dinner with me on Saturday evening to celebrate?' Graham suggested with a smile.

This wasn't the first time he had invited her out to dinner at the weekend, but so far she had always refused, because James was always at home. Instinc-tively she knew that Graham's invitation did not extend to her husband. The words of refusal were trembling on her lips as they turned into the pub car park where she had left her car. When they left it had been the only vehicle there, now with a shock she recognised James's BMW parked alongside it, and even more shocking was the sight of James standing beside it, his dark hair ruffled in the breeze, his face drawn into an expression of intense anger.

'Jenna . . . ' Graham's voice dragged her attention from her husband to himself, and she realised that he was still waiting for a response to his invitation.

'I don't know, Graham,' she replied in a faintly dis-tracted voice. 'I'll have to ring you.' In her heart of hearts she knew she would not accept his invitation, but with James looking at them both with those icily cold blue eyes she was too wrought up even to think of replying to Graham properly.

James didn't even allow Graham the courtesy of helping her out of his car. His hand was on the door handle the moment the other man brought the car to a halt.

'James . . . What a surprise!' How fluttery and ner-vous her voice sounded, Jenna realised, deploring her weakness in her reaction to him. Why on earth was she behaving like a guilty wife when she had done nothing wrong?

'Allingham!' Graham spoke curtly avoiding James's

eyes, Jenna noticed, suddenly feeling sorry for her friend. He looked uneasy and uncomfortable in James's presence, and he did not compare favourably with her husband physically either, but despite that she felt a rush of warm sympathy towards him, and a corresponding flood of resentment against James.

'What a surprise,' she reiterated shortly, as she got out of the car. 'I thought you weren't coming back until later.'

'The client I was going to have lunch with couldn't make it.' On the surface James was completely urbane, but Jenna could sense the rage simmering underneath. By what right was he angry with her? she wondered bitterly. She had done nothing wrong, unless he considered lunching with another man to be 'wrong'. She wasn't James's property, she reminded herself, bitterly angry with him all of a sudden. How dare he come looking for her like this, humiliating her in front of Graham? Humiliating Graham with his totally unreasonable anger. And *why* was he angry? James was hardly the man to play the role of jealous husband — in order to experience jealousy one first must experience love. Her mouth compressed into tight resentment.

'What are you doing here, James?' she demanded angrily, two dark spots of colour burning on her cheeks.

'Looking for you. Sarah was concerned when you didn't return after lunch. She said you'd been having trouble with your car — something about the brakes. She was concerned that you might have had an accident.'

It was plausible — just. She had complained to Sarah that her car was giving her trouble. She bit her lip, suddenly feeling at an acute disadvantage.

'Well, as you can see I'm still in one piece,' she said in brittle tones. 'Graham took me to see a set of Chippendale dining-room furniture he knew I'd be interested in.' The moment the explanation was offered, Jenna hated herself for offering it. Doing so was tantamount to admitting that she had a need to excuse her actions to James, when the reverse was the truth. What need did she have to make any excuses or explanations of her behaviour to him? None. None at all!

'And were you?' he asked silkily. 'Interested, I mean.'

For some reason Jenna felt as though the question had some hidden meaning in it that made her heart beat uncomfortably fast. It was almost as though James knew of her own inner turmoil, of her secret curiosity at lunchtime about her own reaction to Graham. About what it would be like if he ever attempted to kiss her or make love to her. To cover her inner confusion she said curtly, 'Yes, I was.' Her chin jutted defiantly as she added, 'In fact, I've bought the entire set — ten chairs and a matching table. It will be just right for the dining-room.'

'I'm sure, if you say so, it will,' James agreed smoothly. 'Since your car isn't entirely reliable, why don't I take you home with me, and we'll arrange for the garage to pick yours up in the morning and look it over?' He nodded coolly towards Graham dismissing him as though he were no more than a schoolboy, Jenna thought bitterly, while she fumed impotently at James's side, unable to do anything other than offer a palliative smile as she accompanied James towards his own car.

She controlled her rage for just as long as she could, which was only about as long as it took for James to drive away from the pub car park, and then her feelings exploded out of control. Her face contorted with intense anger as she demanded furiously, 'Just what was all that about, James? How dare you treat me like a child, embarrassing me like that in front of Graham? Dragging me home for all the world as though . . . '

'As though you were my wife,' he supplied ironically, adding with menacing softness, 'oh, but I thought that's what you are. Forgive me if I'm in error, Jenna.'

'I may be your wife, but I'm not your exclusive property,' she threw at him, forced to take another tack. 'What did you think I was doing with Graham, James? Going to bed with him?'

Too late she saw the dark glitter spring into his eyes as he turned to look at her. The smouldering rage she could sense banked down beneath the icy control he was exhibiting both frightened and exhilarated her. Shocked, Jenna realised that she wanted to quarrel with him, that she wanted to provoke him to the point where his control was shattered into pieces, where he was as vulnerable to his emotions as he made her vulnerable to her desires. It was an intolerable burden this mingling of anguish and hatred that rode her beyond the point where she was capable of thinking rationally never mind behaving rationally.

'Is that what you want to do?' he asked at last, 'because if it is I —— '

'You'll what?' Jenna demanded hotly. 'Punish me by abusing my body?' She laughed wildly. 'Haven't you done that enough already, James? Do you really find it so impossible to believe that I might want tenderness as an antidote to your cruelty?'

'My cruelty!' He laughed harshly. 'My God, Jenna, I don't know how you can say that to me. But let's get one thing straight here and now. You won't see Graham Wilde again,' he told her grimly, 'and I mean that.'

Jenna couldn't speak. She was too disbelievingly furious to do so, but one thing was clear to her — James wasn't going to tell her how to run her life. First thing tomorrow she was going to telephone Graham and accept his invitation for Saturday. And if that invitation extended to sharing a bed with him as well as a meal? a tiny inner voice demanded relentlessly ... Then she would accept, Jenna told herself. James was going to learn that she wasn't going to allow him to dictate to her, to humiliate her, to subjugate her with his sexuality. She shuddered delicately and looked resolutely out of the window. Dear God, how she hated him! Hated him and hated herself for what he was turning her into.

CHAPTER THIRTEEN

JENNA rang Graham the following morning to accept his invitation for dinner on Saturday night. James was in the Georgian wing talking to the men working there, so Jenna knew that there was no chance of his interrupting her.

It was wrong that she should be made to feel guilty about telephoning Graham. She was completely free to make her own friends and spend her time with them if she wished. Even so, after she had replaced the receiver she was nagged by a feeling of having fallen below her own standards somehow and it enraged her that James should have forced her to behave in a way that made her feel she had been underhand. She was caught in a trap and she was reacting to it as instinctively as any wild animal might, twisting and turning desperately to fight free. But what was the trap? Her marriage or her enslavement to the sexual desire James seemed able to arouse within her at will? Even last night although she had been furious with him . . . Angrily she refused to allow her thoughts to form. She didn't want to think about last night or all the other nights when James's hands against her skin aroused her to such a pitch that nothing was more important than the hectic, remorseless need inside her to make love with him.

Shuddering she went back to her desk and tried to work, but it was useless. Lucy's arrival gave her a welcome excuse to push the bills to one side and greet her.

'Tell me all about London,' she invited. 'What did you do?'

'Lots of shopping,' Lucy laughed. 'James said he'd never seen so many parcels when he came to pick me up. Definitely not a case of like mother like daughter . . . ' She made a face. 'I've spent nearly half my allowance already and I haven't even done any Christmas shopping yet.'

The allowance was James's idea — it would, he had said, help Lucy to feel more adult and responsible, and Jenna had acceded to it.

'Well, you know what James said,' she warned Lucy. 'No more until the New Year once this quarter's been spent.'

'I know. I'll have to get myself a holiday job, I think . . . You and I aren't a bit alike when it comes to clothes and money, are we?' Lucy mused before Jenna could comment on this new mature attitude. 'I mean, I'm hopelessly extravagant, and I love clothes and make-up and you . . . '

A sharp pang of pain ached through her as Jenna looked at the smiling teenager. Lucy was perched on her desk wearing an oversize sweatshirt and jeans, one slim leg balancing her chin while the other swung free.

She was so like Rachel at the same age and, like Lucy, Rachel had loved clothes and make-up. So had she . . . but once Lucy had been born there had been no time and, most of all, no money for such fripperies, and somehow over the years she had lost that heedless adolescent pleasure in buying herself new things. Now, new clothes were something she bought out of need rather than pleasure. Since she had come back from the Caribbean she had reverted to wearing jeans and cool tops most of the time. The only new clothes she owned were the ones James had bought her and the only time she had worn any of them had been when she had been going out with Graham.

To stem the guilty sensation spreading through her veins, she smiled at Lucy. 'At your age there was nothing I loved more than a new outfit but somehow over the years . . .'

'Tell me about this New Year's Eve ball we're having,' Lucy interrupted eagerly. 'James was talking about it on the drive home.'

'Well, the Georgian wing will be finished for Christmas and we'll move into it then so that work can start on the older part of the house, and James thought it would be a good idea to celebrate the completion of the Georgian wing with a fancy dress ball.

'We've decided to make it a charity affair — I've been in touch with the vicar's wife and she was telling me that they've been trying to raise funds to buy some new equipment for the local children's hospital. From the enquiries I've made so far I think it will be a well subscribed event.'

'Oh . . . fancy dress!' Lucy exclaimed. 'Fantastic! What sort of costume will you have?' she demanded. 'It will have to be something special. I know! Something Georgian to fit in with the décor. Where will you get it?'

'Hold on. I haven't got anywhere near thinking about what I'm going to wear yet,' Jenna was laughing in spite of herself. 'But I suppose you're right,' she conceded, 'it will have to be something Georgian, although I'm not sure what or where it will come from. A hire firm, I suppose.'

'Oh, no, you want something really special,' Lucy argued. 'Something that no one else has ever worn . . . I know . . .' She scrambled down from the desk and ran over to the bookcases, searching along them until she found what she wanted. 'This has got some drawings in it of fashionable clothes in Georgian times,' Lucy announced, carrying the book back to the desk. 'Why don't you get someone to make you up a copy of one of them?'

On the point of denouncing Lucy's suggestion as potentially far too expensive, the words died on Jenna's lips as James walked into the room and asked casually, 'Make up a copy of what?'

Before Jenna could speak Lucy was enthusiastically pouring out her idea to him.

'Mmm. I think you've got something there, brat,' he agreed, taking the book off her and flicking thoughtfully through the pages.

'It will be far too expensive.' Even to her own ears Jenna knew her voice sounded acid and defensive.

She expected James to argue with her, but instead he simply closed the book and shrugged, saying coolly, 'Well, you know best, Jenna.' He turned to Lucy and smiled down at her in a way that for some reason made Jenna's heart ache.

'I'm going in to York this morning — how about you and Sarah coming with me?'

'Great!'

The house felt empty without them, and although Jenna tried to concentrate on the work she was doing for the renovation of the older parts of the house she found she could not.

James had already engaged an architect to design the conservatory-cum-swimming-pool that he wanted, and his plans had been presented the previous week. They were very well done Jenna had to admit, and the conservatory as he conceived it would fit admirably into the design of the house. As James had suggested, he had designed a building that was, in effect, a replica of a traditional Georgian orangery. Jenna suspected that

James had gone into York to see the architect and approve his plans, and although one half of her was relieved that he hadn't suggested she go with him, another . . .

Moving restlessly around the room she asked herself what was the matter with her. The only place she and James communicated was in bed, and that was a form of communication she bitterly resented. For the rest of the time he was coolly indifferent towards her, apart from those brief and disturbing flashes she had of a smouldering anger that seemed to lurk dangerously beneath his surface calm.

Saturday seemed to come round all too soon. Jenna's conscience would not allow her to forget that she had deliberately gone behind James's back in arranging to have dinner with Graham. Irrationally she blamed him for this irregularity in her own behaviour. If he had not made her so bitterly resentful and angry she would never have agreed to have dinner with Graham at all. But she *had* agreed, and some stubborn streak inside her insisted that she go through with it.

Uneasily she pushed aside the troubling knowledge that Graham was already far more emotionally involved with her than she had realised. She had been made very aware of that the morning she rang him to accept his invitation. She had thought he realised that there could only be friendship between them, and perhaps a light-hearted flirtation.

A dangerous thrill of excitement raced through her blood as she forced herself to accept the fact that Graham was probably thinking more in terms of an affair than a flirtation. Part of her instinctively and fastidiously drew back from such a commitment and yet, wouldn't it set her free from the powerful sexual hold

James had over her if she could discover that another man could arouse her?

She liked Graham, liked him very much; she was flattered by his attention and admiration and had even wondered what it would be like to be kissed by him. Therefore she was hardly indifferent to him. Even so, an affair?

But it need not come to that, and if she stopped seeing Graham now, James would think that once again he had won. She told herself stubbornly that that was not going to happen. Graham was her friend and she was going to go on seeing him and to hell with what James thought — and to hell with the consequences!

As chance would have it James was out when she dressed for her date. Having showered and donned fresh underwear — one of the pretty silk sets James had provided for her trousseau — she sat down to put on her make-up.

Lucy came in while she was doing so, and asked curiously, 'Where are you going? James never said you were going out tonight.'

Jenna carefully smoothed taupe shadow on to her eyelids. 'No, we're not. At least, I'm not going out with James.'

'Oh.' Lucy looked disturbed, and Jenna gave her a rather forced smile. 'It's just a business dinner. I shan't be back late. What are you and Sarah going to do?'

'Watch the new Indiana Jones video,' Lucy told her with relish, 'and then play our new tapes. That's one good thing about living here, we can play our records just as loud as we like!'

'You'll end up deaf by the time you're forty,' Jenna told her wryly, standing up and opening her wardrobe doors.

She had decided to wear a misty, lavender-hued

floral dress in finely pleated cotton muslin, with a matching short-sleeved casual jacket that fastened at the waist with knotted ties.

She put it on, feeling the cool, silky slide of the fragile fabric against her legs.

'Wow! That looks great,' Lucy told her admiringly. 'When did you buy it?'

James had bought it for her — he had handed it to her one evening after he had been in London. Jenna had never worn it before, and it gave her a heady feeling of recklessness tinged spicily with guilt to wear it now.

'James bought it for me,' she told her niece, glancing at her watch. 'Look, I'm going to be late, if I don't go now. Make sure that you and Sarah have a proper supper, there's plenty of food in the fridge.'

As Jenna picked up her bag and slipped on delicate white mules Lucy bent to kiss her cheek.

She had changed so much in the last couple of months, no longer a resentful moody enemy, but a teasing, happy teenager slowly blossoming into womanhood. If for no other reason she ought to be grateful to James for what he had done for Lucy, Jenna told herself, and then quickly checked the thought. She wasn't going to weaken now. She was determined that James was going to learn that he could not lay down the law and tell her who she could and could not see.

She had arranged to meet Graham at his home. He had a small flat above his antique shop, and as she walked round to the rear entrance that led to it, a stormcloud of butterflies fluttered painfully in her stomach.

'On time as usual.' Graham had the door open before she even knocked. He had obviously just showered, and his hair was still damp, his white shirt open at the throat revealing a muscular chest. The butterflies in

Jenna's stomach fluttered harder, and she carefully averted her gaze. 'Your husband didn't mind your dining with me tonight then?'

Avoiding his eyes, Jenna shrugged. 'James does not have the right to dictate to me how I run my life,' she told him coolly. 'I'm a grown woman, not a child.'

'I'm very glad to hear you say it.' He was standing behind her now and she could feel the heat of his breath against her nape.

Instinct told her that in another moment he would kiss her, and she moved away, saying quickly, 'You'll see that I've got my car back. They managed to locate the problem and put it right almost straight away. Where are we dining?'

If Graham was disappointed by her reaction he did not betray it. 'A new place that's been recommended to me. I don't know what it's like, but apparently they serve an excellent *nouvelle cuisine* menu.'

Nouvelle cuisine! Jenna's heart leapt and twisted inside her like a stranded fish. Against her will she was forced to remember the meals she and James had eaten in their honeymoon suite. Those too had been *nouvelle cuisine* . . . delicate, light morsels designed to tempt even the most flagging appetite.

'Jenna?'

The sharp query in Graham's voice brought her back to the present. 'Sorry . . . I was thinking about something else. It sounds lovely,' she added, giving him a smile.

'But nowhere near as lovely as you look.'

There was a deepening, husky timbre to his voice that warned Jenna to tread carefully.

'That's very complimentary of you, kind sir,' she responded lightly. 'You look rather dashing yourself.'

Once again, Graham responded to the light warning

in her voice. 'I'll just get my jacket,' he told her, 'and then we can be on our way.'

While he was gone, Jenna glanced round his small sitting-room. It was pleasantly furnished, and had a masculine, bookish air about it; very much the room of a man who was a bachelor. It made her wonder slightly why Graham was still unmarried. He must be well into his thirties . . . Had he been married at some time perhaps? It struck her how little she knew about him and how incurious she was. Too incurious perhaps to be genuinely emotionally involved enough with him to contemplate an affair?

'Autumn's on the way,' Graham commented as they drove out of York. 'Some of the leaves are already turning.'

They made desultory conversation as he drove them to their destination — a renovated barn by a quiet millpond.

The restaurant was well patronised, and the food every bit as excellent as Graham had been told, but throughout the meal Jenna was conscious of an increasing tension emanating not just from her but from Graham as well.

It was gone eleven when they finally finished their liqueurs and paid the bill.

Jenna had dawdled deliberately over her meal, knowing that by now James would have guessed just what she had done. She tried to picture his reaction and found disturbingly that she could not.

The tension between them increased as Graham drove them back to York.

As he parked his car at the back of his shop next to Jenna's he turned to her and said huskily, 'Jenna, will you come up and have a nightcap before you go?'

This was the moment. Jenna knew it as surely as

though he had spelled it out for her. If she said yes now she was saying yes to far more than a mere nightcap. The choice was still hers. She knew that Graham would not press or force her in any way. Part of her urged her to refuse, to leave now before any real damage was done, but another part of her, unbearably goaded by James and everything that he had done to her, pushed her on into reckless responsiveness.

'Yes . . . yes, I will . . . '

The soft, breathy words seemed to fall into a pool of thick silence. For a moment neither of them spoke and then Graham was galvanised into action, unclipping his seat-belt and getting out of the car, helping Jenna from her seat as he opened her door, taking her arm possessively through his own as he led her up the flight of stairs to his door.

The moment they were inside the door he took her in his arms, kissing her with a passionate abandon she found instantly stifling and offensive. Unbelievably, all those sensations she had expected to feel in James's embrace and had not done so, surfaced now, as Graham's mouth continued to savage her own.

She was filled with a mindless, clawing panic, a terrifying fear that obliterated all reason and logic. She began to fight wildly against his constraining arms, blind to everything but her need to be free. He released her immediately, and with her release came a return to sanity. She didn't know which of them was shaking the most, Jenna thought guiltily. In the half-light of the room she could see Graham's pale face, and shaking body. She bit her lip torn between anguish and despair. She had hurt him and that was the last thing she had intended to do, but she had been so blindly, so selfishly intent on punishing James that she had not spared a thought for anything else.

She reached out and touched his arm tentatively and winced when she saw the anger laced with bitterness darken his eyes. 'I'm sorry,' she apologised huskily, knowing there was no way she could explain away her terrified lack of response to him with mere social phrases. It must have been as blindingly obvious to him as it had been to her that she was not able to respond to him, and hate herself though she might for hurting him, there was no way she could wipe away from either of their memories what had happened.

'I think you'd better go.' He sounded angry and terse and Jenna could not blame him. Although she had not actually led him on she had certainly, tonight at least, encouraged him to think that she would welcome his love-making.

As she turned towards the door he added bitterly, 'If that's the way you treat your husband, I'm surprised that he's so desperate to keep you.'

Jenna turned and hesitated. James? Desperate to keep her? Her mouth compressed. If he was, it was not for the reason that Graham so obviously supposed.

'I was not aware that he was,' her voice sounded more defeated than she realised and she caught Graham's responsive sigh as he said tightly,

'Well, let's just say he was desperate enough to come round here the other day and tell me to keep away from you.'

Jenna was stunned, left wordless and totally be-mused. *James* had called round to see Graham and told him *that*! She could hardly believe it.

'But you never said,' she protested weakly. 'You . . . '

'I didn't what?' Graham sounded angry and bitter. 'Tell you that your precious husband threatened me with physical violence if I so much as laid a finger on you? What would you have done if I had? I wanted you,

Jenna,' he told her fiercely '... and tonight you let me think you wanted me too. There was no room in the things I wanted to say to you to talk about your husband.'

Slowly, Jenna opened the door and walked down the steps. James had actually threatened Graham. She could hardly believe it. She let herself into her car and started the engine, dismayed to see that already it was gone twelve.

She drove all the way home in a tense, numb state of shock. Her mouth she discovered when she touched her tongue to its aching contours was bruised from the violence of Graham's kiss. She shuddered faintly at the memory of it. Well, she had had more than one shock tonight. If nothing else she had learned that what she felt about James, what he was able to arouse inside her, wasn't something that could be magically conjured up by just any man.

She stopped the car outside the house and started to tremble wildly as the truth burst upon her. *She loved him.* She loved James. No . . . She denied the thought even as it was born, but it refused to die. How *could* she love him? How could she *not*? a tiny derisive voice whispered. How could she not *know* that she loved him? Why else did she fight so hard and fiercely against him, if she was not motivated by fear, a fear that sprang from the deep inner knowledge that he threatened her indifference to his sex, that he made her feel all the things she had sworn she would never . . . ever feel?

'Jenna!'

The cool crispness of James's voice as he strolled out of the house and towards the car acted on her sensitive nerve endings like a cruel lash. She recoiled from the sound of it almost visibly and in the light streaming out of the open door she saw his eyes narrow and harden as

he observed first her recoil and then the swollen fullness of her lips.

'So, the wanderer returns. Are you going to stay there
all night or do you intend to come in?'

His derisive tones lacerated her aching heart, unleashing a healing flood of anger. On shaking legs, she
got out of the car and walked towards him. How dare he
treat her like a child incapable of running her own life?
How dare he tell Graham he wasn't to see her again?
And most of all how dare he make her fall in love with
him?

'I'm not a child, James,' she told him curtly. 'I am
perfectly capable of running my own life. There was no
need for you to wait up for me.'

'I quite agree,' came his bland reply. 'I was just on my
way back from an evening stroll.' He stood aside to
allow her to precede him into the house, and then Jenna
headed straight for the stairs. She knew that he would
have to stop to lock the front door and she fully intended that by the time he came upstairs, she would be fast
asleep — in her own bed. She still had her own room,
although James insisted on her sleeping with him. Well,
tonight . . .

In her heart of hearts, Jenna knew her actions were
motivated more by cowardice than defiance. How
could she sleep next to him and not betray to him how
she felt about him? It would be an unbearable form of
torture to be anywhere near him. And if he should . . .
Her whole body shuddered at the mere thought of his
touching her.

Cursing the fact that there was no lock on her bedroom door, Jenna undressed rapidly, not bothering to
hang up her dress, or take another shower. Quickly
pulling her nightdress over her head, she slid beneath
the sheets, switching off the bedside lamp as she did so.

It was torture to lie there feigning sleep, trying to slow down the frantic thud of her heart, her ears listening for the slightest indication that James had come upstairs.

When he did arrive, he was so quiet that she didn't hear a sound until he pushed open the communicating door between their rooms. Lying tensely beneath the covers, she monitored his progress towards the bed. As he leaned over her to snap on the light, she could smell the male heat of his body. He was angry, she realised intuitively despite the calm indifference he was manifesting outwardly.

'Did you have a pleasant evening?'

Jenna swallowed nervously. So there was going to be no fiction allowed that she might be asleep. Without looking at him, she shrugged and said huskily, 'It was okay . . . '

'Only "okay"? Dear me, I shall have to see if I can improve on that, won't I?'

There was a wealth of menace in his voice as he reached for her, and Jenna tensed, trying to buy time by saying hoarsely, 'I will not have you telling me who I may and may not have as friends, James, nor will I have you threatening those people who are my friends.'

'So . . . ' He sounded more indifferent than perturbed. 'He told you that, did he?'

His hands wrenched away the bedclothes with a muted violence that made her nerve endings ache, and then fastened on her shoulders, lifting her round so that he could look at her.

His eyes rested briefly on hers and then lingered on her mouth. It felt sore and tender and Jenna had to fight the impulse to touch her tongue to its bruised contours.

She heard James make a savage sound beneath his breath and then his mouth was on hers, grinding her sore lips back against her teeth, savaging, brutalising, punishing, she recognised wildly, as she struggled to push him away from her, knowing as she did so that despite what he was doing to her, she was experiencing none of the terror she had felt in Graham's arms. She felt humiliation and pain, yes ... anger too ... but strangely, no fear.

At last he released her throbbing mouth, his eyes glinting fiercely blue as he stared at her.

'You hurt me ... ' Her fingers touched her sore mouth.

'Damn you, do you think I don't know that?' His fingers cupped her face, forcing her to look at him. 'Did you let him make love to you, Jenna? Did you? Or was this ... ' his thumb touched her bruised mouth, 'as far as he got?'

'We didn't make love.' She stared back at him defiantly, loathing him for his dominance of her, for his ability to make her ache for his possession even when he was ill-treating her. She hated him for all the things he made her realise about herself that she had never previously known, for making her aware of woman's infinite capacity to respond to man in all his many moods, both cruel and kind, and she hated herself even more. And because of that she lied to him, adding huskily, 'But I wanted to.'

The words seemed to drop into a bottomless abyss and hang there echoing into the taut silence.

'Well, then, so you shall.'

She shivered beneath the silvered menace of his voice, wanting to call back the lie, but forbidden by her pride to do so. 'And this time, Jenna,' he added with soft surety, 'I promise you, you will know who I am.'

He hadn't forgiven her for telling him about her dream lover. Jenna knew that. She wished now she hadn't been so stupid as to come to bed. She would have been safer downstairs. Now . . . she gulped nervously.

There wasn't any way she could avoid the grip he had on her waist. Instinctively she wanted to fight him, but just as instinctively she sensed that was exactly what he wanted her to do and that if she did he would take great pleasure in physically subduing her. As though he read her mind, he laughed savagely, and whispered tauntingly, 'Yes, struggle if you want to, Jenna! I can't tell you what it does to me to hear those delicious panting cries you make when you try to pretend that I don't arouse you.'

He didn't *have* to tell her, Jenna already knew, and she was instantly horrified by the way her body responded to the mental pictures he was drawing. She loved him and she hated herself for it. How could she love a man who treated her in this way? Who used her as a sexual convenience, who derived pleasure from tantalising her?

She felt one of his hands move from her waist to the strap of her nightdress and forced herself to lie still as he slid it from her shoulder. The fragile fabric fell away to reveal the creamy curve of her breast. A feverish, nerve-racking tension possessed her. She wanted to lie still to remain outwardly, at least, completely unmoved by his sadistic torture, but as always her body betrayed her and as she felt him move she twisted desperately away, hating the soft laughter she could see lifting his chest.

'Ah, that's more like my firebrand of a wife.'

'I don't want you. Go away!'

Jenna was not really surprised when he laughed, but what did surprise her was the harshness of that sound, where she had expected to hear either amusement or contempt. He must know how pathetically defiant a lie

it was but instead of deriding her he only said softly,
'But you will, Jenna, I promise you that. You will want
me . . . and when you do, then you can tell me to go
away.'

He bent his head, his mouth caressing not, as she had
expected, the tip of her exposed breast but the sensitive
skin of her throat, her shoulders, the tender flesh on the
inside of her arm, the valley between her breasts. Each
delicately light movement of his mouth was a delicious
form of torment which very quickly became less delicious and more of a refined form of torture. Her body
throbbed and ached with the need that only he seemed
to be able to conjure up in it.

When he stopped kissing her and raised his head to
look into her eyes and demand, 'Undress me, Jenna,'
her pride revolted and she turned her head away in
mute denial of his command. Only she knew just how
much she longed to reach out and embrace him, desperately trying to deny the fiery need swiftly consuming
her. It was like trying to hold back the tide and even her
teeth seemed to ache with the tension she was imposing
upon her body.

James's mouth was caressing her throat again now;
the delicate skin beneath her ear, her cheek, the eyelids,
and then when she thought she would die from the agony of his slow torment, his mouth brushed her own.
Pleasure surged through her only to be arrested as the
brief contact was broken almost before she had been
able to enjoy it. Again and again his mouth tormented
her in the same way, until she was frantic, mindless
with a need that blotted out everything else.

This time when his mouth brushed hers, she clung
fiercely to him winding her fingers into his hair, holding
his mouth against her own, kissing him with an intensity she couldn't begin to hide. Beneath his palm her heart

thudded erratically, and she ached to be rid of the constraining layers of clothes.

This time the command he repeated against her mouth acted upon her as though it was something she had been programmed to obey. Like a sleepwalker she reached out to unfasten the buttons on his shirt, shuddering in mute pleasure as her fingertips touched his skin. A surge of heat flooded over her skin and she felt her tenuous self-control slip. Against the screaming command of her brain she pressed her lips to the male flesh exposed by her hands. Propping his head up on one hand James watched her, but Jenna was barely aware of his scrutiny. She reached the final button on his shirt and pushed the fabric off his shoulders an aching mixture of pleasure and pain swelling inside her body. She found the buckle of his belt and unfastened it, her fingers trembling slightly as she slid down his zip. His body hardened immediately beneath her hand, distracting her from her task, making her long to stop and caress him, her own flesh aching in acknowledgement of his desire.

He waited until she had removed the rest of his clothes and then reached for her, tumbling her on to the bed, impatiently pulling off her nightdress to expose her body to his ardent gaze. Jenna trembled beneath the look he gave her, her breathing shallow and rapid.

'You want me.' He murmured the words against her mouth, adding, 'Tell me, Jenna . . . tell me you want me . . .'

She didn't want to obey him. Her body quivered and tensed as she fought to keep the admission locked up inside her, but James was trailing his fingers down over her treacherous skin, stroking the full swollenness of her breasts, teasing their erect crests until she was dizzy,

As he withdrew from her she curled up into a defensive ball, willing him to go to his own room, but instead of leaving, he leaned over her, grasping her face in his hand and demanded savagely, 'Now tell me that you wanted Wilde, Jenna.'

All at once her control shattered. Tears spurted weakly from her eyes and she pulled away from him. 'Why are you doing this to me?' she demanded huskily. 'Why?'

She heard him laugh harshly as he moved away from her. 'If you're not woman enough to know, there isn't much point in my telling you.'

He meant that he was motivated simply by physical desire, she thought dully. And, no doubt, male-like he resented her refusal to admit that his desire kindled her own. Now at last she knew why she had always been on edge with him, so determined to hold him at bay . . . It was because all along she had sensed how attracted she was to him; how dangerously ready to fall in love with him. That antagonism that had prickled within her at their first meeting had held more than a sharp edge of desire, but she had not wanted to admit it. Her dream, if she was honest with herself, had not been about the man in the portrait, but about James. Pure fantasy stuff. Her sleeping mind's way of trying to show her what she really wanted. She was just on the point of sliding into an exhausted sleep when she felt James move.

No doubt he was going back to his own bed. She closed her eyes determined not to watch him go, and then gasped as she felt him lift her.

Cradled against his chest she glowered furiously at him. 'Just what do you think you're doing?' she demanded.

'Taking you to where you belong,' he told her softly. 'My bed . . . '

A terrible weakness assailed her. There was nothing she wanted more right now than to go to sleep in James's arms. More tears stormed the back of her throat but she suppressed them. Why weep for what she could not have? Surely she had learned the futility of that long ago? James would never love her.

The enormity of what she had committed herself to tormented her dreams. She saw the years ahead of her, loveless, empty years when she would have James's love-making for just as long as it took him to grow bored with her and then what? What would happen when the girls were grown and he had no further use for her? But of course, she was forgetting the main reason he had married her. She was forgetting the old Hall. And then Jenna knew that as much as the house meant to her it was not all-important. She would give it up, and willingly, to escape from the torture of being James's unwanted wife. In her sleep she turned away from him and curled up into a tight defensive ball, completely unaware of the fact that he was awake and watching her, a brooding bitterness darkening his eyes as his gaze slid over her hunched shoulders.

He reached out and touched her, caressing the exposed curve of her shoulder, his voice wryly bitter as he murmured, 'So, even in sleep you reject me, Jenna. I wonder what it would take to make you turn gladly into my arms for once.' His mouth compressed and he moved away from her, lying on his back with his hands locked behind his head, lost in the pain of his own thoughts.

CHAPTER FOURTEEN

'JENNA, Lucy tells me that you've forbidden her to go to a friend's party this weekend.'

Jenna looked away from James and into the fire. They had started lighting it in the evenings only a week ago when September drifted out into a cold October. Or did she simply feel so cold because of the empty wasteland that was her life, Jenna wondered soberly.

James seemed to be spending more and more time in London, coming home only at weekends. Sarah and Lucy were both busy with their own lives, Lucy at her new day school, and Sarah with the promise of art school to lure her to spend most of her spare time poring over either her books or at her easel.

'Jenna?'

The sharp note of disapproval in James's voice hurt her, but she wasn't going to let him see it. She had not been quite certain what to do when Lucy came home and told her that she had been invited to a party at a schoolfriend's home, especially when she had learned that the girl's parents would be away from home that weekend. The spectre of what had happened to Rachel still haunted her, and while she knew that she could not keep Lucy a girl for ever, she wanted to protect her for as long as she could.

It pained her that Lucy had not accepted her embargo on the party but had gone to James instead. She had been getting on so much better with Lucy recently, and now it seemed she had spoiled it all. An irrational surge of jealousy against James prompted her to say bitterly, 'Yes, I heard you, James, but you seem to forget that you are not Lucy's father.'

She got up from the dinner table as she spoke and went over to the fire, bending to put another log on it. It had been raining all day and outside the trees dripped monotonously. It was also windy and cold, the weather echoing her own inner despair. James had only been home a matter of hours, having arrived just in time for dinner. How long would it be before he started making excuses not to come home at all, but stayed in London over the weekend as well? Before they were married he had stated his intention of doing most of his work from the Hall, but now he seemed to have changed his mind. He took so little interest in the house that Jenna sometimes wondered why he had ever wanted it.

But she knew the answer to that of course. Did owning the property that had once belonged to the man who had so wronged his mother ease any of his anguish? It was not a question she could ask him. They were like two strangers forced to live in close proximity to one another, and Jenna did not know how she could bear it for much longer. James no longer even seemed to desire her. The last time he had made love to her had been the night she had been out with Graham.

She hadn't seen Graham since that night, nor did she want to. She paced restlessly round the room, wishing she could find the courage to tell James that she wanted their marriage to come to an end. She could not endure the slow torment of living with him, of loving him and of knowing that he felt nothing for her in return. It was slowly destroying her. Now that she no longer had her resentment of him to buoy her up she sometimes felt as though her life had totally disintegrated.

She heard his chair scrape back as he stood up, but

didn't bother to turn to look at him, and was therefore startled when he drawled bitingly, 'No, Jenna, I am not Lucy's father, but by the same token *you* are not her mother.'

For one disbelieving moment Jenna thought she must be imagining things. She stared at James, forgetting her resolution not to look at him, her mouth opening slightly. In those early days of their marriage she had tensed herself against a remark of this kind, sure that he must know that he was her first and only lover, and then when no such remark had ever been forthcoming, she had surmised that James must not, after all, have been aware of her virginity and that her belief that he was had sprung only from her own fear of discovery. Therefore, it came as a double shock now to discover that he had known all along, and, moreover, that he had kept that knowledge to himself.

'I . . . You . . . '

He let her struggle for a few seconds and then said sardonically, 'I shouldn't bother trying to lie about it if I were you, Jenna. Surely you can't really believe I don't know a virgin when I make love to one?'

All the breath seemed to have been squeezed out of her lungs. It was actually physically painful to try to drag air into them. A roaring sense of despair engulfed her, followed by an intense surge of anger. 'If you knew, then why didn't you say something before now? Or were you keeping it in reserve, as an alternative means of torture once the novelty of making me submit to your love-making had waned?' she demanded savagely.

She saw his mouth compress and knew instantly she had pushed him too far.

'Submit?' He said the word slowly as though tasting it. 'What a very odd memory you have, my dear. Or perhaps it's your understanding of the English language that is at fault?' His voice was liquid soft with menace and contempt, and Jenna felt herself go hot all over as she remembered her wanton response to him the last time they had made love.

'Quite so.' His mouth was twisted and for a second it seemed as though there was something more than mere bitterness in his eyes as they met hers, but before Jenna could define his expression he had looked away and then at last he answered her original question, his voice stripped of all emotion as he said coolly, 'As to why I said nothing, I could well ask you that same question, couldn't I?'

When she remained stubbornly silent, he added bitingly, 'I know exactly whose child Lucy is, Jenna. She's your sister's. It was all there in the records, Lucy is registered as your sister's child, father unknown . . . '

He turned his back on her, his voice suddenly savage with anger and something else she couldn't name as he demanded bitingly, 'Did you really think I would not *know* she could not possibly be *yours*?'

'But you said nothing,' Jenna said stupidly, hating him suddenly for the torment she had endured in the early days of their marriage, waiting for him to denounce her, and then her feeling of relief when she thought he must not know. How she had deluded herself!

He swung round, his eyes dark, glittering with an anger almost as intense as her own. 'Perhaps I was waiting for you to tell me!'

Her eyes betrayed her shock, and he laughed harshly.'But no, of course, that would never occur to you *would it*? *I* would be the last person you would confide in, even though a simpleton could have realised the truth. Or do you really think me so crass a lover that I did not know? Is that it, Jenna?'

He had *wanted* her to tell him about Lucy? Jenna could not understand why. Surely it was enough that he knew the truth. And how had he intended to use that truth? As a weapon to force her to give up her claim to the Hall.

'I have known whose child Lucy is almost from the moment we returned from the Caribbean,' he told her softly, 'and all that time, my dear wife, I have waited for you to tell me the truth yourself.' This time there was no mistaking the irony in his voice. 'I have waited . . . and still continue to wait.'

'But why?'

The words burst from her before she could check them, and it seemed so incredible that she should actually see pain and bitterness reflected in his eyes that she was sure she must have imagined them.

'Perhaps as a gesture of trust?' His lips twisted slightly.

Her mouth had gone completely dry, a nagging, haunting pain making her chest ache for something elusive and lost. Concealing her expression from him, she asked thickly, 'Why should you want my trust?'

She thought she heard him sigh as he murmured softly, 'Why indeed?' and then his voice hardened as he said in a more normal tone, 'But if I can't have your trust, then at least I shall have the truth.'

His cool control, the purposeful determination she read in his eyes, and the hard grimness of his mouth combined to arouse inside Jenna an even deeper fear. She wanted to run from the room and hide herself from him. She felt as though she were being forced to face every menacing, hideous monster that had ever lurked in her nightmares, as though she were standing in the path of some primeval force of destruction from which she could not escape.

Goaded beyond endurance her self-control snapped and she cried out, 'What is it you want to know? How my sister was raped by Charles Deveril? Is that what you want me to tell you? How she was abused and humiliated by the same man who humiliated your own mother? Is that what you want me to tell you, James? She was eighteen, that was all . . . only a girl, but because of that family she died. We came here to see Sir Alan . . . ' Her voice was high and tight with hysteria now, James really forgotten, as she was sucked back into the past, reliving the terror and pain of those months before Rachel's death.

'Everyone liked her, you know. She wasn't like me, she was soft and gentle. I came here with her, but Sir Alan virtually threw us out. He threatened Rachel, told her that no one would ever believe her story, that they'd say that she had encouraged his son to abuse her, but it wasn't like that. I know . . . Rachel would never . . . ' She caught back a bitter sob, her eyes wide and dark as they looked past the man standing watching her, not seeing him, instead seeing her sister's pale face and swollen body.

'She wouldn't let me tell anyone. She was too frightened. I was frightened too. I was there when she went into labour . . . I went with her to the hospital . . . I could hear her screaming . . . ' Her voice dropped, her body shuddering with remembered agony. 'I wanted to go to her, but they wouldn't let me . . . '

Her eyes focused abruptly and she saw that James was standing immediately in front of her, his face pale, the bones beneath the skin harshly delineated.

'Do you know what it was *like* . . ?' She was virtually screaming the words at him. 'Can you imagine what I felt like to have to stand there and hear my sister scream in mortal agony? My sister, who never did anything to hurt anyone . . . who was so gentle and good . . . '

She was breathing hard, sobbing almost, unaware of
the fact that she was beating her fists on James's chest
until he took her wrists in a gentle grip.

'Jenna, Jenna . . . Stop now . . . '

She took a deep, painfully racking breath and glared
at him with angry, bitter eyes. 'Oh, no. You wanted to
know . . . well, I'll tell you . . . I'll tell you what I haven't
told anyone else . . . anyone . . . I wanted to see Rachel,
but they wouldn't let me. I pushed my way past the
nurses and into the ward. She was lying there. There
was blood everywhere, on the sheets, on the floor . . . '

'Jenna . . . '

'No!' She said it savagely, her eyes wild with her
tormenting memories. 'You wanted to know. Well, now
you do. No, I did not give birth to Lucy, but my sister
did; she's part of her, all I have left of her, and —— '

'You must have been so young . . . '

She heard the words dimly, and forced herself to
respond. 'Fifteen. I was fifteen.' Her voice seemed to
come from a long distance. 'They wanted her to be
adopted, but I wouldn't let them. Bill and Nancy helped
me. I had to keep her.' She said it urgently, as though
James was someone she had to convince of the right-
ness of her actions. 'She was Rachel's child . . . Rachel
would have wanted . . . Rachel . . . '

Tears spurted from her eyes and poured unceasingly
down her face. Jenna tried to stem their flow and discovered it was impossible. Something unfamiliar had
happened to her. She felt curiously weak and empty
somehow as though something she had carried within
her for years had gone. And then she realised what it
was — it was her pain, the pain of losing Rachel, the
guilt and fear she had known because of her sister's
death, because she had not been able to do anything to

help her. She swayed giddily, suddenly glad of the protective bulk of James's body against her own. She wanted to stay here with him for ever, she thought dreamily,
safe . . . But she was not safe with James and she never
would be. All the life seemed to have drained out of her.
It was more than she could cope with right now to move
away from him. Like a limp doll Jenna allowed herself
to be lifted in his arms and carried from the room.

With a curious sense of being apart from herself she
felt James place her on her bed. No, not *her* bed, but his
own, she realised, raising her head to glance incuriously
round his room.

She couldn't remember their coming upstairs, and as
though he knew what she was thinking, James said
tightly, 'You fainted. I think you need a drink,' he added
in that same strangely tight voice. 'I think we both do.'

Jenna wanted to protest that she didn't want anything but she was too weak to do so. Telling him about
Rachel's death had been like a dam breaking, sweeping
away the hurt and the pain that had built up over the
years, and now she just felt empty somehow, lifeless
and unable to so much as co-ordinate a single thought.
All she wanted to do was simply to lie here.

'Jenna.'

James was back, carrying two brandy glasses. He saw
the face she pulled and his own expression relaxed
slightly from its hard remoteness. 'Come on, let me help
you.' He put the glasses down and leaned over her,
lifting her shoulders from the bed and supporting her
with the soft pillows.

'I don't want anything to drink, James.' She turned
her face away from him. 'I'm all right.'

Her ears just caught the sound he made, something
between derision and . . . anguish? But she wouldn't let
herself believe that. Why should James feel anguish on

her behalf, or Rachel's? It had all been a long time ago.

Despite her denial, Jenna found herself taking a small sip of the reviving brandy when James held the glass to her lips. It burned fiercely down to her stomach, making her shudder in faint distaste.

'Was that why you wanted the old Hall so much?' James asked her quietly.

'At first,' Jenna admitted, 'at least that was my intention. Bill and Nancy were horrified. Neither of them wanted to see me making decisions based on a desire for revenge.' Amazingly she could talk quite calmly now: the storm of emotion and pain that had threatened to destroy her earlier had cleansed her of the past, removing all the dark bitterness that had tormented her for so long. She would never forget what had happened to Rachel, but now at last she was no longer haunted by the bitter hatred that had tainted her life since her sister's death.

'But, ridiculously in some ways, the moment I saw the old Hall properly, I fell in love with it. I told myself I was doing it for Lucy's sake, that it was rightfully hers. I told myself it would make good sense from a business point of view, but in reality, I wanted the house for myself. It called out to me, satisfying some need inside me.'

'You talk as though those feelings are now all in the past,' James told her, watching her.

Jenna shrugged, suddenly aware that she was treading on ground as delicate as eggshells. If she wasn't careful, James would lure her into betraying the real reason the Hall no longer held her heart — namely, the fact that it now belonged to him. She fought to revive her earlier resentment and anger against him, but they had both gone. She could feel nothing . . . just a vast emptiness.

'I don't know what I feel at the moment,' she told him

at last. She gave a wry smile, and then raised her eyes to his face. 'Your godmother told me all about your mother.' She saw his expression change, become shuttered and dark, and instinctively she reached out to touch him . . . hurt because he so obviously did not welcome her knowing. 'I'm sorry if you'd rather she hadn't told me,' she whispered tensely, 'but please don't be angry with her, she was acting with the best of motives. She wanted me to understand why you wanted the old Hall so desperately.'

'Yes,' his mouth curled wryly, 'she would, she and my mother were very close.'

They sat in silence for a moment and then he added huskily, almost as though the words were dragged out of him, 'I couldn't believe it when she died . . . I loved her so much, and yet in a way I hated her for . . . '

'Dying and leaving you alone with a burden you were too young to handle?' Jenna supplied for him, recognising in his admission a trace of her own feelings on Rachel's death. She too had experienced that mingling of pain and anger, and with it both guilt and resentment.

He looked at her and for a moment Jenna felt as though for the first time they were really seeing one another. Hope fluttered tentatively inside her and then James ruined it all by saying curtly, 'You realise that Lucy will have to be told the truth.'

'No!' The denial was wrenched from her already aching throat in a husky cry of pain.

'Yes, Jenna,' James replied firmly. 'She has to know.'

'But she thinks that you are her father.'

'Does she?'

The wry doubt in his voice reinforced Jenna's own private belief that Lucy did not behave towards him as she would have expected her to react to her father.

'I think she finds me a convenient substitute, but as to whether or not she genuinely thinks I am her father . . . '

'But it was because you believed she did that you married me,' Jenna pointed out in bewilderment.

'That was one of the reasons, but since then I've had more opportunity to observe her.'

Cold icicles of dread formed down Jenna's spine. Was this James's way of telling her that he wanted their marriage to end? Was he using the truth about Lucy's parenthood as a means of escape? Pride kept her from asking him.

'She'll have to be told, Jenna,' he softened the words with a brief smile, and added huskily, 'but not to-night . . . ' He was looking at her mouth and a tingling reaction of delight heated Jenna's skin. Unwittingly provocative, her lips parted.

James's fingers touched her throat, and slid upwards to cup her jaw. Against her mouth he murmured hyp-notically, 'Tell me to stop if you don't want this.'

Dizzy with emotional exhaustion, she had no energy left to fight against her need and love. Her mouth clung welcomingly to his, her body shivering in delight beneath the light touch of his hands.

When they had made love before, it had always been with an element of raw savagery and Jenna had never totally overcome her own inner rage and confusion that James should be able to make her respond in such a way, until passion had blotted those feelings from her mind, but this time that elemental anger wasn't there.

James's touch was gentle, tender, reverent almost, the slow spiralling dance of desire building up between them so achingly beautiful that it brought a tight lump of pain to her throat.

This time when she caressed and kissed James's body

he seemed somehow less invulnerable, less hard and unyielding, his voice a soft, husky litany of pleasure against her skin as he muttered hoarse words of praise and delight at her touch.

They seemed almost to be making love in slow motion, as though there was all the time in the world to enjoy and relish each simple caress, with no urgent rush to satisfy their mutual craving for satisfaction.

Long before she felt the hard warmth of James's body sliding over her own Jenna had abandoned reason and reality in favour of emotion and fantasy. She was here in James's arms where she had longed to be for so many empty weeks, and he was touching her, making love to her as though he did indeed cherish and adore her. It was a precious dream she did not want to relinquish, and her body opened willingly to the first thrust of his, moving in perfect time to his demands, sharing with him the sweetly piercing pleasure of escalating desire.

Her hands moved over his back, clinging lovingly to the hard muscles as she wrapped her arms around him, kissing the salt skin of his throat, loving the moist heat of his shoulder as her mouth moved slowly over it. His tongue touched her ear, investigating each delicate convolution and she shuddered in fierce pleasure, muffling the small sounds of delight she couldn't subdue against the heat of his skin.

'Don't do that!' His voice was hoarse and strained, sending shivers of reaction racing over her skin as he pressed his lips to her ear. 'Don't try to hide from me how you feel, Jenna. I want to hear it,' he told her thickly, cupping her face with hands that trembled slightly, momentarily stilling the arousing movements of his body within her own. 'I want to hear your pleasure . . . I want to see it . . . taste it . . . ' He groaned suddenly and then kissed her with a suppressed violence that shattered her languorous spiral of desire and turned it instead into a white-hot, aching need that twisted and coiled inside her, making her arch pleadingly against his body and respond feverishly to his kiss.

Her blood sang through her veins, her breathing constricted. Huskily she cried out his name, lost to everything but the intensity of the feeling inside her. A terrifying heat burned her skin, turning it slick with sweat so that it clung to James's. He groaned something unintelligible against her mouth and moved fiercely within her, demanding and getting her response to his urgency. She was racing towards the outer limits of the universe with no means of controlling her pace, with nothing to hold on to except James . . . She clung desperately to him, her body convulsing in the first primitive spasms of pleasure.

'Jenna!' He cried out her name and it seemed to echo hollowly round the room as his body released a fierce heat within her and shuddered to a climax that matched her own.

Tears ran freely down her face, but they were not tears of pain or anguish, simply tears of joy and release. There would never be anything else in her life to equal this pleasure, this giving of herself wholly and completely to the man she loved. But who did not love her, she told herself on the edge of exhausted sleep. James did not love her.

She woke up once towards dawn, and knew immediately that James was also awake. His mouth touched her throat, his hand gently cupping her breast, slowly caressing the warm fullness of it. She made a lazy sound of pleasure deep in her throat and turned into his arms.

'Tell me something . . . ' His voice reverberated against her ear and she curled in sleepy appreciation of his reaction to her.

'What?'

'Tonight when we made love, was I the one you took into your body, Jenna, or was it still your fantasy lover?'

Still her fantasy lover? Jenna frowned in the darkness. Did James still really believe that lie she had told him when they were first married? Surely he must have guessed that she had used it merely as a means of defence, as a protection against the desire he had aroused within her? She frowned a little more, remembering how on previous occasions he had also demanded to know who had been in her mind while he made love to her body. A curious tension gripped her. Could it be possible that he could . . . but no . . . It was just male sexual jealousy, nothing more.

She wanted to tell him the truth, but she sensed that to do so would be to leave herself too vulnerable to him. It would be safer and wiser to let him go on doubting. All at once their earlier quarrel came back to her. James wanted her to tell Lucy the truth. He wanted to end their marriage, she was sure of it. Last night had simply been an expression of a man's physical need, nothing more.

She thought for a moment before answering his question, and then glad of the darkness to conceal her expression from him she said lightly, 'Does it matter? Lots of women have fantasies about men other than their husbands.'

She wanted to cry out in protest as he withdrew from her turning over on to his side, unbearably hurt by his mocking, 'No, I suppose not, especially when it has such an extremely erotic effect on you.'

She only realised how angry he was when he added bitingly, 'Perhaps the next time we make love you'd like me to be my ancestor physically as well mentally. Maybe I could hire the appropriate costume . . . It would be quite interesting to see what effect that has on you, if

simply imagining that I'm him can . . . ' He broke off as
Jenna burst out, 'Stop it . . . stop it!' and laughed
savagely before saying finally, 'There are those who do
say that there's a remarkable family resemblance between us, but I can't say that I find your response to me
exactly flattering. Not when I know that in reality
you're making love to a man who's been dead for over a
hundred years.'

Jenna felt as though she had been physically and
mentally mauled. James had hurt her before, but it had
been nothing like this. She crept out of his bed and went
into her own room, gathering up her discarded clothes
as she did so. They could not continue to live like this.
The thought struck her that perhaps James was making
life as impossible for her as he could in the hope that she
might be the one to leave, to leave him with the Hall.

Strangely enough, the thought of losing the house
did not affect her at all.

'Where's Lucy?'

They were having breakfast, James was reading his
paper, Sarah had a book open in front of her, but now
both of them looked up as Jenna came in with some
fresh coffee. Munching a piece of toast, Sarah said in
surprise, 'Oh, didn't you know? She's gone out. She left
just after she spoke to you, James,' Sarah added, turning
to her step-brother. 'I saw you both coming in from outside. It isn't like Lucy to be such an early bird, normally I
have to drag her out of bed.'

A cold fist closed round Jenna's heart. She looked into
James's face but could discern nothing from it. He had
threatened last night that if she did not tell Lucy the
truth herself, he would do it for her.

Had he carried out that threat? Had he told Lucy the
truth about her parenthood?

Jenna ached to demand the truth from him, and couldn't repress a small sigh of relief when Sarah finished her coffee and said lightly, 'I'm going to see how they're getting on with the work on the hall ceiling. See you both later.'

When she had gone, before Jenna could say a word, James frowned and said thoughtfully, 'Has it struck you that Sarah could have a crush on young Bob? She seems to spend an awful lot of her time watching him work.'

'Never mind Sarah,' Jenna exploded. 'What about Lucy? You told her, didn't you? Didn't you?' she demanded, standing up and pacing anxiously, coming to an abrupt halt in front of the window which she stared out of blindly. 'You can't wait to get rid of me, can you? You don't give a damn about Lucy, you never did. All you wanted was this place. Well, you can have it and welcome. I couldn't live here with you now, even if you begged me, not after what you've done. How could you?' she whispered in a choked voice turning to look at him, her face white with strain. 'How could you? Didn't you think of the effect it might have on her of —— '

She gasped in shock as he got up from the table and came towards her, grasping her shoulders and shaking her almost violently.

'Just what in hell are you talking about?' he demanded thickly. 'Just what sort of man do you think I am, Jenna?' He released her, his face contorting in a brief expression of disgust. 'I don't need to ask that really, do I? You've already told me. Well, for your information I didn't tell Lucy the truth — you did. She overheard part of our conversation last night, it seems. I found her wandering round the garden early this morning. Like her, although for different reasons, I hadn't been able to sleep. I guessed at once that she knew.'

Jenna said nothing. She couldn't have spoken to save

her life. She sank down on to the cushioned window-seat, her body trembling with aching despair. 'What did she say to you?' she asked in a husky voice. 'What . . . '

'She asked me if what she had heard was true — apparently she didn't hear all of it, only the first bit. She was so shocked that she didn't stop to listen to any more. I told her as much as I could.'

'Oh, my God, she must hate me,' Jenna said quietly, pressing her hands to her face. 'For her to find out like that.'

'She took it surprisingly well . . . '

'Then, where is she?' Jenna cried desperately. 'Where has she gone? James, she's missing!'

'She's gone to see Bill and Nancy. I drove her there. She wanted to talk to someone who knew what had happened. I suggested Nancy and Bill and she agreed. She'll be quite safe with them, Jenna.'

All at once it was too much for her. She started to cry silently, tears soaking her skin, her whole body shaking with shock and reaction. James got up and came towards her, but she flinched automatically from him. She heard him swear and then suddenly she was in his arms, his eyes almost black as they glittered into her own with fierce anger.

'For God's sake, why can't you trust me a little?' he grated. 'Why must I always be cast as the villain of the piece? Your dislike of my sex as a whole I can understand — now! but you seem to have singled me out for special treatment. What have I ever done . . . '

'What?' Now that she knew Lucy was safe, some of her fear slipped away from her bringing in its wake restorative anger. 'What about forcing me to marry you, humiliating me by making me . . . ' She bit her lip.

'By making you what?'

'It doesn't matter,' she said wearily, 'it's all over now, James. You can have the old Hall, I just don't care any longer.'

'Damn you, Jenna,' he swore softly, shaking her again. 'I'm not letting you go. I love you far too much, and if you'd just give yourself a chance you might admit that you're not totally indifferent to me . . . '

For minutes the shock of what she was hearing totally stunned her. Was there a slight plea in those final words? Jenna's head spun as she tried to take in what he was saying.

'You *love* me! But you *can't* . . . ' she whispered in complete bewilderment.

'Why not? Unlike you *I* have all the normal human frailties, Jenna. I think I fell in love with you the first time I saw you. The day you so obviously mistook me for some uncouth country lout,' he added wryly, with a tight smile. 'Remember?'

Did she? Of course she did . . . and everything that had happened between them since.

'But you — you never said — you . . . '

His harshly derisive laughter silenced her. 'Said what, Jenna? That I loved you? When did you ever give me a chance? You fought me every inch of the way. I had to trap you into marrying me and even then you demanded that it be a marriage in name only.' His eyes met hers and he said softly, 'Surely you realised then how I felt about you? I made a pretty poor show of concealing it and that's a fact!'

'You said you wanted me and . . . ' she shrugged helplessly.

'And you believed that was all?' He sounded incredulously angry. 'Dear God, what sort of woman are you, Jenna?'

He saw the colour surge up under her skin and

muttered something fierce under his breath, cupping her face, and taking her mouth with his own, kissing her with a feverish need that spoke more clearly than any words could have done.

'There,' he said hoarsely when he finally released her. 'If I can't tell you, I can at least show you. I love you, Jenna,' he murmured against her mouth. 'More than anything else in this life. Yes, I wanted the old Hall originally because of my mother, but that was only a fleeting insipid emotion compared with the way I want you. I didn't want this to happen. I never planned to fall in love. I had seen what it did to my mother. We have an awful lot in common, you and I, if you really think about it,' he added softly. 'We've both been hurt by events in our lives outside our own control. Don't shut me out, Jenna. We could build something good together. You may not love me now . . . '

She started to shake in his arms, and after initially tightening they fell away from her. He took a step away and said with his back to her, his voice raw with weariness, 'All right, Jenna, if a divorce is what you want . . . '

'James, no . . . ' It was the pain in his voice that gave her the courage to cross the chasm of self-doubt and vulnerability that separated them. She touched his arm with her fingertips, instantly aware of the hardness of the muscles beneath his skin. He turned to look at her, and she saw suddenly how tense and strained he looked.

'No, what?' he asked her, his mouth wry and twisted. 'I can't go on like this, Jenna,' he told her. 'The strain of having to stay away from you, of not being able to touch you, of not having you as my wife in every real sense of the word, of having to guard everything I say to you in case I betray the truth, and, worst of all, to know that when I do get you in my arms it isn't me who's holding you but some damned —— '

'James, no.' She said it more urgently this time, clutching his arm so that he had to look at her. 'That was a lie,' she told him quietly. 'It's true that I did dream I had a lover and that he was dressed much as one might expect to find your ancestor dressed, but his face was your face, James, his hands on my body your hands — even though at the time I fought to deny it even to myself. You're my dream lover, James,' she told him softly, 'and I love you more than I can say.'

When they kissed it was as though it was for the first time, with no restraints or doubts between them. The sensation of James trembling with emotion in her arms was one that illuminated and humbled her. She ached to cradle him in her arms, against her body, to pour out for him the full measure of her love, to wrap him in her warmth and remove from his heart all pain.

'So many mistakes . . . ' His fingertip traced her gently swollen lips. 'So much unhappiness. I could have killed Wilde when you told me you wanted him to be your lover,' he told her slowly. 'And it sickened me to know that I was capable of so much violence towards a fellow human being.' He paused and then said quietly, 'Jenna, about your sister . . . I wish there was some way I could ease that hurt for you but —— '

Her fingers against his mouth silenced him. 'You have done,' she assured him. 'Last night . . . telling you about it acted as some sort of catharsis. I can't explain it properly to you, I only know that for the first time since it happened I feel empty of all the bitterness and pain. It's gone, James. I finally feel free of the past.' A frown pleated her forehead. 'I just wish that Lucy . . . '

The sharp peal of the telephone cut across her words. James answered it and listened silently for several seconds. 'Fine, we'll come and get her now.'

'That was Nancy,' he told Jenna when he had replaced the receiver. 'Lucy is ready to come home. Jenna, why don't you wait for her here?' he suggested softly. 'This will be hard enough for both of you. I'll go and collect her alone, shall I?'

She nodded her head wearily, knowing that what he was saying made sense. He came over to her, kissing her gently, and in spite of her anguish her heart flooded with love.

She was sitting in Lucy's bedroom when they came back. She heard the car doors slam and then slow footsteps on the stairs. When Lucy pushed the door open Jenna could only look at her, and then without a word Lucy ran towards her, tears cascading down her face. Jenna opened her arms instinctively hugging the lithe teenage body to her own.

'I never knew . . . I never knew . . . ' Lucy sobbed against her shoulder. 'You gave up so much for me.'

It was not what she had expected. She had been braced for recriminations, for anguish and despair, but never for this.

Holding Lucy away from her Jenna looked into her niece's crumpled face. 'Lucy, what I did, I did out of love, love for my sister and love for her child . . . you,' she said softly, 'and although I've been at fault in not telling you the truth about your father, I did it because —— '

'Because you didn't want me to be frightened that I might grow up like him,' Lucy supplied for her. 'James explained it all to me.'

Poor child, how dreadful it must be for her to have to accept that James whom she adored was not her father, and that he in reality . . .

'I don't really mind, you know,' she said, surprising

Jenna with the accuracy with which she had read her mind. 'About James not being my father. I never really felt that he was. It was just with all that gossip about it in the papers I couldn't help hoping that it was true, but deep inside I knew somehow that it wasn't. That's why I call him James . . . ' She grimaced shamefacedly. 'I didn't want to tell you, though, because I knew if you knew, you and James wouldn't get married!'

Jenna was stunned for a moment and then she pulled herself together enough to say huskily, 'Lucy, about your mother and father . . . '

'Bill and Nancy have told me everything. I understand that my father was sick in some way and that he couldn't help what he did, and I know enough about myself to know that I'm not like him. Children can't always like their parents, or parents their children.'

'You would have loved your mother,' Jenna told her softly. 'Everyone did!'

Lucy's eyes lit up. 'Tell me about her. Have you any photographs? Was she . . . '

Jenna laughed. 'Oh, Lucy, there is so much I *want* to tell you about her, so much about her that I want to share with you. All these years I've longed to talk about her, but I couldn't. You're very like her, you know, but I think you have more of my personality.'

'You mean we're both survivors,' Lucy said wryly. 'James said she died when I was born.'

It was obvious that Lucy had not overheard their entire conversation and Jenna made a mental promise to herself that she would never know exactly what had happened.

'Yes, she did,' she agreed calmly. 'But before she died she knew about you and she asked me to look after you.'

'I wasn't really eavesdropping, you know,' Lucy mur-

mured when she digested this. 'I was hungry because
Sarah and I had had an early supper and I came down
for something to eat. I heard you and James quarrelling.
I meant to move away and then I heard you saying that
James wasn't my father. When he said you weren't my
mother, I couldn't believe it. I went back upstairs,
then . . .'

'What were you planning to do when James found
you in the garden?' Jenna asked her gently.

'Nothing much, I was just plucking up the courage to
come and ask you if it was true.' She saw Jenna's face
and hugged her reassuringly. 'Oh, no, I'd never have
done anything silly. Life's too precious to throw away.
I've been an awful brat recently, haven't I? But I'm
much more mature now,' she added naïvely.

Jenna had to laugh. 'Ah, yes, three months or so
makes a very big difference,' she teased, and yet in a
way wasn't that quite true? She as much as Lucy had
matured tremendously in a very short period of time —
the period of time she had known James . . .

James. A small smile curved Jenna's mouth, her eyes
suddenly dreamy. 'You're thinking about James,' Lucy
accused with startling accuracy. 'I know because that's
how he looks when he's thinking about you!'

'Well now, madam wife, that's a very fetching costume
you're wearing!'

They were in their new bedroom in the Georgian
wing. They had moved in on time just before Christmas
and tonight was New Year's Eve. Their charity ball had
been exceptionally well subscribed, and Jenna had just
put on her outfit. Down the hall in the large bedroom
that they shared Sarah and Lucy were also getting
dressed. For the first time tonight Sarah would be walking without her crutches.

'I'm glad you like it.' Jenna pirouetted mischievously in front of her husband, laughing as he caught her round her waist and pulled her towards him. The dress in question was a flimsy Regency ballgown, all gauzy drapes falling from the beribboned Empire waistline under her bust. The soft aqua colour suited her, the tiny puff sleeves sliding provocatively off her silky shoulders. The pearls, which had been her Christmas present from James, glowed warmly against her throat and ears.

'Time we went down, I think,' James murmured against her mouth, the words husky and indistinct. His hand slid from her waist, to the gently rounded curve of her stomach, concealed by the floating lines of her dress.

She had told him about their child at the end of November. At first she had been disappointed by the way he received the news. She had hoped he would be as overjoyed as she was herself, but when he had told her later in bed, that if she had any fears about the birth, that if she did not want to continue with the pregnancy, she had understood at once that it was because of his love for her that he had been so reticent. Strangely, perhaps, she was not at all frightened. She wanted to have James's children . . . she wanted them to be a family . . . to banish any lingering shadows from the old Hall, and now she thought indulgently, there could be no prouder father-to-be.

'The older they are the worse they are,' Lady Carmichael had told Jenna drily over Christmas. 'You'd think from James's expression when he looks at you, thinking no one else is looking, that he's the first man ever to have achieved conception.'

'Ready?' asked James.

Nodding her head, Jenna followed him through their bedroom door. On her way past the girls' room she tapped on the door and glanced inside. Both of them looked lovely in their pretty Victorian-style dresses, their long hair demurely ringleted.

'Don't be long,' she warned them. 'Everyone will start arriving soon.'

James was waiting for her on the stairs, and a grin curled her mouth as she saw that he was posing beneath the portrait.

'Well?' he demanded with a mock injured air when she made no comment. 'Don't you think it's a good likeness?'

He had had the clothes worn in the portrait copied, without her knowing it, and tonight had put them on for the first time. The resemblance was remarkable, but there were subtle differences, easily discernible by a woman who looked with the eyes of love.

'Isn't this what you wanted?' he whispered against her ear, pulling her into his arms. 'Your favourite fantasy come true . . . your dream lover?'

Wriggling out of his embrace, Jenna tapped him on the chin with the fan she was carrying. 'Fie, sir, you are too bold,' she cautioned him in simpering tones, adding with a soft giggle, 'Ask me that again later tonight, James. I just might be able to give you an answer!' She looked at him out of the corner of her eye and grinned wickedly. 'I shouldn't dance too much if I were you, you're going to need plenty of stamina.'

'You'll regret saying that,' he threatened softly, but both of them knew it was just a game. There was no fantasy lover in Jenna's life, only a very real and live one — in the shape of her husband.

Tonight they would bring in the New Year, and with it she would finally put aside all the miseries of the old. There was so much to look forward to, and she could hardly wait for it to begin. Tonight they would celebrate what was to come with their friends and neighbours. Later, alone, they would celebrate those same things together, reaffirming their love for one another and the life they had created between them.

On the last stair, Jenna paused, and James reached for her automatically. 'James . . . ' she eyed him thoughtfully and said as seriously as she could, 'do you think you could manage to lure me away from the ball? Could you . . ?'

'Do you really want to find out? If so, it can quite easily be arranged.' He picked her up as he spoke and turned to go back up the stairs, just as they heard the first car crunch over the drive. 'Just in the nick of time!'

Jenna pouted and then as she prepared herself to go and greet their first guests she whispered against his ear, 'But never mind, there's always later!'

'Always . . . ' James kissed the tips of her fingers lightly as he released her. 'That word has a very delightful permanent sound to it, Jenna. And that's how I want you . . . permanently . . . for always . . . '

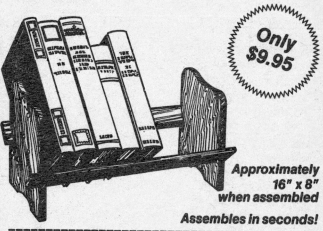